THE COLLECTED WORKS OF WILLIAM FAULKNER

*

A FABLE

A FABLE

William Faulkner

1969

CHATTO & WINDUS

LONDON

Published by
Chatto and Windus Ltd
42 William iv Street
London Wc 2

First published by Chatto & Windus 1955
First published in this edition 1969

Copyright 1950, 1954 by William Faulkner
All rights reserved under International and
Pan-American Copyright Conventions
Published in the United States by
Random House, Inc., New York
and distributed in Canada by
Random House of Canada, Limited, Toronto

SBN 7011 0670 0

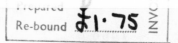
Printed in Great Britain by
William Lewis (Printers) Ltd, Cardiff

TO MY DAUGHTER

JILL

To William Bacher and Henry Hathaway of Beverly Hills, California, who had the basic idea from which this book grew into its present form; to James Street in whose volume, *Look Away*, I read the story of the hanged man and the bird; and to Hodding Carter and Ben Wasson of the Levee Press, who published in a limited edition the original version of the story of the stolen race-horse, I wish to make grateful acknowledgment.

W. F.

WEDNESDAY

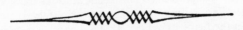

LONG before the first bugles sounded from the barracks within the city and the cantonments surrounding it, most of the people in the city were already awake. They did not need to rise from the straw mattresses and thin pallet beds of their hive-dense tenements, because few of them save the children had even lain down. Instead, they had huddled all night in one vast tongueless brotherhood of dread and anxiety, about the thin fires of braziers and meagre hearths, until the night wore at last away and a new day of anxiety and dread had begun.

The original regiment had been raised in this district, raised in person, in fact, by one of those glorious blackguards who later became Napoleon's marshals, who delivered the regiment into the Emperor's own hand, and along with it became one of the fiercest stars in that constellation which filled half the sky with its portent and blasted half the earth with its lightning. And most of its subsequent replacements had been drawn from this same district, so that most of these old men were not only veterans of it in their time, and these male children already dedicated to it when their time should come, but all these people were parents and kin, not only the actual old parents and kin of the doomed men, but fathers and mothers and sisters and wives and sweethearts whose sons and brothers and husbands and fathers and lovers might have been among the doomed men except for sheer blind chance and luck.

Even before the bugles' echoes died away, the warrened purlieus were already disgorging them. A French or British or American aviator (or a German either for that matter, if he had had the temerity and the luck) could have watched it best: hovel and tenement voiding into lane and alley and nameless *cul-de-sac*, and lane and alley and *cul-de-sac* compounding into streets as the trickles became streams and the streams became rivers, until the whole city seemed to be pouring down the broad boulevards converging

9

like wheel spokes into the *Place de Ville*, filling the *Place* and then, pressed on by the weight of its own converging mass, flowing like an unrecoiling wave up to the blank gates of the *Hôtel* where the three sentries of the three co-embattled nations flanked the three empty flagstaffs awaiting the three concordant flags.

They met the first troops here. It was a body of garrison cavalry, drawn up across the mouth of the wide main boulevard leading from the *Place* to the old gate in what had once been the city's ancient eastern wall, already in position and waiting as though the murmur of the flood's beginning had preceded it, right into the bedroom of the town-major himself. But the crowd paid no attention to the cavalry. It just continued to press on into the *Place*, slowing and stopping now because of its own massy congested weight, merely stirring and shifting constantly and faintly within its own mass while it stared, mazed and patient in the rising light, at the *Hôtel* door.

Then the sunrise gun crashed from the old citadel above the city; the three flags broke simultaneously from nowhere and climbed the three staffs. What they broke and climbed and peaked in was still dawn, hanging motionless for a moment. But when they streamed on the first morning breeze, they streamed into sunlight, flinging into sunlight the three mutual colours—the red for courage and pride, the white for purity and constancy, the blue for honour and truth. Then the empty boulevard behind the cavalry filled suddenly with sunlight which flung the tall shadows of the men and the horses outward upon the crowd as though the cavalry were charging it.

Only it was the people advancing on the cavalry. The mass made no sound. It was almost orderly, merely irresistible in the concord of its frail components like a wave in its drops. For an instant the cavalry—there was an officer present, though a sergeant-major seemed to be in charge—did nothing. Then the sergeant-major shouted. It was not a command, because the troop did not stir. It sounded like nothing whatever, in fact: unintelligible: a thin forlorn cry hanging for a fading instant in the air like one of the faint, sourceless, musical cries of the high invisible larks now filling the sky above the city. His next shout though was a command. But it was already too late; the crowd had already underswept the military, irresistible in that passive and invincible humility, carrying its fragile bones and flesh into the iron orbit of the hooves and sabres with an almost inattentive, a humbly and passively contemptuous disregard, like martyrs entering an arena of lions.

For another instant, the cavalry held. And even then, it did not break. It just began to move in retrograde while still facing forward, as though it had been picked up bodily—the white-rolled eyes of the short-held horses, the high, small faces of the riders gaped with puny shouting beneath the raised sabres, all moving backward like the martial effigies out of a gutted palace or mansion or museum being swept along on the flood which had obliterated to instantaneous rubble the stone crypts of their glorious privacy. Then the mounted officer freed himself. For a moment, he alone seemed to be moving, because he alone was stationary above the crowd which was now parting and flowing on either side of him. Then he actually was moving, forward, breasting the still short-bitted horse, iron-held, into and through the moving crowd; a voice cried once somewhere beneath the horse—a child, a woman, possibly a man's voice eunuch-keened by fear or pain—as he forced the horse on, feinting and dodging the animal through the human river which made no effort to avoid him, which accepted the horse as water accepts a thrusting prow. Then he was gone. Accelerating now, the crowd poured into the boulevard. It flung the cavalry aside and poured on, blotting the intersecting streets as it passed them as a river in flood blots up its tributary creeks, until at last that boulevard too was one dense seething voiceless lake.

But before that, the infantry had already arrived, debouching from the *Place de Ville* on the crowd's rear long before the cavalry officer could have reported to the officer of the day, who would have dispatched the orderly, who would have summonsed the batman, who would have interrupted at his ablutions and shaving the adjutant, who would have waked the town-major in his nightcap, who would have telephoned or sent a runner to the infantry commander in the citadel. It was a whole battalion, armed except for packs, emerging from the *Place de Ville* in close route column, led by a light tank with its visor closed for action, which, as it advanced parted the crowd like a snowplough, thrusting the divided parting back from either kerb like the snowplough's jumbled masses, the infantry deploying into two parallel files behind the advancing tank, until at last the whole boulevard from the *Place* to the old gate was clear and empty again between the two thin lines of interlocked bayonetted rifles. A slight commotion rose at one point behind the dyke of bayonets, but its area was not ten feet and it did not spread, and only those near it knew that anything was happening or had happened. And when a platoon sergeant stooped under the interlocked rifles and shouldered his way in, there was not much to see either: only a young woman, a girl, thin and poorly dressed, who had fainted. She lay as she had fallen: a thin huddle of shabby, travel-stained garments, as if she had come a long distance and mostly on foot or in farm carts, lying in the narrow grave-shaped space they had made for her to fall in, and, if such had been her intention, die in, while those who apparently had made no room for her to stand erect and breathe in, stood looking quietly down at her as people will, until someone makes the first move. The sergeant made it.

'At least pick her up,' he said savagely. 'Get her up out of the street where she won't be trampled.' A man moved then, but as he and the sergeant stooped, the woman opened her eyes; she even tried to help as the sergeant hauled her to her feet, not roughly, just impatient at the stupidly complicating ineptitude of civilians at all times, particularly at this one now which kept him from his abandoned post. 'Who does she belong to?' he said. There was no answer: only the quiet attentive faces. Apparently he had expected none. He was already glancing about, though he had probably already seen that it would be impossible to get her out of the crowd, even if anyone had offered to take charge of her. He looked at her again; he started to speak again, to her this time, but stopped himself, furious and contained—a thick man of forty, moustached like a Sicilian brigand and wearing the service and campaign ribbons of three continents and two hemispheres on his tunic, whose racial stature Napoleon had shortened two or three inches a hundred years ago as Caesar had shortened that of the Italians and Hannibal that of the nameless pediment-pieces of his glory—a husband and father who should (perhaps even could and would) have been a custodian of wine casks in the Paris Halles if he and the Paris Halles had been cast on some other stage than this. He glanced again at the patient faces. 'Doesn't anybody—'

'She's hungry,' a voice said.

'All right,' the sergeant said. 'Has anybody—' But the hand had already extended the bread. It was the heel of a loaf, soiled and even a little warm from the pocket it had been carried in. The sergeant took it. But when he offered it to her, she refused it, quickly, glancing quickly about with something like fright in her face, her eyes, as if she were looking for an avenue of escape. The sergeant thrust the bread into her hands. 'Here,' he said harshly, with that roughness which was not unkindness but just impatience, 'eat it. You'll have to stay and look at him too, whether you want to or not.'

But she refused again, repudiating the bread, not the gift of it but the bread itself, and not to whoever had offered it, but to herself. It was as if she were trying to keep her eyes from looking at the bread, and knew that she could not. Even while they watched her, she surrendered. Her eyes, her whole body, denied her mouth's refusal, her eyes already devouring the bread before her hand reached to take it, snatching it from the sergeant and holding it to her face between both hands as though to hide either the bread from a ravisher, or her voracity from those who watched her, gnawing at the bread like a species of rodent, her eyes darting constantly above the concealing hands, not quite furtive, not quite secret: just anxious, watchful, and terrified—a quality which glowed and faded and then glowed again like a coal she breathed on. But she was all right now, and the sergeant had begun to turn away, when the same voice spoke again. Without doubt, it belonged to the hand which had tendered the bread, though if the sergeant remarked it now, he gave no sign. But without doubt he did remark now that the face did not belong here at all, not now, at this time, this place —not just in France, but in forty kilometres of the Western front, on this or any Wednesday in late May in 1918—a man not so young actually, but rather simply youthful-looking, and this not merely in contrast to the other men among (or above rather; he was that tall, that unblemished) whom he stood, sound and erect and standing easily in a faded smock and rough trousers and stained shoes like a road-mender or perhaps a plasterer, who, to be here on this day on this place on the earth, must have been a soldier invalided safely and securely and forever out since the fifth day of August almost four years ago now, yet who, if this was so, didn't show it, and if the sergeant remarked it or thought it, there was only the flicker of his glance to reveal that he had. The first time the man spoke, he had addressed the sergeant; this time, the sergeant had no doubt of it.

'But now she has eaten bread,' the man said. 'With that morsel, she should have bought immunity from her anguish, not?'

In fact, the sergeant had turned away, already in motion, when the voice, the murmur, stopped him—the murmur not so much gentle as just quiet, not so much tentative as bland, and possessing, for last of all the qualities, innocence: so that in the second, the instant of pause before he even began to turn back, he could see, feel all the quiet attentive faces watching, not him nor the speaker either, but as though looking at something intangible which the man's voice had created in the very air between them. Then the sergeant saw it too. It was the cloth he wore. Turning and looking back, not only at the man who had spoken but at all the faces surrounding him, it seemed to him that he was looking, out of a sort of weary, prolonged, omniscient grief and sorrow so long borne and accustomed that, now when he happened to remember it, it was no longer even regret, at the whole human race across the insuperable barrier of the vocation and livelihood to which twenty years ago he had not merely dedicated but relinquished too, not just his life, but his bones and flesh; it seemed to him that the whole ring of quiet attentive faces was stained with a faint, ineradicable, reflected horizon-blue. It had always been so; only the tint had changed—the drab and white of the desert and the tropics, the sharp full red-and-blue of the old uniform, and now the chameleon-azure of this present one since three years ago. He had expected that, not only expected, but accepted, relinquishing volition and the fear of hunger and decision, to the extent of even being paid a few sure sous a day for the privilege and right, at no other cost than obedience and the exposure and risk of his tender and brittle bones and flesh, of immunity forever for his natural appetites. So for twenty years now he had looked at the anonymous denizens of the civilian world from the isolation, insulation, of that unchallengeable immunity, with a sort of contempt as alien intruders, rightless, on simple sufferance, himself and his interknit and interlocked kind in the impregnable fraternity of valour and endurance breasting through it behind the sharp and cleaving prow of their stripe and bars and stars and ribbons, like an armoured ship (or, since a year ago now, a tank) through a shoal of fish. But now something had happened. Looking about at the waiting faces (all except the young woman's; she alone was not watching him, the end of the heel of bread still cupped against her chewing face between her slender dirt-stained hands, so that it was not he alone, but the two of them, himself and the kinless and nameless girl, who seemed to stand in a narrow well of unbreathing), it seemed to him with a kind of terror that it was himself who was the alien, and not just alien but obsolete; that on that day twenty years ago, in return for the right and the chance to wear on the battle-soiled breast of his coat the battle-grimed symbolical candy-stripes of valour and endurance and fidelity and physical anguish and sacrifice he had sold his birthright in the race of man. But he did not show it. The candy-stripes themselves were the reason that he could not, and his wearing of them the proof that he would not.

'And so?' he said.

'It was the whole regiment,' the tall man said dreamily, in his murmurous, masculine, gentle, almost musing baritone. 'All of it. At zero, nobody left the trench except the officers and a few N.C.O.'s. That's right, not?'

'And so?' the sergeant said again.

'Why didn't the boche attack?' the tall man said. 'When they saw that we were not coming over? that something had happened to the attack? The drum-fire was all right, and the rolling barrage too, only when it lifted and the moment came, only the section leaders had climbed out of the trench, but that the men themselves were not coming? They must have seen that, not? When you have been facing another front only a thousand metres away for four years, you can see an attack fail to start, and probably why. And you can't say it was because of the barrage; that's why you get out of the trench in the first place and charge: to get out from under somebody's shelling—sometimes your own, not?'

The sergeant looked only at the tall man; he needed to do no more since he could feel the others—the quiet, attentive, quietly-breathing faces, listening, missing nothing. 'A field marshal,' the sergeant said in a bitter contemptuous voice. 'Maybe it's time somebody looked into that uniform you are wearing.' He held out his hand. 'Let's have a look at them.'

The tall man looked calmly and peacefully down at him a moment longer. Then his hand went somewhere under the smock and reappeared and extended the papers, folded once, stained and soiled and dog-eared at the crease. The sergeant took and opened them. Yet even then, he did not seem to be looking at the papers; his glance instead now flicking rapidly again about the other motionless intent faces, while the tall man still looked down at him, serene and waiting, and then speaking again, remote, calm, almost absently, conversational:

'And at noon yesterday, our whole front stopped except for token artillery, one gun to a battery each ten thousand metres, and at fifteen hours the British and the Americans stopped too, and when it got quiet you could hear the boche doing the same thing, so that by sundown yesterday there was no more gunfire in France except the token ones since they had to leave them for a little longer yet since all that silence, falling suddenly out of the sky on the human race after going on four years, might have destroyed it—' Rapidly and in one motion, the sergeant refolded the papers and extended them back toward the man, or apparently so, since before the man could raise his hand to take them, the sergeant's hand had grasped the front of his smock, gripping as one the crumple of the papers and the wadded mass of the rough cloth, jerking, though actually it was not the tall man but the sergeant who moved, the sergeant's brigand face nose to nose with the other's, his rotting discoloured teeth gaped for speech, though still empty of it because the other man was still talking in that calm unhurried murmur: 'And now General of Division Gragnon is bringing the whole lot of them back here to ask the Generalissimo to let him shoot them, since that much peace and silence, falling without warning on the human race—'

'Not even a field marshal,' the sergeant said in his furious, seething voice: 'an advocate.' He said, in that harsh furious murmur no louder than the other man's had been, to which the static attentive faces ringing them about seemed not to listen or even hear any more than they had listened to or heard the other man while he spoke, any more than the young woman herself did or was, still gnawing and tearing steadily at the bread behind her huddled hands, but only watching them, intent and incurious as deaf people. 'Ask the bastards you have come here to look at if they think anybody has quit.'

'I know that too,' the other said. 'I just said so. You saw my papers.'

WEDNESDAY

'So will the provost-marshal's adjutant,' the sergeant said, and flung, not the other man, but himself away and turned again, still clutching the crumpled papers and using his elbows and hands both this time to open his path back to the boulevard; then he stopped again suddenly and jerked his head up, and as they watched, he seemed to raise his whole body in order to look past and above the crowded heads and faces, in the direction of the old city gate. Then they all heard it, not only the sergeant already ducking back under the interlocked rifles, but even the young woman, who even stopped chewing behind her cupped hands to listen too, when as one the heads and the packed bodies turned away from her and toward the boulevard, not because so light on them had been the impact of her trouble and the spectacle of its alleviation, but because of the sound now coming up the boulevard from the old city gate like a wind beginning. Except for the shouts of the section leaders of the deployed infantry aligning each kerb, the sound was not voices yet so much as a sigh, an exhalation, travelling from breast to breast up the boulevard. It was as if the night's anxiety, quiescent for a time beneath the simple weight of waiting, now that the new day was about to reveal the actuality which in darkness had only been a dread, was gathering itself to flow over them like the new day itself in one great blinding wave, as the first car entered the city.

It contained the three generals. It came fast, so fast that the shouts of the section leaders and the clash of rifles as each section presented arms and then clashed back to 'at ease,' were not only continuous but overlapping so that the car seemed to progress on one prolonged crash of iron as on invisible wings with steel feathers —a long, dusty open car painted like a destroyer and flying the pennon of the supreme commander of all the allied armies, the three generals sitting side by side in the tonneau amid a rigid glitter of aides—the three old men who held individual command over each of the three individual armies, and the one of that three who, by mutual consent and accord, held supreme command over all (and, by that token and right, over everything beneath and on and above the distracted half-continent)—the Briton, the American, and between them the Generalissimo: the slight grey man with a face wise, intelligent, and unbelieving, who no longer believed in anything but his disillusion and his intelligence and his limitless

17

power—flashing across that terrified and aghast amazement and then gone, as the section leaders shouted again and the boots and the rifles crashed back to simple alert.

The lorries were right behind it. They were coming fast too, in close order and seemingly without end, since this was the whole regiment. But still there was no concerted, no definite, human sound yet, not even the crashing ejaculation of salute this time, but only the stir, the shift of movement in the crowd itself, pacing the first lorry in that silence which was still aghast and not quite believing, in which the anguish and terror seemed to rise to each lorry as it approached, and enclose it as it passed, and follow it as it sped on, broken only now and then when someone—a woman— cried out at one of the passing faces—a face which, because of the lorry's speed, had already passed and vanished before recognition became a fact, and the roar of the next lorry had already drowned it before the recognition became a cry, so that the lorries seemed to be travelling even faster than the car, as though the car, with half a continent supine before its bonnet, possessed the gift of leisure, where the lorries, whose destination could be computed in seconds now, had only the spur of shame.

They were open, with high, slatted sides as though for the transportation of cattle, packed like cattle with standing men, bare-headed, disarmed, stained from the front lines, with something desperate and defiant in the unshaven and sleepless faces which glared down at the crowd as if they had never seen human beings before, or could not see these now, or at least could not recognise them as human beings. They were like the faces of sleepwalkers looking backward across nightmares, recognising no one and no familiar things, glaring down across the fleeing irrevocable instant as if they were being hurried to execution itself, flashing on, rapid and successive and curiously identical, not despite the fact that each had an individuality and a name, but because of it; identical not because of an identical doom, but because each carried into that mutual doom a name and an individuality, and that most complete privacy of all: the capacity for that solitude in which every man has to die—flashing on as if they had no part nor interest in, and were not even aware of, the violence and speed with which or in which they rigidly moved, like phantoms or apparitions or perhaps figures cut without depth from tin or cardboard

and snatched in violent repetition across a stage set for a pantomime of anguish and fatality.

And now there was a concerted sound: a faint yelling beginning
somewhere in the *Place de Ville*, which the first lorry would be
reaching about now. It was high, thin with distance, prolonged,
not vindictive but defiant, with at the same time a curiously impersonal quality, as if the men it came from were not making, producing it, but merely passing through it as through a sudden noisy
though harmless burst of spring rain. It came in fact from the
Hôtel de Ville, which the first lorries were now passing, where the
three sentries now stood at attention beneath the three flags hanging windless now in the following stillness of the dawn breeze, and
where on the stone steps before the door the old generalissimo, the
other two generals having followed him out of the halted car, had
now stopped and turned, the two lesser generals stopping and turning with him, both on a step higher than his and so taller than he,
both as grey as he, both slightly behind him though not behind
each other, while the first lorry passed, and the hatless, dishevelled,
somnambulistic men in it, waked perhaps at sight of the three flags
or perhaps by the simple isolation of the three old men after the
crowded boulevard, but waking anyway, and in that same instant
divining, identifying the three gaudy panoplied old men, not merely by their juxtaposition to the three flags but by their isolation, like
that of three plague carriers in the empty centre of an aghast and
fleeing city, or perhaps the three survivors of a city swept by plague,
immune and impervious, gaudy and panoplied and seemingly as
harmless in time as a photograph posed and fading since these fifty
or sixty years—but—the men in the lorries—anyway waking, as
one man, and as one man yelling, shaking their clenched hands
down at the three impassive figures, the yelling passing from lorry
to lorry as each entered the yelling and sped on, until the last one
seemed to trail behind it a cloud of doomed and forlorn repudiation filled with gaped faces and threatening fists like the fading
cloud of its own dust.

It was like dust, still hanging in the air long after the object—
the motion, the friction, the body, the momentum, speed—which
had produced it was gone and vanished. Because the whole boulevard was filled with yelling now, no longer defiant but just amazed
and incredulous, the two back-flung parallel banks of massed bodies

and wan faces gaped and frantic with adjuration. Because there was still one more lorry. It came fast too; although there were two hundred yards between it and the last one preceding it, this one seemed to be travelling twice as fast as the others, just as the others had seemed to be travelling twice as fast as the pennoned car containing the three generals. Yet it seemed to move in complete silence. There was something almost furtive about it. Where the others had seemed to pass noisily, violently almost, in a kind of defiant valedictory of shame and despair, this one came and was gone with a sort of noiseless, celeritous effacement, as if the men who drove it abhorred, not its destination at all, but rather its contents.

It was open, like the others, indistinguishable from the others, except by its cargo. Because, where the others had been packed with standing men, this one carried only thirteen. They were hatless and dirty and battle-stained too, but they were manacled, chained to one another and to the lorry itself like wild beasts, so that at first glance they looked not merely like foreigners but like creatures of another race, another species; alien, bizarre, and strange, even though they wore on their collar-tabs the same regimental numerals, to the rest of the regiment which had not only preceded them by that reduceless gap but which had even seemed to be fleeing from them, not only by their chains and isolation, but by their very expressions and attitudes too: where the faces in the other fleeing lorries had been dazed and spent, like those of men too long under ether, the faces of these thirteen were merely grave, attentive, watchful. Then you saw that four of the thirteen were really foreigners, alien not only by their gyves and isolation to the rest of the regiment but, against the whole panorama of city and soil across which the lorry was rushing them—the faces of four mountain men in a country which had no mountains, of peasants in a land which no longer had a peasantry; alien even among the other nine among whom they were chained and shackled, since where the other nine were grave and watchful and a little—not too much—concerned, three of the four who were not Frenchmen were merely a little puzzled, alert too, almost decorous, curious and interested: the mountain peasants whom they resembled, entering for the first time a strange valley market town, say; men overtaken suddenly by an uproar in a tongue which they had no hope of comprehending and, indeed, not much interest in, and therefore no concern in its significance—three of the four who were not Frenchmen, that is, because now the crowd itself had discerned that the fourth one was alien still somehow even to the other three, if only in being the sole object of its vituperation and terror and fury. Because it was to—against—this one man that the crowd was raising its voices and its clenched hands, having barely glanced at the other twelve. He stood near the front, his hands resting quietly on the top rail, so that the loop of chain between his wrists and the corporal's stripes on his sleeve were both visible, with an alien face like all the other twelve, a mountain peasant's face like the last three, a little younger than several of them, looking down at the fleeing sea of eyes and gaped mouths and fists with the same watchfulness as the other twelve, but with neither the bafflement nor the concern—a face merely interested, attentive, and calm, with something else in it which none of the others had: a comprehension, understanding, utterly free of compassion, as if he had already anticipated without censure or pity the uproar which rose and paced and followed the lorry as it sped on.

It crossed in its turn the *Place de Ville*, where the three generals still stood like a posed camera group on the steps of the *Hôtel*. Perhaps this time it was the simple juxtaposition of the three flags which were just beginning to stir in the reversed day wind, since certainly none of the other three who were not Frenchmen, and possibly none of the whole twelve, seemed to remark the significance of the three dissimilar banners, nor even to see the three starred and braided old men standing beneath them. It was only the thirteenth man who seemed to notice, see, remark; only the gaze of the corporal in passing as he and the old supreme general, whom no man in any of the other lorries could say had ever looked definitely at any one of them, stared full at each other across the moment which could not last because of the vehicle's speed—the peasant's face above the corporal's chevrons and the shackled wrists in the speeding lorry, and the grey inscrutable face above the stars of supreme rank and the bright ribbons of honour and glory on the *Hôtel* steps, looking at each other across the fleeing instant. Then the lorry was gone. The old generalissimo turned, his two confreres turning with him, flanking him in rigid protocol; the three sentries clashed and stamped to present arms as the limber and glittering young aide sprang and opened the door.

This time, the commotion went almost unnoticed, not only because of the yelling and uproar, but because the crowd itself was moving now. It was the young woman again, the one who had fainted. She was still gnawing at the bread when the last lorry came up. Then she ceased, and those nearest remembered later that she moved, cried out, and tried to run, to break through the crowd and into the street as if to intercept or overtake the lorry. But by that time, they were all moving toward the street, even those at whose backs she was clawing and scrabbling and at whose faces she was trying to cry, say something through the mass of chewed bread in her mouth. So they stopped remembering her at all, and there remained only the man who had given her the bread, upon whose chest she was still hammering with the hand which still clutched the fragment of the morsel, while she tried to cry something at him through the wet mass in her mouth.

Then she began to spit the chewed bread at him, not deliberately, intentionally, but because there was not time to turn her head aside and void her mouth for speech, already screaming something at him through the spew and spray of mastication. But the man was already running too, wiping his face on his sleeve, vanishing into the crowd as it burst at last through the interlocked rifles and poured into the street. Still clutching what remained of the bread, she ran too. For a while, she even kept up with them, running and darting between and among them with an urgency apparently even greater than theirs, as the whole mass of them poured up the boulevard after the fleeing lorries. But presently the ones she had passed began to overtake her in turn and pass her: soon she was running in a fading remnant of dispersal, panting and stumbling, seeming to run now in spent and frantic retrograde to the whole city's motion, the whole world's, so that when she reached the *Place de Ville* at last, and stopped, all mankind seemed to have drained away and vanished, bequeathing, relicting to her the broad, once-more empty boulevard and the *Place* and even, for t⁀ ıt moment, the city and the earth itself—a slight woman, not much more than a girl, who had been pretty once, and could be again, with sleep and something to eat and a little warm water and soap and a comb, and whatever it was out of her eyes, standing in the empty *Place*, wringing her hands.

MONDAY * MONDAY NIGHT

W HEN the choice to accept or refuse to command the attack
was first offered him, the general commanding the division
which contained the regiment said immediately: 'Of course.
Thanks. What is it?' Because it seemed to him that here at last
was the chance which he had needed and wanted for more years
than he cared to remember, so many years in fact that he had, as
he realised now, given up hope of ever getting. Because at some
moment in his past which even he could not specifically postulate,
something had happened to him, or at least to his career.

It seemed to him that he had been intended by fate itself to be
the perfect soldier: pastless, unhampered, and complete. His first
recollection had been a Pyrenean orphanage run by a Catholic
sisterhood, where there was no record of his parentage whatever,
even to be concealed. At seventeen, he was an enlisted private; at
twenty-four, he had been three years a sergeant and of such destined promise that his regimental commander (himself a self-made
man who had risen from the ranks) gave no one any rest until the
protégé also had his chance for officers' school; by 1914 he had
established a splendid record as a desert colonel of Spahis, and,
immediately in France itself, the beginning of an unimpeachable
one as a brigadier, so that to those who believed in him and watched
his career (he had no influence either, and no friends too save
those, like the obscure colonel of his sergeantcy, whom he had
made, earned himself by his own efforts and record) there seemed
no limit to his destiny save the premature end of the war itself.

Then something happened. Not to him: he had not changed,
he was still competent, still unhampered and complete. He seemed
merely to have lost or mislaid somewhere, at some point, the old
habit or mantle or aura or affinity for almost monotonous success
in which he had seemed to move as in his garments, as if not he
but his destiny had slowed down, not changed: just slowed down
for the time being: which idea his superiors themselves seemed to

hold, since he got in due time (in fact, a little sooner than some) the next star for his hat and not only the division which went with it but the opportunities too, indicating that his superiors still believed that at any moment now he might recover, or rediscover, the secret of the old successfulness.

But that was two years ago, and for a year now even the opportunities had ceased, as though at last even the superiors had come around to his own belief that the high tide of his hopes and aspirations had fluxed three years ago, three years before the last backwash of his destiny finally ebbed from beneath him, leaving him stranded a mere general of division still in a war already three years defunctive. It—the war—would hang on a while yet, of course; it would take the Americans, the innocent newcomers, another year probably to discover that you cannot really whip Germans: you can only exhaust them. It might even last another ten years or even another twenty, by which time France and Britain would have vanished as military and even political integers and the war would have become a matter of a handful of Americans who didn't even have ships to go back home in, battling with branches from shattered trees and the rafters from ruined houses and the stones from fences of weed-choked fields and the broken bayonets and stocks of rotted guns and rusted fragments wrenched from crashed aeroplanes and burned tanks, against the skeletons of German companies stiffened by a few Frenchmen and Britons tough enough like himself to endure still, to endure as he would always, immune to nationality, to exhaustion, even to victory—by which time he hoped he himself would be dead.

Because by ordinary he believed himself incapable of hoping: only of daring, without fear or qualm or regret within the iron and simple framework of the destiny which he believed would never betray him so long as he continued to dare without question or qualm or regret, but which apparently had abandoned him, leaving him only the capacity to dare, until two days ago when his corps commander sent for him. The corps commander was his only friend in France, or anywhere else above earth, for that matter. They had been subalterns together in the same regiment into which he had been commissioned. But Lallemont, though a poor man too, had along with ability just enough of the sort of connections which not only made the difference between division and corps command at the same length of service, but placed Lallemont quite favourably for the next vacant army command. Though when Lallemont said, 'I've something for you, if you want it,' he realised that what he had thought was the capacity to dare was still soiled just a little with the baseless hoping which is the diet of weaklings. But that was all right too: who, even though apparently abandoned by destiny, still had not been wrong in dedicating his life as he had: even though abandoned, he had never let his chosen vocation down; and sure enough in his need, the vocation had remembered him.

So he said, 'Thanks. What?' Lallemont told him. Whereupon for a moment he believed that he had not understood. But this passed, because in the next one he saw the whole picture. The attack was already doomed in its embryo, and whoever commanded it, delivered it, along with it. It was not that his trained professional judgment told him that the affair, as the corps commander presented it, would be touch-and-go and hence more than doubtful. That would not have stopped him. On the contrary, that would have been a challenge, as if the old destiny had not abandoned him at all. It was because that same trained judgment saw at once that this particular attack was intended to fail: a sacrifice already planned and doomed in some vaster scheme, in which it would not matter either way, whether the attack failed or not: only that the attack must be made: and more than that, since here the whole long twenty-odd years of training and dedication paid him off in clairvoyance; he saw the thing not only from its front and public view, but from behind it too: the cheapest attack would be one which must fail, harmlessly to all if delivered by a man who had neither friends nor influence to make people with five stars on the General Staff, or civilians with red rosettes in the Quai d'Orsay, squirm. He didn't for even one second think of the old grey man in the *Hôtel de Ville* at Chaulnesmont. He thought for even less time than that: *Lallemont is saving his own neck*. He thought—and now he knew that he was indeed lost—*It's Mama Bidet*. But he only said:

'I can't afford a failure.'

'There will be a ribbon,' the corps commander said.

'I don't have enough rank to get the one they give for failures.'

'Yes,' the corps commander said. 'This time.'

'So it's that bad,' the division commander said. 'That serious. That urgent. All between Bidet and his baton is one infantry division. And that one, mine.' They stared at each other. Then the corps commander started to speak. The division commander didn't permit him to. 'Stow it,' the division commander said. That is, that's what he conveyed. What he spoke was a phrase pithy, succinct and obscene out of his life as an N.C.O. in the African regiment recruited from the prison- and gutter-sweepings of Europe before he and the corps commander had ever seen each other. He said: 'So I have no choice.'

'You have no choice,' the corps commander said.

The division commander always watched his attacks from the nearest forward observer's post; it had been his habit always; that was a part of his record too. This time, he had one especially prepared, on an elevation, revetted and sandbagged behind a steel plate, with one telephone line direct to corps headquarters and another to the artillery commander; here, synchronised watch in hand while the preliminary barrage wailed and screeched overhead on to the German wire, he looked down upon his own front line and on the opposite one which even those who had assigned him the attack didn't intend to breach, as from a balcony seat at the opera. Or box seat, and not just any box, but the royal one: the victim by regal dispensation watching in solitary splendour the preparations for his execution, watching not the opera's final scene, but his own before he moved, irrevocable and forever, into some back-area job in that region whose function was to arm and equip the combat divisions who reaped the glorious death and the immortal renown; from now on, his to reap every hope save glory, and every right save the chance to die for it. He could desert, of course, but where? To whom? The only people who would accept a failed French general would be people so far free of the war: the Dutch, who were off the normal course of German invasions, and the Spanish, who were too poor even to make a two-day excursion to it, as the Portuguese did, for excitement and change of scene—in which case—the Spanish one—he would not even be paid for risking his life and what remained of his reputation, until he corrected that: thinking how war and drink are the two things man is never too poor to buy. His wife and children may be shoeless; someone will always buy him drink or weapons, thinking *More than that.*

*The last person a man planning to set up in the wine trade would approach
for a loan would be a rival wine-dealer. A nation preparing for war can
borrow from the very nation it aims to destroy.*

Then he didn't even have a failure. He had a mutiny. When
the barrage lifted, he was not even observing the scene beneath
him, but was already looking at his watch-face. He didn't need to
see the attack. After watching them from beneath his stars for
three years now, he had become an expert, not merely in forecast-
ing failure, but in predicting almost exactly when, where, at what
point in time and terrain, they would become void and harmless—
this, even when he was not familiar with the troops making the
attack, which in the present case he was, having selected this particular regiment the day before because he knew, on the one hand,
not only the condition of the regiment but its colonel's belief in
it and the record of his success with it; and on the other, its value
as measured against each of the other three in the division; he
knew it would deliver the attack near enough to the maximum
demanded of him, yet if the foreordained failure meant its temporary wreckage or even permanent ruin, this would weigh less in
the strength and morale of the division than that of any of the
other three; he could never, breathing, have been convinced or
even told that he had chosen the regiment out of his division exactly
as the group commander had chosen the division out of his
armies.

So he simply followed the jerking watch-hand, waiting for it to
establish the point when all the men who were to get through the
wire would be beyond it. Then he looked up and saw nothing,
nothing at all in the space beyond the wire which by now should
have been filled with running and falling men; he saw only a few
figures crouching along his own parapet, not advancing at all but
apparently yelling, screaming and gesticulating, downward into the
trench—the officers and N.C.O.'S, the company and section leaders
who obviously had been betrayed as he had been. Because he knew
at once what had happened. He was quite calm; he thought without passion or even astonishment: *So this was reserved for me too*
as he dropped the binocular back into its case on his chest and
snapped the cover down and spoke to the aide beside him, indicating the line to Corps Headquarters: 'Say that the attack failed to
leave the trench. Tell them to ratify me to Artillery. Say I'm on

27

my way out now,' and took the other telephone himself and spoke down it: 'Gragnon. I want two barrages. Re-range one on the enemy wire. Range the other on the communication trenches behind the ——th Regiment and continue until you have a remand from Corps,' and put the telephone down and turned toward the exit.

'Sir!' the aide at the other telephone cried, 'here's General Lallemont himself!' But the division commander didn't even pause, not until the tunnel broached at last into light, and then only long enough to listen for a moment to the screeching crescendo of shells overhead, listening with a sort of impersonal detached attentiveness, as if he were a messenger, a runner, sent there to ascertain whether or not the guns were still firing, and to return and report. It had been twenty years now, the first scrap of braid not even tarnished on his sleeve, since he had accepted, established as the first stone in the edifice of his career: *A commander must be so hated, or at least feared by his troops that, immunised by that fury, they will attempt any odds, any time, any where.* He stood, not stopped, just paused, his face lifted too, like the runner taking that simple precaution against the possibility that those to whom he would report might demand the authority of his eyes too, or order him to walk the whole distance back again to rectify the oversight, thinking: *Except that I didn't intend that they should hate me so much they would refuse to attack at all because I didn't think then that a commander could be hated that much, apparently didn't know even this morning that soldiers could hate that much, being soldiers;* thinking quietly: *Of course. Countermand the barrage, stop it, let them come over; the whole thing will be obliterated then, effaced, and I need only say that they were ready for me before my attack ever started, with none to refute me since those who could will no longer be alive;* thinking with what he considered not even sardonicism nor even wittiness, but just humour: *With a regiment which has already mutinied holding the line, they will overrun and destroy the whole division in ten or fifteen minutes. Then even those who are giving him the baton will appreciate the value of their gift*—already walking again, on for another thousand metres, almost to the end of the communication trench where his car would be waiting; and this time he did stop, utterly; he didn't know how long it had been going on nor even how long he had been hearing it: no puny concentration now of guns behind one single regimental front; it seemed to him that he could hear the fury spreading battery to battery in both directions along the whole front until every piece in the entire sector must be in frantic action. *They did come over,* he thought. *They did. The whole line has collapsed; not just one mutinied regiment, but the whole line of us;* already turned to run back up the trench before he could catch himself, telling himself, *It's too late; you can't get back in time now*—catching himself back into sanity, or at least into trained military logic and reason, even if he did have to use what he thought was humour (and this time called wittiness too, the wit perhaps of despair) in order to do it: *Nonsense. What reason could they have had for an assault at this moment? How could the boche have known even before I did that one of my regiments was going to mutiny? And even if they did know it, how could they afford to give Bidet his German marshalcy at the rate of just one regiment at a time?*—walking on again, saying quietly aloud this time: 'That's the clatter a falling general makes.'

Two field howitzers were firing almost over his waiting car. They had not been there at dawn when he left it, and his driver could not have heard him if he had spoken, which he did not: one peremptory gesture as he got in, sitting rigid and calm and parallel now for a while to the pandemonium of guns stretching farther than hearing did; still quite calm when he got out of the car at Corps Headquarters, not even seeing at first that the corps commander was already waiting for him at the door, then reversing in midstride and returning to the car, still striding rigidly on when the corps commander overtook him and put one hand on his arm and began to draw him aside toward where the corps car waited. The corps commander spoke the army commander's name. 'He's waiting for us,' he said.

'And then, Bidet,' the division commander said. 'I want authority from Bidet's own lips to shoot them.'

'In with you,' the corps commander said, touching him again, almost shoving him into the car, then following, closing the door himself, the car already in motion, so that the orderly had to leap for the running board; soon they were moving fast too beside, beneath the horizon's loud parallel, the division commander rigid, erect, immobile, staring ahead, while the corps commander, leaning back, watched him, or what was visible of the calm and invincible face. 'And suppose he refuses,' the corps commander said.

'I hope he does,' the division commander said. 'All I ask is to be sent under arrest to Chaulnesmont.'

'Listen to me,' the corps commander said. 'Can't you see that it will not matter to Bidet whether it failed or not or how it failed or even whether it was made or not? That he will get his baton just the same, anyway?'

'Even if the boche destroys us?'

'Destroys us?' the corps commander said. 'Listen.' He jerked his hand toward the east where, fast though they were moving, the division commander might have realised now that the uproar still reached farther and faster than hearing moved. 'The boche doesn't want to destroy us, any more than we would want, could afford, to destroy him. Can't you understand: either of us, without the other, couldn't exist? That even if nobody was left in France to confer Bidet's baton, some boche would be selected, even if there remained only one private, and elevated high enough in French rank to do it? That Bidet didn't choose you for this because you were Charles Gragnon, but because you were General of Division Gragnon at this time, this day, this hour?'

'Us?' the division commander repeated.

'Us!' the corps commander said.

'So I failed, not in a front line at six this morning, but the day before yesterday in your headquarters—or maybe ten years ago, or maybe forty-seven years ago.'

'You did not fail at all,' the corps commander said.

'I lost a whole regiment. And not even by an attack: by a provost marshal's machine-gun squad.'

'Does it matter how they will die?'

'It does to me. How it dies is the reason it died. That's my record.'

'Bah,' the corps commander said.

'Since what I lost was merely Charles Gragnon. While what I saved was France—'

'You saved us,' the corps commander said.

'Us?' the division commander repeated again.

'Us,' the corps commander said in that voice harsh and strong with pride: 'the lieutenants, the captains, the majors and colonels and sergeants all with the same privilege: the opportunity to lie some day in the casket of a general or a marshal among the flags of our nation's glory in the palace of the Invalides—'

'Except that the Americans and British and Germans don't call theirs "Invalides".'

'All right, all right,' the corps commander said, '—merely in return for fidelity and devotion and accepting a little risk, gambling a petty stake which, lacking glory, was no better than any vegetable's to begin with, and deserved no less of obscurity for its fate. Failed,' he said. 'Failed. Charles Gragnon, from sergeant to general of division before he was forty-five years old—that is, forty-seven—'

'And then lost.'

'So did the British lieutenant general who commanded that army in Picardy two months ago.'

'And whatever boche it was who lost contact or mislaid his maps and compass in Belgium three years ago,' the division commander said. 'And the one who thought they could come through at Verdun. And the one who thought the Chemin des Dames would be vulnerable, having a female name.' He said: 'So it's not we who conquer each other, because we are not even fighting each other. It's simple nameless war which decimates our ranks. All of us: captains and colonels, British and American and German and us, shoulder to shoulder, our backs to the long invincible wall of our glorious tradition, giving and asking . . . Asking? not even accepting quarter—'

'Bah,' the corps commander said again. 'It is man who is our enemy: the vast seething moiling spiritless mass of him. Once to each period of his inglorious history, one of us appears with the stature of a giant, suddenly and without warning in the middle of a nation as a dairymaid enters a buttery, and with his sword for paddle he heaps and pounds and stiffens the malleable mass and even holds it cohered and purposeful for a time. But never for always, nor even for very long: sometimes before he can even turn his back, it has relinquished, dis-cohered, faster and faster flowing and seeking back to its own base anonymity. Like that out there this morning—' Again the corps commander made the brief indicative gesture.

'Like what out there?' the division commander said; whereupon the corps commander said almost exactly what the group commander would say within the next hour:

'It cannot be that you don't even know what happened.'

A FABLE

'I lost Charles Gragnon.'

'Bah,' the corps commander said. 'We have lost nothing. We were merely faced without warning by an occupational hazard. We hauled them up out of their ignominious mud by their boot-straps; in one more little instant they might have changed the world's face. But they never do. They collapse, as yours did this morning. They always will. But not us. We will even drag them willy-nilly up again, in time, and they will collapse again. But not us. It won't be us.'

The army commander was waiting too; the car had barely to stop for him. As soon as it was in motion again, the division commander made for the second time his request in the flat, calm, almost dispassionate voice: 'I shall shoot them, of course.' The army commander didn't answer. The division commander had not expected him to. He would not have heard any answer because he was not even listening to the other two voices murmuring to each other in brief, rapid, half-finished phrases as the corps commander briefed, reviewed to the army commander by number and designation, the regiments in the other divisions on either flank of his own, until the two voices had locked block into regimental block the long mosaic of the whole army front.

And—not only no sound of guns here, but never at any time— they were challenged at the chateau gates and entered the park, a guide on the running board now so that they didn't even pause at the carved rococo entrance but went on around to the side, across a courtyard bustling with orderlies and couriers and popping motorcycles, passing—and the division commander neither noticed nor cared here either—two cars flying the pennons of two other army commanders, and a third car which was British, and a fourth one which had not even been manufactured on this side of the Atlantic, and on to a *porte-cochere* at the back of the chateau and so directly into the shabby cluttered cubicle not much larger than a clothes press, notched into the chateau's Italianate *bijou* like a rusted spur in a bride's cake, from which the group commander conducted the affairs of his armies.

They were all there: the commanders of the two other armies which composed the group of armies, their heavy moustaches, al-ready shaped to noon's spoon, richly luxuriant from the daily ritual of soup; the English chief of staff who could have looked no more indomitably and rigidly youthful if the corset had been laced in full view on the outside of his tunic, with his bright ribbons and wisps of brass and scarlet tabs and his white hair and moustache and his blue eyes the colour of icy war; and the American colonel with the face of a Boston shipping magnate (which indeed he was, or at least the entailed scion of one)—or rather, an eighteenth-century face: the face of that predecessor or forefather who at twenty-five had retired rich from the quarter deck of a Middle Passage slaver, and at thirty had his name illuminated in coloured glass above his Beacon Hill pew. He was the guest, the privileged, since for three years it had not even been his nation's war, who had brought already into the conclave the privileged guest's air of prim, faintly spinsterish disapproval—an air, quality, appearance too, almost Victorian in fact, from his comfortable old man's shoes and the simple leather puttees of a Northumberland drover (both —shoes and puttees—beautifully polished but obviously purchased at different times and places and so never to match in colour, and neither matching the ordnance belt which obviously had been acquired in two places also, making four different tones of leather) and the simple flareless breeches cut from the same bolt as the short-tailed jacket rising unblemished by any brass to the high-boned throat with its prim piping of linen collar backside foremost like the dog-collar of a priest. (There was an anecdote about that uniform, or rather about its wearer, the colonel, going the rounds of messes six months ago, about how, shortly after the American headquarters had been set up, a junior officer—no Bostonian, this: a New Yorker—had appeared before the colonel one morning in the Bedford cords of a British officer and a long-skirted tunic cut by a London tailor, though it did have the high closed throat; the colonel would meet many duplicates of it later, but not then because that was 1917; the youth appearing a little sheepishly, probably a little fearfully, wishing perhaps, as many another pioneer has done, that he had let someone else be first, before the cold banker's eyes of his superior, saying presently: 'You think I shouldn't have done it? It's bad form, taste, aping—'; then the colonel, pleasant, immediate: 'Why not? They taught us the art of war in 1783 by losing one to us; they should not object lending us the clothes in 1917 to win one for them.')

And, cynosure of all, the Mama Bidet, the General Cabinet, the Marshal d'Aisance of the division commander's calm and ice-like implacability not for justice for himself but for vindication of his military record, who—the group commander—had brought twenty-five years ago into the African sun glare not a bent for war (that would reveal later) and not even a simple normal thirst for glory and rank, but a cold, pitiless preoccupation with the functioning of that mucous-lined orifice inside his army breeches, which accompanied (even preceded) him from troop to squadron to regiment to brigade, division and corps and army and army group as he advanced and rose, more immune to harm as his stars increased in number and his gift for war found field and scope, but no more pitiless—the short, healthy, pot-bellied little man who looked like a green grocer retired happy and cheerful at fifty, and then ten years later dressed not too willingly for a masquerade in the ill-fitting private's tunic without a single ribbon on it nor even any insigne of rank, whose real name had been an authority for fifteen years among textbook soldiers on how to keep troops fit, and a byword for four years among field commanders on how to fight them.

He didn't ask the division commander to sit down when the army- and corps-commanders did; as far as the division commander could have affirmed, the group commander had not even remarked his presence, leaving him to stand while that unbidden and uncaring part of his attention recorded the tedious recapitulation of regiments and divisions, not merely by their positions in the front but by their past records and the districts of their derivation and their officers' names and records, the army commander talking, rapid and succinct, nothing still of alarm in the voice and not very much of concern: just alertness, precision, care. Nor, watching—or not specifically watching the group commander because he was not really watching anything: just looking steadily at or toward the group commander as he had been doing ever since he entered, aware suddenly that he not only could not remember when he had blinked his eyes last, but that he felt no need to blink them—did it seem to the division commander that the group commander was listening either, though he must have been, quietly and courteously and inattentively; until suddenly the division commander realised that the group commander had been looking at him for several seconds. Then the others seemed to become aware of it too; the army commander stopped talking, then said:

'This is Gragnon. It was his division.'

'Ah yes,' the group commander said. He spoke directly to the division commander in the same tone, pleasant and inflectionless: 'Many thanks. You may return to your troops,' and turned again to the army commander. 'Yes?' Then for another half minute, the army commander's voice; and now the division commander, rigid and unblinking, was looking at nothing at all, rigid and unblinking still until the army commander's voice stopped again, the division commander not even bothering to bring vision back behind his eyes even after the group commander spoke to him again: 'Yes?'

Standing not quite at attention, looking not at anything but merely staring at rigid eye level above the group commander's head, the division commander made his formal request for permission to have the whole regiment executed. The group commander heard him through. There was nothing whatever in the group commander's face.

'Endorsed as received,' he said. 'Return to your troops.' The division commander did not move. He might not have heard even. The group commander sat back in his chair and spoke to the army commander without even turning his head: 'Henri, will you conduct these gentlemen to the little drawing room and have them bring wine, whisky, tea, whatever they fancy?' He said to the American colonel in quite passable English: 'I have heard of your United States Coca-Cola. My regrets and apologies that I do not have that for you yet. But soon we hope, eh?'

'Thank you, General,' the colonel said in better than passable French: 'The only European terms we decline to accept are German ones.'

Then they were gone; the door closed behind them. The division commander had not moved. The group commander looked at him. His voice was still merely pleasant, not even quizzical: 'A general of division. You have come a long way from Africa, Sergeant Gragnon.'

'So have you,' the division commander said, '—Mama Bidet.'— speaking in his cold, flat voice, with no inflection nor emphasis either, the name given not secretly so much as merely when he was out of earshot, or perhaps not even that but simply from the

35

inviolable security of their rankless state, by the men in ranks to the group commander soon after he came out as a subaltern into the African regiment in which the division commander was already a sergeant: 'A long way, Monsieur the General Cabinet, Monsieur soon-to-be the Marshal d'Aisance.' And still nothing in the group commander's face; his voice was still calm, yet there now crept into it a shadow of something else, something speculative and even a little astonished, though the division commander would prove that he at least had not remarked it. Then the group commander said:

'I seem to have been more right than even I knew or hoped. When you came in, I felt that perhaps I owed you an apology. Now I am sure of it.'

'You demean yourself,' the division commander said. 'How could a man doubting his own infallibility get that many stars? And how could a man with that many stars retain any doubts about anything?'

The group commander looked at the division commander for another moment. Then he said: 'It can't be possible that you don't even see that it has already ceased to matter whether these three thousand men or these four men die or not. That there is already more to this than the execution of twice three thousand men could remedy or even change.'

'Speak for yourself,' the division commander said. 'I have seen ten times three thousand dead Frenchmen.' He said, 'You will say, "Slain by other Frenchmen"?' He said, repeated, rote-like, cold, unemphasised, almost telegraphic: '*Comité des Forges. De Ferrovie. S.P.A.D.* The people at Billancourt. Not to mention the English and Americans, since they are not French, at least not until they have conquered us. What will it matter to the three thousand or the ten times three thousand, when they are dead? Nor matter to us who killed them, if we are successful?'

'By "successful" you mean "victorious",' the group commander said. 'And by "we" of course, you mean France.'

In his flat, cold voice the division commander repeated the simple, explicit, soldiery expletive of the Cambronne legend.

'A fact, but not a rejoinder,' the group commander said.

The division commander said the word again. 'For me, a ribbon tomorrow; for you, a baton before you die. Since mine is worth only a regiment, yours will certainly be cheap at that.'

MONDAY

Presently the group commander said: 'What you are really asking me for is to endorse you for a court-martial. You're offering me the choice between sending you to the commander-in-chief, and compelling you to go yourself.' The division commander did not move. He was not going to. They both knew it. 'Return to your headquarters,' the group commander said. 'You will be notified there when the Marshal will see you at Chaulnesmont.'

He returned to Corps Headquarters with the corps commander, and got his own car; he would probably not even remember that the corps commander did not ask him to lunch. He would not have cared. He would have declined anyway. The group commander had told him to return to his own headquarters: an order. He was probably not even aware that he was disobeying it, getting into his car and saying briefly to the driver: 'The line.' Though it would be too late. It was nearing two o'clock; the regiment would long since have been evacuated and disarmed and replaced; it would be too late to watch it pass now and so see for himself that it was done, just as he had paused in the communication trench to make sure that the artillery was still firing. He was going back as a chef might return two or three hours afterward to the kitchen where a dish he had been preparing had burned or perhaps exploded, not to help nor even advise in tidying up, but merely to see what might remain with some of the litter removed; not to regret it, because that would be a waste of regret, but just to see, to check; not even thinking about it, not thinking about anything, immobile and calm in the moving car, carrying inside him like a liquid sealed in a vacuum bottle that cold, inflexible undeviable determination for justice to his rank at any cost, vindication of his record at all.

So at first he did not realise what had startled, shocked him. He said sharply: 'Stop' and sat in the halted car in the ringing silence which he hadn't even heard yet because he had never heard anything here before but guns: no longer a starred, solitary man in a staff car behind the French battle-front, but a solitary boy lying on his stomach on a stone wall outside the Pyrenean village where, for all any records stated or knowledge remembered, he had been born an orphan; listening now to the same cicada chirring and buzzing in a tangle of cordite-blasted weeds beyond the escarpment landmarked since last winter by the skeleton tail of a crashed German aeroplane. Then he heard the lark too, high and invisible,

37

almost liquid but not quite, like four small gold coins dropped
without haste into a cup of soft silver, he and the driver staring at
each other until he said, loud and harsh: 'Drive on!'—moving on
again; and sure enough, there was the lark again, incredible and
serene, and then again the unbearable golden silence, so that he
wanted to clap his hands to his ears, bury his head, until at last
the lark once more relieved it.

Though the two batteries at the camouflaged corner were not
firing now, they were not only still there, but a section of heavy
howitzers was flanked on them, the gunners watching him quietly
as he approached, chop-striding, bull-chested, virile, in appearance
impervious and indestructible, starred and exalted and, within this
particular eye-range of earth, supreme and omnipotent still, yet
who, because of those very stars, didn't dare ask whoever was senior
here when he had ceased to fire, let alone where his orders to do
so had come from, thinking how he had heard all his military life
about the ineradicable mark which war left on a man's face, without ever having seen it himself, but at least he had seen now what
peace did to men's faces. Because he knew now that the silence
extended much further than one divisional front or even than the
two flanking ones; knowing now what the corps commander and
the group commander both had meant when they had said in
almost the same words: 'It cannot be that you don't even know
what is happening,' thinking *I am not even to have a court-martial
for incompetence. Now that the war is over, they won't have to allow me
a court because nobody will care any longer, nobody compelled by simple
military regulations to see that my record receives justice.*

'Who commands here?' he said. But before the captain could
answer, a major appeared from beyond the guns. 'Gragnon, here,'
the division commander said. 'You're standing to, of course.'

'Yes, General,' the major said. 'That was the order which came
up with the remand. What is it, General? What's happening?'—
saying the last of it to the division commander's back, because he
had already turned, striding on, rigidly erect and only a little blind;
then a battery did fire, two kilometres and perhaps more to the
south: a salvo, a ragged thud; and, chop-striding, unhurried, burly
and virile and indestructible, there occurred inside him a burst, a
giving-away, a flow of something which if he had still been the
unfathered unmothered boy secure in the privacy of his abandoned

Pyrenean wall, would have been tears, no more visible then than now, no more then than now of grief, but of inflexibility. Then another battery fired, one salvo, less than a kilometre away this time, the division commander not faltering, merely altering direction in midstride and instead of entering the communication trench he rapidly climbed the escarpment, into the pocked field beyond it, not running still but walking so fast that he was a considerable distance away when the next battery fired, this time one of those he had just left, firing its salvo in its turn as if whoever had created the silence were underlining it, calling men's attention to it with the measured meaningless slams, saying with each burst of puny uproar, 'Hear it? Hear it?'

His first brigade's headquarters was the cellar of a ruined farm. There were several people there, but he was not inside long enough to have recognised any of them, even if he had wanted to or tried. Almost immediately he was outside again, wrenching his arm from the hand of the aide who had been with him in the observation post when the attack failed. But he did take the flask, the brandy insentient as stale water in his throat, slightly warm from the aide's body-heat, tasteless. Because here at last was one of the rare moments in the solitude and pride of command when he could be General Gragnon without being General of Division Gragnon too. What—' he said.

'Come,' the aide said rapidly. But the division commander jerked his arm from the aide's hand again, not following but preceding the aide for a short distance into the farmyard, then stopping and turning.

'Now,' he said.

'They didn't even tell you?' the aide said. He didn't answer, immobile, bull-like and indestructible; and, bull-like and indestructible, quite calm. The aide told him. 'They are stopping it. Our whole front—I don't meant just our division and corps, but the whole French front—remanded at noon except for air patrols and artillery like that yonder at the corner. And the air people are not crossing: just patrolling up and down our front, and the orders to the artillery were to range, not on the boche, but between us and them, on what the Americans call no-man's land. And the boche is doing the same thing with his artillery and air, and the order is out for the British and Americans to remand at fifteen hours, to

see if the boche will do the same thing in front of them.' The
division commander stared at him. 'It's not just our division: it's
all of them: us and the boche too.' Then the aide saw that even
now the division commander did not understand. 'It's the men,'
the aide said. 'The ranks. Not just that regiment, nor even our
division, but all the private soldiers in our whole front, the boche
too, since he remanded too as soon as our barrage lifted, which
would have been his chance to attack since he must have seen that
our regiment had refused, mutinied; he went further than we have,
because he is not even using artillery: only his air people, not crossing either, just patrolling up and down his front. Though of course
they won't know for sure about the British and the Americans and
the boche in front of them until fifteen hours. It's the men; not
even the sergeants knew, suspected anything, had any warning.
And nobody knows if they just happened to set a date in advance
which coincided with our attack, or if they had a prearranged
signal which our regiment put up when it knew for certain that it
was going over this morning—'

'You lie,' the division commander said. 'The men?'

'Yes. Everybody in the line below sergeant—'

'You lie,' the division commander said. He said with a vast, a
spent, an indomitable patience: 'Can't you understand? Can't you
see the difference between a single regiment getting the wind up
—a thing which can and might happen to any regiment, at any
time; to the same regiment which took a trench yesterday and
which tomorrow, simply because it turned tail today, will take a
village or even a walled town? And you try to tell me this' (using
again the succinct soldiery noun). 'The men,' he said. 'Officers—
marshals and generals—decreed that business this morning and
decreed it as a preordained failure; staff officers and experts made
the plans for it within the specifications of failure; I supplied the
failure with a mutinying regiment, and still more officers and
generals and marshals will collect the cost of it out of my reputation. But the men. I have led them in battle all my life. I was
always under the same fire they were under. I got them killed: yes;
but I was there too, leading them, right up to the day when they
gave me so many stars that they could forbid me to any more. But
not the men. They understand even if you cannot. Even that
regiment would have understood; they knew the risk they took

40

when they refused to leave the trench. Risk? Certainly. Because I could have done nothing else. Not for my reputation, not even for my own record or the record of the division I command, but for the future safety of the men, the rank and file of all the other regiments and divisions whose lives might be thrown away to-morrow or next year by another regiment shirking, revolting, refusing, that I was going to have them executed—' thinking, *Was. I'm already saying was; not am: was*, while the aide stared at him in incredulous amazement.

'Is it possible?' the aide said. 'Do you really contend that they are stopping the war just to deprive you of your right, as commander of the division, to execute that regiment?'

'Not my reputation,' the division commander said quickly, 'not even my own record. But the division's record and good name. What else could it be? What other reason could they have—' blinking rapidly and painfully while the aide took the flask from his pocket and uncapped it and nudged it against the division commander's hand. 'The men,' the division commander said.

'Here,' the aide said. The division commander took the flask.

'Thanks,' he said; he even started to raise the flask to his lips. 'The men,' he said. 'The troops. All of them. Defying, revolting, not against the enemy, but against us, the officers, who not only went where they went, but led them, went first, in front, who desired for them nothing but glory, demanded of them nothing but courage . . .'

'Drink, General,' the aide said. 'Come now.'

'Ah, yes,' the division commander said. He drank and returned the flask; he said, 'Thanks,' and made a motion, but before he could complete it the aide, who had been in his military family since he got his first brigadier's star, had already produced a handkerchief, immaculate and laundered, still folded as the iron pressed it. 'Thanks,' the division commander said again, taking the handkerchief and wiping his moustache, and then stood again, the handkerchief open now in his hand, blinking rapidly and painfully. Then he said, simply and distinctly: 'Enough of this.'

'General?' the aide said.

'Eh? What?' the division commander said. Then he was blinking again, steadily though not painfully now, not really fast. 'Well—' he said. He turned.

41

'Shall I come too?' the aide said.

'No, no,' the division commander said, already walking on. 'You stay here. They may need you. There might be something else . . .' his voice not fading but simply ceasing, already chop-striding again, virile and impregnable, the gunners now standing along the crest of the opposite escarpment as he approached, carrying the loose handkerchief in his hand as though bearing under orders a flag of truce of which he himself was inflexibly ashamed and grieved. The major saluted him. He returned it and got into the car. It moved at once; the driver had already turned it around. The boche crash was not far; soon they reached it. 'Stop here,' he said. He got out. 'Drive on. I'll overtake you in a moment,' not even waiting for the car to move but already climbing the bank into the cordite-blasted weeds, still carrying the handkerchief. This was the place; he had marked it, though naturally his sudden advent would have alarmed the tiny beast. But it would still be here; by squatting and hunting patiently enough, parting the weed-stems gently enough, he could probably see it in the Pyrenean grass, crouching and unterrified, merely waiting for him to become still, resume the solitude which was his origin and his ancestry and his birthright, the Sisters—the Father himself when he would arrive with his inconsolable dedicated eyes and his hands gentle enough but sonless, which had never caressed nor struck in anger and love and fear and hope and pride, boy's flesh sprung from his flesh and bearing his immortality in the same intolerant love and hope and pride, wiser perhaps than the Sisters were, less tender than they were tender, but no less compassionate, knowing nothing as the Sisters knew nothing too— saying: 'The Mother of Christ, the Mother of all, is your mother'; not enough, because he didn't want the mother of all nor the mother of Christ either: he wanted the mother of One; only necessary to become still and wait until the tiny creature was accustomed to his sudden advent, then the first sound would come, tentative, brief: a rising, almost an interrogative inflection, almost a test as if to learn if he were really there and ready; then he would whisper the one word against the noon-fierce stone under his face: and he had been right: not the Pyrenean cicada of course, but certainly its northern sister, the miniature sound insistent and impersonal and constant and unobtrusive, steadfast somewhere among the jumble of rusted engine and guns and blackened wires and charred sticks—a purring sound such as he imagined might be made by the sleeping untoothed mouth itself around the sleeping nipple.

His divisional headquarters was what its owner called his country house, built by a man who had made several millions on the Paris Bourse and returned to the district of his birth to install an Argentine mistress, establishing not only the symbol and monument, but bringing the proof of his success back to the scene of his childhood and youth, his I-told-you-so to the elders, mayor and doctor and advocate and judge, who had said he would never amount to anything; and who was well served not only in his patriotism but in his devotion too, when the military demanded the use of it, since the Argentine had quitted Paris only under pressure in the first place.

The message from Corps Headquarters was waiting for him: *Chaulnesmont. Wednesday 15 hours. You are expected. You will confine yourself to quarters until the motor car calls for you*, crumpling the message and the aide's handkerchief into his tunic pocket; and, home again (what home he had ever had since when, at eighteen, he had first donned the uniform which from then on would be his home as the turtle's shell is its domicile), there opened before him an attenuation, an emptiness, of the next five or six or seven hours until it would be dark. He thought of drink. He was not a drinking man; he not only never thought of it until he saw it; it was as though he had forgot it existed until someone actually put it into his hand, as the aide had done the flask. But he dismissed the idea as immediately and completely and for exactly the same reason as if he had been a drinking man: although he had officially ceased to be General of Division Gragnon the moment he received the corps commander's order for him to put himself under arrest, General of Division Gragnon would have to continue to exist for another five or six or seven hours, perhaps even for another day or two yet.

Then suddenly he knew what he would do, quitting the official quarters for his private ones, passing his own bedroom—a small, panelled closet called by the millionaire the gunroom and containing a shotgun which had never been fired and a mounted stag's head (not a very good one) and a stuffed trout, both bought in the same shop with the gun—and went on to the room in which

43

three of his aides slept—the love nest itself, which seemed to retain even yet something of the Argentine, though none could have
said what it was, since nothing remained of her, unless it was some
inconsolable ghost perhaps or what northerners conceived, believed, to be antipodal libidinous frenzy—and found the volume
in the battered chest in which it was the duty of one of the aides
to transport about with them the unofficial effects of the headquarters entourage. And now the book's dead owner was present
again too: a former member of his staff, a thin, overtall, delicately-
and even languidly-made man regarding whose sexual proclivities
the division commander had had his doubts (very likely wrong) without really caring one way or the other, who had entered the (then)
brigadier's military family shortly before he received his division,
who, the general discovered, was the nameless product of an
orphanage too—which fact, not the book, the reading itself, the
division commander would admit to himself, with a sort of savage
self-contempt in his secret moments, was what caused him to be
so constantly aware of the other not quite sipping and not quite
snatching and certainly not buried in the book because he was a
satisfactory aide, until at last it seemed to the division commander
that the battered and dog-eared volume was the aide and the man
himself merely that aide's orderly: until one evening while they
were waiting for a runner from the front lines with a return con-
cerning some prisoners which a brigadier had neglected to sign (the
aide was his divisional Judge Advocate General), he asked and
then listened in cold, inattentive amazement to the answer he got:

'I was a couturier. In Paris—'

'A what?' the division commander said.

'I made women's clothes. I was good at it. I was going to be
better some day. But that wasn't what I wanted. I wanted to be
brave.'

'Be what?' the division commander said.

'You know: a hero. Instead, I made women's clothes. So I
thought of becoming an actor—Henry V—Tartuffe better than
nothing—even Cyrano. But that would be just acting, pretence—
somebody else, not me. Then I knew what to do. Write it.'

'Write it?'

'Yes. The plays. Myself write the plays, rather than just act out
somebody else's idea of what is brave. Invent myself the glorious

deeds and situations, create myself the people brave enough to perform and face and endure them.'

'And that woudn't have been make-believe too?' the general said.

'It would have been me that wrote them, invented them, created them.' Nor did the general discern humility either: a quality humble yet dogged too, even if it was sheep-like. 'I would at least have done that.'

'Oh,' the general said. 'And this is the book.'

'No, no,' the aide said. 'Another man wrote this one. I haven't written mine yet.'

'Haven't written it yet? You have had time here'; not even knowing that he had expressed the contempt nor even that he had tried to conceal it, or that perhaps he might have tried. And now the aide was not humble, not even dogged; certainly the general would not have recognised despair, though he might indomitability:

'I don't know enough yet. I had to wait to stop the books to find out—'

'In books? What in books?'

'About being brave. About glory, and how men got it, and how they bore it after they got it, and how other people managed to live with them after they got it; and honour and sacrifice, and the pity and compassion you have to have to be worthy of honour and sacrifice, and the courage it takes to pity, and the pride it takes to deserve the courage—'

'Courage, to pity?' the general said.

'Yes. Courage. When you stop to pity, the world runs over you. It takes pride to be that brave.'

'Pride in what?' the general said.

'I don't know yet. That's what I'm trying to find out.' Nor did the general recognise serenity then, since he probably called it something else. 'And I will find it. It's in the books.'

'In this book?' the general said.

'Yes,' the aide said, and he died, or that is, the general found him missing one morning, or rather failed to find him at all one morning. It was two hours before he found where the aide was, and another three or four hours before he learned exactly what the aide had done, and he never did learn why and how the aide had come to be there, inside the lines, where a general of division's

Assistant Judge Advocate General had no right nor business whatever, sitting—this was how the runner told it—beside a regimental
runner behind a wall near a corner much used by staff cars, on
which, so the runner claimed he had told the aide, the enemy had
registered a gun only that morning. And everybody had been
warned of it, yet the car came on anyway, still coming on even
after the aide sprang to his feet and began to wave his arms to stop
the car. But it refused to stop, still coming on even after the aide
ran out into the open road, still trying to wave the car off even
after the runner said that he could hear the shell coming, and that
the aide himself must have heard it also; and how the aide could
not possibly have known that the car contained not only a wealthy
American expatriate, a widow whose only son was in a French air
squadron a few kilometres away and who was supporting near Paris
an asylum for war-orphaned children, but a well-connected Paris
staff-major too. And there had been nothing to pin the medal on
when it came through, and nothing to identify to bury it with
either, so that the medal also was still in the battered chest which
the aide's successors in their succession superintended from post to
post; and the division commander took the book out and read the
title and then read it again in mounting exasperation, reading it
aloud, saying aloud almost, *All right. Blas wrote it. But what's the
name of the book?* until he realised that the word he was looking
at was the name of the book and therefore the book would have
to be about a man, thinking *Yes*, remembering scraps, fragments,
echoes from that night two years ago, saying the name aloud this
time: '*Gil Blas*,' listening, concentrated, if perhaps there might
come out of the closed pages, through the cover itself and into the
simple name, something, some echo of the thunder, the clanging
crash, the ringing bugles and the horns, the—*What was it?* he
thought. *The glory, the honour and the courage and the pride—*

He returned to his bedroom, carrying the book. Save for his field
cot and chest and desk, the furniture still belonged to the owner
of the house and of the Argentinian. It had the look of having
been bought all in one shop too, probably over the telephone. He
drew the single chair into the light from the window beside the
stuffed fish and sat down and began to read, slowly, rigidly, not
moving his lips even, inflexible in fortitude and suffering as if he
were sitting fifty years ago for his portrait. After a while it was

dusk. The door opened, hesitated, opened more and quietly and a batman entered and came to the table and prepared to light the lamp on it, the division commander not even looking up to say 'Yes,' even when the soft blob of light plopped and burst sound-less and brilliant on the open page in his hands, still reading when the batman went out, still reading until the tray was on the table beside the lamp and the batman had gone again. Then he put the book carefully down and turned to the tray, immobile again for a second, facing, somewhat as he had faced the book before open-ing it, the tray bearing the covered dish and the loaf and plate and cutlery and glass, and the bottle of wine and one of rum and one of *cassis* which he had been looking at on this tray for three years now—the same bottles which he had never touched, the same corks started each day and then driven home again and even dusted freshly over, the same liquid level in each as when vintner and distiller had bottled them. Nor did he use the knife and fork when he ate alone from the tray like this, eating not with voracity, noth-ing at all really gross about the feeding: simply putting the food rapidly and efficiently into himself with his fingers and sops of the bread. Then with only the slightest pause, not of indecision but simply to remember which pocket, he drew out the aide's handker-chief and carefully wiped his moustache and fingers and tossed the handkerchief on to the tray and thrust the chair away from the table and took up the book and paused again, immobile, the book half raised, though none could have said whether he was looking at the open page or out the open window which he now faced, looking at or listening to the spring-filled darkness, the myriad peaceful silence, which it framed. Then he raised the book farther and entered, strode into it as a patient enters a dentist's office for the last petty adjustment before paying the bill, and read again, rigid and inflexible above the pages' slow increment in which he missed, skipped, elided, no single word, with a cold, incredulous, respectful amazement, not at the shadows of men and women, because they were inventions and naturally he didn't believe them—besides being in another country and long ago and therefore even if they had been real, they could never impinge, affect, the course of his life and its destruction—but at the capacity and industry and (he admitted it) the competence of the man who could remember all this and write it down.

He waked immediately, completely prescient. He even picked up the fallen book before looking at his watch; no start of concern or dismay, as though he knew beforehand that he would be able to reach the château in plenty of time before dawn. Not that it would make any difference; he had simply planned to see the group commander tonight, and slept without intending to sleep and waked without needing to be waked, in plenty of time to see the group commander while technically at least it was still tonight.

So it was not dawn yet when the sentry at the lodge passed him (he was alone in the car, driving himself) through the gates and into the drive running straight and over-arched now through the spring darkness loud with predawn nightingales, up to the château A successful highwayman had established its site and the park it sat in; a distant connection of a French queen had restored it in the Italian style of his native land; his marquis descendants had owned it: then the Republic: then a marshal of Napoleon: then a Levantine millionaire; for the last four years now, for all practical purposes, it had been the property of the general commanding the circumambient group of French armies. And the division commander had not noticed the nightingales until he was inside the park and it may have been at this moment that he realised that he himself would never own either: army command or château, or nightingales for doomed division commanders, coming to resign their pasts and their futures both, to listen to. And still not dawn when he slammed the car to a stop before the dark pile less of Louis than Florentine and more of baroque than either, jerking it up exactly as he would the over-ridden horse and getting out and flinging the door backward behind him against the night's silence as he would have flung the reins to a groom without even pausing to see if the animal's head were secure or not, then mounting the broad shallow steps to the stone terrace with its carved balustrade and urns garlanded in carven stone. Nor was even all the old gothic quite absent either: a pile of horse-droppings two or three days old on the terrace beside the door, as if the old princely highwayman himself had returned, or perhaps had only left day before yesterday, which the division commander glanced at in passing, thinking how forage grown from this northern chalk-loam soil merely gave a horse windy size, distending the animal simply by its worthless passing bulk: nothing of speed and bottom like the hard, lean, light desert-bred ones bone- and flesh-bred to endure on almost nothing, contemptuous even of that. And not just horses: man too, thinking *Able was I ere I saw France again*, thinking how always a man's simple longevity outlives his life and we are all our own paupers, derelict; thinking, as men had thought and said before him, that no soldier should be permitted to survive his first engagement under fire and then not thinking at all, chop-striding to the door and rapping on it, deliberate, peremptory, and loud.

He saw the candle, heard the feet. The door opened: no dishevelled Faubourg Saint Germain aide, this, but a private soldier: a middle-aged man in unlaced infantry boots and dangling braces, holding his trousers up with the other candleless hand over a soiled lavender civilian shirt whose collarless neckband was clasped by a tarnished brass button the size and shape of a wolf's fang. Even the man appeared no different; certainly the shirt was not: he (the division commander) might have been looking at both that day fifteen years ago when Bidet got his captaincy at last and an instructorship at the *École Militaire*, and he and the wife, who had followed him a subaltern to Africa even though she herself got no further than a loft in the Oran native town, could sleep every night under the same roof again at last, the same soldier but with a baize apron over the soiled violet shirt, scrubbing the stoop or the staircase while the wife stood over him like a sergeant herself, with a vast bunch of keys at her waist to jangle at each of his convulsive starts when she would murmur at him, and in the same baize apron waiting on table at meals; and apparently the same soldier (or at least one as large) but certainly the same shirt eight years later when Bidet was a colonel with enough pay to keep a horse too, waiting on table with a white apron now over the collarless shirt and the vast bunch of keys jangling against authentic satin now or even the true funereal silk at each of his convulsive starts, the same heavy boots under the apron bringing amid the viands the smell of stable manure now, the same giant thumb in the bowls of soup.

He followed the candle into the same bedroom at which the knightly highwayman, along with the shade of the imperial marshal, would have looked in contemptuous unbelief, in which the marquis-descendants of the Florentine might or might not have slept, but in which the Levantine without doubt did, and saw something else which, he realised now, he had not expected to find changed either, though the man who wore them had. Standing at the foot of the bed, he faced across the fretted garlanded painted footboard the group commander sitting against the piled pillows in the same flannel nightcap and nightshirt which he too had brought to Africa that day twenty-five years ago when he had had to leave his wife under the broiling eaves of the Oran native house because they had no money then (he the only child of the widow living—or trying to—on the pension of her husband, a Savoyard schoolmaster, she one of the six daughters of a retired sergeant-major of marines) while the husband was absent for almost two years on his first subaltern's tour of outpost duty—facing the man who even now did not look like a French soldier and who on that first day twenty-five years ago seemed to have been completely and, more, criminally miscast, looking then himself like a consumptive schoolteacher, condemned not just to simple failure but to destitution and suicide too, who weighed then less than a hundred pounds (he was stouter now, almost plump in fact, and somewhere in his career like that of a delayed rocket, the glasses had vanished too) and wearing spectacles of such fierce magnification that he was almost blind without them, and even with them too since for a third of the time the lenses were sweated to opaqueness and he spent another third wiping them dry with the end of his burnous in order to see at all before sweating them blind again, and who had brought into the field life of that regiment of desert cavalry something of the monastery, something of the cold fierce blinkless intolerant glare which burns at midnight in the dedicated asepsis of clinical or research laboratories: that pitiless preoccupation with man, not as an imperial implement, least of all as that gallant and puny creature bearing undismayed on his frail bones and flesh the vast burden of his long inexplicable incomprehensible tradition and journey, not even in fact as a functioning animal but as a functioning machine in the same sense that the earthworm is: alive purely and simply for the purpose of transporting, without itself actually moving, for the distance of its corporeal length, the medium in which it lives, which, given time, would shift the whole earth that infinitesimal inch, leaving at last its own blind insatiate jaws chewing nothing above the spinning abyss: that cold, scathing, contemptuous preoccupation with body vents and orifices and

mucous membrane as though he himself owned neither, who declared that no army was better than its anus, since even without
feet it could still crawl forward and fight, and so earned his nickname because of his inflexible belief in his doctrine—a nickname
spoken at first in contempt and derision, then in alarm and anger
and then rage and then concerned and impotent fury since his
inflexible efforts to prove his doctrine soon extended beyond his
own platoon, into troops and squadrons where, still a simple junior
lieutenant of cavalry and not even a medical officer, he had no
right nor business at all; and then spoken no longer in ridicule nor
even contumely and anger anywhere, because presently the whole
African establishment knew how, sitting in a tent, he had told his
regimental commander how to recover two scouts captured one
night by a band of mounted tribesmen who vanished afterward
like antelope; and it worked, and later, still sitting in a tent, told
the general himself how to avail to a hitherto dry outpost a constant supply of drinking water, and that worked too; and moved
from the classroom colonelcy to the command of a field division
in 1914 and three years later was the competent and successful
commander of an army group and already unofficially next but one
to a marshal's baton while still less than fifty-five years old, sitting
in his flannel nightshirt and cap in the gaudy bed in the rococo
room lighted by the cheap candle in its tin candlestick which the
batman had set on the bedside table, like an ex-grocer alderman
surprised, but neither alarmed nor even concerned, in a sumptuous
bordello.

'You were right,' the division commander said. 'I won't go to
Chaulnesmont.'

'You have wrestled all night,' the group commander said. 'With
what angel?'

'What?' the division commander said. He blinked for only a
second. Then he said, firmly and calmly, like a man stepping firmly
forward into complete darkness, drawing a folded paper from his
tunic as he did so and dropping it on to the group commander's
covered knees: 'It didn't take that long.'

The group commander didn't touch the paper. He merely looked
at it. He said pleasantly: 'Yes?'

'It's my resignation,' the division commander said.

'You think it's over, then?'

'What?' the division commander said. 'Oh. The war. No, it's not over. They'll have something I can do as a civilian. I was even a fair veterinary in the old days, farrier, too. Or maybe I could even run a production line (that's what they call it, isn't it?) in a munitions plant.'

'And then?' the group commander said.

The division commander looked at him, though only for a second. 'Oh, when it is over, you mean? I'm leaving France then. Maybe to the South Pacific. An island . . .'

'Like Gaugin,' the group commander said gently.

'Who?'

'Another man who one day discovered that he had had enough of France too and went to the South Pacific and became a painter.'

'This is another place,' the division commander said immediately. 'There won't be enough people on this one to need their houses painted.'

The group commander reached his hand and took up the folded paper and turned and, the paper still folded, held the corner of it to the candle-flame until it took fire and then burst blazing, the group commander holding it for a second longer before he dropped it hissing into the chamber-pot beside the bed and in the same motion slid himself down the pillows until he was reclining again, already drawing the covers up. 'Chaulnesmont,' he said. 'At three tomorrow—Bah, it's already tomorrow.' And then the division commander was aware of it too: the alteration, day, the invincible oblivious tomorrow which follows always, undeviable by man and to man immune; no longer ago than yesterday saw him and his fury, the first tomorrow will have forgotten both. It was even a second or so before he realised that the group commander was still talking to him: '—if the world thinks it wishes to stop fighting for twenty-five or thirty years, let it. But not this way. Not like a group of peasants in a half-mown field suddenly shouldering their scythes and lunch-pails and walking off. Chaulnesmont this afternoon.'

'Because there are rules,' the division commander said harshly. 'Our rules. We shall enforce them, or we shall die—the captains and the colonels—no matter what the cost—'

'It wasn't we who invented war,' the group commander said. 'It was war which created us. From the loins of man's furious ineradicable greed sprang the captains and the colonels to his necessity. We are his responsibility; he shall not shirk it.'

'But not me,' the division commander said.

'You,' the group commander said. 'We can permit even our own rank and file to let us down on occasion; that's one of the prerequisites of their doom and fate as rank and file forever. They may even stop the wars, as they have done before and will again; ours merely to guard them from the knowledge that it was actually they who accomplished that act. Let the whole vast moil and seethe of man confederate in stopping wars if they wish, so long as we can prevent them learning that they have done so. A moment ago you said that we must enforce our rules, or die. It's no abrogation of a rule that will destroy us. It's less. The simple effacement from man's memory of a single word will be enough. But we are safe. Do you know what that word is?'

The division commander looked at him for a moment. He said: 'Yes?'

'Fatherland,' the group commander said. Now he raised the top of the covers, preparatory to drawing them back over his head and face. 'Yes, let them believe they can stop it, so long as they don't suspect that they have.' The covers were already moving; now only the group commander's nose and eyes and the nightcap remained in sight. 'Let them believe that tomorrow they will end it; then they won't begin to ponder if perhaps today they can. Tomorrow. And still tomorrow. And again tomorrow. That's the hope you will vest them in. The three stars that Sergeant Gragnon won by his own strength, with help from man nor God neither, have damned you, General. Call yours martyrdom for the world; you will have saved it. Chaulnesmont this afternoon.'

And now the division commander was no longer a general, still less the sergeant of twenty-five years ago whose inflexible pride it had been to accept odds from no man. 'But to me,' he said. 'What will happen to me?'

And now even the nightcap had vanished and only the muffled voice came from beneath the covers. 'I don't know,' it said. 'It will be glorious.'

TUESDAY NIGHT

SOME time after midnight that Tuesday (it was Wednesday now) two British privates were resting on the firestep of a frontline trench below the Bethune slagheap. Two months ago they were looking at it not only from another angle but from another direction; until then, the line's relation to it seemed fixed to a longer life than memory's. But since the breakthrough there had been no fixed line at all. The old corridor had still remained of course, roofed over with the shriek and stink of cordite, but attached to the earth only at the two ends; the one somewhere on the Channel and the other somewhere up the roof of France, so that it seemed to belly before the Teutonic gale like a clothesline about to carry away in a wind. And since three o'clock yesterday afternoon (yesterday morning rather, noon when the French quit) it had merely hung in its spent bulge against the arrested weight of the Germanic air, even roofless now since with dark the last patrolling aircraft had gone to roost and there remained only the flares arching up from behind the flickerless wire with a faint hiss, a prolonged whispered sniff, to bloom and parachute and hang against the dark with the cold thick texture and colour of the working lights in a police morgue, then sliding silently down the black air like drops of grease on a window-pane, and far away to the north the spaced blink and thump of a single gun, a big one, with no following burst at all, as though it were firing at the Channel, the North Sea itself fifty miles away, or perhaps at some target even vaster and more immune than that: at Cosmos, space, infinity, lifting its voice against the Absolute, the ultimate I-Am, harmless: the iron maw of Dis, toothless, unwearyable, incapable, bellowing.

One of the privates was a sentry. He stood on the firestep, leaning slightly against the wall beside the sand-bagged aperture in which his rifle lay loaded and cocked and with the safety off. In civil life he had indubitably been a horse-groom, because even in khaki and even after four years of infantryman's war he still moved, stood in an aura, effluvium of stalls and tack-rooms—a hard-faced jockey-sized man who seemed to have brought on his warped legs even into the French and Flemish mud something of hard, light, razor-edge horses and betting-rings, who even wore the steel helmet at the same vicious rake of the filthy heavy-checked cap which would have been the badge of his old dead calling and dedication. But this was only inference, from his appearance and general air, not from anything he ever told anyone; even his mates in the battalion who had stayed alive long enough to have known him four years knew nothing about his past, as if he did not have one, had not even been born until the fourth of August, 1914—a paradox who had no business in an infantry battalion at all, and an enigma to the extent that six months after he entered the battalion (this was about Christmas, 1914) the colonel commanding it had been summoned to Whitehall to make a specific report on him. Because the authorities had discovered that eleven privates in the battalion, had made the man beneficiary of the soldiers' life assurance policies; by the time the colonel reached the war ministry, the number had increased to twenty, and although the colonel had made an intensive two-days' investigation of his own before leaving the battalion, he knew little more than they in London did. Because the company officers knew nothing about it, and from the N.C.O.'s he got only rumour and hearsay, and from the men themselves, only a blank and respectful surprised innocence as to the man's very existence, the sum of which was that the (eleven when the war office got its first report, and twenty by the time the colonel reached London, and—the colonel had been absent from the battalion twelve hours now—nobody knew how many more by this time) men had approached the battalion sergeant-major all decorously and regularly and apparently of their own free will and desire, and made the request which, since none of them had legal heirs, was their right to make, and the Empire's duty to acquiesce to. As for the man himself—

'Yes,' the staff-major who was doing the informal questioning said. 'What did he say about it?' and then, after a moment: 'You didn't even question him?'

This time, the colonel did shrug. 'Why?' he said.

'Quite,' the major said. 'Though I should have been tempted—if only to learn what he can be selling them.'

'I should rather know what the ones who have legal heirs and can't make over the insurance are paying him instead,' the colonel said.

'Their souls, obviously,' the major said. 'Since their deaths are already pledged.' And that was all. In the whole King's Regulations, through which had been winnowed and tested and proved every conceivable khaki or blue activity and posture and intention, with a rule provided for it and a penalty provided for the rule, there was nothing to cover it: who (the man) had infringed no discipline, trafficked with no enemy, failed to shine no brass nor wrap properly any puttee nor salute any officer. Yet still the colonel sat there, until the major, a little more than curious now, said, 'What? Say it.'

'I can't,' the colonel said. 'Because the only word I can think of is love'—explaining that: the stupid, surly, dirty, unsocial, really unpleasant man, who apparently neither gambled nor drank (during the last two months, the battalion sergeant-major and the colonel's orderly sergeant had sacrificed—unofficially, of course—no little of their own free time and slumber too, walking suddenly into dugouts and rest billets and estaminets, ascertaining that), who, in the light of day, seemed to have no friends at all, yet each time the sergeant-major or the orderly sergeant entered one of the dugouts or billets, they would find it jammed with men. And not the same men either, but each time there would be a new set of faces, so that in each period between two pay-days, the entire battalion roll could have been called by anyone detailed to sit beside the man's bunk; indeed, on pay-day itself, or for a day or two days after it, the line, queue, had been known to extend into the street, as when people wait to enter a cinema, while the dugout, the room, itself would be jammed to the door with men standing or sitting or squatting about the bunk or corner in which the man himself lay quite often asleep, morose and resigned and not even talking, like people waiting in a dentist's anteroom—waiting, that was it, as both the sergeant-major and the sergeant realised, if for nothing else except for them—the sergeant-major and the sergeant —to leave.

'Why don't you give him a stripe?' the major said. 'If it's devotion, why not employ it for the greater glory of English arms?'

'How?' the colonel said. 'Try to buy with one file, the man who already owns the battalion?'

'Perhaps you should assign your own insurance and pay-book over to him.'

'Yes,' the colonel said. 'If he gives me time to.' And that was all. The colonel spent fourteen hours with his wife. At noon the next day, he was in Boulogne again; at six that afternoon, his car entered the village where the battalion was in rest billets. 'Stop here,' the colonel said, and sat for a moment in the car, looking at the queue of men which was moving infinitesimally toward and through the gate into one of those sweating stone courtyards which for a thousand years the French have been dotting about the Picard and Artois and Flanders countryside, apparently for the purpose of housing between battles the troops of the allied nations come to assist in preserving them. *No*, the colonel thought, *not a cinema; the anticipation is not great enough, although the urgency is twice as strong. They are like the parade outside a latrine.* 'Drive on,' he said.

The other private was a battalion runner. He was sitting on the firestep, his unslung rifle propped beside him, himself half-propped, half-reclining against the trench-wall, his boots and puttees not caked with the drying mud of trenches but dusted with the recent powdery dust of roads; even his attitude showed not so much indolence, but fatigue, physical exhaustion. Except that it was not spent exhaustion, but the contrary: with something tense behind it, so that the exhaustion did not seem to possess him, but rather he seemed to wear it as he did the dust, sitting there for five or six minutes now, all of which he had spent talking, and with nothing of exhaustion in his voice either. Back in the old spanking time called peace, he had been not only a successful architect, but a good one, even if (in private life) an aesthete and even a little precious; at this hour of those old dead days, he would have been sitting in a Soho restaurant or studio (or, his luck good, even in a Mayfair drawing room or even—at least once or twice or perhaps three times—boudoir), doing a little more than his share of the talking about art or politics or life or both or all three. He had been among the first London volunteers, a private at Loos; without even a lance corporal's stripe on his sleeve, he had extricated his platoon and got it back alive across the Canal; he commanded the platoon for five days at Passchendaele and was confirmed in it, posted from the battlefield to officers' school and had carried his single pip for five months into 1916 on the night when he came off duty and entered the dugout where his company commander was shaving out of a Maconochie tin.

'I want to resign,' he said.

Without stopping the razor nor even moving enough to see the other's reflection in the mirror, the company commander said, 'Don't we all.' Then he stopped the razor. 'You must be serious. All right. Go up the trench and shoot yourself through the foot. Of course, they never really get away with it. But—'

'I see,' the other said. 'No, I don't want to get out.' He touched the pip on his left shoulder rapidly with his right finger tips and dropped the hand. 'I just don't want this any more.'

'You want to go back to ranks,' the company commander said. 'You love man so well you must sleep in the same mud he sleeps in.'

'That's it,' the other said. 'It's just backward. I hate man so. Hear him?' Again the hand moved, an outward motion, gesture, and dropped again. 'Smell him, too.' That was already in the dug-out also, sixty steps down though it was: not just the rumble and mutter, but the stench too, the smell, the soilure, the stink of simple usage: not the dead bones and flesh rotting in the mud, but because the live bones and flesh had used the same mud so long to sleep and eat in. 'When I, knowing what I have been, and am now, and will continue to be—assuming of course that I shall continue among the chosen beneath the boon of breathing, which I probably shall, some of us apparently will have to, don't ask me why of that either—can, by the simple coincidence of wearing this little badge on my coat, have not only the power, with a whole militarised government to back me up, to tell vast herds of man what to do, but the impunitive right to shoot him with my own hand when he doesn't do it, then I realise how worthy of any fear and abhorrence and hatred he is.'

'Not just your hatred and fear and abhorrence,' the company commander said.

'Right,' he said. 'I'm merely the one who can't face it.'

'Won't face it,' the company commander said.

'Can't face it,' he said.

'Won't face it,' the company commander said.

'All right,' he said. 'So I must get back into the muck with him. Then maybe I'll be free.'

'Free of what?' the company commander said.

'All right,' he said. 'I don't know either. Maybe of having to perform forever at inescapable intervals that sort of masturbation about the human race people call hoping. That would be enough. I had thought of going straight to Brigade. That would save time. But then, the colonel might get his back up for being overslaughed. I'm looking for what K.R. and O. would call channels, I suppose. Only I don't seem to know anybody who ever read that book.'

It was not that easy. The battalion commander refused to endorse him; he found himself in the presence of a brigadier twenty-seven years old, less than four years out of Sandhurst today, in a Mons Star, M.C. and bar, D.S.O. and a French *Croix de Guerre* and a thing from the Belgian monarch and three wound stripes, who could not—not would not, could not—even believe what he was hearing, let alone understand what his importuner was talking about, who said, 'I daresay you've already thought of shooting yourself in the foot. Raise the pistol about sixty inches first. You might as well get out front of the parapet too, what? Better still, get past the wire while you're about it.'

But it was quite simple, when he finally thought of the method. He waited until his leave came up. He would have to do that; desertion was exactly what he did not want. In London he found a girl, a young woman, not a professional, not really a good-standing amateur yet, two or three months pregnant from any one of three men, two of whom had been killed inside the same fortnight and mile by Nieppe Forest, and the other now in Mesopotamia, who didn't understand either and therefore (so he thought at the time) was willing to help him for a price—a price twice what she suggested and which represented his whole balance at Cox's—in a plot whose meretricity and shabbiness only American moving pictures were to match: the two of them taken in *delicto* so outrageously *flagrante* and public, so completely unequivocal and incapable of other than one interpretation, that anyone, even the field-rank moralists in charge of the conduct of Anglo-Saxon-derived junior officers, should have refused point blank to accept or even believe it.

It worked though. The next morning, in a Knightsbridge bar-racks anteroom, a staff officer spokesman offered, as an alternative to preserve the regiment's honour, the privilege which he had re-requested of his company commander and then the battalion com-mander, and finally of the brigadier himself in France three months ago; and three nights later, passing through Victoria station to file into a coach full of private soldiers in the same returning train which had brought him by officers' first class up from Dover ten days ago, he found he had been wrong about the girl, whom at first he didn't even remember after she spoke to him. 'It didn't work,' she said.

'Yes,' he said. 'It worked.'

'But you're going back. I thought you wanted to lose the com-mission so you wouldn't have to go back.' Then she was clinging to him, cursing him and crying too. 'You were lying all the time, then. You wanted to go back. You just wanted to be a poor bloody private again.' She was pulling at his arm. 'Come on. The gates are still open.'

'No,' he said, holding back. 'It's all right.'

'Come on,' she said, jerking at him. 'I know these things. There's a train you can take in the morning; you won't be reported absent until tomorrow night in Boulogne.' The line began to move. He tried to move with it. But she clung only the harder. 'Can't you see?' she cried. 'I can't get the money to give back to you until tomorrow morning.'

'Let go,' he said. 'I must get aboard and find a corner to sleep in.'

'The train won't go for two hours yet. How many of them do you think I've seen leave? Come on. My room isn't ten minutes from here.'

'Let go now,' he said, moving on. 'Good-bye.'

'Just two hours.' A sergeant shouted at him. It had been so long since an N.C.O. had spoken to him this way that he did not realise at once he was meant. But he had already freed himself with a sud-den sharp hard movement; a carriage door was open behind him; then he was in the compartment, dropping his pack and rifle on to a jumble of others, stumbling among a jumble of legs, pulling the door behind him as she cried through the closing gap: 'You haven't told me where to send the money.'

'Good-bye,' he said, closing the door, leaving her on the step, clinging on somehow even after the train was moving, her gaped urgent face moving parallel beyond the voiceless glass until an M.P. on the platform snatched her off, her face, not the train, seeming to flee suddenly with motion, in another instant gone.

He had gone out in 1914 with the Londoners. His commission was in them. This time, he was going out to a battalion of Northumberland Borderers. His record had preceded him; a corporal was waiting on the Boulogne quai to take him to the R.T.O. anteroom. The lieutenant had been with him at officers' school.

'So you put up a job on them,' the lieutenant said. 'Don't tell me: I don't want to know why. You're going out to the —th. I know James (the lieutenant colonel commanding it). Cut my teeth with him in the Salient last year. You don't want to go in a platoon. What about a telephonist—a sergeant-major's man?'

'Let me be a runner,' he said. So a runner he was. The word from the R.T.O. lieutenant had been too good; not just his record but his past had preceded him to the battalion also, up to the lieutenant colonel himself before he had been a week in the battalion, possibly because he, the runner, was entitled to wear (he did not wear it since it was the officer's branch of the decoration and, among the men he would now mess and sleep with, that ribbon up on his private's tunic would have required too much breath) one of the same candy-stripes which the colonel (he was not a professional soldier either) did; that, and one other matter, though he would never believe that the two were more than incidentally connected.

'Look here,' the colonel said. 'You haven't come here to stir up anything. You ought to know that the only possible thing is to get on with it, finish it and bloody well have done. We already have one man who could be a trouble-maker—unless he oversteps in time for us to learn what he is up to.' He named the man. 'He's in your company.'

'I couldn't,' the runner said. 'They won't talk to me yet. I probably couldn't persuade them to anything even if they would talk to me and I wanted to.'

'Not even (the colonel named the private again)? You don't know what he's up to either?'

'I don't think I'm an agitator,' the runner said. 'I know I'm not a spy. This is gone now, remember,' he said, touching his shoulder lightly with the opposite hand.

'Though I doubt if you can stop remembering that you once had it,' the colonel said. 'It's your own leg you're pulling, you know. If you really hate man, all you need do is take your pistol back to the latrines and rid yourself of him.'

'Yes, sir,' the runner said, completely wooden.

'Hate Germans, if you must hate someone.'

'Yes, sir,' the runner said.

'Well? Can't you answer?'

'All the Germans with all their kith and kin are not enough to make up man.'

'They are for me—now,' the colonel said. 'And they had better be for you too now. Don't force me to compel you to remember that pip. Oh, I know it too: the men who, in hopes of being recorded as victorious prime- or cabinet-ministers, furnish men for this. The men who, in order to become millionaires, supply the guns and shells. The men who, hoping to be addressed some day as Field Marshal or Viscount Plugstreet or Earl of Loos, invent the gambles they call plans. The men who, to win a war, will go out and dig up if possible, invent if necessary, an enemy to fight against. Is that a promise?'

'Yes,' the runner said.

'Right,' the colonel said. 'Carry on. Just remember.' Which he did, sometimes when on duty but mostly during the periods when the battalion was in rest billets, carrying the unloaded rifle slung across his back which was his cognizance, his badge of office, with somewhere in his pocket some—any—scrap of paper bearing the colonel's or the adjutant's signature in case of emergency. At times he managed lifts from passing transport—lorries, empty ambulances, an unoccupied sidecar. At times while in rest areas he even wangled the use of a motorbike himself, as if he actually were a dispatch rider; he could be seen sitting on empty petrol tins in scout- or fighter- or bomber-squadron hangars, in the material sheds of artillery or transport parks, at the back doors of field stations and hospitals and divisional châteaux, in kitchens and canteens and at the toy-sized zinc bars of village estaminets, as he had told the colonel, not talking but listening.

TUESDAY NIGHT

So he learned about the thirteen French soldiers almost at once —or rather, the thirteen men in French uniforms—who had been known for a year now among all combat troops below the grade of sergeant in the British forces and obviously in the French too, realising at the same moment that not only had he been the last man below sergeant in the whole Allied front to hear about them, but why: who five months ago had been an officer too, by the badges on his tunic also forever barred and interdict from the right and freedom to the simple passions and hopes and fears—sickness for home, worry about wives and allotment pay, the weak beer and the shilling a day which won't even buy enough of that; even the right to be afraid of death—all that confederation of fellowship which enables man to support the weight of war; in fact, the surprise was that, having been an officer once, he had been permitted to learn about the thirteen men at all.

His informant was an A.S.C. private more than sixty years old, member of and lay preacher to a small nonconformist congregation in Southwark; he had been half porter and half confidential servant with an unblemished record to an Inns of Court law firm, as his father had been before him and his son was to be after, except that at the Old Bailey assizes in the spring of 1914 the son would have been sent up for breaking and burglary had not the presiding judge been not only a humanitarian but a member of the same philatelist society to which the head of the law firm belonged; whereupon the son was permitted to enlist instead the next day and in August went to Belgium and was reported missing at Mons all in the same three weeks and was accepted so by all save his father, who received leave of absence to enlist from the law firm for the single reason that his employers did not believe he could pass the doctors; eight months later the father was in France too; a year after that he was still trying to get, first, leave of absence; then, failing that, transfer to some unit near enough to Mons to look for his son, although it had been a long time now since he had mentioned the son, as if he had forgot the reason and remembered only the destination, still a lay preacher, still half night-watchman and half nurse, unimpeachable of record, to the succession of (to him) children who ran a vast ammunition dump behind St. Omer, where one afternoon he told the runner about the thirteen French soldiers.

'Go and listen to them,' the old porter said. 'You can speak foreign; you can understand them.'

'I thought you said that the nine who should have spoken French, didn't, and that the other four couldn't speak anything at all.'

'They don't need to talk,' the old porter said. 'You don't need to understand. Just go and look at him.

'Him?' the runner said. 'So it's just one now?'

'Wasn't it just one before?' the old porter said. 'Wasn't one enough then to tell us the same thing all them two thousand years ago: that all we ever needed to do was just to say, Enough of this—us, not even the sergeants and corporals, but just us, all of us, Germans and Colonials and Frenchmen and all the other foreigners in the mud here, saying together: Enough. Let them that's already dead and maimed and missing be enough of this—a thing so easy and simple that even human man, as full of evil and sin and folly as he is, can understand and believe it this time. Go and look at him.'

But he didn't see them, not yet. Not that he couldn't have found them; at any time they would be in the British zone, against that khaki monotone, that clump of thirteen men in horizon blue, even battle-stained, would have stood out like a cluster of hyacinths in a Scottish moat. He didn't even try yet. He didn't dare; he had been an officer himself, even though for only five months, and even though he had repudiated it, something ineradicable of it still remained, as the unfrocked priest or repentant murderer, even though unfrocked at heart and reformed at heart, carries forever about him like a catalyst the indelible effluvium of the old condition; it seemed to him that he durst not be present even on the fringe of whatever surrounding crowd, even to walk, pass through, let alone stop, within the same air of that small blue clump of hope; this, even while telling himself that he did not believe it, that it couldn't be true, possible, since if it were possible, it would not need to be hidden from Authority; that it would not matter whether Authority knew about it or not, since even ruthless and all-powerful and unchallengeable Authority would be impotent before that massed unresisting undemanding passivity. He thought: *They could execute only so many of us before they will have worn out the last rifle and pistol and expended the last live shell,* visualising it:

first, the anonymous fringe of subalterns and junior clerks to which he had once belonged, relegated to the lathes and wheels to keep them in motion rifling barrels and filling shell-cases; then, the frenzy and the terror mounting, the next layer: the captains and majors and secretaries and attachés with their martial harness and ribbons and striped trousers and brief cases among the oil cans and the flying shafts; then the field officers: colonels and senators and Members; then, last and ultimate, the ambassadors and ministers and lesser generals themselves frantic and inept among the slowing wheels and melting bearings, while the old men, the last handful of kings and presidents and field marshals and spoiled-beef and shoe-peg barons, their backs to the last crumbling rampart of their real, their credible, their believable world, wearied, spent, not with blood-glut at all but with the eye-strain of aiming and the muscle-tension of pointing and the finger-cramp of squeezing, fired the last puny scattered and markless fusillade as into the face of the sea itself. It's not that I don't believe it, he said. It's because it can't be true. We can't be saved now; even He doesn't want us any more now.

So he believed that he was not even waiting: just watching. It was winter again now, the long unbroken line from Alps to sea lying almost quiescent in mud's foul menopause; this would be the time for them, with even front-line troops free for a little while to remember when they were warm and dry and clean; for him and the other twelve—(thinking, almost impatiently, *All right, all right, they are thirteen too*)—a soil not only unfallow now but already tumescent even, having a little space to think now, to remember and to dread, thinking (the runner) how it was not the dying but the indignity of the method: even the condemned murderer is better off, with an hour set and fixed far enough in the future to allow time to summon fortitude to face it well, and privacy to hide the lack in case the fortitude failed; not to receive both the sentence and its execution all in one unprepared flash, not even at rest but running, stumbling, laden with jangling iron like a pack-mule in the midst of death which can take him from any angle, front, rear or above, panting, vermin-covered, stinking with his own reek, without even privacy in which to drop the dung and water he carried. He even knew what he was watching for: for the moment in the stagnancy when Authority would finally become aware of the clump of alien incongruous blue in its moat. Which would be at any time now; what he was watching was a race. Winter was almost over; they—the thirteen—had had time, but it was running out. It would be spring soon: the jocund bright time beginning to be mobile and dry underfoot; and even before that they in the Whitehalls and Quai d'Orsays and Unter den Somethings and Gargleplatzes would have thought of something anew, even if it had to be something which had already failed before. And suddenly he knew why it would not matter to Authority whether they knew about the thirteen men or not. They didn't need to, having not only authority but time too on their side; no need for them to hunt down and hoick out and execute a mere thirteen men: their very avocation was its own defender and emollient.

And it had run out. It was already spring; the Americans (1918 now) were in it now, rushing frantically across the Atlantic Ocean before it was too late and the scraps were all gone, and the breakthrough had come: the old stale Germanic tide washing again over the Somme and Picard towns which you might have thought had served their apprenticeship, washing along the Aisne a month later so that clerks in Paris bureaus were once more snapping the locks on the worn and homeless attaché-cases; May and even the Marne again, American troops counter-attacking this time among the ruined towns which you would think might have had absolution too. Except that he was not thinking now; he was too busy; for two weeks now he and his heretofore unfired rifle had been in an actual platoon, part of a rearguard, too busy remembering how to walk backward to think, using in place of the harassing ordeal of thought a fragment out of the old time before he had become incapable of believing, out of Oxford probably (he could even see the page) though now it seemed much younger than that, too young to have endured this far at all:

lo, I have committed fornication.
But that was in another country; and besides,
the wench is dead

So when it finally happened, he had no warning. The wave had stopped, and he was a runner again; he had got back from Division Headquarters at dawn and two hours later he was asleep in the bunk of a man on a fatigue party, when an orderly summoned him to the office. 'You can drive a motorbike,' the colonel said.

He thought *You should know*. He said: 'Yes, sir.'

'You're going to Corps Headquarters. They want couriers. A lorry will pick up you and the others at Division.'

He didn't even think *Other what?* He just thought *They have killed the serpent, and now they have got to get rid of the fragments*, and returned to Division Headquarters, where eight more runners from the other battalions and a lorry waited, the nine of them by that special transport to serve as special couriers out of Corps Headquarters which by ordinary bristled with couriers, not warned still, knowing no more yet, not even wondering, not even caring; fixed behind a faint wry grimace which was almost smiling in the midst of what was not ruin at all because he had known it of old too long, too long of old: *Yes*, he thought, *a bigger snake than even they had anticipated having to destroy and efface*. Nor did he learn any more at Corps Headquarters, nor during the next two hours while at top speed now he delivered and exchanged and received dispatches from and to people whom even his travels had never touched before—not to orderly room N.C.O.'s but in person to majors and colonels and sometimes even generals, at transport and artillery parks, with columns of transport and artillery camouflaged beside roads and waiting for darkness to move, at batteries in position and Flying Corps wing offices and forward aerodromes —no longer even wondering now behind that fixed thin grimace which might have been smiling: who had not for nothing been a soldier in France for twenty-one months and an officer for five of them, and so knew what he was looking at when he saw it: the vast cumbrous machinery of war grinding to its clumsy halt in order to reverse itself to grind and rumble in a new direction—the proprietorless wave of victory exhausted by its own ebb and returned by its own concomitant flux, spent not by its own faded momentum but as though bogged down in the refuse of its own success; afterward, it seemed to him that he had been speeding along those back-area roads for days before he realised what he had been travelling through; he would not even recall afterward at what moment, where, what anonymous voice from a passing lorry or another motorbike or perhaps in some orderly room where he lay one dispatch down in the act of taking up another, which said:

'The French quit this morning—' merely riding on, speeding on into the full burst of sun before he realised what he had heard.

It was an hour after noon before he finally found a face: that of a corporal standing before a café in a village street—a face which had been in the anteroom of the old battalion when he was an officer in it: and slowed the machine in and stopped, still straddling it; it was the first time.

'Nah,' the corporal said. 'It was just one regiment. Fact is, they're putting one of the biggest shoots yet in Jerry's support and communications along the whole front right this minute. Been at it ever since dawn—'

'But one regiment quit,' the runner said. 'One did.' Now the corporal was not looking at him at all.

'Have a wet,' the corporal said.

'Besides,' the runner said gently, 'you're wrong. The whole French front quit at noon.'

'But not ours,' the corporal said.

'Not yet,' the runner said. 'That may take a little time.' The corporal was not looking at him. Now the corporal said nothing whatever. With a light, rapid gesture the runner touched one shoulder with the opposite hand. 'There's nothing up here now,' he said.

'Have a wet,' the corporal said, not looking at him.

And an hour later he was close enough to the lines to see the smoke-and-dust pall as well as hear the frantic uproar of the concentrated guns along the horizon; at three o'clock, though twelve miles away at another point, he heard the barrage ravel away into the spaced orderly harmless-seeming poppings as of salutes or signals, and it seemed to him that he could see the whole long line from the sea-beaches up the long slant of France to old tired Europe's rooftree, squatted and crouched with filthy and noisome men who had forgot four years ago how to stand erect any more, amazed and bewildered and unable to believe it either, forewarned and filled with hope though (he knew it now) they must have been; he thought, said aloud almost: *Yes, that's it. It's not that we didn't believe: it's that we couldn't, didn't know how any more. That's the most terrible thing they have done to us. That's the most terrible.*

That was all, then. For almost twenty-four hours in fact, though he didn't know it at the time. A sergeant-major was waiting for them as they returned, gathered again at Corps Headquarters that night —the nine from his Division and perhaps two dozen others from other units in the Corps. 'Who's senior here?' the sergeant-major said. But he didn't even wait on himself: he glanced rapidly about at them again and with the unerring instinct of his vocation chose a man in the middle thirties who looked exactly like what he probably was—a demoted lance corporal out of a 1912 Northwest Frontier garrison. 'You're acting sergeant,' the sergeant-major said. 'You will indent for suppers and bedding here.' He looked at them again. 'I suppose it's no use to tell you not to talk.'

'Talk about what?' one said. 'What do we know to talk about?'

'Talk about that,' the sergeant-major said. 'You are relieved until reveille. Carry on.' And that was all then.

They slept on a stone floor in a corridor; they were given breakfast (a good one; this was a Corps Headquarters) before reveille went even; what bugles they—he, the runner—heard were at other Division and Corps Headquarters and parks and depots where the motorcycle took him during another day like yesterday in his minuscule walking-on (riding-on) part in bringing war to a pause, a halt, a stop; morning noon and afternoon up and down back areas not beneath a pall of peace but a thrall of dreamlike bustling for a holiday. The night again, the same sergeant-major was waiting for them—the nine from his Division and the two dozen others. 'That's all,' the sergeant-major said. 'Lorries are waiting to take you back in.' *That's all*, he thought. *All you have to do, all you need to do, all He ever asked and died for eighteen hundred and eighty-five years ago*, in the lorry now with his group of the thirty-odd others, the afterglow of sunset fading out of the sky like the tideless shoreless sea of despair itself ebbing away, leaving only the peaceful grief and the hope; when the lorry stopped and presently he leaned out to see what was wrong—a road which it was unable to cross because of transport on it, a road which he remembered as running southeast from up near Boulogne somewhere, now so dense with hooded and lightless lorries moving nose to tail like a line of elephants that their own lorry had to put them down here, to find their ways home as best they might, his companions dispersing, leaving him standing there in the last of afterglow while the vans crawled endless past him, until a head, a voice called his name from one of them, saying, 'Hurry, get up quick . . . something to show you,' so that he had to run to overtake it and had already begun to swing himself up before he recognised it: the old watchman from the St. Omer ammunition dump, who had come to France four years ago to search for his son and who had been the first to tell him about the thirteen French soldiers.

Three hours after midnight he was sitting on the firestep where the sentry leaned at the aperture while the spaced star-shells sniffed and plopped and whispered down the greasy dark and the remote gun winked and thudded and after a while winked and thudded again. He was talking in a voice which, whatever else it contained, exhaustion was not it—a voice dreamy and glib, apparently not only inattentive to itself but seemingly incapable of compelling attention anywhere. Yet each time he spoke, the sentry without even removing his face from the aperture would give a start, a motion convulsive and intolerable, like someone goaded almost beyond endurance.

'One regiment,' the runner said. 'One French regiment. Only a fool would look on war as a condition; it's too expensive. War is an episode, a crisis, a fever the purpose of which is to rid the body of fever. So the purpose of a war is to end the war. We've known that for six thousand years. The trouble was, it took us six thousand years to learn how to do it. For six thousand years we laboured under the delusion that the only way to stop a war was to get together more regiments and battalions than the enemy could, or vice versa, and hurl them upon each other until one lot was destroyed and, the one having nothing left to fight with, the other could stop fighting. We were wrong, because yesterday morning, by simply declining to make an attack, one single French regiment stopped us all.'

This time the sentry didn't move, leaning—braced rather—against the trench-wall beneath the vicious rake of his motionless helmet, peering apparently almost idly through the aperture save for that rigidity about his back and shoulders—a kind of immobilit*· on top of immobility—as though he were braced not against the dirt wall but rather against the quiet and empty air behind him. Nor had the runner moved either, though from his speech it was almost as if he had turned his face to look directly at the back of the sentry's head. 'What do you see?' he said. 'No novelty, you think?—the same stinking strip of ownerless valueless frantic dirt between our wire and theirs, which you have been peering at through a hole in a sandbag for four years now? The same war which we had come to believe did not know how to end itself, like the amateur orator searching desperately for a definitive preposition? You're wrong. You can go out there now, at least during the next fifteen minutes, say, and not die probably. Yes, that may be the novelty: you can go out there now and stand erect and look about you—granted of course that any of us really ever can stand erect again. But we will learn how. Who knows? In four or five years we may even have got our neck-muscles supple enough simply to duck our heads again in place of merely bowing them to await the stroke, as we have been doing for four years now; in ten years, certainly.' The sentry didn't move, like a blind man suddenly within range of a threat, the first warning of which he must translate through some remaining secondary sense, already too late to fend with. 'Come,' the runner said. 'You're a man of the world. Indeed, you have been a man of this world since noon yesterday, even if they didn't bother to tell you so until fifteen o'clock. In fact, we are all men of this world now, all of us who died on the fourth day of August four years ago—'

The sentry moved again with that convulsive start; he said in a harsh thick furious murmur: 'For the last time. I warned you.'

'—all the fear and the doubt, the agony and the grief and the lice— Because it's over. Isn't it over?'

'Yes!' the sentry said.

'Of course it's over. You came out in ... fifteen, wasn't it? You've seen a lot of war too. Of course you know when one is over.'

'It is over!' the sentry said. 'Didn't you hear the ——ing guns stop right out there in front of you?'

'Then why don't we go home?'

'Can they draw the whole ——ing line out at once? Leave the whole ——ing front empty at one time?'

'Why not?' the runner said. 'Isn't it over?' It was as if he had fixed the sentry as the matador does the bull, leaving the animal capable only of watching him. 'Over. Finished. Done. No more parades. Tomorrow we shall go home; by this time tomorrow night we shall have hoicked from the beds of our wives and sweethearts the manufacturers of walking-out shoe-pegs and Enfield primers—'

He thought rapidly *He's going to kick me*. He said, 'All right. Sorry. I didn't know you had a wife.'

'No more I have,' the sentry said in his shaking whisper. 'So will you stow it now? Will you for bleeding Christ?'

'Of course you haven't. How wise you are. A girl in a High Street pub, of course. Or perhaps a city girl—a Greater City girl, Houndsditch or Bermondsey, towarding forty but not looking within five years of it, and's had her troubles too—who hasn't?—but suppose she does, who wouldn't choose her and lucky, who can appreciate a man, to one of these young tarts swapping cove for cove with each leave train—'

The sentry began to curse, in the same harsh spent furious monotone, cursing the runner with obscene and dull unimagination out of the stalls and tack-rooms and all the other hinder purlieus of what must have been his old vocation, until at the same moment the runner sat quickly and lightly up and the sentry began to turn back to the aperture in a series of jerks like a mechanical toy running down, murmuring again in his shaking furious voice: 'Remember. I told you' as two men came around the traverse and up the trench in single line, indistinguishable in their privates' uniforms save for the officer's stick and the sergeant's chevrons.

'Post?' the officer said.

'Two-nine,' the sentry said. The officer had lifted his foot to the firestep when he saw, seemed to see, the runner.

'Who's that?' he said. The runner began to stand up, promptly enough but without haste. The sergeant pronounced his name.

'He was in that special draft of runners Corps drew out yesterday morning. They were dismissed to dugouts as soon as they reported back tonight, and told to stop there. This man was, anyway.'

'Oh,' the officer said. That was when the sergeant pronounced the name. 'Why aren't you there?'

'Yes, sir,' the runner said, picking up the rifle and turning quite smartly, moving back down the trench until he had vanished beyond the traverse. The officer completed his stride on to the firestep; now both the helmets slanted motionless and twinlike between the sandbags while the two of them peered through the aperture. Then the sentry said, murmured, so quietly that it seemed impossible that the sergeant six feet away could have heard him:

72

'Nothing more's come up I suppose, sir?' For another half minute the officer peered through the aperture. Then he turned and stepped down to the duckboards, the sentry turning with him, the sergeant moving again into file behind him, the officer himself already beginning to move when he spoke:

'When you are relieved, go down your dugout and stay there.' Then they were gone. The sentry began to turn back toward the aperture. Then he stopped. The runner was now standing on the duckboards below him; while they looked at each other the starshell sniffed and traced its sneering arc and plopped into parachute, the faint glare washing over the runner's lifted face and then, even after the light itself had died, seeming to linger still on it as if the glow had not been refraction at all but water or perhaps grease; he spoke in a tense furious murmur not much louder than a whisper:

'Do you see now? Not for us to ask what nor why but just go down a hole in the ground and stay there until they decide what to do. No: just how to do it because they already know what. Of course they won't tell us. They wouldn't have told us anything at all if they hadn't had to, hadn't had to tell us something, tell the rest of you something before the ones of us who were drawn out yesterday for special couriers out of Corps would get back in tonight and tell you what we had heard. And even then, they told you just enough to keep you in the proper frame of mind so that, when they said go down the dugouts and stay there you would do it. And even I wouldn't have known any more in time if on the way back in tonight I hadn't blundered on to the lorry train.

'No: that's wrong too; just known in time that they are already up to something. Because all of us know by now that something is wrong. Don't you see? Something happened down there yesterday morning in the French front, a regiment failed—burked—mutinied, we don't know what and are not going to know what because they aren't going to tell us. Besides, it doesn't matter what happened. What matters is, what happened afterward. At dawn yesterday a French regiment did something—did or failed to do something which a regiment in a front line is not supposed to do or fail to do, and as a result of it, the entire war in Western Europe took a recess at three o'clock yesterday afternoon. Don't you see? When you are in battle and one of your units fails, the last thing you do, dare do, is quit. Instead, you snatch up everything else you've got and fling it in as quick and hard as you can, because you know that that's exactly what the enemy is going to do as soon as he discovers or even suspects you have trouble on your side. Of course you're going to be one unit short of him when you meet; your hope, your only hope, is that if you can only start first and be going the fastest, momentum and surprise might make up a little of it.

'But they didn't. Instead, they took a recess, remanded: the French at noon, us and the Americans three hours later. And not only us, but Jerry too. Don't you see? How can you remand in war, unless your enemy agrees too? And why should Jerry have agreed, after squatting under the sort of barrage which four years had trained him to know meant that an attack was coming, then no attack came or failed or whatever it was it did, and four years had certainly trained him to the right assumption for that; when the message, signal, request—whatever it was—came over suggesting a remand, why should he have agreed to it, unless he had a reason as good as the one we had, maybe the same reason we had? The same reason; those thirteen French soldiers apparently had no diffi-culty whatever going anywhere they liked in our back-areas for three years, why weren't they across yonder in Jerry's too, since we all know that, unless you've got the right properly signed paper in your hand, it's a good deal more difficult to go to Paris from here than to Berlin; any time you want to go east from here, all you need is a British or French or American uniform. Or perhaps they didn't even need to go themselves, perhaps just wind, moving air, carried it. Or perhaps not even moving air but just air, spreading by attrition from invisible and weightless molecule to molecule as disease, smallpox spreads, or fear, or hope—just enough of us, all of us in the mud here saying together, Enough of this, let's have done with this.

'Because—don't you see?—they can't have this. They can't per-mit this, to stop it at all yet, let alone allow it to stop itself this way —the two shells in the river and the race already under way and both crews without warning simply unshipping the oars from the locks and saying in unison: We're not going to pull any more. They can't yet. It's not finished yet, like an unfinished cricket or rugger match which started according to a set of mutually accepted rules formally and peaceably agreed on, and must finish by them, else the whole theory of arbitration, the whole tried and proven step-by-step edifice of politics and economy on which the civilised concord of nations is based becomes so much wind. More than that: that thin and tensioned girder of steel and human blood which carries its national edifice soaring glorious and threatful among the stars, in dedication to which young men are transported free of charge and even with pay, to die violently in places that even the map-makers and -dividers never saw, that a pilgrim stumbling on it a hundred or a thousand years afterward may still be able to say, Here is a spot that is (anyway was once) forever England or France or America. And not only can't, dare not: they won't. They have already started not to. Because listen. On the way back up tonight, I got a lift in a lorry. It was carrying AA shells. It was in a column almost three miles long, all chock full of AA shells. Think of it: three miles of AA shells; think of having enough shells to measure it in miles, which apparently they did not have in front of Amiens two months ago. But then, naturally it takes more ammunition to recess a war for ten minutes than to stop a mere offensive. The lorry was in charge of an old man I knew who had been waiting for three years at an ammo dump at St. Omer for his application to go through for leave and permission to go to Mons and search for his son who hadn't or didn't or couldn't or didn't want to—anyway, failed to—come back that afternoon four years ago. He showed me one of the shells. It was blank. Not dud: blank, complete and intact except that there was no shrapnel in it; it would fire and even burst, harmless. It looked all right on the outside; I doubt if its father in his West End club (or Birmingham or Leeds or Manchester or wherever people live who make shells) would have known the difference, and only a dyed-in-the-wool archie bloke could. It was amazing, really; they must have worked like beavers all last night and today too there at the dump, altering, gelding three miles of shells—or maybe they had them all ready beforehand, in advance; maybe after four years, even Anglo-Saxons can learn to calculate ahead in war—' talking, the voice not dreamy now: just glib and rapid, he (the runner) in the moving lorry now, the three of them, himself, the old man and the driver, crowded into the close and lightless cab so that he could feel the whole frail length of the old man's body tense and exultant against him, remembering how at first his voice had sounded as cracked and

75

amazed as the old man's, but soon no more: the two voices running along side by side as logical in unreason, rational and inconsequent as those of two children:

'Perhaps you'd better tell me again. Maybe I have forgot.'

'For the signal!' the old man cried. 'The announcement! To let the whole world know that He has risen!'

'A signal of AA shells? Three miles of AA shells? Wouldn't one gun be enough to herald Him? And if one gun, why hold His resurrection up long enough to run three miles of shells through it? Or if one shell to each gun, why only three miles of guns? Why not enough for every gun between Switzerland and the Channel? Aren't the rest of us to be notified too? To welcome Him too? Why not just bugles, horns? He would recognise horns; they wouldn't frighten Him.'

'Don't the Book itself say he will return in thunder and lightning?'

'But not gunpowder,' the runner said.

'Then let man make the noise!' the cracked voice cried. 'Let man shout hallelujah and jubilee with the very things he has been killing with!'—rational and fantastic, like children, and as cruel too:

'And fetch your son along with Him?' the runner said.

'My son?' the old man said. 'My son is dead.'

'Yes,' the runner said. 'That's what I meant. Isn't that what you mean too?'

'Pah,' the old man said; it sounded almost like spitting. 'What does it matter, whether or not He brings my son back with Him? My son, or yours, or any other man's? *My* son? Even the whole million of them we have lost since that day four years ago, the billion since that day eighteen hundred and eighty-five years ago. The ones He will restore to life are the ones that would have died since eight o'clock this morning. My son? *My* son?'—then (the runner) out of the lorry again (The column had stopped. It was near the lines, just under them in fact, or what had been the front line until three o'clock this afternoon; the runner knew that at once, although he had never been here before. But he had not only been an infantryman going in and out of them for twenty-odd months, for seven months he had been a runner going in and out of them every night, so he had no more doubt of where he was

than would the old wolf or lynx when he was near a trap-line.),
walking up the column toward the halted head of it, and stopped
in shadow and watched the M.P.'s and armed sentries splitting
the column into sections with a guide for each leading lorry, each
section as it was detached turning from the road into the fields and
woods beyond which lay the front; and not long to watch this
either, because almost at once a corporal with his bayonet fixed
came quickly around the lorry in whose shadow he stood.

'Get back to your lorry,' the corporal ordered.

He identified himself, naming his battalion and its vector.

'What the bleeding —— are you doing down here?' the corporal
said.

'Trying to get a lift.'

'Not here,' the corporal said. 'Hop it. Sharp, now'—and (the
corporal) still watching him until darkness hid him again; then
he too left the road, into a wood, walking toward the lines now;
and (telling it, sprawled on the firestep beneath the rigid and
furious sentry almost as though he drowsed, his eyes half-closed,
talking in the glib, dreamy, inconsequent voice) how from the
shadows again he watched the crew of an anti-aircraft battery,
with hooded torches, unload the blank shells from one of the lorries,
and tumble their own live ammunition back into it, and went on
until he saw the hooded lights again and watched the next lorry
make its exchange; and at midnight was in another wood—or what
had been a wood, since all that remained now was a nightingale
somewhere behind him—not walking now but standing with his
back against the blasted corpse of a tree, hearing still above the
bird's idiot reiteration the lorries creeping secretly and steadily
through the darkness, not listening to them, just hearing them,
because he was searching for something which he had lost, mislaid,
for the moment, though when he thought that he had put the
digit of his recollection on it at last, it was wrong, flowing rapid
and smooth through his mind, but wrong: *In Christ is death at
end in Adam that began:*—true, but the wrong one: not the wrong
truth but the wrong moment for it, the wrong one needed and
desired; clearing his mind again and making the attempt again,
yet there it was again: *In Christ is death at end in Adam that—*
still true, still wrong, still comfortless; and then, before he had
thought his mind was clear again, the right one was there, smooth

77

and intact and instantaneous, seeming to have been there for a whole minute while he was still fretting its loss:

—but that was in another country;
and besides, the wench is dead

And this time the flare went up from their own trench, not twenty yards away beyond the up traverse, so near this time that after the green corpse-glare died the sentry could have discerned that what washed over the runner's face was neither the refraction assumed nor the grease it resembled, but the water it was: 'A solid corridor of harmless archie batteries, beginning at our parapet and exactly the width of the range at which a battery in either wall would decide there wasn't any use in even firing at an aeroplane flying straight down the middle of it, running back to the aerodrome at Villeneuve Blanche, so that to anyone not a general it would look all right—and if there was just enough hurry and surprise about it, maybe even to the men themselves carrying the shells running to the guns ramming them home and slamming the blocks and pulling the lanyards and blistering their hands snatching the hot cases out fast enough to get out of the way of the next one, let alone the ones in front lines trying to cringe back out of man's sight in case the aeroplane flying down the corridor to Villeneuve wasn't carrying ammunition loaded last night at whatever the hun calls his Saint Omer, it would still look and sound all right, even if the hun continued not falling all the way back to Villeneuve because Flying Corps people say archie never hits anything anyway—

'So you see what we must do before that German emissary or whatever he will be can reach Paris or Chaulnesmont or wherever he is to go, and he and whoever he is to agree with, have agreed, not on what to do because that is no problem: only on how, and goes back home to report it. We don't even need to start it; the French, that one French regiment, has already taken up the load. All we need is not to let it drop, falter, pause for even a second. We must do it now, tomorrow—tomorrow? it's already tomorrow it's already today now—do as that French regiment did, the whole battalion of us: climb over this parapet tomorrow morning and get through the wire, with no rifles, nothing, and walk toward

78

Jerry's wire until he can see us, enough of him can see us—a regiment of him or a battalion or maybe just a company or maybe even just one because even just one will be enough. You can do it. You own the whole battalion, every man in it under corporal, beneficiary of every man's insurance in it who hasn't got a wife and I.O.U.'s for their next month's pay of all the rest of them in that belt around your waist. All you'll need is just to tell them to when you say, Follow me; I'll go along to the first ones as soon as you are relieved, so they can see you vouch for me. Then others will see you vouch for me when I vouch for them, so that by daylight or by sunup anyway, when Jerry can see us, all the rest of Europe can see us, will have to see us, can't help but see us—' He thought: *He's really going to kick me this time, and in the face.* Then the sentry's boot struck the side of his jaw, snapping his head back even before his body toppled, the thin flow of water which sheathed his face flying at the blow like a thin spray of spittle or perhaps of dew or rain from a snapped leaf, the sentry kicking at him again as he went over backward on to the firestep, and was still stamping his boot at the unconscious face when the officer and the sergeant ran back around the traverse, still stamping at the prone face and panting at it:

'Will you for Christ's sake now? Will you? Will you?' when the sergeant jerked him bodily down to the duckboards. The sentry didn't even pause, whirling while the sergeant held him, and slashing his reversed rifle blindly across the nearest face. It was the officer's, but the sentry didn't even wait to see, whirling again back toward the firestep though the sergeant still gripped him in one arm around his middle, still—the sentry—striking with the rifle-butt at the runner's bleeding head when the sergeant fumbled his pistol out with his free hand and thumbed the safety off.

'As you were,' the officer said, jerking the blood from his mouth, on to his wrist and flinging it away. 'Hold him.' He spoke without turning his head, toward the corner of the down traverse, raising his voice a little: 'Two-eight. Pass the word for corporal.'

The sentry was actually foaming now, apparently not even conscious that the sergeant was holding him, still jabbing the rifle-butt at or at least toward the runner's peaceful and bloody head, until the sergeant spoke almost against his ear.

'Two-seven . . . for corporal,' a voice beyond the down traverse said; then fainter, beyond that, another:

'Two-six . . . corporal.'

'Use yer boot,' the sergeant muttered. 'Kick his ——ing teeth in.'

MONDAY * TUESDAY
WEDNESDAY

HE had already turned back toward the aerodrome when he saw the Harry Tate. At first he just watched it, merely alerting himself to overshoot it safely; they looked so big and were travelling so slowly that you always made the mistake of over-estimating them if you were not careful. Then he saw that the thing obviously not only hoped but actually believed that it could cut him off—a Harry Tate, which usually had two Australians in it or one general-and-pilot, this one indubitably a general since only by some esoteric factor like extreme and even overwhelming rank could an R.E.8 even hope to catch an S.E. and send it to earth.

Which was obviously what this one intended to do, he throttling back now until the S.E. was hanging on its airscrew just above stalling. And it was a general: the two aeroplanes broadside on for a second or so, a hand in a neat walking-out glove from the observer's seat gesturing him peremptorily downward until he waggled his wings in acknowledgment and put his nose down for home, thinking, *Why me? What've I done now? Besides, how did they know where I was?*—having suddenly a sort of vision of the whole sky full of lumbering R.E.8's, each containing a general with a list compiled by frantic telephone of every absent unaccounted-for scout on the whole front, hunting them down one by one out of back-areas and harrying them to earth.

Then he reached the aerodrome and saw the ground signal-strip laid out on it; he hadn't seen one since ground school and for a goodish while he didn't even know what it was; not until he saw the other aeroplanes on the ground or landing or coming in to land did he recognise it to be the peremptory emergency signal to all aircraft to come down, landing in his turn faster and harder than people liked to land S.E.'s because of their unhappy ground habits, taxi-ing in to the tarmac where, even before he could switch off, the mechanic was shouting at him: 'The mess, sir! Right away! The major wants you at the mess right away!'

A FABLE

'What?' he said. 'Me?'

'Everyone, sir,' the mechanic said. 'The whole squadron, sir. Best hurry.'

He jumped down to the tarmac, already running, so young in breathing that he wouldn't be nineteen for another year yet and so young in war that, although the Royal Air Force was only six weeks old, his was not the universal tunic with RFC badges superimposed on the remnants of old regimental insigne which veteran transfers wore, and he didn't even own the old official Flying Corps tunic at all: his was the new RAF thing not only unmartial but even a little epicene, with its cloth belt and no shoulderstraps like the coat of the adult leader of a neo-Christian boys' club and the narrow pale blue ring around each cuff and the hat-badge like a field marshal's until you saw, remarked, noticed the little modest dull gold pin on either side of it like lingerie-clips or say the christening's gift-choice by godfathers whose good taste had had to match their pocketbooks.

A year ago he was still in school, waiting not for his eighteenth birthday and legal age for joining up, but for his seventeenth one and the expiration, discharge, of a promise to his widowed mother (he was the only child) to stick it out until then. Which he did, even making good marks, even while his mind, his whole being, was sleepless and athirst with the ringing heroic catalogue: Ball: McCudden: Mannock: Bishop: Barker: Rhys Davies: and above all, simply: England. Three weeks ago he was still in England, waiting in Pilot's Pool for posting to the front—a certificated stationary engine scout pilot to whom the King had inscribed *We Reposing Trust and Confidence in Our Trusty and Well-Beloved Gerald David* . . . but already too late, gazetted not into the RFC but into the RAF. Because the RFC had ceased to exist on April Fool's day, two days before his commission came through: whereupon that March midnight had seemed to him a knell. A door had closed on glory; immortality itself had died in unprimered anticlimax: not his to be the old commission in the old glorious corps, the brotherhood of heroes to which he had dedicated himself even at the cost of that wrench to his mother's heart; not his the old commission which Albert Ball had carried with him into immortality and which Bishop and Mannock and McCudden still bore in their matchless record; his only the new thing not flesh nor fowl nor good red herring: who had waited one whole year acquiescent to his mother's unrational frantic heart fiercely and irrevocably immune to glory, and then another year in training, working like a beaver, like the very proverbial Trojan, to compensate for his own inability to say no to a woman's tears.

It was too late; those who had invented for him the lingerie pins and the official slacks in place of pink Bedfords and long boots and ordnance belt had closed the door even to the anteroom of heroes. In Valhalla's un-national halls the un-national shades, Frenchman and German and Briton, conqueror and conquered alike—Immelman and Guynemer, Boelcke and Ball identical not in the vast freemasonry of death but in the closed select one of flying, would clash their bottomless mugs, but not for him. Their inheritors—Bishop and Mannock and Voss and McCudden and Fonck and Barker and Richthofen and Nungesser—would still cleave the earth-foundationed air, pacing their fleeing shadows on the scudding canyon-walls of cumulae, furloughed and immune, secure in immortality even while they still breathed, but it would not be his. Glory and valour would still exist of course as long as men lived to reap them. It would even be the same valour in fact, but the glory would be another glory. And that would be his: some second form of Elysium, a cut above dead infantry perhaps, but little more: who was not the first to think *What had I done for motherland's glory had motherland but matched me with her need*.

And now apparently even what remained was to be denied him: three weeks spent in practice, mostly gunnery (he was quite good at it, astonishing even himself), at the aerodrome; one carefully chaperoned trip—the major, Bridesman, his flight commander, himself and one other new and unblooded tyro—up to the lines to show them what they looked like and how to find the way back; and yesterday he was in his hut after lunch trying to compose a letter to his mother when Bridesman thrust his head in and gave him the official notice which he had been waiting for now ever since his seventeenth birthday: 'Levine. Jobs tomorrow. Eleven o'clock. Before we take off, I'll try again to remind you to try to remember what we have been trying to tell you to remember.' Then this morning he had gone up for what would be the last of his unchallenged airy privacy, the farewell to his apprenticeship, what might be called the valedictory of his maidenhood, when the general in the Harry Tate sent him back to earth, to spring down almost before the aeroplane stopped rolling and, spurred again by the mechanic, run to the mess, already the last one, since everyone else was there except the flight which was still out, finding the major already talking, one knee crooked easily across the corner of the table; he (the major) had just got back from Wing Headquarters, where he had met the general commanding, who had come straight from Poperinghe: the French had asked for an armistice; it would go into effect at noon—twelve hours. But it meant nothing: they (the squadron) were to remember that; the British hadn't asked for any armistice, nor the Americans either; and having known the French, fought beside them for almost four years now, he (the major) didn't yet believe it meant anything with them. However, there would be a truce, a remand, for an hour or two hours or perhaps a whole day. But it was a French truce; it wasn't ours—looking about at them, nonchalant and calm and even negligent, speaking in that same casual negligent voice and manner with which he could carry the whole squadron through a binge night, through exuberance and pandemonium and then, with none realising it until afterward, back into sufficient sobriety to cope with the morrow's work, which was not the least of the reasons why, even though no hun-getter, he was one of the most popular and capable squadron commanders in France, though he (the child) had not been there long enough to know that. But he did know that here was the true authentic voice of that invincible island which, with not merely the eighteen years he had but the rest of his promised span which he might very likely lose doing it, he would in joy and pride defend and in gratitude preserve: 'Because we aren't quitting. Not us nor the Americans either. It's not over. Nobody declared it for us; nobody but us shall make our peace. Flights will stand by as usual. Carry on.'

He didn't think *Why* yet. He just thought *What*. He had never heard of a recess in war. But then, he knew so little about war; he realised now that he knew nothing about war. He would ask Bridesman, glancing about the room where they were already beginning to disperse, and in the first moment realising that Bridesman was not there, and in the next one that none of the flight commanders was there: not only Bridesman, but Witt and Sibleigh too, which in Witt's case obviously meant that he still had C Flight out on the mid-morning job, and which—the fact that C Flight was still carrying on with the war—ratified the major's words; C Flight hadn't quit, and if he knew Bridesman (and after three weeks he certainly should) B hadn't either; glancing at his watch now: half after ten, thirty minutes yet before B would go up; he would have time to finish the letter to his mother which Bridesman had interrupted yesterday; he could even—since the war would officially begin for him in thirty minutes—write the other one, the succinct and restrained and modestly heroic one to be found among his gear afterward by whoever went through it and decided what should be sent back to his mother: thinking how the patrol went up at eleven and the remand would begin at twelve, which would leave him an hour—no, it would take them ten minutes to get to the lines, which would leave fifty minutes; if fifty minutes was long enough for him to at least make a start after Bishop's and McCudden's and Mannock's records, it would be long enough for him to get shot down in too: already moving toward the door when he heard engines: a flight: taking off: then running up to the hangars, where he learned that it was not even B Flight, shouting at the sergeant, incredulous and amazed:

'Do you mean that all three flight commanders and all the deputies have gone out in one patrol?' and then heard the guns begin, not like any heavy firing he had ever heard before, but furious and simultaneous and vast in extent—a sound already in existence to the southeast before audibility began and still in existence to the northwest when audibility ceased. 'They're coming over!' he shouted. 'The French have betrayed us! They just go out of the way and let them through!'

'Yes, sir,' the flight sergeant said. 'Hadn't you better get along to the office? They may be wanting you.'

'Right,' he said, already running, back up the vacant aerodrome beneath the sky furious with the distant guns, into the office which was worse than empty: the corporal not only sitting as always behind the telephone, but looking at him across the dogeared copy of *Punch* which he had been looking at when he saw him first three weeks ago. 'Where's the major?' he cried.

'Down at Wing, sir,' the corporal said.

'Down at Wing?' he cried, incredulous, already running again:

through the opposite door, into the mess, and saw the rest of the squadron's new replacements like himself all sitting quietly about as though the adjutant had not merely arrested them but was sitting guard over them at the table with his pipe and wound stripe and observer's O and single wing above the Mons Star ribbon, and the squadron chessboard and the folded sheet of last Sunday's *Times* chess problem laid out before him; and he (the child) shouting, 'Can't you hear them? Can't you?' so that he couldn't hear the adjutant at all for his own noise, until the adjutant began to shout too:

'*Where have you been?*'

'Hangars,' he said. 'I was to go on the patrol.'

'Didn't anyone tell you to report to me here?'

'Report?' he said. 'Flight Sergeant Conventicle—— No,' he said

'You're——'

'Levine.'

'Levine. You've been here three weeks. Not long enough to have learned that this squadron is run by people especially appointed and even qualified for it. In fact, when they gave you those badges, they gave you a book of rules to go with them, to prevent you needing ever to rack your brains like this. Perhaps you haven't yet had time to glance through it.'

'Yes,' he said. 'What do you want with me?'

'To sit down somewhere and be quiet. As far as this squadron is concerned, the war stopped at noon. There'll be no more flying here until further notice. As for those guns, they began at twelve hours. The major knew that beforehand. They will stop at fifteen hours. Now you know that in advance too—'

'Stop?' he said. 'Don't you see—'

'Sit down!' the adjutant said.

'—if we stop now, we are beat, have lost——'

'*Sit down!*'

He stopped then. Then he said: 'Am I under arrest?'

'Do you want to be?'

'Right,' he said. He sat down. It was twenty-two minutes past twelve hours; now it was not the Nissen walls which trembled, but the air they contained. Presently, or in time that is, it was thirteen hours, then fourteen, all that distant outside fury reduced now to a moiling diastole of motes where the sun slanted into the western windows; getting on for fifteen hours now and the squadron itself reduced to a handful of tyros who barely knew in which direction the front lay, under command of a man who had never been anything but a poor bloody observer to begin with and had even given that up now for a chessboard—the other new men who had—must have—brought out from England with them the same gratitude and pride and thirst and hope—Then he was on his feet, hearing the silence still falling like a millstone into a well; then they were all moving as one, through the door and outside into that topless gape from which the walls and roof of distant gunfire had been ripped, snatched, as a cyclone rips the walls and roof from the rectangle of vacancy which a moment ago had been a hangar, leaving audibility with nothing now to lean against, outbursting into vacuum as the eardrums crack with altitude, until at last even that shocking crash died away.

'That seems to be it,' a voice said behind him.

'Seems to be what?' he said. 'It's not over! Didn't you hear what the major said? The Americans aren't quitting either! Do you think Monaghan' (Monaghan was an American, in B Flight too; although he had been out only ten weeks, he already had a score of three and a fraction) 'is quitting? And even if they do—' and stopped, finding them all watching him, soberly and quietly, as if he were a flight commander himself; one said:

'What do you think, Levine?'

'Me?' he said, 'About what?' *Ask Collyer*, he thought. *He's running the nursery now;* bitterly too now: *Ask Collyer*—the pipe, the balding head, the plump bland face which at this moment was England's sole regent over this whole square half-mile of French dirt, custodian of her honour and pride, who three years ago had probably brought out to France (he, Collyer, according to squadron folklore, had been ridden down by a Uhlan with a lance inside the war's first weeks and turned flying observer and came out again and within a week of that managed somehow to live through a F.E. crash after his pilot was dead and since then, carrying the same single pip and—the legend said—the same cold pipe, had been a squadron adjutant) the same feeling, belief, hunger—whatever you want to call it—as intolerant and unappeasable as his own, and then lost it or put it aside as he had put the war itself forever away, secure and immune in his ground job where no thirst for victory nor tumescence of valour could trouble him more; thinking, *Oh yes, ask Collyer*, finishing the thought which the cessation of the guns had interrupted inside the mess: *He has quit too. He gave up so long ago that he doesn't even remember now that he hasn't even lost anything.—I heard the death of England* he said quietly to himself, then aloud: 'Think about what? That noise? Nothing. That's what it sounds like, doesn't it?'

At five o'clock the major was delivered almost on to the office stoop by the general commanding the brigade's Harry Tate. Just before sunset two lorries drove on to the aerodrome; watching from his hut he saw infantry with rifles and tin hats get down and parade for a moment on the dusty grass behind the office and then disperse in squads and at sunset the patrol of flight commanders and deputies which had gone out at noon in the similitude of B Flight had not returned, three times longer than any patrol ever stayed out or than any S.E. could stay up on its petrol. And he dined with a mess (the major was not present though a few of the older men—including the infantry officer—were; he didn't know where they had been nor when returned) half of whom he knew knew nothing either and the other half he didn't know how much they knew or cared—a meal which was not long before the adjutant got up and stopped just long enough to say, not speaking to the older people at all: 'You aren't confined to quarters. Just put it that almost any place you can think of is out of bounds.'

'Even the village?' someone said.

'Even Villeneuve Blanche, sink of iniquity though it be not. You might all go home with Levine and curl up with his book. That's where he should be.' Then he stopped again. 'That means the hangars too.'

'Why should we go to the hangars this time of night?' one said.

'I don't know,' the adjutant said. 'Don't.' Then the others dispersed but not he, he was still sitting there after the orderlies had cleared the mess for the night and still there when the motor car came up, not stopping at the mess but going on around to the office and through the thin partition he heard people enter the office and then the voices: the major and Bridesman and the other two flight commanders and no S.E. had landed on this aerodrome after dark even if he hadn't heard the car. Nor could he have heard what the voices were saying even if he had tried, just sitting there

when the voices stopped short and a second later the door opened
and the adjutant paused an instant then came on, pulling the door
after him, saying: 'Get along to your hut.'

'Right,' he said, rising. But the adjutant came on into the mess,
shutting the door behind him; his voice was really kind now.

'Why don't you let it alone?'

'I am,' he said. 'I don't know how to do anything else because I
don't know how it can be over if it's not over nor how it can be not
over if it's over—'

'Go to your hut,' the adjutant said. He went out into the darkness, the silence, walking on in the direction of the huts as long
as anyone from the mess might still see him, then giving himself
another twenty steps for good measure before he turned away toward the hangars, thinking how his trouble was probably very
simple, really: he had never heard silence before; he had been thirteen, almost fourteen, when the guns began, but perhaps even at
fourteen you still could not bear silence: you denied it at once and
immediately began to try to do something about it as children of
six or ten do: as a last resort, when even noise failed, fleeing into
closets, cupboards, corners under beds or pianos, lacking any other
closeness and darkness in which to escape it; walking around the
corner of the hangar as the challenge came, and saw the crack of
light under the hangar doors which were not only closed but pad-
locked—a thing never before seen by him or anyone else in this
or any squadron, himself standing quite still now with the point
of the bayonet about six inches from his stomach.

'All right,' he said. 'What do I do now?'

But the man didn't even answer. 'Corporal of the guard!' he
shouted. 'Post Number Four!' Then the corporal appeared.

'Second Lieutenant Levine,' he said. 'My aeroplane's in this
hangar—'

'Not if you're General Haig and your sword's in there,' the
corporal said.

'Right,' he said, and turned. And for a moment he even thought
of Conventicle, the Flight Sergeant; he had been a soldier long
enough by now to have learned that there were few, if any, military situations which the simple cry of 'Sergeant!' would not re-
solve. It was mainly this of course, yet there was a little of something else too: the rapport, not between himself and Conventicle

perhaps, but between their two races—the middle-aged bog-com-plected man out of that race, all of whom he had ever known were named Evans or Morgan except the two or three named Deuter-onomy or Tabernacle or Conventicle out of the Old Testament—that morose and musical people who knew dark things by simply breathing, who seemed to be born without dread or concern into knowledge of and rapport with man's sunless and subterrene origins which had better never have seen light at all, whose own misty and music-ed names no other men could pronounce even, so that when they emerged from their fens and fastnesses into the rational world where men still tried to forget their sombre beginnings, they permitted themselves to be designated by the jealous and awesome nouns out of the old fierce Hebraic annals in which they as no other people seemed at home, as Napoleon in Austria had had his (the child's) people with their unpronounceable names fetched before him and said 'Your name is Wolf' or 'Hoff' or 'Fox' or 'Berg' or 'Schneider,' according to what they looked like or where they lived or what they did. But he considered this only a moment. There was only one sure source, knowing now that even this one would not be too certain. But nothing else remained: Bridesman's and Cowrie's hut (That was one of the dangled prerequisites for being brave enough to get to be a captain: half a hut to yourself. The major had a whole one.), Cowrie looking at him from the pillow as Bridesman sat up in the other cot and lit the candle and told him.

'Certainly it's not over. It's so far from over that you're going on jobs tomorrow. Does that satisfy you?'

'All right,' he said. 'But what happened? What is it? An armed sentry stopped me at the hangars thirty minutes ago and turned out the guard and the hangar doors were locked and a light inside and I could hear people doing something, only I couldn't pass the bayonet and when they drove me away I heard a lorry and saw a torch moving about down at that archie battery this side the village and of course that's fresh ammo being hurried up since archie quit at noon today too and naturally they'll need a lot of ammo to quit with too—'

'If I tell you, will you let be and go to your hut and go to bed?'

'Right,' he said. 'That's all I ever wanted: just to know. If they've beat us, I want to stand my share too—'

'Beat us be blowed. There's nobody in this war any longer capable of beating anyone, unless the Americans might in time—'

'And welcome,' Cowrie said. But Bridesman was still talking:

'A French regiment mutinied this morning—refused to go over. When they—the French—began to poke about to learn why, it seems that—But it's all right.'

'How all right?'

'It was only their infantry disaffected. Only troops holding the line. But the other regiments didn't do anything. The others all seemed to know in advance that the one was going to refuse, but all the others seemed to be just waiting about to see what was going to happen to it. But they—the French—took no chances. They pulled the regiment out and replaced it and moved up guns and put down a heavy barrage all along their front, just like we did this afternoon. To give ourselves time to see what was what. That's all.'

'How that's all?' he said. Cowrie had put a cigarette into his mouth and, raised on to one elbow, was reaching for the candle when the hand stopped, less than a fraction of a second before it moved on. 'What was the hun doing all this time?' He said quietly: 'So it's over.'

'It's not over,' Bridesman said harshly. 'Didn't you just hear what the major said at noon today?'

'Oh, yes,' he said serenely. 'It's over. All the poor bloody stinking infantry everywhere, Frenchmen, Americans, Germans, us . . . So that's what they're hiding.'

'Hiding?' Bridesman said. 'Hiding what? There's nothing to hide. It's not over, I tell you. Didn't you just hear me say we have a job tomorrow?'

'All right,' he said. 'It's not over. How can it be not over then?'

'Because it isn't. What do you think we put down that barrage for today—we and the French and the Americans too—the whole front from the Channel in—blasting away a half year's supply of ammo for except to keep the hun off until we can know what to do?'

'Know to do what? What are they doing in our hangar tonight?'

'Nothing!' Bridesman said.

'What are they doing in B Flight's hangar, Bridesman?' he said. The cigarette pack lay on the packing case which served for a table between the two cots. Bridesman half turned and reached his hand, but before he had touched the pack Cowrie, lying back on one arm beneath his head, without looking around extended the cigarette already burning in his own hand. Bridesman took it.

'Thanks,' he said. Bridesman looked at him again. 'I don't know.' He said harsh and strong: 'I don't want to know. All I know is, we have a job tomorrow and you're on it. If you've a good reason for not going, say it and I'll take someone else.'

'No,' he said. 'Good night.'

'Good night,' someone said.

But it wasn't tomorrow. There was nothing tomorrow: only dawn and then daylight and then morning. No dawn patrol went out because he would have heard it, being already and long since awake. Nor were there any aeroplanes on the tarmac when he crossed to the mess for breakfast, and nothing on the blackboard where Collyer occasionally saw fit to scrawl things in chalk which no one really ever read, himself sitting long at the cleared table where Bridesman would more or less have to see him sooner or later, provided he wanted to. From here he could see across the aerodrome to the blank and lifeless hangars and watch the two-hourly relief of the pacing guards through the long coma-ed fore-noon, the morning reft of all progress beneath the bland sky and the silence.

Then it was noon; he watched the Harry Tate land and taxi up to the office and switch off, and the trench coat get down from the observer's seat and remove the helmet and goggles and toss them into the cockpit and draw out the stick and the red and brazen hat. Then all of them at lunch: the general and his pilot and the infantry officer and the whole squadron, the first lunch he could remember from which at least one flight and sometimes two were not absent, the general saying it not quite as well as the major because it took him longer, but saying the same thing:

'It's not over. Not that we needed the French. We should simply have drawn back to the Channel ports and let the hun have Paris. It wouldn't be the first time. 'Change would have got windy, but it wouldn't have been their first time either. But that's all past now. We have not only kept the hun fooled, the French have got their backs into it again. Call this a holiday, since like all holidays it will be over soon. And there are some of you I think won't be sorry either'—naming them off because he did keep up with records, knew them all '—Thorpe, Osgood, De Marchi, Monaghan—who are doing damned well and will do better because the French have had their lesson now and so next time it will be the long vac. proper because when the guns stop next, it will be on the other side of the Rhine. Plenty of revs, and carry on.' And no sound, though maybe no one expected any, everyone following outside to where the Harry Tate's engine was already ticking over and the major helped put the stick and the red hat back into the cockpit and get the helmet out and get it on the general and the general back into the Harry Tate and the major said 'Shun!' saluting and the general jerked his thumbed fist upward and the Harry Tate trundled away.

Then afternoon, and nothing either. He still sat in the mess where Bridesman could see or find him if he liked, not waiting now any less than he had been waiting during the forenoon, because he knew now that he had not been waiting then, had not believed it then, not to mention that Bridesman had had to look at him at lunch because he had sat right across the table from him. The whole squadron did in fact: sat or idled about the mess—that is, the new ones, the tyros, the huns like himself—Villeneuve Blanche, even Villeneuve, which what Collyer called that sink, still out of bounds (which fact—the out of bounds—was probably the first time in all its history that anyone not born there had specifically wanted to go there). He could have gone to his hut too; there was a letter to his mother in it that he had not finished yet, except that now he could not finish it because the cessation of the guns yesterday had not only deleted all meaning from the words but effaced the very foundation of their purpose and aim.

But he went to the hut and got a book out and lay down on his cot with it. Perhaps it was simply to show, prove to, the old flesh, the bones and the meat, that he was not waiting for anything. Or perhaps to teach them to relinquish, abnegate. Or perhaps it was not the bones and meat so much as the nerves, muscles, which had been trained by a government in a serious even though temporary crisis to follow one highly specialised trade, then the government passed the crisis, solved the dilemma needing it, before he had had the chance to repay the cost of the training. Not glory: just to repay the cost. The laurel of glory, provided it was even moderately leafed, had human blood on; that was permissible only when

93

motherland itself was at stake. Peace abolished it, and that man who would choose between glory and peace had best let his voice be small indeed—

But this was not reading; *Gaston de la Tour* at least deserved to be read by whoever held it open looking at it, even lying down. So he read, peaceful, resigned, no longer thirsting now. Now he even had a future, it would last forever now; all he needed was to find something to do with it, now that the only trade he had been taught—flying armed aircraft in order to shoot down (or try to) other armed aircraft—was now obsolete. It would be dinner time soon, and eating would exhaust, get rid of, a little of it, four, perhaps, counting tea, even five hours out of each twenty-four, if one only remembered to eat slowly enough, then eight off for sleeping or even nine if you remembered to go slowly enough about that too, would leave less than half to have to cope with. Except that he would not go to tea or dinner either today; he had yet almost a quarter-pound of the chocolate his mother had sent last week and whether he preferred chocolate to tea and dinner would not matter. Because they—the new ones, the tyros, the huns—would probably be sent back home tomorrow, and he would return to London if he must without ribbons on his coat, but at least he would not go back with a quarter-pound of chocolate melting in his hand like a boy returning half asleep from a market fair. And anyone capable of spreading eating and sleeping over fourteen hours of twenty-four, should be able to stretch *Gaston de la Tour* over what remained of this widowed day, until it met the night: the dark: and the sleep.

Then tomorrow, it had just gone three Pip Emma, he was not only not waiting for anything, it had been twenty-four hours now since he had had to remind himself that he was not waiting for anything, when the orderly room corporal stood suddenly in the door of the hut.

'What?' he said. 'What?'

'Yes, sir,' the corporal said. 'A patrol, sir. Going up in thirty minutes.'

'The whole squadron?'

'Captain Bridesman just said you, sir.'

'In only thirty minutes?' he said. 'Damn it, why couldn't— Right,' he said. 'Thirty minutes. Thanks.' Because he would have to finish the letter now, and it was not that thirty minutes was not long enough to finish it in, but that they were not long enough to get back into the mood, belief in which the letter had been necessary. Except for signing it and folding it into the envelope, he would not even have needed to get the letter out. Because he remembered it:

. . . not dangerous at all, really. I knew I could fly before I came out, and I have got to be pretty good on the range and even Captain Bridesman admits now that I'm not a complete menace to life in formation, so maybe when I settle down I might be of some value in the squadron after all

And what else could one add? What else say to a woman who was not only a mother, but an only and half-orphan mother too? Which was backward, of course, but anybody would know what he meant; who knew? perhaps one of the anybody could even suggest a postscript: like this say:

P.S. A delightful joke on you: they declared a recess at noon two days ago and if you had only known it, you would not have needed to worry at all from then until three o'clock this afternoon; you could have gone out to tea two afternoons with a clear conscience, which I hope you did, and even stayed for dinner too though I do hope you remembered what sherry always does to your complexion

Except that there was not even time for that. He heard engines; looking out, he saw three buses outside now in front of the hangar, the engines running and mechanics about them and the sentry standing again in front of the closed hangar doors. Then he saw a strange staff-car on the grass plot beside the office and he wrote 'love, David' at the foot of the letter and folded and licked it into the envelope and in the mess again now he saw the major's batman cross toward the office carrying an armful of flying kit; apparently Bridesman hadn't left the office at all, except that a moment later he saw Bridesman coming up from the hangars already dressed for the patrol, so the gear was not his. Then the office door opened and Bridesman came out, saying, 'All right, get your—' and stopped, because he already had it: maps, gloves, helmet, scarf, his pistol inside the knee pocket of the Sidcott. Then they were outside, walking toward the three aeroplanes in front of B hangar.

'Just three,' he said. 'Who else is going?'

'The major,' Bridesman said.

'Oh,' he said. 'Why did he pick me?'

'I don't know. Out of a hat, I think. I can wash you out if you don't like it. It won't matter. I think he really picked you out of a hat.'

'Why should I not like it?' he said. Then he said, 'I just thought—' and then stopped.

'Thought what?' Bridesman said.

'Nothing,' he said. Then he was telling it, he didn't know why: 'I thought that maybe the major found out about it somehow, and when he wanted one of the new blokes on this job, he remembered about me—' telling it: that morning when he had been supposed simply to be out practising, contour chasing probably, and instead had spent that forty or fifty seconds right down on the carpet with the unarmed aeroplane over the hun trenches or at least what he thought was the hun front line: 'You don't get frightened then; it's not until later, afterward. And then— It's like the dentist's drill, already buzzing before you have even opened your mouth. You've got to open your mouth and you know you're going to all right, only you know at the same time that neither knowing you are going to, nor opening it either, is going to help because even after you have closed it again, the thing will buzz at you again and you'll have to open it again the next moment or tomorrow or maybe it won't be until six months from now, but it will buzz again and you will have to open again because there's nowhere else you can go . . .' He said: 'Maybe that's all of it. Maybe when it's too late and you can't help yourself any more, you don't really mind getting killed—'

'I don't know,' Bridesman said. 'You didn't get even one bullet hole?'

'No,' he said. 'Maybe I shall this time.' And this time Bridesman did stop.

'Listen,' Bridesman said. 'This is a job. You know what jobs in this squadron are for.'

'Yes. To find huns.'

'And then bust them.'

'You sound like Monaghan: "Oh, I just ran up behind and busted the ass off the son of a bitch." '

'You do that too,' Bridesman said. Come on.' They went on. But he had needed only one glance at the three aeroplanes.

'Your bus is not back yet,' he said.

'No,' Bridesman said. 'I'm taking Monaghan's.' Then the major came and they took off. As he passed the office, he saw a smallish closed van turn in from the road, but he didn't have time to look then, not until he was off and up and from the turn could really look down. It was the sort of van provost marshals' people used; and climbing for formation, he saw not one car but two behind the mess—not ordinary muddy staff cars but the sort which detached Life and Horse Guards officers on the staffs of corps- and army-commanders were chauffeured about in. Now he drew in opposite Bridesman across the major's tail-plane, still climbing but to the southward, so that they would approach the lines squarely, and did so, still climbing; Bridesman waggled his wings and turned away and he did likewise long enough to clear the Vickers, into Germany or anyway toward Germans, and traversed the Lewis on its quadrant and fired it off too and closed in again. Now the major turned back northwest parrallel above the front, still climbing and nothing below now to reveal, expose it as front lines although he hadn't seen it but twice to have learned to know it again—only two kite balloons about a mile apart above the British trenches and two others almost exactly opposite them above the German ones, no dust no murk no burst and drift of smoke purposeless and un-origined and convoluted with no sound out of nothing and already fading and already replaced, no wink of guns as he had seen them once though perhaps at this height you didn't see flashes anyway: nothing now but the correlative to a map, looking now as it would look on that day when as the general said the last gun would cease beyond the Rhine—for that little space before the earth with one convulsive surge would rush to cover and hide it from the light of day and the sight of man—

He broke off to turn when the major did. They were crossing now, still climbing, right over the upper British balloon, heading straight for the German one. Then he saw it too—a white salvo bursting well below them and in front and then four single bursts

97

pointing away eastward like four asterisks. But he never had time
to look where it was pointing because at the same instant German
archie burst all around them—or would have, because the major
was diving slightly now, going east. But still he could see nothing
yet except the black hun archie. It seemed to be everywhere; he
flew right through a burst of it, cringing, shrinking convulsively
into himself while he waited for the clang and whine which he had
heard before. But maybe they were going too fast now, he and the
major really diving now, and he noticed for the first time that
Bridesman was gone, he didn't know what had become of him
nor when, and then he saw it: a two-seater: he didn't know what
kind because he had never seen a German two-seater in the air
before nor any other German for that matter. Then Bridesman
came vertically down in front of him and putting his nose down
after Bridesman, he discovered that the major had vanished and
forgot that too, he and Bridesman going almost straight down, the
German right under them now, going west; he could see Bridesman's tracer going right into it until Bridesman pulled out and
away, then his own tracer though he never could seem to get right
on the two-seater before he had to pull out and away too, the
archie already waiting for him before he was clear even, as though
the hun batteries were simply shooting it up here without caring
whom it hit or even watching to see. One actually seemed to burst
between his upper and lower right-hand planes; he thought, *Maybe
the reason I don't hear any clang is because this one is going to shoot me
down before I have time to.* Then he found the two-seater again.
That is, not the aeroplane but the white bursts of British archie
telling him or them where it was, and an S.E. (it would have to be
the major; Bridesman couldn't possibly have got that far by now)
diving toward the bursts. Then Bridesman was just off his wing-
tip again, the two of them going full out now in the pocking cloud
of black archie like two sparrows through a swirl of dead leaves;
and then he saw the balloons and noticed or remembered or perhaps simply saw the sun.

He saw them all—the two-seater apparently emerged neatly and
exactly from between the two German balloons and, in its aureole
of white archie, flying perfectly straight and perfectly level on a
line which would carry it across No-man's Land and exactly between the two British ones, the major behind and above the two-

seater and Bridesman and himself perhaps a mile back in their cloud of black archie, the four of them like four beads sliding on a string and two of them not even going very fast because he and Bridesman were up with the major almost at once. And perhaps it was the look on his face, the major glancing quickly at him, then motioning him and Bridesman back into formation. But he didn't even throttle back and then Bridesman was following him, the two of them passing the major and he thought, *Maybe I was wrong, maybe the hun archie doesn't clang and it was ours I heard that day*, still thinking that when, slightly ahead of Bridesman, they closed that gap too and flew into the white archie enclosing the two-seater before someone could tell the gunners they could stop now too, the last white wisp of it vanishing in the last fading drift about him and Bridesman now and there was the two-seater flying straight and level and sedate toward the afternoon sun and he pressed the button and nudged and ruddered the tracer right on to it, walking the tracer the whole length of it and return—the engine, the back of the pilot's head then the observer sitting as motionless as though in a saloon car on the way to the opera, the unfired machine gun slanting back and down from its quadrant behind the observer like a rolled umbrella hanging from a rail, then the observer turned without haste and looked right into the tracer, right at him, and with one hand deliberately raised the goggles—a Prussian face, a Prussian general's face; he had seen too many caricatures of the Hohenzollern Crown Prince in the last three years not to know a Prussian general when he saw one—and with the other hand put up a monocle at him and looked at him through it, then removed the monocle and faced front again.

Then he pulled away and went past; there was the aerodrome right under them now, until he remembered the archie battery just outside the village where he had seen the torch last night and heard the lorry; from the tight vertical turn he could look straight down at the gunners, shaking his hand at them and yelling: 'Come on! Come on! This is your last chance!' and slanted away and came back diving, walking the tracer right through the gun and the pale still up-turned discs of the faces watching him about it; as he pulled up he saw another man whom he had not seen before standing just on the edge of the wood behind the battery; the gentlest nudge on stick and rudder brought this one squarely into the Aldis

99

itself this time and, pulling up at last to get over the trees, he knew that he should have got something very close to a possible ten somewhere about that one's navel. Then the aerodrome again; he saw the two-seater squaring away to land, the two S.E.'s above and behind it, herding it down; he himself was too high even if he had not been much too fast; even after the vicious sideslip he might still wipe off the S.E.'s frail undercarriage, which was easy enough to do even with sedate landings. But it held, stood up; he was down first, rolling now and for a moment he couldn't remember where he had seen it, then he did remember, beginning to turn as soon as he dared (Some day they would put brakes on them; those who flew them now and lived would probably see it.) and turning: a glimpse of brass and scarlet somewhere near the office and the infantry in column coming around the corner of the office; he was taxi-ing fast now back along the tarmac past the hangars where three mechanics began to run toward him until he waved them off, taxi-ing on toward the corner of the field and there it was where he had seen it last week and he switched off and got down, the two-seater on the ground too now and Bridesman and the major landing while he watched, the three of them taxi-ing on in a clump like three waddling geese toward the office where the scarlet and brass gleamed beautiful and refulgent in the sun in front of the halted infantry. But he was running a little heavily now in his flying boots and so the ritual had already begun when he arrived—the major and Bridesman on foot now with the adjutant and Thorpe and Monaghan and the rest of B Flight, in the centre of them the three Poperinghe a.d.c.'s splendid in scarlet and brass and glittering Guards badges, behind them the infantry officer with his halted platoon deployed into two open files, all facing the German aeroplane.

'Bridesman,' he said but at that moment the major said ' 'Shun!' and the infantry officer shouted 'Present—*harms*!' and at salute now he watched the German pilot jump down and jerk to attention beside the wing while the man in the observer's seat removed the helmet and goggles and dropped them somewhere and from somewhere inside the cockpit drew out a cap and put it on and did something rapidly with his empty hand like a magician producing a card and set the monocle into his eye and got down from the aeroplane and faced the pilot and said something rapid in German and the pilot stood himself back at ease and then snapped something else at the pilot and the pilot jerked back to attention and then with no more haste than when he had removed the helmet but still a little quicker than anyone could have stopped it drew a pistol from somewhere and even aimed it for a second while the rigid pilot (he looked about eighteen himself) stared not even at the pistol's muzzle but at the monocle and shot the pilot through the centre of the face and turned almost before the body jerked and began to fall and swapped the pistol to the other gloved hand and had started to return the salute when Monaghan jumped across the pilot's body and flung the other German back into the aeroplane before Bridesman and Thorpe caught and held him.

'Fool,' Bridesman said. 'Don't you know hun generals don't fight strangers?'

'Strangers?' Monaghan said. 'I'm no stranger. I'm trying to kill the son of a bitch. That's why I came two thousand miles over here: to kill them all so I can get to hell back home!'

'Bridesman,' he said again but again the major said ' 'Shun there! Shun!' and at salute again he watched the German straighten up (he hadn't even lost the monocle) and flip the pistol over until he held it by the barrel and extend it butt first to the major who took it, and then draw a handkerchief from his cuff and brush off the breast and sleeve of his tunic where Monaghan had touched him and look at Monaghan for just a second with nothing behind the monocle at all as he put the handkerchief back into the cuff and clicked and jerked as he returned the salute and walked forward straight at the group as though it were not there and he didn't even need to see it part and even scramble a little to get out of the way for him to stride through, the three Guards officers falling in behind, between the two open infantry files, toward the mess; the major said to Collyer:

'Move this. I don't know whether they want it or not, but neither do we, here.'

'Bridesman,' he said again.

'Pah,' Bridesman said, spitting, hard. 'We shan't need to go to the mess. I've a bottle in the hut.' Then Bridesman overtook him. 'Where are you going?'

'It will only take a moment,' he said. Then apparently Bridesman saw, noticed the aeroplane too.

'What's wrong with your bus? You got down all right.'

'Nothing,' he said. 'I left it there because there's an empty petrol tin in the weeds we can set the tail up on.' The tin was there: a faint and rusting gleam in the dying end of day. 'Because it's over, isn't it? That's what they want with that hun general of course. Though why they had to do it this way, when all somebody needed was just to hold out a white sheet or tablecloth; they must have a tablecloth at Pop and surely Jerry's got one at his headquarters that he took away from a Frenchwoman; and somebody owes something for that poor bloodstained taxi-driver he— Which was not like the book either: he did it backward; first he should have unpinned the iron cross from his own coat and hung it on the other one and then shot him—'

'You fool,' Bridesman said. 'You bloody fool.'

'All right. This will only take a moment.'

'Let it be,' Bridesman said. 'Just let it be.'

'I just want to see,' he said. 'Then I shall. It won't take but a moment.'

'Will you let it be then? Will you promise?'

'Of course. What else can I do? I just want to see'—and set the empty petrol tin in position and lifted the S.E.'s tail and swung it around on to the tin and it was just right: in a little better than flying angle: almost in a flat shallow glide, the nose coming down just right; and Bridesman really saying No now.

'I'll be damned if I will.'

'Then I'll have to get . . .' he hesitated a second: then rapidly, cunningly: '. . . Monaghan. He'll do it. Especially if I can overtake the van or the staff-car or whichever it is, and borrow the Jerry general's hat. Or maybe just the monocle will be enough— no: just the pistol to hold in my hand.'

'Take your own word for it,' Bridesman said. 'You were there. You saw what they shot at us, and what we were shooting at that two-seater. You were right on him for five or six seconds once. I watched your tracer rake him from the engine right on back through the monocle.'

'So were you,' he said. 'Get in.'

'Why don't you just let it be?'

'I have. Long ago. Get in.'

'Do you call this letting be?'

'It's like a cracked record on the gramophone, isn't it?'

'Chock the wheels,' Bridesman said. He found two chocks for the wheels and steadied the fuselage while Bridesman got into the cockpit. Then he went around to face the nose and it was all right; he could see the slant of the cowl and the Aldis slanting a little since he was taller than most, a little high still. But then he could raise himself on his toes and he intended to put his arms over his face anyway in case there was something left of whatever it was they had loaded the cartridges with last night by the time it had travelled twenty feet, though he never had actually seen any of them strike, bounce off the two-seater, and he had been right on top of it for the five or six seconds Bridesman had talked about. And the airscrew was already in open position so the constantinesco would be working or not working or whatever it was doing when it let bullets pass. So all he had to do was line up the tube of the Aldis on Bridesman's head behind the wind screen, except that Bridesman was leaning out around the screen, talking again: 'You promised.'

'That's right,' he said. 'It will be all right then.'

'You're too close,' Bridesman said. 'It's still tracer. It can still burn you.'

'Yes,' he said, backing away, still facing the little black port out of which the gun shot, 'I wondered how they did that. I thought tracer was the bullet itself burning up. However did they make tracer without a bullet in it? Do you know? I mean, what are they? Bread pellets maybe? No, bread would have burned up in the breach. Maybe they are wood pellets dipped in phosphorus. Which is a little amusing, isn't it? Our hangar last night locked tight as . . . . with an armed guard walking back and forth in the dark and the cold outside and inside somebody, maybe Collyer; a chess player ought to be good with a knife, whittling sounds philosophical too and they say chess is a philosopher's game, or maybe it was a mechanic who will be a corporal tomorrow or a corporal who will be a sergeant tomorrow even if it is over because they can give a corporal another stripe even on the way home or at least before he is demobbed. Or maybe they'll even still keep the Air Force since a lot of people came into it out of the cradle before they had time to learn to do anything else but fly, and even in peace these ones will still have to eat at least now and then—' still backing away

because Bridesman was still waving him back, still keeping the
Aldis aligned; '—out here three years, and nothing, then one night
he sits in a locked hangar with a penknife and a lapful of wooden
blocks and does what Ball nor McCudden nor Mannock nor
Bishop nor none of them ever did: brought down a whole German
general: and get the barnacle at Buckingham Palace his next leave
—except that there won't be any, there's nothing now to be on
leave from, and even if there was, what decoration will they give
for that, Bridesman?—All right,' he said, 'all right, I'll cover my
face too—'

Except that he wouldn't really need to now; the line of fire
was already slanting into the ground, and this much farther away
it would cross well down his chest. And so he took one last sight
on the Aldis for alignment and bowed his head a little and crossed
both arms before his face and said, 'All right.' Then the chattering
rattle, the dusky rose winking in miniature in the watch-crystal on
his lifted wrist and the hard light stinging (They were pellets of
some sort; if he had been three feet from the muzzle instead of
about thirty, they would have killed him as quickly as actual bullets
would have. And even as it was, he had leaned into the burst, not
to keep from being beaten back but to keep from being knocked
down: during which—the falling backward—the angle, pattern,
would have walked up his chest and he would probably have taken
the last of the burst in his face before Bridesman could have stopped
it.) bitter *thock-thock-thock-thock* on his chest and the slow virulent
smell of burning cloth before he felt the heat.

'Get it off!' Bridesman was shouting. 'You can't put it out! Get
the Sidcott off, damn it!' Then Bridesman was wrenching at the
overall too, ripping it down as he kicked out of the flying boots
and then out of the overall and the slow invisible smouldering
stink. 'Are you satisfied now?' Bridesman said. 'Are you?'

'Yes, thanks,' he said. 'It's all right now. Why did he have to
shoot his pilot?'

'Here,' Bridesman said, 'get it away from the bus—' catching up
the overall by one leg as though to fling it away until he caught
hold of it.

'Wait,' he said. 'I've got to get my pistol out. If I don't, they'll
charge me with it.' He took the pistol from the Sidcott's knee-
pocket and dropped it into his tunic pocket.

'Now then,' Bridesman said. But he held on.

'Incinerator,' he said. 'We can't leave it lying about here.'

'All right,' Bridesman said. 'Come along.'

'I'll put it in the incinerator and meet you at the hut.'

'Bring it on to the hut and let the batman put it in the incinerator.'

'It's like the cracked record again, isn't it?' he said. Then Bridesman released his leg of the Sidcott though he didn't move yet.

'Then you'll come along to the hut.'

'Of course,' he said. 'Besides, I'll have to stop at the hangars and tell them to roll me in.—But why did he have to shoot his pilot, Bridesman?'

'Because he is a German,' Bridesman said with a sort of calm and raging patience. 'Germans fight wars by the rule-books. By the book, a German pilot who lands an undamaged German aeroplane containing a German lieutenant general on an enemy aerodrome is either a traitor or a coward, and he must die for it. That poor bloody bugger probably knew while he was eating his breakfast sausage and beer this morning what was going to happen to him. If the general hadn't done it here, they would probably shoot the general himself as soon as they got their hands on him again. Now get rid of that thing and come on to the hut.'

'Right,' he said. Then Bridesman went on and at first he didn't dare roll up the overall to carry it. Then he thought what difference could it possibly make now. So he rolled up the overall and picked up his flying boots and went back to the hangars. B's was open now and they were just rolling in the major's and Bridesman's buses; the rule-book wouldn't let them put the German two-seater under a British shed probably, but on the contrary it would doubtless compel at least six Britons (who, since the infantry were probably all gone now, would be air mechanics unaccustomed both to rifles and having to stop up all night) to pass the night in relays walking with guns around it. 'I had a stoppage,' he told the first mechanic. 'There was a live shell in. Captain Bridesman helped me clear it. You can roll me in now.'

'Yes sir,' the mechanic said. He went on, carrying the rolled overall gingerly, around the hangars and on in the dusk toward the incinerator behind the men's mess, then suddenly he turned sharply again and went to the latrines; it would be pitch dark

inside, unless someone was already there with a torch (Collyer had
a tin candlestick; passed going or coming from the latrines, cloistral
indeed he would look, tonsured and with his braces knotted about
his waist under his open warm). It was dark and the smell of the
Sidcott was stronger than ever inside. He put the flying boots
down and unrolled it but even in the pitch dark there was nothing
to see: only the slow thick invisible burning; and he had heard
that too: a man in B Flight last year who had got a tracer between
the bones of his lower leg and they were still whittling the bone
away as the phosphorus rotted it; Thorpe told him that next
time they were going to take off the whole leg at the knee to see
if that would stop it. Of course the bloke's mistake was in not
putting off until day after tomorrow say, going on that partol
(Or tomorrow, for that matter. Or today, except that Collyer
wouldn't have let him.), only how could he have known that a
year ago, when he himself knew one in the squadron who hadn't
discovered it until people shot blank archie at him and couldn't
seem to believe it even then? rolling up the Sidcott again and
fumbling for a moment in the pitch dark (It wasn't quite dark
after you got used to it. The canvas walls had gathered a little
luminousness, as if delayed day would even begin inside them after
it was done outdoors.) until he found the boots. Outside, it was
not at all night yet; night wouldn't even begin for two or three
hours yet and this time he went straight to Bridesman's hut, pausing only long enough to lay the rolled Sidcott against the wall
beside the door. Bridesman was in his shirt sleeves, washing; on
the box between his and Cowrie's beds a bottle of whisky sat
between his and Cowrie's toothmugs. Bridesman dried his hands
and without stopping to roll down his sleeves, dumped the two
tooth-brushes from the mugs and poured whisky into them and
passed Cowrie's mug to him.

'Down with it,' Bridesman said. 'If the whisky's any good at all,
it will burn up whatever germs Cowrie put in it or that you'll
leave.' They drank. 'More?' Bridesman said.

'No, thanks. What will they do with the aeroplanes?'

'What will what?' Bridesman said.

'The aeroplanes. Our buses. I didn't have time to do anything
with mine. But I might have, if I had had time. You know: wash
it out. Taxi it into something—another aeroplane standing on the

tarmac, yours maybe. Finish it, do for two of them at once, before
they can sell them to South America or the Levantine. So nobody
in a comic-opera general's suit can lead the squadron's aeroplanes
in some air force that wasn't even in this at all. Maybe Collyer'll
let me fly mine once more. Then I shall crash it—'

Bridesman was walking steadily toward him with the bottle.
'Up the mug,' Bridesman said.

'No, thanks. I suppose you don't know just when we'll go home.'

'Will you drink, or won't you?' Bridesman said.

'No, thanks.'

'All right,' Bridesman said. 'I'll give you a choice: drink, or shut
up—let be—napoo. Which will you have?'

'Why do you keep on saying let be? Let be what? Of course I
know the infantry must go home first—the p.b.i. in the mud for
four years, out after two weeks and no reason to be glad or even
amazed that you are still alive, because all you came out for is to
get your rifle clean and count your iron rations so you can go back
in for two weeks, and so no reason to be amazed until it's over.
Of course they must go home first, throw the bloody rifle away
forever and maybe after two weeks even get rid of the lice. Then
nothing to do forever more but work all day and sit in pubs in the
evenings and then go home and sleep in a clean bed with your
wife—'

Bridesman held the bottle almost as though he was going to
strike him with it. 'Your word's worth damn all. Up the mug.'

'Thanks,' he said. He put the mug back on the box.—'All right,'
he said. 'I've let be.'

'Then cut along and wash and come to the mess. We'll get one
or two others and go to Madame Milhaud's to eat.'

'Collyer told us again this morning none of us were to leave the
aerodrome. He probably knows. It's probably as hard to stop a
war as it is to start one. Thanks for the whisky.' He went out. He
could already smell it even before he was outside the hut and he
stooped and took up the overall and went to his hut. It was empty
of course; there would probably be a celebration, perhaps even a
binge in the mess tonight. Nor did he light the lamp: dropping
the flying boots and shoving them under his bed with his foot,
then he put the rolled Sidcott carefully on the floor beside the
bed and lay down on it, lying quietly on his back in that spurious

semblance of darkness and the time for sleeping which walls held, smelling the slow burning, and still there when he heard Burk cursing something or someone and the door banged back and Burk said,

'Holy Christ, what's that stink?'

'It's my Sidcott,' he said from the bed while someone lit the lamp. 'It's on fire.'

'What the bloody hell did you bring it in here for?' Burk said. 'Do you want to burn down the hut?'

'All right,' he said, swinging his legs over and getting up and then taking up the overall while the others watched him curiously for a moment more, Demarchi at the lamp still holding the burning match in one hand. 'What's the matter? No binge tonight?' Then Burk was cursing Collyer again even before Demarchi said,

'Collyer closed the bar.' He went outside; it was not even night yet, he could still read his watch: twenty-two hours (no, simple ten o'clock P.M. now because now time was back in mufti too) and he went around the corner of the hut and put the overall on the ground beside the wall, not too close to it, the whole north-west one vast fading church window while he listened to the silence crowded and myriad with tiny sounds which he had never heard before in France and didn't know even existed there because they were England. Then he couldn't remember whether he had actually heard them in English nights either or whether someone had told him about them, because four years ago, when such peaceful night-sounds were legal or at least *de rigeur*, he had been a child looking forward to no other uniform save that of the Boy Scouts. Then he turned; he could still smell it right up to the door and even inside too though inside of course he couldn't really have sworn whether he actually smelled it or not. They were all in bed now and he got into pyjamas and put out the lamp and got into bed properly, rigid and quiet on his back. The snoring had already begun—Burk always snored and always cursed anyone who told him he did—so he could near nothing but night passing, time passing, the grains of it whispering in a faint rustling murmur from or into whatever it was it ran from or into, and he swung his legs quietly over again and reached under the bed and found the flying boots and put them on and stood up and found his warm quietly and put it on and went out, already smelling it before he reached the door and on around the corner and sat down with his back against the wall beside the overall, not any darker now than it had been at twenty-two (no, ten P.M. now), the vast church window merely wheeling slowly eastward until almost before you knew it now it would fill, renew with light and then the sun, and then tomorrow.

But they would not wait for that. Already the long lines of infantry would be creeping in the darkness up out of the savage bitter fatal stinking ditches and scars and caves where they had lived for four years now, blinking with amazement and unbelief, looking about them with dawning incredulous surmise, and he tried listening, quite hard, because surely he should be able to hear it since it would be much louder, noisier than any mere dawning surmise and unbelief: the single voice of all the women in the Western world, from what used to be the Russian front to the Atlantic Ocean and beyond it too, Germans and French and English and Italians and Canadians and Americans and Australians— not just the ones who had already lost sons and husbands and brothers and sweethearts, because that sound had been in the air from the moment the first one fell, troops had been living with that sound for four years now; but the one which had begun only yesterday or this morning or whenever the actual instant had been, from the women who would have lost a son or brother or husband or sweetheart today or tomorrow if it hadn't stopped and now wouldn't have to since it had (not his women, his mother of course because she had lost nothing and had really risked nothing; there hadn't been that much time)—a sound much noisier than mere surmise, so much noisier that men couldn't believe it quite yet even, where women could and did believe anything they wanted to, making (didn't want to nor even need to make) no distinction between the sound of relief and the sound of anguish.

Not his mother in the house on the River beyond Lambeth where he had been born and lived ever since and from which, until he died ten years ago, his father would go in to the City each day to manage the London office of a vast American cotton establishment; they—his father and mother—had begun too late if he were the man on whom she was to bestow her woman's capacity for fond anguish, she the woman for whom (as history insisted— and from the talk he had had to listen to in messes he was inclined to admit that at least history believed it knew what it was talking about—men always had) he was to seek garlands or anyway sprigs of laurel at the cannon's mouth. He remembered, it was the only time, he and two others were celebrating their commissions, pooled their resources and went to the Savoy, and McCudden came in, either just finished getting some more ribbons or some more huns, very likely both, in fact indubitably both, and it was an ovation, not of men but of women, the three of them watching while women who seemed to them more beautiful and almost as myriad as angels flung themselves upward like living bouquets about that hero's feet; and how, watching, they thought it whether they said it aloud or not: 'Wait.'

But there hadn't been time; there was only his mother still, and he thought with despair how women were not moved one jot by glory and when they were mothers too, they were even irascible about uniforms. And suddenly he knew that his mother would be the noisiest of any anywhere, the noisiest of all, who had never for one instant had any intention of losing anything in the war and now had been proved in the sight of the whole world to have been right. Because women didn't care who won or lost wars, they didn't even care whether anybody did. And then he knew that it really didn't matter, not to England: Ludendorff could come on over Amiens and turn for the coast and get into his boats and cross the Channel and storm whatever he thought fit between Goodwin Sands and Land's End and Bishop's Rock and take London too and it wouldn't matter. Because London signified England as the foam signifies the beer, but the foam is not the beer and nobody would waste much time or breath grieving, nor would Ludendorff have time to breathe either or spend gloating, because he would still have to envelop and reduce every tree in every wood and every stone in every wall in all England, not to mention three men in every pub that he would have to tear down brick by brick to get to them. And it would not matter when he did, because there would be another pub at the next crossroads with three more men in it and there were simply just not that many Germans nor anybody else in Europe or anywhere else, and he unrolled the Sidcott; at first there had been a series of little smouldering overlapping rings across the front of it, but now it had become one single sprawling ragged loop spreading, creeping up toward the collar and down toward the belt and across toward each armpit, until by morning the whole front would be gone probably. Because it was constant, steadfast, invincible and undeviable; you could depend on it as Ball had, and McCudden and Bishop and Rhys Davies and Barker, and Boelcke and Richthofen and Immelman and Guynemer and Nungesser and the Americans like Monaghan who had been willing to die even before their country was actually in it to give them a roster of names to brag about; and the troops on the ground, in the mud, the poor bloody infantry—all of them who hadn't asked to be safe nor even to not to be let down again tomorrow always by the brass hats who had done the best they could too probably, but asked only that the need for the unsafeness and the fact that all of them had dared it and a lot of them had accepted it and in consquence were now no more, be held by the nations at Paris and Berlin and Washington and London and Rome immune and unchallengeable above all save brave victory itself and as brave defeat, to the one of which it would give glory and from the other efface the shame.

TUESDAY * WEDNESDAY

THE next time anyone might have seen or noticed her to remember would have been at the old eastern city gate. And they would have noticed her then only because she had been there so long, standing beside the arch and staring at each face as it entered, then looking quickly on to the next one even before the first one had passed her.

But nobody noticed her to remember. Nobody except her lingered about the gate to notice anything. Even the ones who were still crowding steadily up to pass through the gate had already entered the city in mind and spirit long before their bodies reached it, their anxiety and dread already one with the city's vast and growing reservoir of it, while their bodies still choked the slow converging roads.

They had begun to arrive yesterday, Tuesday, when news of the regiment's mutiny and arrest first reached the district and before the regiment itself had even been brought back to Chaulnesmont for the old supreme generalissimo himself to decide its fate. They continued to pour into the city all that night, and this morning they still came, on the heels of the regiment, in the very dust of the lorries which had rushed it back to the city and into it and through it without stopping, coming on foot and in clumsy farm carts, to crowd through the gate where the young woman stood scanning each face with strained and indefatigable rapidity —villagers and farmers, labourers and artisans and publicans and clerks and smiths: other men who in their turn had served in the regiment, other men and women who were parents and kin of the men who belonged to it now and, because of that fact, were now under close guard beneath the threat of execution in the prisoners' compound on the other side of the town—other men and women who, but for sheer blind chance and luck, might have been the parents and kin this time, and—some of them—would certainly be the next.

TUESDAY

It was little they knew on that first day when they left their homes, and they would learn but little more from the others on the same mutual errand of desperation and terror whom they met or overtook or were overtaken by before they reached the city: only that at dawn yesterday morning the regiment had mutinied, refused to make an attack. It had not failed in an attack: it had simply refused to make one, to leave the trench, not before nor even as the attack started, but afterward—had, with no prewarning, no intimation even to the most minor lance-corporal among the officers designated to lead it, declined to perform that ritual act which, after four years, had become as much and as inescapable a part of the formal ritual of war as the Grand March which opens the formal ball each evening during a season of festival or carnival —the regiment had been moved up into the lines the night before, after two weeks of rest and refitting which could have disabused even the rawest replacement of what was in store for it, let alone the sudden moil and seethe of activity through which it fumbled in the darkness on the way up: the dense loom and squat of guns, the lightless lurch and crawl of caissons and lorries which could only be ammunition; then the gunfire itself, concentrated on the enemy-held hill sufficient to have notified both lines for kilometres in either direction that something was about to happen at this point, the wire-cutting parties out and back, and at dawn the whole regiment standing under arms, quiet and docile while the barrage lifted from the enemy's wire to hurdle his front and isolate him from reinforcement; and still no warning, no intimation; the company- and section-leaders, officers and N.C.O.'s, had already climbed out of the trench when they looked back and saw that not one man had moved to follow; no sign nor signal from man to man, but the entire three thousand spread one-man deep across a whole regimental front, acting without intercommunication as one man, as—reversed, of course—a line of birds on a telephone wire all leave the wire at the same instant like one bird, and that the general commanding the division of which the regiment was a unit, had drawn it out and put it under arrest, and at noon on that same day, Monday, all activity on the whole French front and the German one opposite it from the Alps to the Aisne, except air patrols and spaced token artillery salvos almost like signal guns, had ceased, and by three o'clock that afternoon, the American and

British fronts and the enemy one facing them, from the Aisne to the sea, had done likewise, and now the general commanding the division of which the regiment was a unit was sending the regiment back to Grand Headquarters at Chaulnesmont, where he himself would appear at three o'clock on Wednesday afternoon (nor did they pause to wonder, let alone doubt, how an entire civilian countryside managed to know two days in advance, not only the purpose and intent but the hour, too, of a high military staff conference) and, with the support or at least acquiescence of his own immediate superiors—the commander of the corps to which the division belonged, and of the army to which the corps belonged—demand in person of the old generalissimo permission to execute every man in it.

That was all they knew now as they hurried toward the city—old people and women and children, parents and wives and kin and mistresses of the three thousand men whom the old generalissimo at Chaulnesmont could destroy tomorrow by merely lifting his finger—a whole converging countryside flowing toward the city, panting and stumbling, aghast and frantic, torn not even between terror and hope, but only by anguish and terror; destinationless even, since they had no hope: not quitting their homes and fields and shops to hurry to the city, but wrenched by anguish and terror, out of their huts and hovels and ditches, and drawn to the city whether they would or not: out of the villages and farms and into the city by simple grief to grief, since grief and anxiety, like poverty, take care of their own; to crowd into the already crowded city with no other will and desire except to relinquish their grief and anxiety into the city's vast conglomerate of all the passions and forces—fear, and grief, and despair, and impotence, and unchallengeable power and terror and invincible will; to partake of and share in all by breathing the same air breathed by all, and therefore both: by the grieving and the begrieved on one hand, and on the other the lone grey man supreme, omnipotent and inaccessible behind the carved stone door and the sentries and the three symbolical flags of the *Hôtel de Ville*, who dealt wholesale in death and who could condemn the whole regiment and miss its three thousand men no more from the myriads he dealt in than he would miss the nod of his head or the reverse of the lifted hand which would save them. Because they did not believe that the war was over. It had gone on too long to cease, finish, over night, at a moment's notice, like this. It had merely arrested itself; not the men engaged in it, but the war itself, War, impervious and even inattentive to the anguish, the torn flesh, the whole petty surge and resurge of victories and defeats like the ephemeral repetitive swarm and swirl of insects on a dung-heap, saying, 'Hush. Be quiet a moment' to the guns and the cries of the wounded too—that whole ruined band of irredeemable earth from the Alps to the sea, studded with faces watching in lipless and lidless detachment for a moment, a day or two days, for the old grey man at Chaulnesmont to lift that hand.

They had got used to the war now, after four years. In four years, they had even learned how to live with it, beside it; or rather, beneath it as beneath a fact or condition of nature, of physical laws—the privations and deprivations, the terror and the threat like the loom of an arrested tornado or a tidal wave beyond a single frail dyke; the maiming and dying too of husbands and fathers and sweethearts and sons, as though bereavement by war were a simple occupational hazard of marriage and parenthood and childbearing and love. And not only just while the war lasted, but after it was officially over too, as if the only broom War knew, or had to redd up its vacated room with, was Death; as though every man touched by even one second's flick of its mud and filth and physical fear had been discharged only under condition of a capital sentence like a fatal disease—so does War ignore its own recessment until it has ground also to dust the last cold and worthless cinder of its satiety and the tag-ends of its unfinished business; whether the war had ceased or not, the men of the regiment would still have had to die individually before their time, but since the regiment as a unit had been responsible for its cessation, the regiment would surely have to die, as a unit, by the old obsolete methods of war, if for no other reason than to enable its executioners to check their rifles back into the quartermasters' stores in order to be disbanded and demobilised. In fact, the only thing that could save the regiment would be the resumption of the war: which was their paradox, their bereavement: that, by mutinying, the regiment had stopped the war; it had saved France (France? England too; the whole West, since nothing else apparently had been able to stop the Germans since the March breakthrough in front of Amiens) and this was to be its reward; the three thousand men who had saved France and the world would lose their lives, not in the act of it, but only after the fact, so that, to the men who had saved the world, the world they saved would not be worth the price they paid for it—not to them, of course, the three thousand men in the regiment; they would be dead: the world, the West, France, all, would not matter to them; but to the wives and parents and children and brothers and sisters and sweethearts who would have lost all in order to save France and the world; they saw themselves no longer as one unit integrated into one resistance, one nation, mutual in suffering and dread and deprivation, against the German threat, but solitary, one small district, one clan, one family almost, embattled against all that Western Europe whom *their* sons and father and husbands and lovers were having to save. Because, no matter how much longer the threat of the war might have continued, some at least of the lovers and sons and fathers and husbands might have escaped with no more than an injury, while, now that the terror and the threat were past, all of their fathers and lovers and husbands and sons would have to die.

But when they reached the city, they found no placid lake of grieving resignation. Rather, it was a cauldron of rage and consternation. Because now they learned that the regiment had not mutinied by mutual concord and design, either planned or spontaneous, but instead had been led, cajoled, betrayed into revolt by a single squad of twelve soldiers and their corporal; that the entire three thousand men had been corrupted into capital crime and through it, right up into the shadow of the rifles which would be its punishment, by thirteen men, four of whom, including the corporal-leader, were not only not Frenchmen by birth, but three of them were not even naturalised Frenchmen. In fact, only one of the four—the corporal—could even speak French. Even the army records did not seem to know what their nationality was; their very presence in a French regiment or the French army in France was contradictory and obfuscated, though indubitably they had, must have, got there through or by means of some carelessly reported or recorded Foreign Legion draft, since armies never really lost anything for good, once it was described and numbered and dated and countersigned on to a scrap of paper; the boot, bayonet, camel or even regiment, might vanish and leave no physical trace, but not the record of it and the name and rank and designation of whoever had it last, or anyway signed for it last. The other nine of the squad were Frenchmen, but only three of them were less than thirty years old, and two of them were over fifty. But all nine of them had unimpeachable service records extending back not only to August, 1914, but on to the day when the oldest of them turned eighteen and was drafted thirty-five years ago.

And by the next morning, Wednesday, they knew the rest of it —how, not only warned and alerted by the barrage that an attack was coming, the German observation posts must have actually seen the men refuse to leave the trench after their officers, yet no counterattack came; and how, even during their best, their priceless opportunity, which was during the confusion and turmoil while the revolted and no-longer-to-be-trusted regiment was having to be relieved in broad daylight, still the enemy made no counter-move, not even a barrage on the communication lines where the relieved and the relieving regiments would have to pass each other, so that, an hour after the regiment had been relieved and put under arrest, all infantry activity in the sector had stopped, and two hours after that, the general commanding the regiment's division and his corps commander and their army commander, and an American staff-colonel and the British commander-in-chief's chief of staff were behind locked doors with the general commanding the entire Group of Armies, where, as report and rumour thickened, it emerged that not only the private soldiers in the division's other three regiments, but those in both the divisions flanking it, knew in advance that the attack was to be made and that the selected regiment was going to refuse. And that (staff- and provost-officers with their sergeants and corporals were moving fast now, spurred by amazement and alarm and incredulity too, while the telephones shrilled and the telegraphs chattered and the dispatch-riders' motorcycles roared in and out of the courtyard) not only were the foreign corporal and his strange conglomerate squad known personally to every private in those three divisions, but for over two years now the thirteen men—the obscure corporal whose name few knew and even they could not pronounce it, whose very presence in the regiment, along with that of the other three apparently of the same Middle-European nationality, was an enigma, since none of them seemed to have any history at all beyond the day when they had appeared, materialised seemingly out of nowhere and nothingness in the quartermaster's store-room where they had been issued uniforms and equipment, and the nine others who were authentic and, until this morning, unimpeachable Frenchmen and French soldiers, had been spending their leaves and furloughs for two years now among the combat-troop rest-billets not only throughout the entire French Army zone, but the American and the British ones too, sometimes individually, but usually as the intact squad—the entire thirteen, three of whom couldn't even speak French, visiting for days and sometimes weeks at a time, not only among French troops, but American and British too; which was the moment when the inspectors and inquisitors in their belts and tabs and pips and bars and eagles and wreaths and stars, realised the—not enormity, but monstrosity, incredibility; the monstrous incredibility, the incredible monstrosity, with which they were confronted: the moment when they learned that during three of these two-week leave-periods, two last year and the third last month, less than three weeks ago, the entire squad had vanished from France itself, vanished one night with their passes and transport and ration warrants from their rest-billets, and reappeared one morning two weeks later in ranks again, with the passes and warrants still unstamped and intact—monstrous and incredible, since there was but one place on earth in almost four years now where thirteen men in uniform could have gone without having their papers stamped, needing no papers at all in fact, only darkness and a pair of wire-cutters; they—the inquisitors and examiners, the inspectors-general and the provost-marshals flanked now by platoons of N.C.O.'s and M.P.'s with pistols riding light to the hand in the unstrapped holsters—were moving rapidly indeed now, with a sort of furious calm, along, among that unbroken line of soiled, stained, unchevroned and braidless men designated only by serial numbers stretching from Alsace to the Channel, who for almost four years now had been standing in sleepless rotation behind their cocked and loaded rifles in the apertures of that one continuous firestep, but who now were not watching the opposite German line at all but, as though they had turned their backs on war, were watching them, the inquisitors, the inspectors, the alarmed and outraged and amazed; until a heliograph in a French observation post began to blink, and one behind the German line facing it answered; and at noon that Monday, the whole French front and the German one opposite it fell silent, and at three o'clock the American and the British fronts and the German one facing them followed suit, so that when night fell, both the dense subterrene warrens lay as dead as Pompeii or Carthage beneath the constant watchful arch and plop of rockets and the slow wink and thud of back-area guns.

So now they had a protagonist for anguishment, an object for execration, stumbling and panting on that Wednesday morning through the kilometres' final converging, above which the city soared into the sunlight the spires and crenellations of its golden diadem, pouring, crowding through the old city gates, becoming one with that vast warrened shadow out of which, until yesterday, the city's iron and martial splendour had serenely stood, but which now had becomed one seethe and turmoil which had overflowed the boulevard at dawn and was still pouring across the city after the fleeing lorries.

As the lorries sped across the city, they soon outdistanced the crowd, though when its vanguard emerged also on to the sunny plain beyond, the lorries were in sight again, fleeing in a sucking swirl of primrose-coloured dust toward the camouflage-painted huddle of the prison-compound a kilometre and a half away.

But for a moment, the crowd seemed unable to discern or distinguish the lorries. It stopped, bunching on to itself like a blind worm thrust suddenly into sunlight, recoiling into arrestment, so that motion itself seemed to repudiate it in one fleeing ripple like a line of invisible wind running down a window of wheat. Then they distinguished or located the speeding dust, and broke, surged, not running now, because—old men and women and children— they had run themselves out crossing the city, and no longer shouting now either because they had spent themselves voiceless too, but hurrying, panting, stumbling, beginning—now that they were clear of the city—to spread out fanwise across the plain, so that already they no longer resembled a worm, but rather again that wave of water which had swept at dawn across the *Place de Ville*.

They had no plan: only motion, like a wave; fanned out now across the plain, they—or it—seemed to have more breadth than depth, like a wave, seeming, as they approached the compound, to increase in speed as a wave does nearing the sand, on, until it suddenly crashed against the wire barrier, and hung for an instant and then burst, split into two lesser waves which flowed in each direction along the fence until each spent itself. And that was all. Instinct, anguish, had started them; motion had carried all of them for an hour, and some of them for twenty-four, and brought them here and flung them like a cast of refuse along the fence (It—the compound—had been a factory once, back in the dead vanished days of what the nations called peace: a rectangle of brick walls covered with peaceful ivy then, converted last year into a training- and replacement-depot by the addition of half a hundred geometric plank-and-paper barracks composed of material bought with American money and sawn into numbered sections by American machines in America, and shipped overseas and clapped up by American engineers and artisans, into an eyesore, monument, and portent of a nation's shocking efficiency and speed, and converted again yesterday into a man-proof pen for the mutinied regiment, by the addition of barricades of electrified wire and searchlight towers and machine-gun platforms and pits and an elevated cat-walk for guards; French sappers and service troops were still weaving more barricades and stringing more of the lethal wire to crown them.) and then abandoned them, leaving them lying along the barrier in an inextricable mass like victims being resurrected after a holocaust, staring through the taut, vicious, unclimbable strands beyond which the regiment had vanished as completely as though it had never existed, while all circumambience—the sunny spring, the jocund morning, the lark-loud sky, the glinting pristine wire (which, even when close enough to be touched, still had an appearance gossamer and ephemeral like Christmas tinsel, giving to the working parties immersed in its coils the inconsequential air of villagers decorating for a parish festival), the empty parade and the blank lifeless barracks and the Senegalese guarding them, lounging haughtily overhead along the catwalks and lending a gaudy, theatrical insouciance to the raffish shabbiness of their uniforms like that of an American blackface minstrel troupe dressed hurriedly out of pawnshops—seemed to muse down at them, contemplative, inattentive, inscrutable, and not even interested.

And that was all. Here they had wanted to come for twenty-four

hours now, and here at last they were, lying like the cast of spent
flotsam along the fence, not even seeing the wire against which
they lay, let alone anything beyond it, for the half-minute perhaps
which it took them to realise, not that they had had no plan when
they came here, nor even that the motion which had served in
lieu of plan, had been motion only so long as it had had room to
move in, but that motion itself had betrayed them by bringing
them here at all, not only in the measure of the time it had taken
them to cover the kilometre and a half between the city and the
compound, but in that of the time it would take them to retrace
back to the city and the *Place de Ville*, which they comprehended
now they should never have quitted in the first place, so that, no
matter what speed they might make getting back to it, they would
be too late. Nevertheless, for still another half minute they lay
immobile against the fence beyond which the fatigue parties,
wrestling slowly among their interminable tinsel coils, paused to
look quietly and incuriously back at them, and the gaudy Senegalese, lounging in lethargic disdain among their machine guns
above both the white people engaged in labour inside the fence
and the ones engaged in anguish outside it, smoked cigarettes and
stroked idly the edges of bayonets with broad dark thumbs and
didn't bother to look at them at all.

Nor could even the aviator stationed and motionless in the hard
blue wind have said exactly where among them the facing-about
began as, like the blind headless earth-brute which, apparently
without any organ either to perceive alarm or select a course to
evade it, can move at instantaneous notice and instantaneous
speed in either direction, the crowd began to flow back to the
city, turning and beginning to move all at one instant as birds do,
hurrying again, weary and indefatigable, indomitable in their
capacity not alone for endurance but for frenzy as well, streaming
immediately once more between two files of troops stretching the
whole distance back to the city—(apparently a whole brigade of
cavalry this time, drawn up and facing, across the cleared path, a
like number of infantry, without packs again but with bayonets
still fixed and with grenades too now, with, one point, the nozzle
and looped hose of a flame thrower, and at the far end of the city,
the cleared path, the tank again, half-seen beyond the arch of the
gate like a surly not-too-courageous dog peering from its kennel)

without seeming to have remarked either the arrival of the troops nor to notice, let alone have any curiosity about, their presence now. Nor did the troops pay any attention to the people, alerted of course, but actually almost lounging on the horses and the grounded rifles while the crowd poured between them, as though to the troops themselves and to those who had ordered them here, the crowd was like the herd of Western cattle which, once got into motion about its own vortex, is its own warrant both of its own security and of the public's peace.

They recrossed the city, back into the *Place de Ville*, filling it again, right up to the spear-tipped iron fence beyond which the three sentries flanked the blank door beneath the three morning-windy flags. They still crowded into the *Place* long after there was no more room, still convinced that, no matter how fast they had come back from the compound, they would be too late, knowing that no courier carrying the order for the execution could possibly have passed them on the road, yet convinced that one must indubitably have done so. Yet they still crowded in, as if the last belated ones could not accept the back-passed word, but must see, or try to see, for themselves that they had missed the courier and were too late; until even if they had wished to stream, stumble, pant back to the compound and at least be where they could hear the volley which would bereave them, there would have been no room to turn around in and begin to run; immobilised and fixed by their own density in that stone sink whose walls were older than Clovis and Charlemagne—until suddenly it occurred to them that they could not be late, it was impossible for them to be late; that, no matter what errors and mistakes of time or direction or geography they might make, they could no more be late for the execution than they could prevent it, since the only reason for the whole vast frantic and anguished influx to the city was to be there when the regiment's division commander arrived to ask the old grey general behind the closed stone door facing them to allow him to have the regiment shot, and the division general was not even due there until three o'clock this afternoon.

So all they needed to do now was just to wait. It was a little after nine o'clock now. At ten, three corporals, an American, a Briton, and a Frenchman, flanked each by an armed soldier of his nation, came out of the archway from the rear of the *Hôtel*, and exchanged each the sentry of his nation and marched the relieved man back through the archway. Then it was noon. Their shadows crept in from the west and centred; the same three corporals came with three fresh sentries and relieved the three posts and went away; it was the hour when, in the old dead time called peace, men went home to eat and rest a little perhaps, but none stirred; their shadows crept eastward, lengthening again; at two o'clock, the three corporals came for the third time; the three sets of three paced and stamped for the third time through the two-hourly ritual, and departed.

This time the car came so fast up the boulevard that it outstripped its own heralding. The crowd had only time to press frantically back and let it enter the *Place* and then anneal behind it as it shot across the *Place* and stopped before the *Hôtel* in a bursting puff of dust. It was a staff car also, but stained with dust and caked with dried mud too, since it had come not only from the army zone, but out of the lines themselves, even if its pennon did bear the five stars of an army commander. Though, after these four years, even the children read that much, and if it had flown no pennon at all, even the children would have recognised two of the men in it—the squat, bull-chested man who commanded the regiment's division, who was already beginning to stand up before the car stopped, and the tall, scholarly-looking man who would be the division commander's army-group commander's chief-of-staff, the division commander springing out of the car before the orderly beside the driver in the front seat had time to get down and open the tonneau door, and already chop-striding his short stiff cavalry legs toward the blank, sentry-flanked entrance to the *Hôtel* before the staff officer had even begun to move.

Then the staff officer rose too, taking up a longish object from the seat beside him, and in the next second they—the crowd—had recognised it, swaying forward out of their immobilised recoil and making a sound now, not of execration, because it was not even directed at the division commander; even before they learned about the foreign corporal, they had never really blamed him, and even with the corporal, although they could still dread the division commander as the postulate of their fear and the instrument of their anguish, they had not blamed him: not only a French soldier, but a brave and faithful one, he could have done nothing else but what he was doing, believed nothing else except what he believed, since it was because of such as he that France had endured this long, surrounded and embattled by jealousy and envy—a soldier: that not only his own honour and that of his division, but the honour of the entire profession of command, from files and squads to armies and groups of them, had been compromised; a Frenchman: that the security of the motherland itself had been jeopardised or at least threatened. Later, afterward, it would seem to them, some of them, that, during the four or five seconds before they recognised the significance of what the staff officer had taken up from the seat of the car, there had been a moment when they had felt in him something almost like pity: not only a Frenchman and a soldier, but a Frenchman and a soldier who had to be a man first, to have been a Frenchman and become a soldier, yet who, to gain the high privilege of being a brave and faithful Frenchman and soldier, had had to forfeit and abdicate his right in the estate of man—where theirs would be only to suffer and grieve, his would be to decree it; he could share only in the bereaving, never in the grief; victim, like they, of his own rank and high estate.

Then they saw what the staff officer had in his hand. It was a sabre. He—the staff officer—had two: wearing one buckled to his ordnance belt, and carrying one, its harness furled about the hilt and sheath, which he was tucking under his arm as he too descended from the car. And even the children knew what that meant: that the division commander too was under arrest, and now they made the sound; it was as though only now, for the first time, had they actually realised that the regiment was going to die—a sound not even of simple agony, but of relinquishment, acceptance almost, so that the division commander himself paused and turned and they seemed to look at, see him too for the first time—victim not even of his rank and high estate, but like them, of that same instant in geography and in time which had destroyed the regiment, but with no rights in its fate; solitary, kinless, alone, pariah and orphan both from them whose decree of orphanage he would carry out, and from them whom he would orphan; repudiated in advance by them from whom he had bought the high privilege of endurance and fidelity and abnegation with the forfeiture of his birthright in humanity, in compassion and pity and even in the right to die—standing for a moment yet, looking back at them, then turned, already chop-striding again toward the stone steps and the blank door, the staff officer with the furled sabre under his arm following, the three sentries clashing to present arms as the division commander strode up the steps and past them and himself jerked open the door's black yawn before anyone else could have moved to do it, and entered—the squat, short figure kinless, indomitable, and doomed, vanishing rigidly and without a backward look, across that black threshold as though (to the massed faces and eyes watching) into Abyss or into Hell.

And now it was too late. If they could have moved, they might at least have reached the compound wire in time to hear the knell; now, because of their own immobilisation, they would have only the privilege of watching the executioner prepare the empty rope. In a moment now, the armed couriers and outriders would appear and kick into life the motorcycles waiting in the areaway; the cars would draw up to the door, and the officers themselves would emerge—not the old supreme general, not the two lesser ones, not even the division commander, compelled to that last full measure of expiation by watching the doom whose mouthpiece he had been—not any of these, but the provost-marshals, the specialists: they who by avocation and affinity had been called and as by bishops selected and trained and dedicated into the immutable hierarchy of War to be major-domos to such as this, to preside with all the impunity and authority of civilised usage over the formal orderly shooting of one set of men by another wearing the same uniform, lest there be flaw or violation in the right; trained for this moment and this end as race-horses are brought delicately, with all man's skill and knowledge and care, up to the instant of the springing barrier and the grandstand's roar, of St. Leger or Derby; the pennoned staff cars would roar away, rapid and distancing, feeding them fading dust once more back to the compound which they knew now they should never have left; even if they could have moved, only by the most frantic speed could they more than reach the compound fence in time merely to hear and see the clapping away of echoes and the wisping away of smoke which made them orphaned and childless and relict, but now they could not even move enough to face about: the whole *Place* one aspic of gaped faces from which rose that sound not yelling but half murmuring and half wailing, while they stared at the grey, tomb-like pile into which the two generals in their panoply and regalia and tools of glory had vanished as into a tomb for heroes, and from which, when something did emerge, it would now be Death —glaring at it, anguished and aghast, unable to move anywhere, unless the ones in front might perhaps fling themselves upon and beneath the cavalcade before it could start, and so destroy it, and, dying themselves with it, bequeath to the doomed regiment at least that further span of breathing comprised in the time necessary to form a new one.

But nothing happened. A courier did appear after a while from the archway, but he was only an ordinary dispatch-rider, and alone; his whole manner declared that he had no concern whatever in anything regarding them or their trouble. He didn't even look at them, so that the sound, never too loud, ceased while he straddled one of the waiting motorcycles and moved away, not even in the direction of the compound but toward the boulevard, pushing the popping mechanism along between his straddled legs, since, in the crowd, there was no chance whatever of running it fast enough to establish its balance, the crowd parting just enough to let him through and then closing behind him again, his urgent, constant adjurations for passage marking his progress, lonely, urgent and irritable, like the crying of a lost wildfowl; after a while two more came out, identical, even to the air of private and leisurely independence, and departed on two more of the machines, their cries too marking their infinitesimal and invisible progress: 'Give way, you bastards—offspring of sheep and camels . . .'

And that was all. Then it was sunset. As they stood in the turning flood of night, the ebb of day rang abruptly with an orderly discordant diapason of bugles, orderly because they all sounded at once, discordant because they sounded not one call, but three: the *Battre aux Champs* of the French the *Last Post* of the English, the *Retreat* of the Americans, beginning inside the city and spreading from cantonment and depot to cantonment and depot, rising and falling within its own measured bruit as the bronze throat of orderly and regulated War proclaimed and affirmed the end of day, clarion and sombre above the parade rite of *Mount* and *Stand Down* as the old guards, custodians of today, relinquished to tomorrow's, the six sergeants themselves appearing this time, each with his old guard or his new, the six files in ordered tramp and wheel facing each its rigid counterpart juxtaposed, the barked commands in the three different tongues ringing in the same discordant unison as the bugles, in staccato *poste* and *riposte* as the guards exchanged and the three sentries of the new ones assumed the posts. Then the sunset gun went from the old citadel, deliberate and profound, as if a single muffled drumstick had been dropped once against the inverted bowl of hollow and resonant air, the sound fading slowly and deliberately, until at last, with no suture to mark its close, it was lost in the murmur of bunting with which the flags, bright blooms of glory myriad across the embattled continent, sank, windless again, down.

They were able to move now. The fading whisper of the gun and the descending flags might have been the draining away of what had been holding them gelid; there would even be time to hasten home and eat, and then return. So they were almost running, walking only when they had to and running again when they could, wan, indomitable and indefatigable, as the morning's ebb flowed back through the twilight, the darkling, the night-assuaged city, toward the warrens and tenements where it had risen. They were like the recessed shift out of a factory furiously abridging the ordered retinue of day and dark producing shells, say, for a retreating yet unconquered army, their eyes bloodshot from the fumes, their hair and garments stinking with the reek, hurrying to eat and then return, already eating the waiting food while they still ran toward it, and already back at the clanking flashing unstopping machines while still chewing and swallowing the food they would not taste.

TUESDAY * WEDNESDAY
WEDNESDAY NIGHT

IT was late spring of 1916 when the runner joined the battalion. The whole brigade had been moved from Flanders down into Picardy, in billets near Amiens, resting and refitting and receiving replacements to be an integer in what would be known afterward as the First Battle of the Somme—an affair which would give even those who had survived to remember Loos and the Canal not only something to blench for, but the discovery that something even remained to blench with.

He had debarked that same dawn from the Dover leave packet. A lorry had given him a lift from Boulogne; he got directions from the first man he met and in time entered the brigade office with his posting order already in his hand, expecting to find a corporal or a sergeant or at most the brigade adjutant, but found instead the brigadier himself sitting at the desk with an open letter, who said:

'Afternoon. As you were a moment, will you?' The runner did so and watched enter a captain whom he was to know as commander of one of the companies in the battalion to which he would be assigned, followed by a thin wiry surly-looking private who, even to the runner's first glance, seemed to have between his bowed legs and his hands the shape of a horse, the brigadier saying pettishly, 'Stand at ease; stand at ease,' then opened the folded letter and glanced at it, then looked at the private and said: 'This came by special courier this morning. From Paris. Someone from America is trying to find you. Someone important enough for the French Government to have located you through channels and then send a special courier up from Paris. Someone named—' and glanced at the letter again: '—Reverend Tobe Sutterfield.'

And now the runner was watching the private too, already looking at him in time not only to hear but to see him say, quick and harsh and immediately final: 'No.'

'Sir,' the captain prompted.

'No what?' the brigadier said. 'An American. A blackamoor minister. You don't know who it is?'

'No,' the private said.

'He seemed to think you might say that. He said to remind you of Missouri.'

'No,' the private said, rigid and harsh and final. 'I was never in Missouri. I don't know anything about him.'

'Say sir,' the captain said.

'That's your last word?' the brigadier said.

'Yes sir,' the private said.

'All right,' the brigadier said. 'Carry on.' Then they were gone and, rigid at attention, the runner felt rather than saw the brigadier open the brigade order and begin to read it and then look up at him—no movement of the head at all: merely an upward flick of the eyes, steady for a moment, then down to the order again: thinking (the runner) quietly: *Not this time. There's too much rank:* thinking: *It won't even be the colonel, but the adjutant.* Which by ordinary could have been as much as two weeks later, since, a runner formally assigned to a combat battalion, his status was the same as any other member of it and he too would be officially 'resting' until they went back up the lines; and, except for coincidence, probably would have been: reporting (the runner) not to the battalion sergeant-major but to Coincidence, entering his assigned billet two hours later, and in the act of stowing his kit into a vacant corner, saw again the man he had seen two hours ago in the brigadier's office—the surly, almost insubordinate stable-aura-ed private who by his appearance would have pined and died one day after he was removed further from Whitechapel than a Newmarket paddock perhaps, yet who was not only important enough to be approached through official channels by some American individual or agent or agency himself or itself important enough to use the French Government for messenger, but important enough to repudiate the approach—seated this time on a bunk with a thick leather money-belt open on one knee and a small dirty dogeared notebook on the other, and three or four other privates facing him in turn, to each of which he counted out a few French notes from the money-belt and then made a notation with the stub of a pencil in the notebook.

And the next day, the same scene; and the day after that, and the one after that, directly after the morning parade for roll-call and inspection; the faces different and varying in number: two, or three, sometimes only one: but always one, the worn money-belt getting a little thinner but apparently inexhaustible, anyway bottomless, the pencil stub making the tedious entries in the grimed notebook; then the fifth day, after noon mess; it was pay-day and, approaching the billet, for a moment the runner thought wildly that part of the pay parade was taking place there: a line, a queue of men extending out into the street, waiting to creep one by one inside, so that the runner had trouble entering his own domicile, to stand now and watch the whole affair in reverse: the customers, clients, patients—whatever they were—now paying the grimed frayed wads of French notes back into the money-belt, the tedious pencil stub still making the tedious entries; and still standing there watching when the orderly, whom he had seen that first morning in the brigade anteroom, entered and broke through the line, saying to the man on the bunk: 'Come on. You're for it this time. It's a bleeding f . . . ing motorcar from Paris with a bleeding f . . . ing prime minister in it'—watching (the runner) the man on the bunk without haste stow the notebook and the pencil-stub into the money-belt and strap it up and turn and roll the belt into the blanket behind him and rise and follow the orderly, the runner speaking to the nearest of the now broken and dispersing line:

'What is it? What's the money for? He's gone now; why don't you just help yourselves while he's not here to put it down against you?' and still getting only the watchful, secretive, already dispersing stares, and not waiting even for that: himself outside too now, in the cobbled street, and saw that too: one of the long black funereal French motorcars such as high government officials use, with a uniformed driver and a French staff-captain in the front seat and a British one and a thin Negro youth on the two small jump seats and behind them in the rear seat, a middle-aged woman in rich furs who could be nothing but a rich American (the runner did not recognise her though almost any Frenchman would since her money partially supported a French air squadron in which her only son was a pilot) and a Frenchman who was not the prime minister but (the runner did recognise this) was at least a high Cabinet secretary for something, and sitting between them, an old Negro in a worn brushed top-hat, with the serene and noble face of an idealised Roman consul; the owner of the money-belt rigid and wooden, staring but at nothing, saluting but saluting no one, just saluting, then rigid and wooden again and ten feet away while the old Negro man leaned, speaking to him, then the old Negro himself descended from the car, the runner watching that too, and not only the runner but the entire circumambience: the six people still in the car, the orderly who had fetched the man from the bunk, the thirty-odd men who had been in the creeping line when the orderly broke through it, having followed into the street to stand before the billet door, watching too, perhaps waiting: the two of them drawn aside now, the owner of the money-belt still rigid, wooden, invincibly repudiant while the serene and noble head, the calm imperial chocolate-coloured face, still talked to him, murmured: barely a minute, then the Negro turned and went back to the car and got into it, the runner not waiting to watch that either, already following the white man back toward the billet, the waiting group before the door parting to let him through, then crowding in after him until the runner stopped the last one by touching, grasping his sleeve.

'The money,' the runner said. 'What is it?'

'It's the Association,' the man said.

'All right, all right,' the runner said, almost testily. 'How do you get it? Can anybody . . .'

'Right,' the man said. 'You take ten bob. Then on the next pay-day you begin paying him sixpence a day for thirty days.'

'If you're still alive,' the runner said.

'Right,' the other said. 'When you have paid up you can start over again.'

'But suppose you're not,' the runner said. But this time the man merely looked at him, so that he said, almost pettishly again:

'All right, all right, I'm not really that stupid; to still be alive a year from now is worth six hundred per cent of anything.' But still the man looked at him, with something so curious in his face, behind his eyes, that the runner said quickly, 'Yes. What?'

'You're new,' the other said.

'Yes,' the runner said. 'I was in London last week. Why?'

'The rate ain't so high, if you're a . . .' the voice stopping, ceasing, the eyes still watching him so curiously, so intently, that it seemed to the runner that his own gaze was drawn, as though by some physical force, down the man's side to where his hand hung against his flank: at which instant the hand flicked out in a gesture, a signal, so brief, so rapid before it became again immobile against its owner's khaki leg that the runner could hardly believe he had seen it.

'What?' the runner said. 'What?' But now the face was closed, inscrutable; the man was already turning away.

'Why don't you ask him what you want to know?' he said. 'He won't bite yer. He won't even make you take the ten bob, if you don't want.'

The runner watched the long car back and fill in the narrow street, to return wherever it came from: nor had he even seen the battalion adjutant yet, who at worse could be no more than captain and very likely not even as old as he: so the preliminaries would not take long, probably not more than this: the adjutant: *Oh, you're that one. Why haven't you got up your M.C.? Or did they take that back too, along with the pip?*

Then he: *I don't know. Could I wear an M.C. on this?*

Then the adjutant: *I don't know either. What else did you want? You're not due here until Orderly Room Monday.*

Then he would ask: who by now had divined who the rich American woman would be, since for two years now Europe— France anyway—had been full of them—the wealthy Philadelphia and Wall Street and Long Island names whose money supported ambulance units and air squadrons in the French front—the committees, organisations, of officially nonbelligerent amateurs by means of which America fended off not Germans but war itself; he could ask then, saying, *But why here? Granted that they have one with at the head of it an old blackamoor who looks like a nonconformist preacher, why did the French Government send him up here in a State motorcar for a two-minute visit with a private soldier in a British infantry battalion?*—oh yes, he could ask, getting nothing probably except the old Negro's name, which he already knew and hence was not what he lacked, needed, must have if there were peace: which took another three days from that Monday when, reporting at Orderly Room, he became officially a member of the battalion family and could cultivate the orderly corporal in charge of the battalion correspondence and so hold at last in his own hands the official document signed by the chief-of-staff at Poperinghe, containing not only the blackamoor's name but the rich and organ-rolling one of the organisation, committee, which he headed: *Les Amis Myriades et Anonymes à la France de Tout le Monde*—a title, a designation, so embracing, so richly sonorous with grandeur and faith, as to have freed itself completely from man and his agonies, majestic in its empyrean capacity, as weightless and palpless upon the anguished earth as the adumbration of a cloud. And if he had hoped to get anything at all, even that much, let alone anything more, from the owner of the money-belt, he would have been wrong indeed there: which (the failure) cost him five shillings in francs: hunting the man down and stopping him by simply getting in front of him and standing there, saying baldly and bluntly:

'Who is Reverend Tobe Sutterfield?' then still standing there for better than another minute beneath the harsh spent vitupera-tion, until he could say at last: 'Are you finished now? Then I apologise. All I really want is ten bob': and watched his name go down into the little dogeared book and took the francs which he would not even spend, so that the thirty sixpences would go back to their source in the original notes. But at least he had established a working, a speaking relationship: because of his orderly-room contact, he was able to use it, not needing to block the way this time to speak:

'Best keep this a staff matter, though I think you should know. We're going back in tonight.' The man looked at him. 'Something is going to happen. They have brought too many troops down here. It's a battle. The ones who thought up Loos can't rest on their laurels forever, you know.' Still the man looked at him. 'It's your money. So you can protect yourself. Who knows? you may be one of the ones to stay alive. Instead of letting us bring you only sixpence a day, demand it all at once and bury it somewhere.' Still the man just looked at him, not even with contempt; suddenly the runner thought, with humility, abasement almost. *He has ethics, like a banker, not to his clients because they are people, but because they are clients. Not pity: he would bankrupt any—all—of them without turning a hair, once they had accepted the gambit; its ethics toward his vocation, his trade, his profession. It's purity. No: it's even more than that: it's chastity, like Caesar's wife*—watching it; the battalion went in that night, and he was right: when it came out again—the sixty-odd per cent which was left of it—it bore forever across its memory like the sear of a heated poker, the name of the little stream not much wider in places than a good downwind spit, and the other Somme names—Arras and Albert, Bapaume and St. Quentin and Beaumont Hamel—ineradicable, to last as long as the capacity for breathing would, the capacity for tears—saying (the runner) this time:

'You mean that all that out there is just a perfectly healthy and normal panic, like a market-crash: necessary to keep the body itself strong and hale? that the ones who die and will still die in it were allotted to do so, like the little brokers and traders without wit or intelligence or perhaps just enough money backing, whose high destiny it is to commit suicide in order to keep the edifice of finance solvent?' And still the other only looked at him not even contemptuous, not even with pity: just waiting until the runner had finished this time. Then he said:

'Well? Do you want the tanner, or don't you?'

The runner took the money, the francs. He spent them, this time, seeing for the first time, thinking, how finance was like poetry, demanding, requiring a giver and a taker too in order to endure; singer and listener, banker and borrower, buyer and seller, both ethical, unimpugnable, immaculate in devotion and faith; thinking *I was the one who failed; I was the debaser, the betrayer*, spending the money this time, usually at one blow, in modest orgies of food and drink for whoever would share it with him, fulfilling his sixpence-by-sixpence contract, then borrowing the ten shillings again, with the single-mindedness of a Roman Catholic at his devotions or expiating a penance: through that fall, that winter; it would be spring soon and now his leave would be coming up again and he thought, quietly, without grief, without regret: *Of course I could go back home, back to London. Because what else can you do to a cashiered subaltern in this year of Our Lord One Nine One Seven but give him a rifle and a bayonet and I already have those*, when, suddenly and peacefully, he knew what he would do with that freedom, that liberty which he no longer had any use for because there was no more any place for it on the earth; and this time he would ask not for shillings but pounds, setting its valuation not in shillings but in pounds, not only on his pilgrimage back to when and where the lost free spirit of man once existed, but on that which made the pilgrimage possible, asking for ten of them and himself setting the rate and interest at ten shillings a day for thirty days.

'Going to Paris to celebrate your f . . . ing D.C.M. are you?' the other said.

'Why not?' he said: and took the ten pounds in francs and with the ghost of his lost youth dead fifteen years now, he retraced the perimeter of his dead life when he had not only hoped but believed, concentric about the once-sylvan vale where squatted the grey and simple stone of Saint Sulpice, saving for the last the narrow crooked passageway in which he had lived for three years, passing the Sorbonne but only slowing, not turning in, and the other familiar Left Bank places—quai and bridge, gallery, garden and café—where he had spent his rich leisure and his frugal money; it was not until the second solitary and sentimental morning, after coffee (and *Figaro*: today was April eighth, an English liner, this time practically full of Americans, had been torpedoed yesterday off Ireland; he thought peacefully, tearless: *They'll have to come in now; we can destroy both hemispheres now*) at the Deux Magots, taking the long way, through the Luxembourg Gardens again among the nursemaids and maimed soldiers (another spring, perhaps by this autumn even, there would be American uniforms too) and the stained effigies of gods and queens, into the rue Vaugirard, already looking ahead to discern the narrow crevice which would be the rue Servandoni and the garret which he had called home (perhaps Monsieur and Madame Gargne, *patron* and *patronne*, would still be there to greet him), when he saw it—the banner, the lettered cloth strip fastened above the archway where the ducal and princely carriages had used to pass, affirming its grandiose and humble declaration out of the old faubourg of aristocrats: *Les Amis Myriades et Anonymes à la France de Tout le Monde*, and, already one in a thin steady trickle of people—soldiers and civilians, men and women, old and young—entered something which seemed to him afterward like a dream: a vestibule, an ante-room, where a strong hale plain woman of no age, in a white coif like a nun, sat knitting, who said:

'Monsieur?'

'Monsieur le président, Madame, s'il vous plaît. Monsieur le

Révérend Sutterfield': and who (the woman) said again, with no pause in the click and flick of the needles:

'Monsieur?'

'Le chef de bureau, Madame. Le directeur. Monsieur Le Révérend Sutterfield.'

'Ah,' the woman said. 'Monsieur Tooleyman': and, still knitting, rose to precede, guide, conduct him: a vast marble-floored hall with gilded cornices and hung with chandeliers and furnished, crowded, heterogeneous and without order, with wooden benches and the sort of battered chairs you rent for a few sous at band concerts in parks, murmurous not with the voices but as though with the simple breathing, the inspiration and suspiration of the people—the soldiers maimed and unmaimed, the old men and women in black veils and armbands and the young women here and there carrying children against or even beneath the complete weeds of bereavement and grieving—singly or in small groups like family groups about the vast room murmurous also still of dukes and princes and millionaires, facing the end of the room across which was suspended another of the cloth banners, the lettered strip like that one above the gateway and lettered like it: *Les Amis Myriades et Anonymes à la France de Tout le Monde:* not looking at the banner, not watching it; not like people in church: it was not subdued enough for that, but perhaps like people in a railway station where a train has been indefinitely delayed; then the rich curve of a stairway, the woman stopping and standing aside, still knitting and not even looking up to speak:

'Prière de monter, monsieur': and he did so: who had traversed a cloud, now mounting to the uttermost airy nepenthelene pinnacle: a small chamber like a duchess's boudoir in heaven converted temporarily to represent a business office in a charade: a new innocent and barren desk and three hard and innocent chairs and behind the desk the serene and noble face in its narrow clasp of white wool rising now from the horizon-blue of an infantry corporal's uniform which by its look had lain only yesterday still on a supply sergeant's shelves, and slightly behind him the pole-thin Negro youth in the uniform and badges of a French sub-lieutenant which looked almost as new, himself facing them across it, the voices also serenely congruous and inconsequential, like dream:

'Yes, it used to be Sutterfield. But I changed it. To make it easier for the folks. From the Association.'

'Oh. Tout le Monde.'

'Yes. Tooleyman.'

'So you came up that day to see . . . I was about to say friend—'

'Yes, he ain't quite ready yet. It was to see if he needed money.'

'Money? He?'

'The horse,' the old Negro said. 'That they claimed we stole. Except that we couldn't have stole it, even if we had wanted to. Because it never belonged to no man to be stole from. It was the world's horse. The champion. No, that's wrong too. Things belonged to it, not it to things. Things and people both. He did. I did. All three of us did before it was over.'

'He?' the runner said.

'Mistairy.'

'Mist what?' the runner said.

'Harry,' the youth said. 'That's how he pronounced it.'

'Oh,' the runner said, with a sort of shame. 'Of course. Mistairy—'

'That's right,' the old Negro said. 'He kept on trying to get me to say just Airy, but I reckon I was too old.' So he told it: what he had seen, watched at first hand, and what he had divined from what he had seen, watched: which was not all; the runner knew that, *thinking, A protagonist. If I'm to run with the hare and be the hounds too, I must have a protagonist, even while the youth,* speaking for the first time, answered that:

'It was the deputy marshal that sent the New Orleans lawyer.'

'The who?' the runner said.

'The Federal deputy marshal,' the youth said. 'The head man of the folks chasing us.'

'All right,' the runner said. 'Tell me.'

It was 1912, two years before the war; the horse was a three-year-old running horse, but such a horse that even the price which the Argentine hide-and-wheat prince paid for it at the Newmarket sale, although an exceptional one, was not an outrageous one. Its groom was the sentry, the man with the ledger and the money-belt. He went out to America with it, whereupon within the next twenty-four months three things happened to him which changed completely not only his life, but his character too, so that when late in 1914 he returned to England to enlist, it was as though somewhere behind the Mississippi Valley hinterland where within the first three months he had vanished, a new man had been born, without past, without griefs, without recollections.

He was not merely included in the sale of the horse, he was compelled into it. And not by the buyer nor even the seller, but by the sold: the chattel: the horse itself, with an imperiousness not even to be temporised with, let alone denied. It was not because he was the exceptional groom, which he might have been, nor even the first-rate one which he actually was. It was because there had developed apparently on sight between the man and the animal something which was no mere rapport but an affinity, not from understanding to understanding but from heart to heart and glands to glands, so that unless the man was present or at least near by, the horse was not even less than a horse: it was no longer a horse at all: not at all intractable and anything but unpredictable, because it was quite predictable in fact; not only dangerous, but in effect, for all its dedicated and consecrated end and purpose —the long careful breeding and selecting which finally produced it to be sold for the price it brought to perform the one rite for which it had been shaped—worthless, letting none save the one man enter the same walls or fence with it to groom or feed it, no jockey or exercise boy to approach and mount it until the man bade it; and even then, with the rider actually up, not even running until—whatever the communication was: voice, touch, whatever —the man had set it free.

So the Argentine bought the groom too, for a sum left in escrow in a London bank, to become the groom's on his return to England after being formally discharged. By the horse of course, since nothing else could, which (the horse) in the end discharged and absolved them all, the old Negro telling this part of it, since this was where he—they—himself and his grandson—came into it:— the horse which before the groom came into its life, merely won races, but which after his advent, began to break records; three weeks after it first felt his hand and heard his voice, it set a mark ('The race was named the Silinger,' the old Negro said. 'It was like our Derby at home.') which seven years later was still standing;

and in its first South American race, although only two weeks out of the ship after a month and a half at sea, it set one not likely to be touched at any time. ('Not nowhere. At no time. By no horse,' the old Negro said.) And the next day it was bought by a United States oil baron for a price which even the Argentine millionaire could not refuse, and two weeks later landed in New Orleans, where the old Negro, a preacher on Sunday and the rest of the week a groom and hostler in the new owner's Kentucky breeding and training stables, met it; and two nights later the train drawing the van containing the horse and the two grooms, the white one and the black one, plunged through a flood-weakened trestle: out of which confusion and mischance were born the twenty-two months from which the English groom emerged at last a practicing Baptist: a Mason: and one of his time's most skillful manipulators of or players at dice.

Sixteen of the twenty-two were the months during which the five separately organised though now grimly unified groups—the Federal Government, the successive state police forces and the railway's and the insurance company's and the oil baron's private detectives—pursued the four of them—the crippled horse and the English groom and the old Negro and the twelve-year-old child who rode it—up and down and back and forth through the section of the Mississippi watershed between Illinois and the Gulf of Mexico and Kansas and Alabama, where on three legs the horse had been running in remote back-country quarter-races and winning most of them, the old Negro telling it, grave and tranquil, serenely and peacefully inconsequential, like listening to a dream, until presently the runner five years afterward was seeing what the Federal deputy marshal had five years ago while in the middle of it: not a theft, but a passion, an immolation, an apotheosis—no gang of opportunists fleeing with a crippled horse whose value, even whole, had ceased weeks back to equal the sum spent on its pursuit, but the immortal pageant-piece of the tender legend which was the crowning glory of man's own legend beginning when his first paired children lost well the world and from which paired prototypes they still challenged paradise, still paired and still immortal against the chronicle's grimed and bloodstained pages: Adam and Lilith and Paris and Helen and Pyramus and Thisbe and all the other recordless Romeos and their Juliets, the world's oldest and

most shining tale limning in his brief turn the warp-legged foul-
mouthed English horse-groom as ever Paris or Lochinvar or any
else of earth's splendid rapers: the doomed glorious frenzy of a
love-story, pursued not by an unclosed office file nor even the
raging frustration of the millionaire owner, but by its own inherent doom, since, being immortal, the story, the legend, was not to
be owned by any one of the pairs who added to its shining and tragic
increment, but only to be used, passed through, by each in their
doomed and homeless turn.

He didn't tell how they did it: only that they did do it: as if,
once it was done, how no longer mattered; that if something must
be done, it is done, and then hardship or anguish or even impos-
sibility no longer signify:—got the frantic and injured horse out
of the demolished car and into the bayou where it could swim
while they held its head above water—'He found a boat,' the old
Negro said. 'If you could call it a boat. Whittled out of a log and
done already turned over before you even put your foot in it.
They called them pirogues. They talked gobble talk there, like
they do here.'—then out of the bayou too, into such complete
invisibility that when the railroad detectives reached the scene the
next morning, it was as if the flood itself had washed the three of
them away. It was a hummock, a small island in the swamp not
a mile from the collapsed trestle, where a work-train and crew had
arrived the next morning to rebuild the bridge and the track, and
from which (They got the horse as far up out of the water as they
could the first night, and the old Negro was left to attend it. 'I
just give it water and kept a mud pack on the hip and tried to
keep the gnats and flies and mosquitoes away,' the old Negro
said.) the groom returned at dawn on the third day, with a block-
and-tackle bearing the railroad company's stencil in the pirogue,
and food for themselves and the horse and canvas for the sling and
cradle and plaster of Paris for the splint—('I know what you're
going to ask now,' the old Negro said. 'Where we got the money
for all that. He got it like he done the boat,' telling that too: the
cockney horse groom who had never been farther from London
than Epsom or Doncaster yet who in two years of America had
become a Mason and a Baptist, who in only two weeks in the
forecastle of the American freighter up from Buenos Aires had
discovered or anyway revealed to himself that rapport with and

affinity for dice, who on the first return to the scene of the wreck had picked up the block-and-tackle simply because he happened to pass it, since his true destination had been the bunk-car where the Negro work-gang slept, waking them, the white man in his swamp-fouled alien jodhpurs and the black ones in undershirts or dungaree pants or in nothing at all, squatting around a spread blanket beneath the smoking lantern and the bank notes and the coins and the clicking and scuttering dice.)—and in the pitch dark—he had brought back no lantern, no light; it would not only have been dangerous to show one, he didn't even need one: scornfully, even contemptuously, who from his tenth year had known the bodies of horses as the blind man knows the room he durst not leave: any more than he would have brought back a veterinary, not only not needing one but he would not have let any hand save his or the old Negro's touch the horse, even if the horse had permitted it—they suspended the horse and set the hip and built the immobilising cast.

Then the weeks while the ruined hip knitted and the search-parties, with every exit to the swamp watched and guarded, continued to drag the bayou beneath the trestle, and to splash and curse among the moccasins and rattlesnakes and alligators of the swamp itself, long after they (the pursuers) had come to believe that the horse was dead for the simple reason that it must be dead, since that particular horse could not be anything else but dead and still be invisible, and that the owner would in the end gain only the privilege of venting his vengeance on the thieves. And once each week, as soon as it was dark enough and the search-parties had withdrawn for the night, the groom would depart in the pirogue, to return before dawn two or three days later with another supply of food and forage; two and three days now because the trestle was repaired at last; once more trains roared hollowly across it in the night and the work-gang and that source of revenue or income was gone, back to New Orleans whence it had come and now the white man was going to New Orleans himself, bucking the professional games on baize-covered tables beneath electric lights and now not even the old Negro—(a horseman, a groom, merely by accident, but by avocation and dedication a minister of God, sworn dedicated enemy of sin yet who apparently without qualm or hesitation had long since drawn and then forgot it the line of his rectitude to include the magnificent ruined horse and all who were willing to serve it)—would know how far he sometimes had to go before he found another spread blanket beneath a smoked lantern or, as a last resort, the electric-lit baize table, where, although in their leathern cup the dice were as beyond impugning as Caesar's wife, the counters—chips, money—still accrued, whether or not to the benison of his gift or to the simple compulsion of his need.

Then months, not only within daily earshot of the trains once more thundering across the repaired trestle but of the search parties themselves (to whom at times either of them could have spoken without even raising his voice), the search continuing long after the ones who did the cursing and splashing and the frantic recoiling from the sluggish thrash or vicious buzz of startled moccasins and rattlesnakes all believed that the horse was long since dead and vanished forever into the sleepless insatiable appetites of eels and gars and turtles and the thief himself fled, out of the country and out of the nation and perhaps even out of the continent and the hemisphere, but continuing nevertheless because the railroad company had for stake an expensive set of triple blocks and over two hundred feet of two-inch cable, and the insurance company owned banks and barge lines and chain stores from Portland, Maine, to Oregon and so could afford not to lose even a one-dollar horse, let alone a fifty-thousand-dollar one, and the horse's owner that bottomless purse which would not miss the value of the sixty race horses he still owned, in order to revenge himself on the thief of the sixty-first, and the Federal police had more at stake than even the state ones who could only share in the glory and the reward: they had a file to be closed out—until one day a United Press flash came, relayed last night from Washington to the Federal deputy, of how a horse, a valuable Thoroughbred and running on three legs, in charge of or at least accompanied by a small bandy-legged foreigner who could barely speak English, and a middle-aged Negro preacher, and ridden by a twelve-year-old Negro boy, had run away from the whole field in a three-furlong race at Weatherford, Texas—('We walked it' the old Negro said. 'At night. It needed that much to get used to itself again. To stop remembering that trustle and get limbered up again and start being a horse. When daylight come, we would hide in the woods again.' And afterwards too, telling that too: how they didn't dare else: run one race and then leave directly afterward without even stopping almost, because as soon as that three-legged horse won a race the whole world would hear about it and they had to stay at least one day ahead of them.)—and got there one day too late, to learn that the Negro preacher and the snarling contemptuous foreigner had appeared suddenly from nowhere exactly in time to enter the three-legged Thoroughbred in a race on which the foreigner had betted sums ranging (by this time) all the way from ten to a thousand dollars, at odds ranging all the way from one to ten to one to a hundred, the three-legged horse breaking so fast from the post that the barrier seemed actually to have sprung behind it, and running so fast that the trailing field appeared, if anything, to be running in another and later race, and so far ahead at the finish that the jockey seemed to have no control over it at all—if anyone, let alone a child of twelve or at most thirteen who rode the race without saddle but simply a bellyband and a surcingle to hold on to (this informant had seen the race), could have held it after the barrier dropped, the horse crossing the finish line at full speed and apparently bent on making another circuit of the track had not the white foreigner, leaning on the rail beyond the finish line, spoken a single word to it in a voice you could not have heard fifteen feet away.

And the next place where they were within even three days of the horse was at Willow Springs, Iowa, and next to that, Bucyrus, Ohio, and the next time they were almost two weeks behind—an inaccessible valley in the East Tennessee mountains three months later, so remote not only from railroads but even telegraphs and telephones too that the horse had been running and winning races for ten days before the pursuit ever heard of it; this was indubitably where he joined, was received into, the order of Masons: since this was the first time they had stopped for longer than one afternoon, the horse able now to run for ten undisturbed days before the pursuit even heard about it, so that, when the pursuers left the valley, they were twice ten days behind the horse, since after two weeks of patient asking and listening up and down that thirty-mile-long mountain-cradled saucer, again, as at the scene of the original disappearance, they had not found one human being who had ever heard of the three-legged horse and the two men and the child, let alone seen them.

So when they heard of the horse next in Central Alabama, it was already gone from there, moving west again, the pursuers still a month behind across Mississippi: across the Mississippi River into Arkansas, pausing only as a bird pauses: not alighting, though the last thing the pause could have been called was hovering since the horse would be running, once more at that incredible, that unbelievable, speed (and at the incredible and unbelievable odds too; by report and rumour the two men—the aged Negro man of God, and the foul-mouthed white one to whom to grant the status of man was merely to accept Darkness' emissary in the stead of its actual prince and master—had won tens of thousands of dollars) as if their mundane progress across America were too slow to register on the eye, and only during those incredible moments against a white rail did the horse and the three adjunctive human beings become visible.

Whereupon the Federal deputy, the titular-by-protocol leader of the pursuit, found that, suddenly and with no warning, something had happened to him which was to happen five years later in Paris to a British soldier even whose name he would never hear. He—the deputy—was a poet, not the writing kind, or anyway not yet, but rather still one of Homer's mere mute orphan godchildren sired by blind chance into a wealthy and political New Orlean family and who, by that family's standards, had failed at Harvard and then wasted two years at Oxford before the family found out about it and fetched him home where, after some months under the threat of the full marshalate, he compromised with his father on the simple deputyship. And so that night—it was in Arkansas, in a new paint-rank hotel room in a little booming logging town, itself less old than last year—he realised what it was about the whole business that he had refused to accept ever since Weatherford, Texas, and then in the next second dismissed it forever because what remained had not only to be the answer but the truth too; or not even *the* truth, but *truth*, because truth was truth: it didn't have to be anything; it didn't even care whether it was so or not even, looking (the deputy) at it not even in triumph but in humility, because an old Negro minister had already seen it with one glance going on two years ago now—a minister, a man of God, sworn and dedicated enemy of man's lusts and follies, yet who from that first moment had not only abetted theft and gambling, but had given to the same cause the tender virgin years of his own child as ever of old had Samuel's father or Abraham his Isaac; and not even with pride because at last he had finally seen the truth even if it did take him a year, but at least pride in the fact that from the very first, as he knew now, he had performed his part in the pursuit with passion and regret. So ten minutes later he waked his second-in-command, and two days later in the New York office he said, 'Give it up. You'll never catch him.'

'Meaning you won't,' the owner of the horse said.

'If you like it that way,' the deputy said. 'I've resigned.'

'You should have done that eight months ago when you quit.'

'Touché then,' the deputy said. 'If that makes you feel better too. Maybe what I'm trying to do now is apologise because I didn't know it eight months ago too.' He said: 'I know about what you have spent so far. You know what the horse is now. I'll give you my check for that amount. I'll buy your ruined horse from you. Call it off.' The owner told him what he had actually paid for the horse. It was almost as much as the public believed. 'All right,' the deputy said. 'I can't give you a check for that much, but I'll sign a note for it. Even my father won't live forever.' The owner pressed a button. A secretary entered. The owner spoke briefly to the secretary, who went out and returned and laid a check on the desk before the owner, who signed the check and pushed it across to the deputy. It was for a sum still larger than the difference between the horse's cost and that of the pursuit to date. It was made out to the deputy.

'That's your fee for catching my horse and deporting that Englishman and bringing my nigger back in handcuffs,' the owner said. The deputy folded the check twice and tore it across twice, the owner's thumb already on the buzzer as the deputy dropped the fragments carefully into an ashtray and was already standing to leave when the secretary opened the door again. 'Another check,' the owner said without even turning his head. 'Add to it the reward for the capture of the men who stole my horse.'

But he didn't even wait for that one, and it was Oklahoma before he (ex now) overtook the pursuit, joining it now as the private young man with money—or who had had it once and lost or spent it—had used to join Marlborough's continental tours (and indeed meeting among them who a week ago had been his companions in endeavour the same cold-fronted unanimity of half-contempt which the private young men would meet among Marlborough's professionals). Then the little bleak railway stations between a cattle-chute and a water-tank, the men in broad hats and heeled boots already clumped about the placard offering for a stolen horse a reward such as even Americans had never seen before—the reproduction of a newspaper photograph made in Buenos Aires of the man and the horse together, with a printed description of both—a face as familiar and recognisable now to the central part of the United States (Canada and Mexico too) as that of a President or a female murderer, but above all, the sum, the amount of the reward—the black, succinct evocation of that golden dream, that shining and incredible heap of dollars to be had by any man for the simple turn of a tongue, always ahead of them (of the pursuit certainly, and, the deputy now believed, of the pursued too), disseminating the poison faster than they advanced, faster even than the meteor-course of love and sacrifice, until already the whole Mississippi-Missouri-Ohio watershed must be corrupt and befouled and at last the deputy knew that the end was in sight: thinking how it was no wonder that man had never been able to solve the problems of his span upon earth, since he has taken no steps whatever to educate himself, not in how to manage his lusts and follies; they harm him only in sporadic, almost individual instances; but in how to cope with his own blind mass and weight: seeing them—the man and the horse and the two Negroes whom they had snatched as it were willy nilly into that fierce and radiant orbit—doomed not at all because passion is ephemeral (which was why they had never found any better name for it, which was why Eve and the Snake and Mary and the Lamb and Ahab and the Whale and Androcles and Balzac's African deserter, and all the celestial zoology of horse and goat and swan and bull, were the firmament of man's history instead of the mere rubble of his past), not even because the rape was theft and theft is wrong and wrong shall not prevail, but simply because, due to the sheer repetition of zeros behind a dollar-mark on a printed placard, everyone within eyerange or tonguespread (which was every human capable of seeing and hearing between Canada and Mexico and the Rockies and the Appalachians) would be almost frantically attuned to the merest whisper regarding the horse's whereabouts.

TUESDAY

No, it would not be much longer now, and for an instant he thought, toyed with the idea, of confounding corruption with corruption: using the equivalent of the check which in New York he had offered to write, to combat the reward, and put that away because that would fail too: not that corrupting corruption would merely spread corruption that much further, but because the idea merely created an image which even a poet must regard as only a poet's fantastic whimsy: Mammon's David ringing for a moment anyway Mammon's Goliath's brazen invincible unregenerate skull. It was not long now, the end was actually in sight when the course, the run (as if it too knew that this was near the end) turning sharply back south and east across Missouri and into the closing V where the St. Francis River entered the Mississippi, haunted still by the ghosts of the old bank-and-railroad bandits who had refuged there; then over, finished, done: an afternoon, a little lost branch-line county seat with a fair grounds and a railless half-mile track, the pursuers crossing the infield in the van of a growing crowd of local people, town and swamp and farm, all men, silent, watching, not crowding them at all yet: just watching; and now for the first time they laid eyes on the thief whom they had pursued now for almost fifteen months: the foreigner, the Englishman leaning in the doorless frame of the fallen stable, the butt of the still-warm pistol protruding from the waistband of his filthy jodhpurs, and behind him the body of the horse shot neatly once through the star on its forhead and beyond the horse the Roman senator's head and the brushed worn frock coat of the old Negro preacher, and beyond him in turn, in deeper shadow still, the still white eyeballs of the child; and that night in the jail cell the ex-deputy (still a lawyer even though the prisoner violently and obscenely repudiated him) said:

'I would have done it too of course. But tell me why—No, I know why. I know the reason. I know it's true: I just want to hear you say it, hear both of us say it so I'll know it's real'—already—or still—speaking even through the other's single vicious obscene contemptuous epithet: 'You could have surrendered the horse at any time and it could have stayed alive, but that was not it: not just to keep it alive, any more than for the few thousands or the few hundred thousands that people will always be convinced you won on it'—stopping then and even waiting, or anyway watching,

exultant and calm while the prisoner cursed, not toward him nor
even just at him, but him, the ex-deputy, steadily and for perhaps
a full minute, with harsh and obscene unimagination, then the ex-
deputy speaking again, rapid and peaceful and soothing: 'All right,
all right. The reason was so that it could run, keep on running,
keep on losing races at least, finish races at least even if it did have
to run them on three legs, did run them on three legs because it
was a giant and didn't need even three legs to run them on but
only one with a hoof at the end to qualify as a horse. While they
would have taken it back to the Kentucky farm and shut it up
in a whorehouse where it wouldn't need any legs at all, not even
a sling suspended from a travelling crane geared by machinery
to the rhythm of ejaculation, since a skillful pander with a tin
cup and a rubber glove'—exultant and quite calm, murmuring:
'Fathering colts forever more; they would have used its ballocks
to geld its heart with for the rest of its life, except that you saved
it because any man can be a father, but only the best, the brave—'
and left in the middle of the spent dull repetitive cursing and from
New Orleans the next morning sent back the best lawyer which
even he, with all the vast scope of his family's political affiliations
and his own semi-professional and social ones, could find—a lawyer
whose like the little lost Missouri town had probably never seen
before, nor anyone else for that matter, as having come four hundred miles to defend a nameless foreign horse thief—telling the
lawyer what he had seen there: the curious, watching attitude of
the town—

'A mob,' the lawyer said, with a sort of unction almost. 'It's a
long time since I have coped with a mob.'

'No no,' the client said quickly. 'They are just watching, waiting
for something, I didn't have time to find out what.'

And the lawyer saw that too. He found more than that: arriving
on the second morning after an all-night drive in his private chauffeured limousine, and within thirty minutes was on the telephone
back to his client in New Orleans, because the man he had come
to defend was gone, vanished, not escaped from the jail but freed
from it, the lawyer sitting at the telephone where he could look
out into the quiet square almost empty of movement, from which
nobody watched him now nor for that matter had ever actually
looked at him, but where he was conscious of them—not so much

148

the dour, slow-speaking, half-Western, half-Southern faces, but of the waiting, the attention.

And not only the white man, the two Negroes were gone too, the lawyer on the New Orleans telephone again that evening, not because it had taken him this long to learn these meagre details, but simply because he realised now that this was all he was going to find out here, by inquiry or purchase or just by simple listening, no matter how much longer he stayed: how the two Negroes had never reached the jail at all but had vanished apparently into thin air somewhere between it and the courthouse, where the ex-deputy's Federal successor had formally relinquished the three prisoners to the local sheriff; only the white man ever to reach the jail, because the ex-deputy had seen him there, and he gone too now, not even freed so much as just vanished, the lawyer discovering five minutes after his arrival that there was no prisoner, and at the end of thirty no felon, and by mid-afternoon no crime even, the body of the horse having vanished too some time during that first night, and nobody had moved it nor seen anyone moving it nor heard of anyone who might have moved it or in fact even knew that it was missing.

But the pursuit had long ago learned about all there was to know about those two weeks in the Eastern Tennessee valley last fall, and the ex-deputy had briefed the lawyer, and so to the lawyer there was no mystery about it; he had already divined the solution: there would be Masons in Missouri too—an opinion which the client in New Orleans didn't even bother to ignore, let alone acknowledge, not the ex-deputy's but the poet's voice actually babbling at his end of the wire while the lawyer was still talking:

'About the money,' the lawyer said. 'They searched him, of course—'

'All right, all right,' the ex-deputy said.—right perhaps, justice certainly, might not have prevailed, but something more important had—

'He had only ninety-four dollars and a few cents,' the lawyer said.

'The old Negro has got the rest of it in the tail of that frock-coat,' the ex-deputy said.—truth, love, sacrifice, and something else even more important than they: some bond between or from man to his brother man stronger than even the golden shackles which coopered precariously his ramshackle earth—

'I'll be damned,' the lawyer said. 'Of course that's where the money is. Why the hell I didn't—Hush, and listen to me a minute. There's nothing more I can do here, so I'm coming back to town as soon as they unlock the garage in the morning and I can get my car. But you are already on the scene, you can do it quicker than I can by telephone from here. Get in touch with your people and get notice spread up and down the valley as quick as you can —placards, descriptions of all three of them—'

'No,' the ex-deputy said. 'You must stay there. If anything further comes out of the charge, it will have to originate there. You must be there to protect him.'

'The only one who will need protection here is the first man who tries to lay a hand on the man who earned as much money as they believe he did, with nothing but his bare hands and a three-legged horse,' the lawyer said. 'He's a fool. If he had stayed here, he could have had the sheriff's badge without even running for it. But I can do everything necessary by telephone from my office until we catch them.'

'I said from the first that you didn't understand,' the ex-deputy said. 'No: that you still did not believe me, even after I tried to tell you. I don't want to find him—them. I had my turn at bat, and struck out. You stay there. That's what you are for,' the ex-deputy said, and hung up. Though still the lawyer didn't move, his end of the connection still open, the smoke from his cigar standing like a balanced pencil on a carven hand until the other New Orleans number answered and he spoke to his confidential clerk, describing the two Negroes, rapid and explicit and succinct:

'Cover all the river towns from St. Louis to Basin Street. Watch the cabin or stable or whatever it is in Lexington. Of course, if he doesn't go back home himself, he might try to send the child back.'

'You're in the middle of a pretty good place to look for him now,' the clerk said. 'If the sheriff there won't—'

'Listen to me,' the lawyer said. 'Listen carefully. He must not reappear here under any condition. He must not be found at all until he can be picked up for something like vagrancy in some city big enough for nobody to know who he is, or care. Under no condition must he come into the clutches of any local officers in any town or hamlet small enough even to have heard of that three-legged horse, let alone seen it. Do you understand?'

A moment: then the clerk: 'So they really did win that much money.'

'Do as I tell you,' the lawyer said.

'Of course,' the clerk said. 'Only you're too late. The owner of the horse has already beat you. The police here have had that notice ever since yesterday, and I imagine the police everywhere have it by now—description, reward and all. They even know where the money is: in the tail-pocket of that preacher's coat the nigger wears. It's too bad every house he passes don't have a wireless, like ships do. Then he would know how valuable he is, and he would have something to trade with you on.'

'Do as I tell you,' the lawyer said; that was the second day; then the third day and the lawyer had established his headquarters or post of command in the judge's chambers next the courtroom in the courthouse, not by the consent or even acquiescence of the judge who was a circuit judge and merely followed the itinerary of his court and did not live in the town and was not even consulted, nor by the acquiescence of the town either but by its will, so that it did not even matter whether the judge was a Mason too or not; and in the barbershop that day the lawyer saw last night's St. Louis paper bearing something which even purported to be a photograph of the old Negro, with the usual description and even a guess at the amount of money in the tail of the frock-coat, the barber, busy with another client, having apparently glanced at least once at the lawyer where he stood looking at the paper, because the barber said, 'That many folks hunting for him ought to find him,' then silence and then a voice from the other end of the shop, speaking to nothing and no one with no inflection: 'Several thousand dollars.'

Then the fourth day, when the Department of Justice investigator and the one from the sheriff's bonding company arrived (the first St. Louis reporter had reached the scene one train ahead of the U.P. man from Little Rock) and from his high small quiet borrowed window the lawyer watched the two strangers and the sheriff and the two men who would be the sheriff's local bondsmen cross the square not to the front door of the bank but around to the discreet side one which led directly to the president's office; five minutes there, then out again, the two strangers stopping while the sheriff and the two local men scattered and vanished, the two strangers looking after them until the Federal man removed his hat and seemed to be studying the inside of it for a moment, a second. Then he turned briskly, leaving the bonding company's man still looking out across the square, and crossed to the hotel and entered it and reappeared with his strapped bag and sat down on the bench opposite the bus stop; and then the bonding company's man moved too and crossed to the hotel and reappeared with his bag.

Then the fifth day and the sixth and even the two reporters had returned to where they came from and there remained in the town no stranger save the lawyer; nor was he a stranger any more now, thought he was never to know by what means the town had learned or divined that he was there not to prosecute but to shield; and at times during that idleness and waiting, he would imagine, envision himself actually in court with the man whom he had not only no expectation but even intention of ever seeing at all—a picture of himself not engaged in just one more monotonous legal victory, but as a—perhaps *the*—figure in a pageant which in reality would be an historical commemoration, in fact, even more than that: the affirmation of a creed, a belief, the declaration of an undying faith, the postulation of an invincible way of life: the loud strong voice of America itself out of the westward roar of the tremendous and battered yet indomitably virgin continent, where nothing save the vast unmoral sky limited what a man could try to do, nor even the sky limit his success and the adulation of his fellow man; even the defence he would employ would be in the old fine strong American tradition of rapine, its working precedent having been already established in this very—or anyway approximate—land by an older and more successful thief than any English groom or Negro preacher: John Murrell himself, himself his own attorney: the rape was not a theft but merely a misdemeanour, since the placard offering the reward before the horse's demise had constituted a legal power of attorney authorising any man's hand to the body of the horse, and its violation had been a simple breach of trust, the burden of the proof of which lay with the pursuers since they would have to prove that the man had not been trying simply to find the owner and restore him his property all the time.

This, out of daydream's idle unexpectation, because the lawyer did not really expect ever to see either of them, since the owner or the Federal Government would indubitably catch them first, right up to the morning of the seventh day when there was a knock at the jail's kitchen door—a knock not much louder than audibility, yet quite firm; and, firm, yet not at all peremptory: just polite, courteous and firm: a knock not often heard at the back door of a small Missouri jail, nor even quite at the back door of an Arkansas or Louisiana or Mississippi plantation house, where it might sooner have been at home, the turnkey's wife wiping her hands on her apron as she turned from the sink and opened the door on a middle-ageless Negro man in a worn brushed frock-coat and carrying a napless tophat, whom she did not recognise because she had not expected to see him there, possibly because he was alone, the boy, the child still standing five minutes later just inside the mouth of the alley beside the jail, where neither he nor the old one gave any sign of recognition whatever, although his grandfather—hand-cuffed now to the turnkey—actually brushed him in passing.

But her husband recognised him at once, not by the face, he scarcely glanced at that, but by the coat: the worn dusty broad-cloth garment which—not the man but the coat, and not even the whole coat but the elbow-deep, suitcase-roomy tails of it—the county and state police of five contiguous commonwealths had been blocking roads and searching farm wagons and automobiles and freight trains and the Jim Crow cars of passenger ones, and charging in pairs and threes with shotguns and drawn pistols through the pool halls and burial associations and the kitchens and bedrooms of Negro tenements for sixty-five hours now, trying to find. As did the town too: the turnkey and his shackled prize had scarcely left the jail before they began to gather behind them a growing tail of men and youths and small boys like that of a rising kite, which in the street leading to the square the turnkey could still tell himself that he was leading, and which while crossing the square toward the courthouse he even still looked as if he was, walking faster and faster, almost dragging the prisoner at the other end of the chain joining them, until at last he broke and even took one step actually running before he stopped and turned to face the pressing crowd, drawing the pistol from its holster all in one blind motion like the hopeless and furious repudiation of the boy turn-ing, once more whole, stainless and absolved, to hurl his toy pistol into the very face of the charging elephant, victim no more of

terror but of pride, and cried in a thin forlorn voice which itself
was like the manless voice of a boy:

'Stop, men! This hyer's the Law!'—who, without doubt if they
had run at him, would have stood his ground, still holding the
pistol which he had not and would not even cock, dying without a
struggle beneath the trampling feet in that one last high second of
his badge and warrant—a small, mild, ordinary man whom you
have seen in his ten thousands walking the streets of little American
towns, and some not so little either, not just in the vast central
valley but on the eastern and western watersheds and the high
mountain plateaus too, who had received his job and office out of
that inexhaustible reservoir of nepotism from which, during the
hundred-odd years since the republic's founding, almost that many
millions of its children had received not just their daily bread but
a little something over for Saturday and Christmas too, since,
coeval with the republic, it was one of the prime foundations—in
this case, from the current sheriff, whose remote kinswoman, to his
unending surprise and unbelief even ten years afterward, the turnkey had somehow managed to marry—a man so quiet so mild and
so ordinary that none remarked the manner in which he accepted
and affirmed the oath when sworn into his office: merely somebody
else's nameless and unknown cousin by blood or maybe just marriage, promising to be as brave and honest and loyal as anyone
could or should expect for the pay he would receive during the next
four years in a position he would lose the day the sheriff went out
of office, turning to meet his one high moment as the male mayfly
concentrates his whole one day of life in the one evening act of
procreation and then relinquishes it. But the crowd was not running at him: only walking, and that only because he was between
them and the courthouse, checking for an instant at sight of the
drawn pistol, until a voice said: 'Take that thing away from him
before he hurts somebody': and they did: a hand, not ungently nor
even unkindly, wrenching the pistol firmly from him, the crowd
moving again, converging on him, the same voice, not impatient so
much as irascible, speaking to him by name this time:

'Gwan, Irey. Get out of the sun': so that, turning again, the turnkey faced merely another gambit, he must choose all over again:
either to acquiesce forevermore to man or sever himself forevermore from the human race by the act—getting either himself or

the prisoner free from one end or the other of the steel chain joining them—which would enable him to flee. Or not flee, not flight;
who to dispute the moment's heroic image even in that last second:
no puny fumbling with a blind mechanical insentient key, but
instead one single lightning-stroke of sword or scimitar across the
betraying wrist, and then running, the scarlet-spurting stump inevictably aloft like an unbowed pennon's staff or the undefeated
lance's headless shank, not even in adjuration but in abdication of
all man and his corruption.

But there was not even time for that; his only choice was against
being trampled as, shoulder to shoulder now with his captive and,
if anything, slightly behind him, they moved on in the centre of
the crowd, across the square and into the courthouse, a firm hand
now grasping him above the elbow and thrusting him firmly on
exactly as he had nightly dreamed ever since he assumed his office
of himself in the act of doing, as soon as he found a felon either
small enough or mild enough to permit him, through the corridor
and up the stairs to the judge's chambers, where the New Orleans
lawyer gave one start of outrage then of astonishment and then the
infinitesimal flicker which never reached his face at all nor even his
eyes, until the same calm merely irascible voice said, 'This ain't big
enough. We'll use the courtroom,' and he (the lawyer) was moving
too, the three of them now—himself, the turnkey and the prisoner
like three hencoops on a flood—filling the little room with a sibi-
lant sound as though all the ghosts of Coke upon Littleton upon
Blackstone upon Napoleon upon Julius Caesar had started up and
back in one inextricable rustle, one aghast and dusty cry, and
through the opposite door into the courtroom itself, where suddenly the lawyer was not only himself free of the crowd, he had
managed (quite skilfully for all his bulk: a man not only tall but
big, in rich dark broadcloth and an immaculate piqué waistcoat
and a black cravat bearing a single pearl like the egg of a celestial
humming bird) to extricate the turnkey and the prisoner too, in
the same motion kneeing the swing gate in the low railing enclosing Bench and witness stand and jury box and counsels' tables,
and thrust the other two through it and followed and let the gate
swing back while the crowd itself poured on into the auditorium.

People were entering now not only through the judge's chambers
but through the main doors at the back too, not just men and

boys now but women also—young girls who already at eight and nine in the morning had been drinking Coca-Cola in the drugstores, and housewives testing meat and cabbages in the groceries and markets, or matching scraps of lace and buttons over drygoods counters—until not just the town but the county itself, all of which had probably seen the three-legged horse run, and most of which had contributed at least one or two each of the dollars (by now the total had reached the thirty thousands) which the two men had won and which the old Negro preacher had escaped with and indubitably concealed—seemed to be converging steadily into the courthouse, ringing with unhurried thunder the corridor and stairs and the cavernous courtroom itself, filling row by row the hard pewlike wooden benches until the last reverberation faded behind the cool frantic pulsing of pigeons in the clock tower on the roof and the brittle chitter and rattle of sparrows in the sycamores and locusts in the yard, and the calm merely irascible voice said—and not from behind any face but as though no one man spoke but rather the room itself: 'All right, Mister. Commence.'

And, standing with his prize behind the railing's flimsy sanctuary, bayed, trapped in fact, between the little wooden barrier which a child could step over in one stride like a degree of latitude or of honesty, and the sacred dais to which, even before he saw it, he had already lost his appeal, not alone except for his two companions nor even despite them, but in fact because of them, for a moment yet the lawyer watched Man pouring steadily into the tabernacle, the shrine itself, of his last tribal mysteries, entering it without temerity or challenge, because why not? it was his, he had decreed it, built it, sweated it up: not out of any particular need nor any long agony of hope, because he was not aware of any lack or long history of agony or that he participated in any long chronicle of frustrated yearning, but because he wanted it, could afford it, or anyway was going to have it whether he could afford it or not: to be no symbol nor cradle nor any mammalian apex, harbour where the incredible cockleshell of his invincible dream made soundings at last from the chartless latitudes of his lost beginnings and where, like that of the enduring sea, the voice of his affirmation roared murmuring home to the atoll-dais of his unanimity where no mere petty right, but blind justice itself, reigned ruthless and inattentive amid the deathless smells of his victories: his stale tobacco spit and his sweat. Because to begin with, he was not *he* but *they*, and *they* only by electing to be, because what he actually was, was *I* and in the first place he was not a mammal and as for his chartless latitudes, he not only knew exactly where he came from six thousand years ago, but that in three score and ten or thereabouts he was going back there; and as for affirmation, the mark of a free man was his right to say *no* for no other reason except *no*, which answered for the unanimity too; and the floor was his because he had built it, paid for it, and who could spit on it if not he. And perhaps the lawyer had even read Dickens and Hugo once long ago when he was a young man, looking now across the flimsy barrier into no brick-and-plaster barn built yesterday by the God-fearing grandfathers of other orderly and decorous and God-fearing Missouri farmers, but back a hundred years into the stone hall older than Orleans or Capet or Charlemagne, filled with the wooden sabots until yesterday reeking with ploughed land and manure, which had stained and fouled the trampled silks and lilies which had lasted a thousand years and were to have endured ten thousand more; and the caps of Mediterranean fishermen, and the smocks of cobblers and porters and road-menders stiffening with the crimson smears of the hands which had rent and cast down the silks and the lilies, looking out at them not even with mere awe and respect, not alone alarm, but with triumph and pride: pride in the triumph of man, and that out of all his kind, time and geography had matched him with this hour:—America, the United States in this April of Our Lord one thousand nine hundred and fourteen, where man had had a hundred and forty years in which to become so used to liberty that the simple unchallenged right to attend its ordered and regimented charades sufficed to keep him quiet and content; looking out at them a moment longer, then he turned and struck the handcuffs a sharp and almost musical blow and thundered down at the turnkey:

'What does this mean? Don't you know that no man shall be put twice in the same jeopardy?' then turned again and spoke into the room in that same voice like the rich snore of an organ: 'This man has been illegally arrested. The law compels his right to consult a lawyer. We will recess for ten minutes,' and turned again and opened the gate in the railing this time by thrusting the other two through it and on ahead of him toward the door to the judge's chambers, not even looking back as five men rose at the back of the room and went out through the main doors, and thrust the Negro and the turnkey into the judge's chambers and followed and shut the door and—the turnkey told this afterward—without even stopping, went on to the opposite door and opened it and was already standing in it when the five men from the courtroom came around the corner.

'Five minutes, gentlemen,' the lawyer said. 'Then we will resume in the courtroom,' and closed the door and came back to where the turnkey and the Negro stood. But he didn't even look at the Negro; and the turnkey, spent, exhausted, almost comatose from courage and excitement, discovered, realised with a kind of outraged unbelief that the lawyer, who had voluntarily given himself only ten minutes to do whatever he intended to do, was apparently going to use up some of them smoking, watching the lawyer produce the cigar from an upper pocket of the white vest which looked as if it had come right out from under the washerwoman's smoothing-iron five minutes ago—a pocket which contained three more just like it. Then the turnkey recognised its brand and therefore its cost—one dollar—because he had owned one once (and on the following Sunday morning smoked it) through the mistake of a stranger under the impression that it was the sheriff who had married his, the turnkey's, sister instead of he who had married the sheriff's brother's wife's niece, recognised it with grief and outrage too, the same thing happening again but this time a thousand times worse: the man who gave him the other cigar had asked nothing of him, whereas he knew now and at last what the lawyer wanted, was after, had been after all the while, setting the price of his, the turnkey's, corruption at that of one-dollar cigar: this was the forty thousand dollars which the nigger had escaped with and hidden so good that even the Federal Government couldn't find it. Then the grief and outrage was not even outrage, let alone grief; it was triumph and pride and even joy too, since not only had the lawyer already lost even before he laid eyes on the nigger, he (the lawyer) wasn't even going to find it out until he (the turnkey) got good and ready to tell him, waiting for the lawyer to speak first, with no organ in the voice either now, which instead was as hard and calm and cold and vacant of trash as that of his wife's uncle-by-marriage:

TUESDAY

'You've got to get him out of town. It's your only chance.' And maybe his (the turnkey's) voice wasn't too calm and maybe to a big-city lawyer it didn't sound too hard either. But even one as big as this one could have heard the finality in it and, if he listened, the scorn and the contempt and the pleasure too:

'I can think of another. In fact, I'm fixing right now to take it.' Then to the nigger: 'Come on': already moving toward the corridor door, drawing the nigger after him, and already reaching from the snap on his belt the ring containing the handcuff key. 'You're thinking of that money. I ain't. Because it ain't mine to think about. It's his, half of it, that is; whether or not a nigger ain't got any business with half of forty thousand dollars ain't none of my business nor yours neither. And soon as I unlock these handcuffs, he can go and get it,' and turned the knob and had opened the door when the voice stopped him—the hard calm not even loud voice behind him sounding like somebody dropping pebbles into a churn:

'Neither am I. Because there's not any money. I'm not even thinking about you. I'm thinking about your bondsmen': and (the turnkey) heard the match and turned in time to watch the flame's haunchy squat at the drawing cigar's tip and the first pale puff of smoke hiding for an instant the lawyer's face.

'That's all right too,' the turnkey said. 'I been living in the jail two years already. So I won't even have to move. I expect I can even stand chain-gang work too.'

'Pah,' the lawyer said, not through smoke but in smoke, by means of smoke, the puff, the spurt, the pale rich costly balloon bursting, vanishing, leaving the hard calm not loud word as durable and single as a piece of gravel or a buckshot: 'When you arrested this man the second time, you broke the law. As soon as you turn him loose, he won't have to hunt for a lawyer because there are probably a dozen of them from Memphis and Saint Louis and Little Rock waiting down there in the yard now, just hoping you will have no more sense than to turn him loose. They're not going to put you in jail. They're not even going to sue you. Because you haven't got any money or know where any is, any more than this nigger does. They're going to sue your bondsmen—whoever they were and whatever it was they thought you could do for them— and your—what is it? brother-in-law?—the sheriff.'

'They were my—' he started to say kinsmen, but they were not, they were his wife's kinsmen; he had plenty of his own, but none of them—or all of them together, for that matter—had enough money in a bank anywhere to guarantee a bond. Then he started to say friends, but they were his wife's family's friends too. But then it didn't matter what he said, because the voice had already read his mind:

'—which makes it harder; you might leave your own kinfolks holding the sack, but these are the sheriff's friends and you've got to sleep in the same bed with his niece every night.' Which was wrong too, since three years and two months and thirteen nights ago now, but that didn't matter either, the cigar smoking in the judge's ashtray now, and the voice: 'Come back here': and he returned, drawing the Negro with him, until they stood facing the white vest with its loop of watch-chain like a section of gold plough-trace, and the voice: 'You've got to get him into a jail somewhere where they can hold him long enough for you to put a charge on him that the law will accept. They can turn him loose the next day or the next minute if they want to; all you want is to have him on record as having been charged with a legal crime or mis-demeanour by a legally qualified officer of a legally constituted court, then when his lawyers sue your bondsmen for false arrest, they can tell them to go chase themselves.'

'What charge?' the turnkey said.

'What's the next big jail from here? Not a county seat: a town with at least five thousand people in it?' The turnkey told him. 'All right. Take him there. Take my car; it's in the hotel garage; I'll telephone my driver from here. Only, you'll—but surely I don't need to tell you how to spirit a prisoner out of the clutches of a mob.' Which was true too, that was a part of the turnkey's dream too; he had planned it all, run it through his mind out to the last splendid and victorious gesture, time and again since that moment two years ago when he had laid his hand on the Book and sworn the oath, not that he really expected it to happen but to be pre-pared against that moment when he should be called upon to prove not merely his fitness for his office but his honour and courage as a man, by preserving and defending the integrity of his oath in the very face of them by whose sufferance he held his office.

'Yes,' he said. 'Only—'

'All right,' the lawyer said. 'Unlock that damn thing. Here, give me the key': and took it from his hand and unlocked the handcuffs and flung them on to the table, where they made again that faint musical note.

'Only—' the turnkey said again.

'Now go around by the corridor and shut the big door to the courtroom and lock it on the outside.'

'That won't stop them—hold them—'

'Don't worry about them. I'll attend to that. Go on.'

'Yes,' he said, and turned, then stopped again. 'Wait. What about them fellows outside the door there?' For perhaps two or three seconds the lawyer didn't say anything at all, and when he did speak, it was as though there was nobody else in the room, or in fact as though he was not even speaking aloud.

'Five men. And you a sworn officer of the law, armed. You might even draw your pistol. They're not dangerous, if you're careful.'

'Yes,' he said, and turned again and stopped again, not looking back: just stopping as he had turned. 'That charge.'

'Vagrancy,' the lawyer said.

'Vagrancy?' he said. 'A man owning half of forty-five thousand dollars?'

'Pah,' the lawyer said. 'He doesn't own half of anything, even one dollar. Go on.' But now it was he who didn't move; maybe he didn't look back, but he didn't move either, talking himself this time, and calm enough too:

'Because this thing is all wrong. It's backwards. The law spirits a nigger prisoner out of jail and out of town, to protect him from a mob that wants to take him out and burn him. All these folks want to do is to set this one free.'

'Don't you think the law should cut both ways?' the lawyer said. 'Don't you think it should protect people who didn't steal forty-five thousand dollars too?'

'Yes,' the turnkey said; and now he looked at the lawyer, his hand on the doorknob again but not turning it yet. 'Only that ain't the question I want to ask anyway. And I reckon you got an answer to this one too and I hope it's a good one—' speaking calm and slow and clear himself too: 'This is all to it. I just take him to Blankton long enough to get a legal charge on the books. Then he can go.'

'Look at his face,' the lawyer said. 'He hasn't got any money. He doesn't even know where any is. Neither of them do, because there never was any and what little there might have been, that cockney swipe threw away long ago on whores and whisky.'

'You still ain't answered,' the turnkey said. 'As soon as the charge is on the books, he can go.'

'Yes,' the lawyer said. 'Lock the courtroom doors first. Then come back for the nigger.' Then the turnkey opened the door; the five men stood there but he didn't even falter: on through and past them; then suddenly, instead of following the corridor to the courtroom's rear door as the lawyer had ordered him, he turned toward the stairs, moving fast now, not running: just moving fast, down the stairs and along the hall to the office of his wife's uncle-in-law, deserted now, and into the office, around the partition and straight to the drawer and opened it and without even faltering, took from beneath the mass of old discharged warrants and incomplete subpoenas and paper clips and rubber stamps and corroded pen points, the spare office pistol and slipped it into the empty holster and returned to the hall and mounted the opposite stairway which brought him to the main courtroom doors and drew them quietly to, even as a face, then three, then a dozen, turned to look at him, and turned the key in the lock and withdrew it and put it into his pocket, already hurrying again, even running now, back to the judge's chambers where the lawyer had put the receiver back on its hook and pushed the telephone away and reached for the cigar in the ashtray and actually looked for the first time at the Negro, drawing the cigar to life in one slow inhale-exhale and through the smoke for the first time examined the calm no-aged Roman senator's face framed in a narrow unclosed circlet of grizzled hair clasping the skull like a Caesar's laurels above the aged worn carefully brushed carefully mended frock coat, and then spoke, the two of them in succinct flat *poste-riposte* that was almost monotone:

'You haven't got any money, have you?'

'No.'

'You don't even know where any is, do you?'

'No.'

'Because there's not any. There never was. And even that little, your white bully boy threw away before you even saw it—'

'You're wrong. And you believe you're wrong too. Because I know—'

'All right. Maybe it was even a whole hundred dollars.'

'More than that.'

'More than thirty thousand dollars?' and only the faintest hesitation here; no faulting: only an interval: the voice still strong, still invincibly unshaken and unshakable:

'Yes.'

'How much more than thirty thousand dollars? . . . All right. How much more than a hundred dollars? . . . Did you ever have a hundred dollars? Ever see a hundred dollars? . . . All right. You know it's more than a hundred dollars, but you don't know how much more. Is that it?'

'Yes. But you don't need to worry—'

'And you came back to get your half of the hundred dollars anyway.'

'I came back to tell him good-bye before he goes back home.'

'Back home?' the lawyer said quickly. 'You mean, England? Did he tell you that?' and the other, insuperably calm, insuperably intractable:

'How could he told me? Because he wouldn't need to. When a man comes to the place where he ain't got anything left worth spending or losing, he always goes back home. But you don't need to worry, because I know what you're fixing to do: lock me up in the jail until he hears about it in the newspapers and comes back. And you're right, because that's what he'll do, because he needs me too. And you don't need to worry about how much money it is; it'll be enough for all the lawyers too.'

'Like the loaves and the fishes?' the lawyer said. But this time it was not an interval; there was no answer at all, serenely nothing, and the interval was the lawyer's to put an end to: 'So he's the one who needs you. Yet he's the one who has the forty thousand dollars. How can anyone with forty thousand dollars need you?' And again the interval, intractable and serene, again the lawyer's to break: 'Are you an ordained minister?'

'I don't know. I bears witness.'

'To what? God?'

'To man. God don't need me. I bears witness to Him of course, but my main witness is to man.'

'The most damning thing man could suffer would be a valid witness before God.'

'You're wrong there,' the Negro said. 'Man is full of sin and nature, and all he does don't bear looking at, and a heap of what he says is a shame and a mawkery. But can't no witness hurt him. Some day something might beat him, but it won't be Satan,' and turned, both of them, at the sound of the door and saw the turnkey inside the room, trying to hold the corridor door, braced against its slow remorseless movement until the yawn's full inswing dismissed him completely into the wall and the five men from the corridor entered, the lawyer already moving before they had got inside the room, crossing to the opposite courtroom door, saying over his shoulder: 'This way, gentlemen,' and opened the door and stood aside holding it: no gesture or motion commanding nor even peremptory as, docile and simultaneous as five sheep, they filed across the room after him like five of the identical targets—ducks or clay pipes or stars—traversing on their endless chain the lilliputian range of a shooting-gallery, and on through the door, the lawyer following on the last one's heels and saying over his shoulder to the turnkey or the Negro or perhaps both or perhaps neither: 'Five minutes,' and followed, on and then through the five men who had stopped, huddled, blocking the narrow passage as if they had walked full tilt, as into an invisible wall, into the room's massed and waiting expectation; and on through the swing gate into the enclosure, to stop facing the room in almost the same prints he had stood in ten minutes ago, solitary this time but anything but alone amid, against, as a frieze or tapestry, that titanic congeries of the long heroic roster who were the milestones of the rise of man—the giants who coerced compelled directed and, on occasion, actually led his myriad moil: Caesar and Christ, Bonaparte and Peter and Mazarin and Alexander, Genghis and Talleyrand and Warwick, Marlborough and Bryan, Bill Sunday, General Booth and Prester John, prince and bishop, Norman, dervish, plotter and khan, not for the power and glory nor even the aggrandisement; these were merely secondarily concomitant and even accidental; but for man: by putting some of him in one motion in one direction, by him of him and for him, to disjam the earth, get him for a little while at least out of his own way—standing there a moment, then two, then three, not accepting but compelling the

entire blast of the cynosure as in the twilit room the mirror concentrates to itself all of light and all else owns visibility only at
second hand; four then five then six, while breathed no sound no
sigh no sound of breathing even save the watch-chain's golden
sough and the thin insistent music of the pearl, still holding as in
his palm like putty, the massed anonymity and the waiting as the
sculptor holds for another moment yet the malleable obedient
unimpatient clay, or the conductor across his balanced untensile
hands the wand containing within its weightless pencil-gleam all
the loud fury and love and anguish.

Then he moved his hand, feeling as he did so the whole vast
weight of the watching and the attention concentrate in one beam
upon it as the magician's hand compels, and took out the watch
and snapped it open, seeing even as he calculated the elapsed creep
of the hands, within the lid's mellow concavity as in the seer's
crystal ball, the shadowy miniatures of the turnkey and the prisoner
who should be well into the square by now and even perhaps
already in the alley leading to the hotel garage; even at the moment
there came into the room the rising roar of an automobile engine,
then the sound of the car itself rushing fast into the square and
across and out of it, rushing on at that contemptuous and reckless
gait at which his insolent Negro driver always drove when, under
his master's orders, the car contained passengers whom the driver
considered beneath him or beneath the car's splendour—a swaggering demi-d'Artagnan of a mulatto murderer whom the lawyer
had let remain in the penitentiary at hard labour for exactly one
year and one day, as the handler wires the dead game bird to the
neck of the disobedient hunting dog, then getting him out on
parole, not that he (the lawyer) held any brief even for the murder
of this particular woman, but because of the way it had been done;
apparently with the razor already naked in his hand, the man had
not driven the woman out of the cabin, but had simply harried
and chivvied her through a scene which, as the lawyer imagined
it, must have had the quality of ballet, until the woman broke and
ran out of the house screaming into the moonlit lane, running
without doubt toward the sanctuary of the white kitchen where
she worked, until the man without haste overtook her, not to catch,
grasp at her, but simply ran past her with one single neat surgeon-
like back-handed slash of the razor, running into, then out of, the

instant's immobility into which all motion flowed in one gesture of formulated epicene, almost finicking, even niggardly fatal violence like the bullfighter's, the two of them running on side by side for two or three paces in the moonlight until the woman fell, the man not even spotted and the blade itself barely befouled, as if he had severed not a jugular but a scream and restored merely to the midnight, silence.

So the lawyer could have stopped now, with one word leaving them once more fixed, as with one twitch of his cape the espada does the bull, and walk again through the door to the judge's chambers and on to the hotel and pack and strap his bag. But he did not: who owed this little more, as the old pagan, before he quaffed it empty, tilted always from the goblet's brimming rim one splash at least upon the hearth, not to placate but simply in recognition of them who had matched him with his hour upon the earth; in one of the houses on one of the best streets in one of the most unassailable sections of New Orleans, he owned a picture, a painting, no copy but proved genuine and coveted, for which he had paid more than he liked to remember even though it had been validated by experts before he bought it and revalidated twice since and for which he had been twice offered half again what he had paid for it, and which he had not liked then and still didn't and was not even certain he knew what it meant, but which was his own now and so he didn't even have to pretend that he liked it, which—so he believed then, with more truth than any save himself knew—he affirmed to have bought for the sole purpose of not having to pretend that he liked it; one evening, alone in his study (wifeless and childless, in the house too save for the white-jacketed soft-footed not tamed but merely tractable mulatto murderer) suddenly he found himself looking at no static rectangle of disturbing Mediterranean blues and saffrons and ochres, nor even at the signboard affirming like a trumpet-blast the inevictable establishment in coeval space of the sum of his past—the house in it unimpeachable street, the membership in clubs some of whose doors were older than the state and behind which his father's name would, could, never have disturbed the air, and the cryptic numbers which opened his lock boxes and monotonous incrementation of his securities-lists—but instead was looking at the cognizance of his destiny like the wind-hard banner of the old Norman earl beneath whose vast shadow not just bankers and politicians clicked and sprang nor governors and lieutenants blenched and trembled but at the groaning tables in whose kitchens and sculleries or even open courtyards and kennels daily sixty thousand who wore no swords and spurs and owned no surnames made the one last supreme sacrifice: the free gift of their pauperism, and (the lawyer) thought: *I didn't really earn this. I didn't have time. I didn't even need to earn it; man out of his boundless and incalculable folly foisted it on me before I even had time to resist him;* and closed the watch and put it back into the waistcoat pocket and then the voice, not even raised, murmurous, ventriloquial, sourceless, as though it were not even he but circumambience, the room, the high unsubstanced air itself somewhere about or among the soaring and shadowy cornices, not speaking to the faces but rather descending, not as sound but as benison, as light itself upon the docile, the enduring, the triumphing heads:

'Ladies, gentlemen—' then not louder: merely sharp peremptory and succinct, like the report of a small whip or a toy pistol: 'Democrats: On the fourth of November two years ago there rose from the ballot boxes of America the sun of a thousand years of peace and prosperity such as the world has never seen; on the fourth day of November two years from now, we will see it set again, if the octopus of Wall street and the millionaire owners of New England factories have their way, waiting and watching their chance to erect once more the barricade of a Yankee tariff between the Southern farmer and the hungry factories and cheap labour of the old world in Europe already entered into its own millennium of peace and reason, freed at last after two thousand years of war and the fear of war, panting only to exchange at a price you can afford to accept, your wheat and corn and cotton for the manufactured goods necessary to your life and happiness and that of your children at a price you can afford to pay, affirming again that inalienable right decreed by our forefathers a hundred and twenty-six years ago of liberty and free trade: the right of man to sell the produce of his own sweat and labour wherever and whenever he wants to, without fear or favour of New York capitalists or New England factory owners already spending like water the money ground out of the child labour of their sweat-shops, to divert to the farthest corners of the earth the just profits of your sweat and labour, so that not your wives and children, but those of African savages and heathen Chinese will have the good roads and the schools and the cream separators and the automobiles—' then already in motion before he stopped speaking, crossing rapidly to the gate in the railing as with one concerted unhaste the entire room stood up, not flowing so much as swaying toward the main doors at the back, since almost at once a voice said from the doors:

'Hit's locked,' the sway not even pausing, only reversing and becoming a flow: one murmurous hollow roaring of feet, not running: merely shuffling yet as the crowd flowed back toward and into the narrow passage leading to the judge's chambers, where the lawyer, passing rapidly through the swing gate, now stood between them and the door; and even as he thought, *My first mistake was moving* he made another.

'Stand back, men,' he said and even raised his hand, palm out, seeing, marking for the first time, faces, individual faces and eyes which least of all were those of individuals now, but rather one single face bearing steadily down on him and overwhelming him until suddenly he was moving backward: no shock, no concussion, but simply enclosed, accepted into one moving envelopment; he stumbled once but immediately what felt like a dozen quick firm impersonal hands steadied and even turned him and then checked him while others reached past him and opened the door to the judge's chambers, not flinging nor even sweeping him aside, but evacuating, voiding him back into the wall as the crowd flowed on across the little room to the opposite corridor door, already emptying the room before they had had time to fill it, so that he knew that the first ones out had gone around to the main courtroom doors and unlocked them, so that not only the corridor but the whole building was murmuring again with the hollow unhurried thunder of feet while he stood for a moment more against the wall with in the centre of the once-immaculate waistcoat the print, not smeared: just blurred, not hurried, just firm and plain and light, of a hand.

And suddenly, in outrage and prescience, he started, actually sprang almost, already knowing what he would see before he reached the window, looking through it down into the square where they had already halted, the turnkey already facing back toward the courthouse as he fumbled inside his coat; except there were three of them now and the lawyer thought, rapid, inattentive and with no surprise: *Oh yes, the child who rode the horse* and looked no more at the turnkey scrabbling clumsily beneath his coat-tail but watched instead the deliberate pour of the crowd from the courthouse portal, already spreading as it converged toward the three waiting figures like the remorseless unhurried flow of spilled ink across a table cloth, thinking (the lawyer) how only when he is mounted on something—anything, from a footstool through a horse or rostrum to a flagpole or a flying machine—is man vulnerable and familiar; that on his own feet and in motion, he is terrible; thinking with amazement and humility and pride too, how no mere immobile mass of him, no matter how large nor apparently doing or about to do no matter what, nor even the mass of him in motion mounted on something which, not he but it, was locomotive, but the mass of him moving of itself in one direction, toward one objective by means of his own frail clumsily jointed legs and feet—not Ghengis' bone horns nor Murat's bugles, let alone the golden voice of Demosthenes or Cicero, or the trumpet-blast of Paul or John Brown or Pitt or Calhoun or Daniel Webster, but the children dying of thirst amid Mesopotamian mirages and the wild men out of the northern woods who walked into Rome carrying even their houses on their backs and Moses' forty-year scavengers and the tall men carrying a rifle or an axe and a bag of beads who changed the colour of the American race (and in the lawyer's own memory the last individual: cowboy who marked the whole of Western America with the ranging dung of his horse and the oxidising hulls of his sardine and tomato cans, exterminated from the earth by a tide of men with wire-stretchers and pockets full of staples); thinking with pride and awe too, how threatful only in locomotion and dangerous only in silence; neither in lust nor appetite nor greed lay wombed the potency of his threat, but in silence and meditation: his ability to move *en masse* at his own impulse, and silence in which to fall into thought and then action as into an open manhole; with exultation too, since none knew this better than the lords proprietors of his massed breathing, the hero-giant precentors of his seething moil, who used his spendthrift potency in the very act of curbing and directing it, and ever had and ever would: in Detroit today an old-time bicycle-racer destined to be one of the world's giants, his very surname an adjectival noun in the world's mouth, who had already put half a continent on wheels by families, and in twenty-five more would have half a hemisphere on wheels individually, and in a thousand would have already effaced the legs from a species just as that long-ago and doubtless at the time not-even-noticed twitch of Cosmos drained the seas into continents and effaced the gills from their fish. But that was not yet; that would be peace, and to attain that, the silence must be conquered too: the silence in which man had space to think and in consequence act on what he believed he thought or thought he believed: the silence in which the crowd walked, flowed steadily across the square toward the three waiting figures and out of which the turnkey cried in his thin high manless voice, dragging the new pistol in its turn from beneath his coat skirts:

'Stop, men! I'm going to count three!' and began to count: 'One —Two—' staring, even glaring at the faces which were not rushing at him nor did they even seem to walk at him, but rather towered down and over him, feeling again the pistol neither wrenched nor snatched but just wrung firmly from him and then other hands had him too. 'You durn fools!' he cried, struggling. But how say it? How tell them? You had to be honourable about money, no matter who had it; if you were not honourable about money, pitying the weak did them no good because about all they got from you then was just pity. Besides, it was already too late to try to tell them, even if there had been no other reason, the firm, quite kind, almost gentle hands not only holding him up but even lifting, raising him, and then they were even carrying him as two kinless bachelors might carry a child between them, his feet remembering earth but no longer touching it; then raising him still further until he could see, between and past the heads and shoulders, the ringed circumference of faces not grim and never angry: just unanimous and attentive, and in the centre of it the old Negro in the worn frock coat and the thin chocolate-coloured adolescent boy with eyeballs of that pure incredible white which Flemish painters knew how to grind; then the owner of the calm irascible voice spoke again and now for the first time the turnkey could see and recognise him: no lawyer or merchant or banker or any other civic leader, but himself a gambler who bucked from choice the toughest game of all: ownership of a small peripatetic sawmill where he had gone to work at the age of fifteen as the sole support of a widowed mother and three unmarried sisters, and now at forty owned the mill and a wife and two daughters and one granddaughter of his own, speaking at last into a silence in which there was not even the sound of breathing:

'How much did you and that fellow really win on that horse? A hundred dollars?'

'More,' the old Negro said.

'A thousand?'

'More than that': and now indeed there was no stir, no breath: only one vast suspension as if the whole bright April morning leaned:

'Was it forty thousand? ... All right. Was it half of forty thousand? How much did you see? How much did you count? Can you count to a thousand dollars?'

'It was a heap,' the old Negro said: and now they breathed: one stir, one exhalation, one movement; the day, the morning once more relinquished, the voice its valedictory:

'There'll be a train at the depot in twenty-five minutes. You be on it when it leaves and don't come back. We don't like rich niggers here.'

'So we got on the train,' the old Negro said, 'and rode to the next station. Then we got out and walked. It was a far piece, but we knowed where he would be now, if they would just let him alone —' the blue haze-cradled valley where the corners of Georgia and Tennessee and Carolina meet, where he had appeared suddenly from nowhere that day last summer with a three-legged racehorse and an old Negro preacher and the Negro child who rode the horse, and stayed two weeks during which the horse outran every other one within fifty miles, and finally one brought all the way from Knoxville to try to cope with it, then (the four of them) vanished again overnight six hours ahead of a horde of Federal agents and sheriffs and special officers like the converging packs of a state- or nation-wide foxhunt.

'And we was right; he must a come straight back there from the Missouri jail because it was still June. They told us about it: a Sunday morning in the church and likely it was the preacher that

seen him first because he was already facing that way, before the
rest of them turned their heads and recognised him too standing
against the back wall just inside the door like he hadn't never
left—' the runner seeing it too, seeing almost as much as the Federal ex-deputy would have seen if he had been there:—the morose,
savage, foul-mouthed, almost inarticulate (only the more so for the
fact that occasionally a fragment of what he spoke sounded a little
like what the valley knew as English) foreigner who moved,
breathed, not merely in an aura of bastardy and bachelordom but
of homelessness too, like a half-wild pedigreeless pariah dog: father-
less, wifeless, sterile and perhaps even impotent too, misshapen,
savage and foul: the world's portionless and intractable and inconsolable orphan, who brought without warning into that drowsing
vacuum an aggregation bizarre, mobile and amazing as a hippo-
drome built around a comet: two Negroes and the ruined remnant
of the magnificent and incredible horse whose like even on four
legs the valley or the section either had never seen before, into
a country where a horse was any milkless animal capable of pulling
a plough or a cart on weekdays and carrying sacks of corn to the
mill on Saturdays and bearing as many of the family as could
cling to its gaunt ridgepole to the church on Sundays, and where
there not only were none, but there never had been any Negroes;
whose people man and boy from sixty-odd down to fourteen and
thirteen, had fifty years ago quitted their misty unmapped eyries to
go for miles and even weeks on foot to engage in a war in which
they had no stake and, if they had only stayed at home, no contact,
in order to defend their land from Negroes; not content merely
to oppose and repudiate their own geopolitical kind and their
common economic derivation, they must confederate with its
embattled enemies, stealing, creeping (once at a crossroads
tavern a party of them fought something resembling a pitched
battle with a Confederate recruiting party) by night through the
Confederate lines to find and join a Federal army, to fight not
against slavery but against Negroes, to abolish the Negro by freeing
him from them who might bring Negroes among them exactly as
they would have taken their rifles down from the pegs or deer
antlers above hearth and doorway to repel, say, a commercial
company talking about bringing the Indians back.

Hearing it too: 'Except it wasn't two weeks we was there that first time. It was fifteen days. The first two they spent just looking at us. They would come from all up and down the valley, walking or on horses and mules or the whole family in the wagon, to set in the road in front of the store where we would be squatting on the gallery eating cheese and crackers and sardines, looking at us. Then the men and boys would go around behind the store where we had built a pen out of rails and scraps of boards and pieces of rope, to stand and look at the horse. Then we begun to run and by the fifth day we had outrun every horse in the whole valley and had done won even one mortagage on a ten-acre corn-patch up on the mountain, and by the seventh day we was running against horses brought all the way in from the next counties across what they called the Gap. Then six days more, with the folks in the valley betting on our horse now, until the fifteenth day when they brought that horse from Knoxville that had run at Churchill Downs back home once, and this time it was not just the valley folks but folks from all that part of Tennessee watching that three-legged horse without even no saddle (we never used no bridle neither: just a one-rein hackamore and a belly-band for this boy to hold on to) outrun that Knoxville horse the first time at five furlongs and the next time at a full mile for double stakes, with not just the folks in the valley but the folks from the other counties too betting on it now, so that everybody or any way every family in that part of Tennessee had a share in what it won—'

'That's when he was taken into the Masons,' the runner said. 'During that two weeks.'

'Fifteen days,' the old Negro said. 'Yes, there was a lodge there. —Then just before daylight the next morning a man on a mule rid down from the Gap, just about a hour ahead of them—' the runner hearing this too as the old Negro himself had heard it a year afterward: when the sun rose the automobile itself stood in front of the store—the first automobile which the soil of the valley had ever imprinted and which some of the old people and children had ever seen, driven part of the way over the gap trail but indubitably hauled and pushed and probably even carried here and there for the rest of the distance, and inside the store the sheriff of the county and the city strangers in their city hats and neckties and shoes, smelling, stinking of excise officers, reveuers, while already the horses and mules and wagons of yesterday flowed back down from the coves and hills, the riders and occupants dismounting at once now, to pause for a moment to look quietly and curiously at the automobile as though at a medium-sized rattlesnake, then crowding into the store until it would hold no more of them, facing not the city strangers standing in a tight wary clump in front of the cold spit-marked stove in its spit-marked sandbox, they had looked at them once and then no more, but rather the sheriff so that, since the sheriff was one of them, bore one of the names which half the valley bore and the valley had all voted for him and in fact, except for his dime-store cravat and their overalls, even looked like them, it was as though the valley merely faced itself.

'They stole the horse,' the sheriff said. 'All the man wants is just to get it back.' But no reply: only the quiet, grave, courteous, not really listening but just waiting faces, until one of the city strangers said in a bitter city voice:

'Wait—' already stepping quickly past the sheriff, his hand already inside the buttoned front of his city coat when the sheriff said in his flat hill voice:

'You wait,' his hand inside the other's buttoned coat too, already covering the other smaller one, plucking it out of the coat and holding easily in the one grasp both the small city hand and the flat city pistol so that they looked like toys in it, not wrenching but merely squeezing the pistol out of the hand and dropping it into his own coat pocket, and said, 'Well, boys, let's get on,' moving, walking, his companions in their white shirts and coat sleeves and pants legs and shoes creased and polished two days ago in Chattanooga hotels, heeling him, compact and close, while the faces, the lane opened: through the store, the lane, the faces closing behind: across the gallery and down the steps, the silent lane still opening and closing behind them until they reached the automobile; 1914 then, and young mountain men had not yet learned how to decommission an automobile simply by removing the distributor or jamming the carburetor. So they had used what they did know: a ten-pound hammer from the blacksmith's shop, not knowing even then the secret of the thing's life beneath the hood and so over-finding it: the fine porcelain dust of shattered plugs and wrenched and battered wires and dented pipes and even the mute half-horseshoe prints of the hammer punctuating the spew of oil and gasoline and even the hammer itself immobile against an overalled leg in plain view; and now the city man, cursing in his furious bitter voice, was scrabbling with both hands at the sheriff's coat until the sheriff grasped both of them in his one and held the man so; and, facing them now across the ruined engine, again it was merely the valley facing itself. 'The automobile don't belong to the government,' the sheriff said. 'It belongs to him. He will have to pay to have it fixed.'

Nor anything yet for a moment. Then a voice: 'How much?'

'How much?' the sheriff said over his shoulder.

'How much?' the city man said. 'A thousand dollars, for all I know. Maybe two thousand—'

'We'll call it fifty,' the sheriff said, releasing the hands and removing the trim pearl-coloured city hat from the city head and with his other hand took from his trousers pocket a small crumple of banknotes and separated one and dropped it into the hat, holding the hat upside down and as though baited with the single bill, toward the nearest of the crowd: 'Next,' he said.

'Except that they had to look quick, because before the preacher could say the benediction so they could get up and even tell him howdy, he was done gone from there too. But quick as he left, it wasn't before the word could begin to spread': telling that too: thirty-seven in the church that morning so in effect the whole valley was and by midafternoon or sundown anyway every cove and hill and run knew he was back: alone: without the horse: and broke, and hungry; not gone again: just disappeared, out of sight: for the time: so that they knew they had only to wait, to bide until the moment, which was that night in the loft above the post-office-store—'It was the lodge-room. They used it for their politics too, and for the court, but mostly for the poker- and crap-games that they claimed had been running there ever since the valley was first settled and the store was built. There was a regular outside staircase going up to it that the lawyers and judges and politicians and Masons and Eastern Stars used, but mainly it was a ladder nailed flat to the back wall outside, leading up to a back window, that everybody in the valley knowed about but not one of them would ever claim he even seen, let alone climbed. And inside there was a jug always full of white mountain whisky setting on the shelf with the water-bucket and the gourd, that everybody in the valley knowed was there just like they done the ladder but that nobody could see while the court or the lodge or a meeting was going on': telling it:

An hour after dark when the six or seven men (including the store's clerk) squatting around the spread blanket on the floor beneath the lantern ('It was Sunday night. They just shot craps on Sunday night. They wouldn't allow no poker.') heard his feet on the ladder and watched him crawl through the window and then didn't look at him any more while he went to the jug and poured himself a drink into the gourd dipper, not watching him exactly as not one of them would have offered him as a gift the actual food or as a loan the money to buy it with, not even when he turned and saw the coin, the half-dollar, on the floor beside his foot where ten seconds ago no coin had been, nor when he picked it up and interrupted the game for two or three minutes while he compelled them one by one to disclaim the coin's ownership, then knelt into the circle and bet the coin and cast the dice and drew down the original half-dollar and pyramided for two more casts, then passed the dice, and rising, left the original coin on the floor where he had found it and went to the trap door and the ladder which led down into the store's dark interior and with no light descended and returned with a wedge of cheese and a handful of crackers and interrupted the game again to hand the clerk one of the coins he had won and took his change and, squatting against the wall and with no sound save the steady one of his chewing, ate what the valley knew was his first food since he returned to it, reappeared in the church ten hours ago; and—suddenly—the first since he had vanished with the horse and the two Negroes ten months ago.

'They just took him back, like he hadn't never even been away. It was more than that. It was like there never had been no more than what they seen now: no horse to win races on three legs and never had been because they probably never even asked him what had become of it, never no two niggers like me and this boy, never no money to ask him how much of it he won like all them folks back there in Missouri done, not even no time between that one a year ago last summer and this one—' no interval of fall and winter and spring, no flame of oak and hickory nor drive of sleet nor foam and rush of laurel and rhododendron down the mountainsides into summer again; the man himself (the runner seeing this too out of the listening, the hearing) unchanged and not even any dirtier: just alone this time (though not as well as the Federal ex-deputy could have seen it)—the same savage and bandy misanthrope in the foul raked checked cap and the cheap imitation tweed jacket and the bagging Bedford cords ('He called them jodhpurs. They would have held three of him. He said they was made in a place called Savile Row for what he called the second largest duke in the Irish peerage.') squatting on the store's front gallery beneath the patent-medicine and tobacco and baking-powder placards and the announcements and adjurations of candidates for sheriff and representative and district attorney; this was 1914, an even year; they had already been defeated and forgotten and there remained only their fading photographs joblotted from the lowest bidder and not looking like them anyway, which no one had expected, but merely like any candidate, which was all that any hoped, dotting the countryside on telephone poles and fences and the wooden rails of bridges and the flanks of barns and already fading beneath the incrementation of time and weather, like ejaculations: a warning: a plea: a cry:

'Just squatting there at first, not doing nothing and not nobody bothering him, even to try to talk to him, until Sunday when he would be in the church again, setting in the last pew at the back where he could get out first after the benediction. He was sleeping on a straw tick in the lodge room over the store and eating out of the store too because he had won that much that first night. He could have had a job; they told me about that too: him squatting on the gallery one morning when some fellow brought a horse in to the blacksmith that he had tried to shoe himself and quicked it in the nigh hind, the horse plunging and kicking and squealing every time they tried to touch it until at last they was trying to cross-tie it up and maybe even have to throw it to pull the quick shoe, until he got up and went in and laid his hand on its neck a minute and talked to it and then just tied the halter rein in the ring and picked up the foot and pulled the shoe and reset it. The blacksmith offered him a steady job right there but he never even answered, just back on the gallery squatting again, then Sunday in the back pew in the church once more where he could get out first, before anybody could try to talk to him. Because they couldn't see his heart.'

'His heart?' the runner said.

'Yes,' the old Negro said. 'Then he did vanish, because the next time they seed him they woudn't have knowed him except for the cap, the coat and them Irish britches gone now and wearing over-halls and a hickory shirt. Except that they would have had to gone out there to seen that, because he was a farmer now, a wage-hand, likely not getting much more than his board and lodging and washing because the place he was working on hadn't hardly sup-ported the two folks that was already trying to live on it—' the runner seeing that now almost as well as the Federal ex-deputy could have seen it—a childless couple of arthritic middle age: two heirs of misfortune drawn as though by some mutual last resort into the confederation of matrimony as inversely two heirs of great wealth or of royalty might have been—a one-room-and-leanto cabin, a hovel almost, clinging paintless to a sheer pitch of mountainside in a straggling patch of corn standing in niggard monument to the incredible, the not just back-but heart-breaking labour which each meagre stalk represented: moloch-effigy of self-sustenance which did not reward man's sweat but merely consumed his flesh;—the man who ten months ago had walked in the company of giants and heroes and who even yesterday, even without the horse and solitary and alone, had still walked in its magnificent gigantic shadow, now in faded overalls milking a gaunt hill cow and splitting firewood and (the three of them, dis-tinguishable at any distance from one another only because one wore the checked cap and another a skirt) hoeing the lean and tilted corn, coming down the mountain to squat, not talking yet not actually mute either, among them on the gallery of the store on Saturday afternoon; and on the next morning, Sunday, again in his back pew in the church, always in that clean fresh rotation of faded blue which was not the regalia of his metamorphosis and the badge of all plodding enduring husbandry, but which hid and concealed even the horse-warped curvature of his legs, obliterating, effacing at last the last breath or recollection of the old swaggering aura bachelor, footfree and cavalier, so that (it was July now) there remained (not the heart) only the foul raked heavily-checked cap talking (not the heart talking of passion and bereave-ment) among the empty Tennessee hills of the teeming metro-politan outland:

'Then he was gone. It was August; the mail rider had brought the Chattanooga and Knoxville papers back over the Gap that week and the next Sunday the preacher made the prayer for all the folks across the water swamped again in battle and murder and sudden death, and the next Saturday night they told me how he taken his last degree in Masonry and how that time they tried to talk to him because the Chattanooga and Knoxville papers was coming over the Gap every day now and they was reading them too: about that battle—'

'Mons,' the runner said.

'Mons,' the old Negro said. '—saying to him, "Them was your folks too, wasn't they?" and getting the sort of answer there wasn't no reply to except just to hit him. And when the next Sunday came, he was gone. Though at least this time they knowed where, so that when we finally got there that day—'

'What?' the runner said. 'It took you from June until August to travel from Missouri to Tennessee?'

'It wasn't August,' the old Negro said. 'It was October. We walked. We would have to stop now and then to find work to earn money to eat on. That taken a while, because this boy never had no size then, and I never knowed nothing but horses and preaching, and any time I stopped to do either one, somebody might have asked me who I was.'

'You mean you had to bring the money to him first before you could even draw travel expenses from it?'

'There wasn't no money,' the old Negro said. 'There never was none, except just what we needed, had to have. Never nobody but that New Orleans lawyer ever believed there was. We never had time to bother with winning a heap of money to have to take care of. We had the horse. To save that horse that never wanted nothing and never knowed nothing but just to run out in front of all the other horses in a race, from being sent back to Kentucky to be just another stud-horse for the rest of its life. We had to save it until it could die still not knowing nothing and not wanting nothing but just to run out in front of everything else. At first he thought different, aimed different. But not long. It was during that time when we was walking to Texas. We was hiding in the woods one day by a creek and I talked to him and that evening I baptised him in the creek into my church. And after that he knowed too that betting was a sin. We had to do a little of it, win a little money to live on, buy feed for it and grub for us. But that was all. God knowed that too. That was all right with Him.'

'Are you an ordained minister?' the runner said.

'I bears witness,' the old Negro said.

'But you're not an ordained priest. Then how could you confirm him into your church?'

'Hush, Pappy,' the youth said.

'Wait,' the runner said. 'I know. He made you a Mason too.'

'Suppose he did,' the old Negro said. 'You and this boy are alike. You think maybe I never had no right to make him a Christian, but you know he never had no business making me a Mason. But which do you think is the lightest to undertake: to tell a man to act like the head Mason thinks he ought to act, that's just another man trying to know what's right to do, or to tell him how the head of Heaven *knows* he ought to act, that's God and *knows* what's right to ease his suffering and save him?'

'All right,' the runner said. 'It was October—'

'Only this time they knowed where he was. "France?" I says, with this boy already jerking at my sleeve and saying, "Come on, Grampaw. Come on, Grampaw." "Which way is that?" I says. "Is that in Tennessee too?"'

' "Come on, Grampaw," this boys says. "I knows where it is." '

'Yes,' the runner said to the youth. 'I'll get to you in a moment too.' He said to the old Negro: 'So you came to France. I won't even ask how you did that with no money. Because that was God. Wasn't it?'

'It was the Society,' the youth said. Only he didn't say 'society': he said 'société'.

'Yes,' the runner said to the youth. He said in French, his best French: the glib smart febrile *argot* immolates into the international *salons* via the nightclubs from the Paris gutter: 'I wondered who did the talking for him. It was you, was it?'

'Someone had to,' the youth said, in still better French, the French of the Sorbonne, the Institute, the old Negro listening, peaceful and serene, until he said:

'His mamma was a New Orleans girl. She knowed gobble talk. That's where he learned it.'

'But not the accent,' the runner said. 'Where did you get that?'

'I don't know,' the youth said. 'I just got it.'

'Could you "just get" Greek or Latin or Spanish the same way?'

'I ain't tried,' the youth said. 'I reckon I could, if they ain't no harder than this one.'

'All right,' the runner said, to the old Negro now. 'Did you have the Society before you left America?' and heard that, without order or emphasis, like dream too: they were in New York, who a year ago had not known that the earth extended farther than the distance between Lexington, Kentucky, and Louisville until they walked on it, trod with their actual feet the hard enduring ground bearing the names Louisiana and Missouri and Texas and Arkansas and Ohio and Tennessee and Alabama and Mississippi—words which until then had been as foundationless and homeless as the ones meaning Avalon or Astalot or Ultima Thule. Then immediately there was a woman in it, a 'lady', not young, richly in furs—

'I know,' the runner said. 'She was in the car with you that day last spring when you came up to Amiens. The one whose son is in the French air squadron that she is supporting.'

'Was,' the youth said. 'Her boy is dead. He was a volunteer, one of the first airmen killed in the French service. That's when she began to give money to support the squadron.'

'Because she was wrong,' the old Negro said.

'Wrong?' the runner said. 'Oh. Her dead son's monument is a machine to kill as many Germans as possible because one German killed him? Is that it? And when you told her so, it was just like that morning in the woods when you talked to the horse-thief and then baptised him in the creek and saved him? All right, tell me.'

'Yes,' the old Negro said, and told it: the three of them traversing a succession almost like avatars: from what must have been a Park Avenue apartment, to what must have been a Wall Street office, to another office, room: a youngish man with a black patch over one eye and a cork leg and a row of miniature medals on his coat, and an older man with a minute red thing like a toy rosebud in his buttonhole, talking gobble talk to the lady and then to the youth too—

'A French consulate?' the runner said. 'Looking for a British soldier?'

'It was Verdun,' the youth said.

'Verdun?' the runner said. 'That was just last year—1916. It took you until 1916—'

'We was walking and working. Then Pappy begun to hear them—'

'There was too many of them,' the old Negro said. 'Men and boys, marching for months down into one muddy ditch to kill one another. There was too many of them. There wasn't room to lay quiet and rest. All you can kill is man's meat. You can't kill his voice. And if there is enough of the meat, without even room to lay quiet and rest, you can hear it too.'

'Even if it's not saying anything but Why?' the runner said.

'What can trouble you more than having a human man saying to you, Tell me why. Tell me how. Show me the way?'

'And you can show him the way?'

'I can believe,' the old Negro said.

'So because you believed, the French Government sent you to France.'

'It was the lady,' the youth said. 'She paid for it.'

'She believed too,' the old Negro said. 'All of them did. The money didn't count no more now because they all knowed by now that just money had done already failed.'

'All right,' the runner said. 'Anyway, you came to France—' hearing it: a ship; there was a committee of at least one or two at Brest, even if they were just military, staff officers to expedite, not a special train maybe but at least one with precedence over everything not military; the house, palace, sonorous and empty, was already waiting for them in Paris. Even if the banner to go above the ducal gates was not ready yet, thought of yet into the words. But that was not long and the house, the palace, was not empty long either: first the women in black, the old ones and the young ones carrying babies, then the maimed men in trench-stained horizon blue, coming in to sit for a while on the hard temporary benches, not always even to see him, since he was still occupied in trying to trace down his companion, his Mistairy, telling that too: from the Paris war office to the Department of State, to Downing Street to Whitehall and then out to Poperinghe, until the man's whereabouts was ascertained at last: who (that Newmarket horse and its legend were known and remembered in Whitehall too) could have gone out as groom to the commander-in-chief himself's horse if he had chosen, but enlisted instead into the Londoners until, having barely learned how to wrap his spiral puttees, he found himself in a posting which would have left him marooned for the duration as groom-farrier-hostler in a troop of Guards cavalry had he not taught the sergeant in charge of the draft to shoot dice in the American fashion and so won his escape from him, and for two years now had been a private in a combat battalion of Northumberland Borderers.

'Only when you finally found him, he barely spoke to you,' the runner said.

'He ain't ready yet,' the old Negro said. 'We can wait. There's plenty of time yet.'

'We?' the runner said. 'You and God too?'

'Yes. Even if it will be over next year.'

'The war? This war? Did God tell you that?'

'It's all right. Laugh at Him. He can stand that too.'

'What else can I do but laugh?' the runner said. 'Hadn't He rather have that than the tears?'

'He's got room for both of them. They're all the same to Him; He can grieve for both of them.'

'Yes,' the runner said. 'Too much of it. Too many of them. Too often. There was another one last year, called the Somme; they give ribbons now not for being brave because all men are brave if you just frighten them enough. You must have heard of that one; you must have heard them too.'

'I heard them too,' the old Negro said.

'*Les Amis à la France de Tout le Monde*,' the runner said. 'Just to believe, to hope. That little. So little. Just to sit together in the anguished room and believe and hope. And that's enough? like the doctor when you're ill: you know he can't cure you just by laying his hands on you and you don't expect him to: all you need is someone to say "Believe and hope. Be of good cheer." But suppose it's already too late for a doctor now; all that will serve now is a surgeon, someone already used to blood, up there where the blood already is.'

'Then He would have thought of that too.'

'Then why hasn't He sent you up there, instead of here to live on hot food in clean bugless clothes in a palace?'

'Maybe because He knows I ain't brave enough,' the old Negro said.

'Would you go if He sent you?'

A FABLE

'I would try,' the old Negro said. 'If I could do the work, it wouldn't matter to Him or me neither whether I was brave.'

'To believe and to hope,' the runner said. 'Oh yes, I walked through that room downstairs; I saw them; I was walking along the street and happened by simple chance to see that placard over the gate. I was going somewhere else, yet here I am too. But not to believe and hope. Because man can bear anything, provided he has something left, a little something left: his integrity as a creature tough and enduring enough not only not to hope but not even to believe in it and not even to miss its lack; to be tough and to endure until the flash, crash, whatever it will be, when he will no longer be anything and none of it will matter any more, even the fact that he was tough and, until then, did endure.'

'That's right,' the old Negro said, peaceful and serene, 'maybe it is tomorrow you got to go back. So go on now and have your Paris while you got a little time.'

'Aha,' the runner said. 'Ave Bacchus and Venus, morituri te salutant, eh? Wouldn't you have to call that sin?'

'Evil is a part of man, evil and sin and cowardice, the same as repentance and being brave. You got to believe in all of them, or believe in none of them. Believe that man is capable of all of them, or he ain't capable of none. You can go out this way if you want to, without having to meet nobody.'

'Thanks,' the runner said. 'Maybe what I need is to have to meet somebody. To believe. Not in anything: just to believe. To enter that room down there, not to escape from anything but to escape into something, to flee mankind for a little while. Not even to look at that banner because some of them probably can't even read it, but just to sit in the same room for a while with that affirmation, that promise, that hope. If I only could. You only could. Anybody only could. Do you know what the loneliest experience of all is? But of course you do: you just said so. It's breathing.'

'Send for me,' the old Negro said.

'Oh yes—if I only could.'

'I know,' the old Negro said. 'You ain't ready yet neither. But when you are, send for me.'

'Are what?' the runner said.

'When you needs me.'

184

'What can I need you for, when it will be over next year? All
I've got to do is just stay alive.'

'Send for me,' the old Negro said.

'Goodbye,' the runner said.

Descending, retracing his steps, they were still there in the vast
cathedral-like room, not only the original ones but the steady
trickle of new arrivals, entering, not even to look at the lettered
banner but just to sit for a while inside the same walls with that
innocent and invincible affirmation. And he had been right: it was
August now and there were American uniforms in France, not as
combat units yet but singly, still learning: they had a captain and
two subalterns posted to the battalion, to blood themselves on
the old Somme names, preparatory to, qualifying themselves to,
lead their own kind into the ancient familiar abbatoir; he thought:
*Oh yes, three more years and we will have exhausted Europe. Then we—
hun and allies together—will transfer the whole business intact to the
fresh trans-Atlantic pastures, the virgin American stage, like a travelling
minstrel troupe.*

Then it was winter; later, remembering it, it would seem to him
that it might actually have been the anniversary of the Son of Man,
a grey day and cold, the grey cobbles of the village *Place de Ville*
gleaming and wimpled like the pebbles beneath the surface of a
brook when he saw the small augmenting crowd and joined it too,
from curiosity then, seeing across the damp khaki shoulders the
small clump of battle-stained horizon blue whose obvious or at
least apparent leader bore a French corporal's insigne, the faces
alien and strange and bearing an identical lostness, like—some of
them at least—those of men who have reached a certain point or
place or situation by simple temerity and who no longer have any
confidence even in the temerity, and three or four of which were
actually foreign faces reminding him of the ones the French
Foreign Legion was generally believed to have recruited out of
European jails. And if they had been talking once, they stopped
as soon as he came up and was recognised, the faces, the heads
above the damp khaki shoulders turning to recognise him and
assume at once that expression tentative, reserved and alert with
which he had become familiar even since the word seeped down

(probably through a corporal-clerk) from the orderly room that he had been an officer once.

So he came away. He learned in the orderly room that they were correctly within military protocol: they had passes, to visit the homes of one or two or three of them in villages inside the British zone. Then from the battalion padre he even began to divine why. Not learn why: divine it. 'It's a staff problem,' the padre said. 'It's been going on for a year or two. Even the Americans are probably familiar with them by now. They just appear, with their passes all regularly issued and visa-ed, in troop rest-billets. They are known, and of course watched. The trouble is, they have done no—' and stopped, the runner watching him.

'You were about to say, "done no harm yet," ' the runner said. 'Harm?' he said gently. 'Problem? Is it a problem and harmful for men in front-line trenches to think of peace, that after all, we can stop fighting if enough of us want to?'

'To think it; not to talk it. That's mutiny. There are ways to do things, and ways not to do them.'

'Render unto Caesar?' the runner said.

'I can't discuss this subject while I bear this,' the padre said, his hand flicking for an instant toward the crown on his cuff.

'But you wear this too,' the runner said, his hand in its turn indicating the collar and the black V inside the tunic's lapels.

'God help us,' the padre said.

'Or we, God,' the runner said. 'Maybe the time has now come for that': and went away from there too, the winter following its course too toward the spring and the next final battle which would end the war, during which he would hear of them again, rumoured from the back areas of the (now three) army zones, watched still by the (now) three intelligence sections but still at stalemate because still they had caused no real harm, at least not yet; in fact, the runner had now begun to think of them as a formally accepted and even dispatched compromise with the soldier's natural undeviable belief that he at least would not be killed, as regimented batches of whores were sent up back areas to compromise with man's natural and normal sex, thinking (the runner) bitterly and quietly, as he had thought before: *His prototype had only man's natural propensity for evil to contend with; this one faces all the scarlet-and-brazen impregnability of general staffs.*

WEDNESDAY

And this time (it was May again, the fourth one he had seen from beneath the brim of a steel helmet, the battalion had gone in again two days ago and he had just emerged from Corps headquarters at Villeneuve Blanche) when he saw the vast black motorcar again there was such a shrilling of N.C.O.'s whistles and a clashing of presented arms that he thought at first it was full of French and British and American generals until he saw that only one was a general: the French one: then recognised them all: in the rear seat beside the general the pristine blue helmet as unstained and innocent of exposure and travail as an uncut sapphire above the Roman face and the unstained horizon-blue coat with its corporal's markings, and the youth in the uniform now of an American captain, on the second jump seat beside the British staff-major, the runner half-wheeling without even breaking stride, to the car and halted one pace short then took that pace and clapped his heels and saluted and said to the staff-major in a ringing voice: 'Sir!' then in French to the French general—an old man with enough stars on his hat to have been at least an army commander: 'Monsieur the general.'

'Good morning, my child,' the general said.

'With permission to address monsieur the director your companion?'

'Certainly, my child,' the general said.

'Thank you, my general,' the runner said, then to the old Negro: 'You missed him again.'

'Yes,' the old Negro said. 'He ain't quite ready yet. And don't forget what I told you last year. Send for me.'

'And don't you forget what I told you last year too,' the runner said, and took that pace backward then halted again. 'But good luck to you, anyway; he doesn't need it,' he said and clapped his heels again and saluted and said again to the staff-major or perhaps to no one at all in the ringing and empty voice: 'Sir!'

And that was all, he thought; he would never see either of them again—that grave and noble face, the grave and fantastic child. But he was wrong. It was not three days until he stood in the ditch beside the dark road and watched the lorries moving up toward the lines laden with what the old St. Omer watchman told him were blank anti-aircraft shells, and not four when he waked, groaning and choking on his own blood until he could turn his head and spit (his lip was cut and he was going to lose two teeth—spitting again, he had already lost them—and now he even remembered the rifle-butt in his face), hearing already (that was what had waked, roused him) the terror of that silence.

He knew at once where he was: where he always was, asleep or on duty either: lying (someone had even spread his blanket over him) on the dirt ledge hacked out of the wall of the tiny cave which was the ante-room to the battalion dugout. And he was alone: no armed guard sitting across from him as he realised now he had expected, nor was he even manacled: nothing save himself lying apparently free on his familiar ledge in that silence which was not only above ground but down here too: no telephonist at the switchboard opposite, none of the sounds—voices, movement, the coming and going of orderlies and company commanders and N.C.O.'s—all the orderly disorder of a battalion p.c. functioning normally in a cramped space dug forty feet down into the earth—which should have been coming from the dugout itself—only the soundless roar of the massed weight of shored and poised dirt with which all subterrene animals—badgers and miners and moles—are deafened until they no longer hear it. His watch (curiously it was not broken) said 10:19, whether Ack Emma or Pip Emma he could not tell down here, except that it could not be, it must not be Pip Emma; he could not, he must not have been here going on twenty hours; the seven which Ack Emma would signify would already be too many. So he knew at least where they would be, the whole p.c. of them—colonel, adjutant, sergeant-major and the telephonist with his temporarily spliced and extended line—topside too, crouching behind the parapet, staring through periscopes across that ruined and silent emptiness at the opposite line, where their opposite German numbers would be crouching also behind a parapet, gazing too through periscopes across that vernal desolation, that silence, expectant too, alerted and amazed.

But he did not move yet. It was not that it might already be too late; he had already refused to believe that and so dismissed it. It was because the armed man might be in the dugout itself, guarding the only exit there. He even thought of making a sound, a groan, something to draw the man in; he even thought of what he would say to him: *Don't you see? We don't know what they are up to, and only I seem to have any fears or alarms. If I am wrong, we will*

*all die sooner or later anyway. If I am right and you shoot me here, we will
all surely die.* Or better still: *Shoot me. I shall be the one man out of this
whole four years who died calmly and peacefully and reposed in dry
clothing instead of panting, gasping, befouled with mud to the waist or
drenched completely in the sweat of exertion and anguish.* But he didn't
do it. He didn't need to. The dugout was empty also. The armed
man might be at the top of the stairs instead of the foot of them
but then there or thereabouts would be where the colonel and
his orderly room and periscope was too; besides, he would
have to face, risk the rifle somewhere and it wouldn't matter
where since it contained only (for him) one bullet while what
he was armed with was capable of containing all of time, all of
man.

He found his helmet at once. He would have no rifle, of course,
but even as he dismissed this he had one: leaning against the wall
behind the sergeant-major's desk (oh yes, what he was armed with
even equipped him at need with that which his own armament
was even superior to) and yes, there it still was in the sergeant-
major's desk: the pass issued to him Monday to pass him out to
Corps Headquarters and then back, so that he didn't even expect
to find a guard at the top of the fifty-two steps leading up and
debouching into the trench: only the transubstantiated orderly
room as he had foreknown—colonel, adjutant, sergeant-major,
telephone periscopes and all, his speech all ready on his tongue
when the sergeant-major turned and looked back at him.

'Latrine,' he said.

'Right,' the sergeant-major said. 'Be smart about it. Then report
back here.'

'Yes sir,' he said and two hours later he was again among the
trees from which he had watched the torches moving about the
archie battery two nights ago; three hours after that he saw the
three aeroplanes—they were S.E.5's—in the sky which had been
empty of aircraft for forty-eight hours now, and saw and heard the
frantic uproar of shells above where the enemy front would be.
Then he saw the German aeroplane too, watched it fly arrow-
straight and apparently not very fast, enclosed by the pocking of
white British archie which paced it, back across No-man's Land,
the three S.E.'s in their pocking of black hun archie zooming and
climbing and diving at the German; he watched one of them hang

on the German's tail for what must have been a minute or two, the two aircraft apparently fastened rigidly together by the thin threads of tracer. And still the German flew steadily and sedately on, descending, descending now even as it passed over him and the battery behind—near—which he lurked opened on it in that frenzy of frantic hysterical frustration common to archie batteries; descending, vanishing just above the trees, and suddenly he knew where: the aerodrome just outside Villeneuve Blanche, vanishing sedately and without haste downward, enclosed to the last in that empty similitude of fury, the three S.E.5's pulling up and away in one final zoom; and, as if that were not enough to tell him what he had to do, he saw one of them roll over at the top of its loop and, frozen and immobile, watched it in its plan as it dove, rushed straight down at the battery itself, its nose flicking and winking with the tracer which was now going straight into the battery and the group of gunners standing quietly about it, down and down past what he would have thought was the instant already too late to save itself from crashing in one last inextricable jumble into the battery, then levelling, himself watching the rapid pattering walk of the tracer across the intervening ground toward him until now he was looking directly into the flicking wink and the airman's helmeted and goggled face behind and above it, so near that they would probably recognise each other if they ever saw each other again—the two of them locked in their turn for a moment, an instant by the thin fiery thread of a similitude of death (afterward he would even remember the light rapid blow against his leg as if he had been tapped rapidly and lightly once by a finger), the aeroplane pulling level and with a single hard snarling downward blast of air, zooming climbing on until the roaring whine died away, he not moving yet, immobile and still frozen in the ravelling fading snarl and the faint thin sulphur-stink of burning wool from the skirt of his tunic.

It was enough. He didn't even expect to get nearer the Ville- neuve aerodrome than the first road-block, himself speaking to the corporal not even across a rifle but across a machine gun: 'I'm a runner from the —th Battalion.'

'I can't help that,' the corporal said. 'You don't pass here.' Nor did he really want to. He knew enough now. Ten hours later in the Villeneuve Blanche gendarme's uniform, he was in Paris, traversing again the dark and silent streets of the aghast and suspended city dense not only with French civil police but the military ones of the three nations patrolling the streets in armed motorcars, until he passed again beneath the lettered banner above the arched gateway.

WEDNESDAY NIGHT

TO the young woman waiting just inside the old eastern city gate that dispersal in the *Place de Ville* made a long faint hollow faraway rushing sound as remote and impersonal as a pouring of water or the wings of a tremendous migratory flock. With her head turned and arrested and one thin hand clutching the crossing of the shabby shawl on her breast, she seemed to listen to it almost inattentively while it filled the saffron sunset between the violet city and the cobalt-green firmament, and died away.

Then she turned back to where the road entered the city beneath the old arch. It was almost empty now, only a trickle approached and entered, the last of them, the dregs; when she turned back to it her face, though still wan and strained, was almost peaceful now, as if even the morning's anguish had been exhausted and even at last obliterated by the day of watching and waiting.

Then she was not even watching the road as her hand, releasing the shawl, brushed past the front of her dress and stopped, her whole body motionless while her hand fumbled at something through the cloth, fumbling at whatever it was as if even the hand didn't know yet what it was about to find. Then she thrust her hand inside the dress and brought the object out—the crust of the bread which the man had given her in the boulevard almost twelve hours ago, warm from her body and which by her expression she had completely forgotten, even the putting it there. Then she even forgot the bread again, clutching it to her mouth in one thin voracious fist, tearing at it with quick darting birdlike snatches as she once more watched the gate which those entering now approached with creeping and painful slowness. Because these were the dregs, the residue—the very old and the very young, belated not because they had had farther to come but because some of them had been so long in life as long ago to have outlived the kin and friends who would have owned carts to lend or share with them, and the others had been too brief in it yet to have friends capable of owning carts and who had already been orphaned of kin by the regiment at Bethune and Souchez and the Chemin des Dames three years ago—all creeping cityward now at the pace of the smallest and weakest.

When she began suddenly to run, she was still chewing the bread, still chewing when she darted under the old twilit arch, running around an old woman and a child who were entering it without breaking stride but merely changing feet like a running horse at a jump, flinging the crust behind her, spurning it with her palm against the hollow purchaseless air as she ran toward a group of people coming up the now almost empty road—an old man and three women, one of them carrying a child. The woman carrying the child saw her and stopped. The second woman stopped too, though the others—an old man on a single crutch and carrying a small cloth-knotted bundle and leaning on the arm of an old woman who appeared to be blind—were still walking on when the young woman ran past them and up to the woman carrying the child and stopped facing her, her wan face urgent and antic again.

'Marthe!' she said. 'Marthe!'

The woman answered, something rapid and immediate, not in French but in a staccato tongue full of harsh rapid consonants, which went with her face—a dark high calm ugly direct competent peasant's face out of the ancient mountainous Central-European cradle, which, though a moment later she spoke in French and with no accent, was no kin whatever to the face of the child she carried, with its blue eyes and florid colouring filtered westward from Flanders. She spoke French at once, as if, having looked at the girl, she realised that, whether or not the girl had ever once understood the other tongue, she was past comprehending or remembering it now. Now the blind woman leading the crippled old man had stopped and turned and was coming back; and now you would have noticed for the first time the face of the second woman, the one who had stopped when the one carrying the child did. It was almost identical with the other's; they were indubitably sisters. At first glance, the second face was the older of the two. Then you saw that it was much younger. Then you realised that it had no age at all; it had all ages or none; it was the peaceful face of the witless.

'Hush now,' the woman carrying the child said. 'They won't shoot him without the others.' Then the blind woman dragged the old man up. She faced them all, but none in particular, motionless while she listened for the sound of the girl's breathing until she located it and turned quickly toward the girl her fierce cataracted stare.

'Have they got him?' she said.

'As we all know,' the woman with the child said quickly. She started to move again. 'Let's get on.'

But the blind woman didn't move, square and sightless in the road, blocking it, still facing the girl. 'You,' she said. 'I don't mean the fools who listened to him and who deserve to die for it. I mean that foreigner, that anarchist who murdered them. Have they got him? Answer me.'

'He's there too,' the woman carrying the child said, moving again. 'Come on.'

But still the blind woman didn't move, except to turn her face toward the woman with the child when she spoke. 'That's not what I asked,' she said.

'You heard me say they will shoot him too,' the woman carrying the child said. She moved again, as though to touch the blind woman with her hand and turn her. But before the hand touched her, the woman who could not even see had jerked her own up and struck it down.

'Let her answer me.' she said. She faced the girl again. 'They haven't shot him yet? Where's your tongue? You were full enough of something to say when you came up.' But the girl just stared at her.

'Answer her,' the woman carrying the child said.

'No,' the girl whispered.

'So,' the blind woman said. She had nothing to blink for or from, yet there was nothing else to call it but blinking. Then her face began to turn rapidly between the girl's and the woman's carrying the child. Even before she spoke, the girl seemed to shrink, staring at the blind woman in terrified anticipation. Now the blind woman's voice was silken, smooth. 'You too have kin in the regiment, eh? Husband—brother—a sweetheart?'

'Yes,' the woman carrying the child said.

'Which one of you?' the blind woman said.

'All three of us,' the woman carrying the child said. 'A brother.'

'A sweetheart too, maybe?' the blind woman said. 'Come, now.'

'Yes,' the woman carrying the child said.

'So, then,' the blind woman said. She jerked her face back to the girl. 'You,' she said. 'You may pretend you're from this district, but you don't fool me. You talk wrong. And you—' she jerked back to face the woman carrying the child again '—you're not even French. I knew that the minute the two of you came up from nowhere back yonder, talking about having given your cart to a pregnant woman. Maybe you can fool them that don't have anything but eyes, and nothing to do but believe everything they look at. But not me.'

'Angélique,' the old man said in a thin quavering disused voice. The blind woman paid no attention to him. She faced the two women. Or the three women, the third one too: the older sister who had not spoken yet, whom anyone looking at her would never know whether she was going to speak or not, and even when she did speak it would be in no language of the used and familiar passions: suspicion or scorn or fear or rage; who had not even greeted the girl who had called the sister by a Christian name, who had stopped simply because the sister had stopped and apparently was simply waiting with peaceful and infinite patience for the sister to move again, watching each speaker in turn with serene inattention.

'So the anarchist who is murdering Frenchmen is your brother,' the blind woman said. Still facing the woman carrying the child, she jerked her head sideways toward the girl. 'What does she claim him as—a brother too, or maybe an uncle?'

'She is his wife,' the woman carrying the child said.

'His whore, maybe you mean,' the blind woman said. 'Maybe I'm looking at two more of them, even if both of you are old enough to be his grandmothers. Give me the child.' Again she moved as unerring as light toward the faint sound of the child's breathing and before the other could move snatched the child down from her shoulder and swung it on to her own. 'Murderers,' she said.

'Angélique,' the old man said.

'Pick it up,' the blind woman snapped at him. It was the cloth-knotted bundle; only the blind woman, who was still facing the three other women, not even the old man himself, knew that he had dropped it. He stooped for it, letting himself carefully and with excruciating slowness hand under hand down the crutch and picked it up and climbed the crutch hand over hand again. As soon as he was up her hand went out with that sightless unerring aim and grasped his arm, jerking him after her as she moved, the child riding high on her other shoulder and staring silently back at the woman who had been carrying it; she was not only holding the old man up, she was actually leading the way. They went on to the old arch and passed beneath it. The last of sunset was gone even from the plain now.

'Marthe,' the girl said to the woman who had carried the child. Now the other sister spoke, for the first time. She was carrying a bundle too—a small basket neatly covered with an immaculate cloth tucked neatly down.

'That's because he's different,' she said with peaceful triumph. 'Even people in the towns can see it.'

'Marthe!' the girl said again. This time she grasped the other's arm and began to jerk at it. 'That's what they're all saying! They're going to kill him!'

'That's why,' the second sister said with that serene and happy triumph.

'Come on,' Marthe said, moving. But the girl still clung to her arm.

'I'm afraid,' she said. 'I'm afraid.'

'We can't do anything just standing here and being afraid,' Marthe said. 'We're all one now. It is the same death, no matter who calls the tune or plays it or pays the fiddler. Come, now. We're still in time, if we just go on.' They went on toward the old dusk-filling archway, and entered it. The sound of the crowd had ceased now. It would begin again presently though, when, having eaten, the city would hurry once more back to the *Place de Ville*. But now what sound it was making was earthy, homely, inturned and appeased, no longer the sound of thinking and hope and dread, but of the peaceful diurnal sublimation of viscera; the very air was coloured not so much by twilight as by the smoke of cooking drifting from windows and doorways and chimneys and from braziers and naked fires burning on the cobbles themselves where even the warrens had overflowed, gleaming rosily on the spitted hunks of horses and the pots and on the faces of the men and children squatting about them and the women bending over them with spoons or forks.

That is, until a moment ago. Because when the two women and the girl entered the gate, the street as far as they could see it lay arrested and immobilised under a deathlike silence, rumour having moved almost as fast as anguish did, though they never saw the blind woman and the old man again. They saw only the back-turned squatting faces about the nearest fire and the face of the woman turned too in the act of stooping or rising, one hand holding the fork or spoon suspended over the pot, and beyond them faces at the next fire turning to look, and beyond them people around the third fire beginning to stand up to see, so that even Marthe had already stopped for a second when the girl grasped her arm again.

'No, Marthe!' she said. 'No!'

'Nonsense,' Marthe said. 'Haven't I told you we are all one now?' She freed her arm, not roughly, and went on. She walked steadily into the firelight, into the thin hot reek of the meat, the squatting expressionless faces turning like the heads of owls to follow her, and stopped facing across the closed circle the woman with the spoon. 'God be with all here this night and tomorrow,' she said.

'So here you are,' the woman said. 'The murderer's whores.'

'His sisters,' Marthe said. 'This girl is his wife.'

'We heard that too,' the woman said. The group at the next fire had left it now, and the one beyond it. But of the three strangers only the girl seemed aware that the whole street was crowding quietly up, growing denser and denser, not staring at them yet, the faces even lowered or turned a little aside and only the gaunt children staring, not at the three strangers but at the covered basket which the sister carried. Marthe had not once even glanced at any of them.

'We have food,' she said. 'We'll share with you for a share in your fire.' Without turning her head she said something in the mountain tongue, reaching her hand back as the sister put the handle of the basket into it. She extended the basket toward the woman with the spoon. 'Here,' she said.

'Hand me the basket,' the woman said. A man in the squatting circle took the basket from Marthe and passed it to her. Without haste the woman put the spoon back into the pot, pausing to give the contents a single circular stir, turning her head to sniff at the rising steam, then in one motion she released the spoon and turned and took the basket from the man and swung her arm back and flung the basket at Marthe's head. It spun once, the cloth still neatly tucked. It struck Marthe high on the shoulder and caromed on, revolving again and emptying itself (it was food) just before it struck the other sister in the chest. She caught it. That is, although none had seen her move, she now held the empty basket easily against her breast with one hand while she watched the woman who threw it, interested and serene.

'You're not hungry,' she said.

'Did that look like we want your food?' the woman said.

'That's what I said,' the sister said. 'Now you don't have to grieve.' Then the woman snatched the spoon from the pot and threw it at the sister. But it missed. That is, as the woman stooped and scrabbled for the next missile (it was a wine bottle half full of vinegar) she realised that the spoon had struck nothing, that none of the three strangers had even ducked, as though the spoon had vanished into thin air as it left her hand. And when she threw the bottle she couldn't see the three women at all. It struck a man in the back and caromed vanishing as the whole crowd surged, baying the three strangers in a little ring of space like hounds holding fixed but still immune some animal not feared but which had completely confounded them by violating all the rules of chase and flight, so that, as hounds fall still and for a moment even cease to whimper, the crowd even stopped yelling and merely held the three women in a ring of gaped suspended uproar until the woman who threw the spoon broke through, carrying a tin mug and two *briquettes* and flung them without aim, the crowd baying and surging again as Marthe turned, half carrying the girl in one arm and pushing the sister on ahead with the other hand, walking steadily, the crowd falling away in front and closing behind so that the flexing intact ring itself seemed to advance as they did like a miniature whirlpool in a current; then the woman, screaming now, darted and stooped to a scatter of horse-droppings among the cobbles and began to hurl the dried globules which might have been *briquettes* too but for hue and durability. Marthe stopped and turned, the girl half hanging from the crook of her arm, the sister's ageless interested face watching from behind her shoulder, while refuse of all sorts—scraps of food, rubbish, sticks, cobbles from the street itself—rained about them. A thread of blood appeared suddenly at the corner of her mouth but she didn't move, until after a time her immobility seemed to stay the missiles too and the gaped crowding faces merely bayed at them again, the sound filling the alley and roaring from wall to wall until the reverberations had a quality not only frantic but cachinnant, recoiling and compounding as it gathered strength, rolling on alley by alley and street to street until it must have been beating along the boulevards' respectable fringes too.

The patrol—it was a mounted provost marshal's party—met them at the first corner. The crowd broke, burst, because this was a charge. The yelling rose a whole octave without transition like flipping over a playing card, as motionless again the three women watched the crowd stream back upon them; they stood in a rushing vacuum while the mass divided and swept past on either hand, in front of and beneath and behind the running horses, the cobble-clashing fire-ringing hooves and the screams dying away into the single vast murmur of the whole city's tumult, leaving the alley empty save for the three women when the N.C.O. leader of the patrol reined his horse and held it, short-bitted, ammoniac and reek-spreading and bouncing a little against the snaffle, while he glared down at them. 'Where do you live?' he said. They didn't answer, staring up at him—the wan girl, the tall calm woman, the quicking and serene approval of the sister. The N.C.O. listened for an instant to the distant tumult. Then he looked at them again. 'All right,' he said harshly. 'Get out of town while you can. Come on now. Get started.'

'We belong here too,' Marthe said. For a second he glared down at them, he and the horse in high sharp fading silhouette against the sky itself filled with anguish and fury.

'Is the whole damned world crowding here to crucify a bastard the army's going to fix anyway?' he said in thin furious exasperation.

'Yes,' Marthe said. Then he was gone. He slacked the horse; its iron feet clashed and sparked on the cobbles; the hot reek

sucked after it, pungent for a fading instant; then even the gallop-
ing had faded into the sound of the city. 'Come,' Marthe said.
They went on. At first she seemed to be leading them away from
the sound. But presently she seemed to be leading them straight
back to it. She turned into an alley, then into another not smaller
but emptier, deserted, with an air about it of back premises. But
she seemed to know where she was going or at least what she was
looking for. She was almost carrying the girl now until the sister
moved up unbidden and exchanged the empty basket to the other
arm and took half the girl's weight and then they went quite
rapidly, on to the end of the alley and turned the wall and there
was what Marthe had gone as directly to as if she had not only
known it was there but had been to it before—an empty stone
stall, a byre or stable niched into the city's night-fading flank.
There was even a thin litter of dry straw on the stone floor and
once inside although the sound was still audible it was as though
they had established armistice with the tumult and the fury, not
that it should evacuate the city in their favour but at least it should
approach no nearer. Marthe didn't speak; she just stood supporting the girl while the sister set down the empty basket and knelt
and with quick deft darting motions like a little girl readying a
doll's house she spread the straw evenly and then removed her
shawl and spread it over the straw and still kneeling helped
Marthe lower the girl on to the shawl and took the other shawl
which Marthe removed from her shoulders and spread it over the
girl. Then they lowered themselves on to the straw on either side
of the girl and as Marthe drew the girl to her for warmth the
sister reached and got the basket, and not even triumphant, with
another of those clumsy darting childlike motions which at the
same time were deft or at least efficient or anyway successful, she
took from the basket which everyone had seen empty itself when
the woman at the fire threw it at her, a piece of broken bread a
little larger than two fists. Again Marthe said nothing. She just
took the bread from the sister and started to break it.

'In three,' the sister said and took the third fragment when
Marthe broke it and put it back into the basket and they reclined
again, the girl between them, eating. It was almost dark now.
What little light remained seemed to have gathered about the
door's worn lintel with a tender nebulous quality like a worn lost

halo, the world outside but little lighter than the stone interior—the chill sweating stone which seemed not to conduct nor even contain but to exude like its own moisture the murmur of the unwearying city—a sound no longer auricularly but merely intellectually disturbing, like the breathing of a sick puppy or a sick child. But when the other sound began they stopped chewing. They stopped at the same instant; when they sat up it was together as though a spreader bar connected them, sitting each with a fragment of bread in one poised hand, listening. It was beneath the first sound, beyond it, human too but not the same sound at all because the old one had women in it—the mass voice of the ancient limitless mammalian capacity not for suffering but for grieving, wailing, to endure incredible anguish because it could become vocal without shame or self-consciousness, passing from gland to tongue without transition through thought—while the new one was made by men and though they didn't know where the prisoners' compound was nor even (nobody had taken time to tell them yet) that the regiment was in a compound anywhere, they knew at once what it was. 'Hear them?' the sister said, serene, in astonished and happy approval, so rapt that Marthe's movement caused her to look up only after the other had risen and was already stooping to rouse the girl; whereupon the sister reached again with that deft unthinking immediate clumsiness and took the fragment of bread from Marthe and put it and her own fragment back into the basket with the third one and rose to her knees and began to help raise the girl, speaking in a tone of happy anticipation. 'Where are we going now?' she said.

'To the Mayor,' Marthe said. 'Get the basket.' She did so; she had to gather up both the shawls too, which delayed her a little, so that when she was on her feet Marthe, supporting the girl, had already reached the door. But even for a moment yet the sister didn't follow, standing clutching the shawls and the basket, her face lifted slightly in rapt and pleased astonishment in the murmurous last of light which seemed to have brought into the damp stone cubicle not merely the city's simple anguish and fury but the city itself in all its impervious splendour. Even inside the stone single-stalled stable it seemed to rise in glittering miniature, tower and spire tall enough and high enough to soar in sunlight still though dark had fallen, high enough and tall enough above earth's old miasmic mists for the glittering and splendid pinnacles never to be in darkness at all perhaps, invincible, everlasting, and vast.

'He will wear a fine sword here,' she said.

Shortly before sunset the last strand of wire enclosing the new compound had been run and joined and the electric current turned into it. Then the whole regiment, with the exception of the thirteen special prisoners who were in a separate cell to themselves, were turned out of the barracks. They were not released, they were evicted, not by simultaneous squads of guards nor even by one single roving detachment moving rapidly, alert compact and heavily armed, from barracks to barracks, but by individual Senegalese. Armed sometimes with a bayoneted rifle and sometimes merely with the naked bayonet carried like a brush knife or a swagger stick and sometimes with nothing at all, they appeared abruptly and without warning in each room and drove its occupants out, hustling them with scornful and contemptuous expedition toward the door, not even waiting to follow but going along with them, each one already well up into the middle of the group before it even reached the door and still pressing on toward the head of it, prodding each his own moving path with the reversed rifle of the bayonet's handle and, even within the ruck, moving faster than it moved, riding head and shoulders not merely above the moving mass but as though on it, gaudy ethiope and contemptuous, resembling harlequined trees uprooted, say, from the wild lands, the tameless antipodal fields, moving rigid and upright above the dull sluggish current of a city-soiled commercial canal. So the Senegalese would actually be leading each group when it emerged into its company street. Nor would they even stop them, not even waiting to pair off in couples, let alone in squads, but seeming to stride once or twice, still carrying the bayoneted rifles or the bayonets like the spears and knives of a lion or antelope hunt, and vanish as individual and abrupt as they had appeared.

So when the regiment, unarmed unshaven hatless and half-dressed, began to coalesce without command into the old sheep-like molds of platoons and companies, it found that nobody was paying any attention to it at all, that it had been deserted even by the bayonets which had evicted it out of doors. But for a while

yet it continued to shuffle and grope for the old familiar align-
ments, blinking a little after the dark barracks, in the glare of
sunset. Then it began to move. There were no commands from
anywhere; the squads and sections simply fell in between the old
file-markers and -closers and began to flow, drift as though by
some gentle and even unheeded gravitation, into companies in the
barracks streets, into battalions on to the parade ground, and
stopped. It was not a regiment yet but rather a shapeless mass in
which only the squads and platoons had any unity, as the coher-
ence of an evicted city obtains only in the household groups which
stick together not because the members are kin in blood but
because they have eaten together and slept together and grieved
and hoped and fought among themselves so long, huddling immobile and blinking beneath the high unclimbable wire and the
searchlights and machine-gun platforms and the lounging scornful
guards, all in silhouette on the sunset as if the lethal shock which
charged the wire ten minutes ago had at the same instant electrocuted them all into inflexible arrestment against the end of time.

They were still huddled there when the new tumult began in
the city. The sun had set, the bugles had rung and ceased, the gun
had crashed from the old citadel and clapped and reverberated
away, and the huddled regiment was already fading into one
neutral mass in the middle of the parade ground when the first faint
yelling came across the plain. But they did nothing at first, except
to become more still, as dogs do at the rising note of a siren about
to reach some unbearable pitch which the human ear will not hear
at all. In fact, when they did begin to make the sound, it was not
human at all but animal, not yelling but howling, huddling still
in the dusk that fading and shapeless mass which might have been
Protoplasm itself, eyeless and tongueless on the floor of the first
dividing of the sea, palpant and vociferant with no motion nor
sound of its own but instead to some gigantic uproar of the primal
air-crashing tides' mighty copulation, while overhead on the catwalks and platforms the Senegalese lounged on their rifles or held
to cigarettes the small windless flames of lighters contrived of
spent cartridge cases, as if the glare of day had hidden until now
that which the dusk exposed: that the electric shock which had
fixed them in carbon immobility had left here and there one random not-yet-faded coal.

The dusk seemed to have revealed to them the lighted window too. It was in the old once-ivied wall of what had been the factory's main building; they might even have seen the man standing in it, though probably the window alone was enough. Not yelling but howling, they began to flow across the compound. But the night moved still faster; the mass of them had already faded completely into it before they had crossed the parade ground, so that it was the sound, the howling, which seemed to roll on and crash and recoil and roar again against the wall beneath the lighted window and the motionless silhouette of the man standing in it, and recoiled and roared again while a hurried bugle began to blat and whistles to shrill and a close body of white infantry came rapidly around the corner and began to push them away from the wall with short jabbing blows of rifle butts.

When the guard came for them, the corporal was still standing at the window, looking down at the uproar. The thirteen of them were in a small perfectly bare perfectly impregnable single-windowed cell which obviously had been a strong room of some sort back in the old dead time when the factory had been merely a factory. A single dingy electric bulb burned in the centre of the ceiling behind a wire cage like the end of a rat-trap. It had been burning when they were herded into the room shortly after dawn this morning, and, since it was American electricity, or that is, was already being charged daily one day in advance to the Service of Supply of the American Expeditionary Force, it had been burning ever since. So as the day succumbed to evening, the faces of the thirteen men sitting quietly on the floor against one wall did not fade wanly back into the shadows but rather instead emerged, not even wan but, unshaven and therefore even more virile, gathering to themselves an even further ghastly and jaundiced strength.

When the first stir of movement went through the compound as the Senegalese began to evict the regiment from the barracks, the thirteen men sitting against the wall of the cell did not appear to respond to it, unless there might have been a further completer stillness and arrestment travelling as though from one to another among twelve of them—the half-turn of a face, the quick almost infinitesimal side-glancing of an eye toward the thirteenth one, the corporal, sitting in the centre of them, who—the corporal—did not move at all until the first roar of yelling rolled across the parade ground and crashed like a wave against the wall beneath the window. Then the corporal rose to his feet, not quietly nor deliberately so much as easily, as mountain men move, and went to the window and, his hands lying as lightly and easily among the bars as they had lain on the lorry's top rail, stood looking down at the yelling. He didn't seem to be listening to it: just looking at it, watching it pour across the compound to break in one inaudible crash beneath the window, in the wan glow from which the men themselves were now visible—the clenched fists, the pale individual faces which, even gaped with yelling he may have recognised, having spent four years crouched with them behind bullet-snicked parapets or trying bitten-tongued to flatten themselves into the stinking muck of shell craters beneath drum fire or rolling barrages or flattened immobile and unbreathing beneath the hiss and whisper of flares on night patrols. He seemed not to listen to it but to watch it, immobile and detached, while the frantic bugle yelped and the whistles shrilled and the infantry section burst on its collapsing flank and whirled it slowly away. He didn't move. He looked exactly like a stone-deaf man watching with interest but neither surprise nor alarm the pantomime of some cataclysm or even universal uproar which neither threatens nor even concerns him since to him it makes no sound at all.

Then heavy boots tramped and clashed in the corridor. The corporal turned from the window and this time the other twelve faces moved too, lifting as one and pacing along the wall the tramp of the invisible feet beyond it until the feet halted, so that they were all looking at the door when it opened and was flung back and a sergeant (they were not Senegalese nor even white infantry this time, but provost marshal's people) stood in it and made a sweeping peremptory gesture with his arm. 'On your feet,' he said.

Still preceding the chief-of-staff, and pausing only long enough for the aide to open the door and get out of the way, the division commander entered the room. It was less large than a modern concert hall. In fact, it had been merely a boudoir back in the time of its dead duchess or marquise, and it still bore the imprint of that princely insensate (and, perhaps one of the duchesses or marquises had thought, impregnable) opulence in its valanced alcoves and pilastered medallioned ceiling and crystal chandeliers and sconces and mirrors and girandoles and buhl étagères and glazed cabinets of faience bibelots, and a white rug into which war-bleached boots sank ankle-deep as into the muck of trenches, say in the cold face of the moon, flooring bland and soft as cloud, that majestic vista at the end of which the three old generals sat.

Backed by a hovering frieze of aides and staff, they sat behind a tremendous oblong table as bare and flat and richly austere as the top of a knight's or a bishop's sacrophagus, all three in the spectacles of old men and each with a thick identical sheaf of clipped papers before him, so that the whole group in their dust- or horizon-coloured clothing and brass-and-scarlet-and-leather harness had a look paradoxical and bizarre, both scholarly and outlandish, like a pack of tameless forest beasts dressed in the regalia and set in the environment of civilised office and waiting in decorous and almost somnolent unhaste while the three old leaders sat for a specified time over the meaningless papers which were a part of the regalia too, until the moment came not to judge nor even condemn but just to fling away the impeding papers and garments and execute.

The windows were open, curtain and casement, so that there came into the room not only the afternoon light and air, but something of the city's tumult too—not sound, because the voices, even the sudden uproar of them which the division commander and the chief-of-staff had just left outside in the *Place de Ville*, didn't reach here. It was rather a sense, a quality as of the light itself, a reflection as of light itself from the massed faces below, refracted upward into the room through the open windows like light from disturbed water, pulsing and quivering faintly and constantly on the ceiling where nobody, not even the clerks and secretaries coming and going steadily on their endless minuscule errands, would notice it without they chanced to look up, unless like now, when something had caused the pulse to beat a little faster, so that when the division commander and the chief-of-staff entered, everyone in the room was looking at the door. Though almost as soon as they entered, that too died away and the refraction merely quivered again.

The division commander had never seen the room before. He did not look at it now. He just entered and paused for a rigid infinitesimal instant until the chief-of-staff came abreast on his right, the sabre between them now under the chief-of-staff's left arm. Then almost in step they trod the rug's blanched vista to the table and halted rigidly together while the chief-of-staff saluted and took from under his arm the dead sabre furled loosely in the dangling buckle-ends of its harness like a badly rolled umbrella, and laid it on the table. And staring rigidly at nothing while the chief-of-staff verbally performed the formal rite of his relinquishment, the division commander thought: *It's true. He knew me at once,* thinking, No: worse: that the old man had already known him long before anyone announced the two of them from an anteroom; that apparently he had come all the long way from that instant in the observation post two mornings back where his career died, merely to prove what all who knew the old marshal's name believed: that the old man remembered the name and face of every man in uniform whom he had ever seen—not only those out of the old regiment into which he had been commissioned from St. Cyr, and the ranking commanders of his armies and corps whom he saw daily, but their staffs and secretaries and clerks, and the commanders of divisions and brigades and their staffs, and regimental and battalion and company officers and their orderlies and batmen and runners, and the privates whom he had decorated or reprimanded or condemned, and the N.C.O. leaders and degreeless file-closers of sections and platoons and squads whose inspection-opened ranks he had merely walked rapidly through once thirty and forty years ago, calling them all 'my child' just as he did his own handsome young personal aide and his ancient batman and his chauffeur: a six-and-a-half-foot Basque with the face of a murderer of female children. He (the division commander) had seen no movement; his recollection on entering was that the old marshal had been holding the sheaf of papers open in his hand. Yet it was not only closed now, it was pushed slightly aside and the old marshal had removed the spectacles, holding them lightly in a mottled old man's hand almost completely hidden inside the round tremendous orifice of an immaculately laundered cuff detachable from an old-fashioned starched white civilian shirt, and looking for just a second into the spectacleless eyes, the division commander remembered something Lallemont had said once: *If I were evil, I would hate and fear him. If I were a saint, I would weep. If I were wise, and both or either, I would despair.*

207

A FABLE

'Yes, General Gragnon?' the old general said.

Staring again not at anything but at simple eye-level above the old general's head, the division commander repeated orally the report which he had already recognised as soon as he entered the room—the verbatim typescripts signed by himself and endorsed by the corps commander, lying now in mimeographed triplicate before the three generals, and finished and stopped for a moment as the lecturer pauses to turn a page or sip from the glass of water, then repeated for the fourth time his official request for the regiment's execution; inflexible and composed before the table on which lay the triumvirate markers of his career's sepulture, the triplicate monument of what the group commander had called his glory, he discharged for the fourth time the regiment from the rolls of his division as though it had vanished two mornings ago in the face of a machine-gun battery or a single mine explosion. He hadn't changed it. It had been right thirty-six hours ago when his honour and integrity as its (or any regiment's) division commander compelled him to anticipate having to make it; it was still right the second after when he discovered that the quality in him which had given him the chance to become commander of a division, in exchange for the dedication of his honour and life, was compelling him to deliver it. So it was still right now for the very reason that it was the same honour and integrity which the beneficence had found worthy to be conferred with the three stars of his major general's rank, rather than the beneficence itself, which was making the demand, the compulsion.

Because the beneficence itself didn't need the gesture. As the group commander himself had practically told him this morning, what he was saying now had no connection at all beyond mere coincidence with what lay on the table. The speech was much older than that moment two days ago in the observation post when he discovered that he was going to have to make it. Its conception was the moment he found he was to be posted to officers' school, its birth the day he received the commission, so that it had become, along with the pistol and sabre and the sublieutenant's badges, a part of the equipment with which he would follow and serve his destiny with his life as long as life lasted; its analogous coeval was that one of the live cartridges constant through the pistol's revolving cylinder, against the moment when he would discharge the

voluntary lien he had given on his honour by expiating what a
civilian would call bad luck and only a soldier disgrace, the bad
luck in it being merely this moment now, when the need compelled the speech yet at the same time denied the bullet. In fact,
it seemed to him now that the two of them, speech and bullet,
were analogous and coeval even in more than birth: analogous in
the very incongruity of the origins from which they moved, not
even shaped yet, toward their mutual end—a lump of dross
exhumed from the earth and become, under heat, brass, and under
fierce and cunning pressure, a cartridge case; from a laboratory, a
pinch, a spoonful, a dust, precipitate of earth's and air's primordial
motion, the two condensed and combined behind a tiny locked
grooved slug and all micrometered to a servant breech and bore
not even within its cognizance yet, like a footman engaged from an
employment agency over the telephone—half Europe went to war
with the other half and finally succeeded in dragging half the
Western Hemisphere along: a plan, a design vast in scope, exalted
in conception, in implication (and hope) terrifying, not even conceived here at Grand Headquarters by the three old generals and
their trained experts and advisers in orderly conference, but conceived out of the mutual rage and fear of the three ocean-dividing
nations themselves, simultaneously at Washington and London
and Paris by some immaculate pollenization like earth's simultaneous leafage, and come to birth at a council not even held at
Grand Headquarters but behind locked and guarded doors in the
Quai d'Orsay—a council where trained military experts dedicated
as irrevocably to war as nuns are married to God, were outnumbered by those who were not only not trained for war, they
were not even braided and panoplied for it—the Prime Ministers
and Premiers and Secretaries, the cabinet members and senators
and chancellors; and those who outnumbered even them: the
board chairmen of the vast establishments which produced the
munitions and shoes and tinned foods, and the modest unsung
omnipotent ones who were the priests of simple money; and the
others still who outnumbered even these: the politicians, the lobby-
ists, the owners and publishers of newspapers and the ordained
ministers of churches, and all the other accredited travelling representatives of the vast solvent organisations and fraternities and
movements which control by coercion or cajolery man's morals

o

and actions and all his mass-value for affirmation or negation—
all that vast powerful terror-inspiring representation which,
running all democracy's affairs in peace, comes indeed into its
own in war, finding its true apotheosis then, in iron conclave now
decreeing for half the earth a design vast in its intention to demolish
a frontier, and vaster still in its furious intent to obliterate a people;
all in conclave so single that the old grey inscrutable supreme
general with the face of one who long ago had won the right to
believe in nothing whatever save man's deathless folly didn't need
to vote at all but simply to preside, and so presiding, contemplated
the plan's birth and then watched it, not even needing to control
it as it took its ordained undeviable course, descending from
nations confederated to nations selected, to forces to army groups
to armies to corps; all that gigantic long complex chronicle, at the
end reduced to a simple regimental attack against a simple elevation of earth too small to show on a map, known only to its own
neighbourhood and even that by a number and a nickname dating
back less than four years to the moment when someone had realised
that you could see perhaps a quarter-mile farther from its summit
than its foot; an attack not allotted to a division but self-compelled
to it by its own geography and logistics because the alternatives
were either here or nowhere, this or nothing, and compelled to
his particular division for the reason that the attack was doomed
and intended as failure and his was the division among all with
which failure could be bought cheapest, as another might be the
division with which a river could be crossed or a village taken
cheapest; he realised now that it had not been necessary for anyone
to have foreseen the mutiny, because the mutiny itself didn't
matter: the failure alone would have been enough, and how and
why it failed, nobody cared, the mutiny flung in as lagniappe to
that end whose sole aim had been to bring him to attention here
before the table on which lay in its furled scabbard the corpse of
his career, to repeat for the fourth time the speech, who had been
denied the bullet, and finish it and stop.

'The whole regiment,' the old marshal said, repeating in his turn,
in a voice inscrutable and pleasant and so void of anything as to seem
almost warm, inattentive, almost impersonal. 'Not just this ringleader and his twelve disciples. By all means, the nine of them who
are Frenchmen, yet who still permitted themselves to be corrupted.'

'There was no ringleader,' the division commander said, harsh and rigid. 'The regiment mutinied.'

'The regiment mutinied,' the old marshal repeated again. 'And suppose we do. What of the other regiments in your division, when they learn of it?'

'Shoot them,' the division commander said.

'And the other divisions in your corps, and the other corps on either side of you.'

'Shoot them,' the division commander said, and stood again inflexible and composed while the old marshal turned and translated quietly and rapidly to the British general and the American on either side of him, then turned back and said to the chief-of-staff:

'Thank you, General.' The chief-of-staff saluted. But the division commander did not wait for him, already about-facing, leaving the chief-of-staff once more the split of a second late since he had to perform his own manoeuvre which even a crack drill-sergeant could not have done smoothly with no more warning than this, having in fact to take two long extra steps to get himself again on the division commander's right hand and failing—or almost—here too, so that it was the old marshal's personal aide who flanked the division commander, the chief-of-staff himself still half a pace behind, as they trod the white rug once more back to the now open door just outside which a provost marshal's officer correct with side-arms waited, though before they reached him, the division commander was even in front of the aide.

So the aide was flanking, not the division commander but the chief-of-staff, pacing him correctly on the left, back to the open door beyond which the provost officer waited while the division commander passed through it.

Whereupon the aide not only effaced from the room the entire significance of the surrendered sabre, he obliterated from it the whole gauche inference of war. As he stepped quickly and lightly and even a little swaggeringly toward the open door beyond which the division commander and the provost officer had vanished, it was as though, in declining in advance to hold the door for the division commander (even though the division commander had already declined the courtesy in advance by not waiting for it), he had not merely retaliated upon the junior general for the junior's affrontment to the senior general's precedence, he had used the junior as the instrument to postulate both himself and the chief-of-staff as being irrevocably alien and invincibly unconcerned with everything the room and those it contained represented—the very tall elegantly thin captain of twenty-eight or thirty with the face and body of a durable matinée idol, who might have been a creature from another planet, anachronistic and immune, inviolable, so invincibly homeless as to be completely and impregnably at home on this or any other planet where he might find himself: not even of tomorrow but of the day before it, projected by reverse avatar back into a world where what remained of lost and finished man struggled feebly for a moment yet among the jumbled ruins of his yesterdays—a creature who had survived intact the fact that he had no place, no business whatever, in war, who for all gain or loss to war's inexorable gambit or that of the frantic crumbling nations either, might as well have been floating gowned and capped (and with the golden tassel of a lordship too, since he looked more like a scion than any duke's son) across an Oxford or Cambridge quadrangle, compelling those watching him and the chief-of-staff to condone the deodorisation of war's effluvium even from the uniforms they wore, leaving them simply costumes, stepping rapidly and lightly and elegantly past the chief-of-staff to grasp the knob and shut the door until the latch caught, then turned the knob and opened the door and clicked not to attention but into a rigid brief inclination from the waist as the chief-of-staff passed through it.

Then he closed the door and turned and started back down the room, then in the same instant stopped again and now apparently essayed to efface from it even the rumour of war which had entered at second hand; motionless for that moment at the top of the splendid diminishing vista, there was about him like an aura a quality insouciant solitary and debonair like Harlequin *solus* on a second- or third-act stage as the curtain goes down or rises, while he stood with his head turned slightly aside, listening. Then he moved, rapid and boneless on his long boneless legs, toward the nearest window. But the old marshal spoke before he had taken the second step, saying quietly in English: 'Leave them open.'

The aide paid no attention whatever. He strode to the window and thurst his whole upper body out as he reached for the out-swung casement and began to swing it in. Then he stopped. He said in French, not loud, in a sort of rapt amazement, dispassion-ate and momentary: 'It looks like a crowd at a race track waiting for the two-sou window to open—if they have such. No, they look as if they are watching a burning pawnshop.'

'Leave it open,' the old general said in English. The aide paused again, the casement half closed. He turned his head and said in English too, perfectly, with no accent whatever, not even of Oxford, not even of Beacon Hill:

'Why not have them inside and be done with it? They can't hear what's going on out there.'

This time the old general spoke French. 'They don't want to know,' he said. 'They want only to suffer. Leave it open.'

'Yes sir,' the aide said in French. He flung the casement out again and turned. As he did so one leaf of the double doors in the opposite wall opened. It opened exactly six inches, by no visible means, and stopped. The aide didn't even glance toward it. He came on into the room, saying in that perfect accentless English, 'Dinner, gentlemen,' as both leaves of the door slid back.

The old general rose when the two other generals did but that was all. When the doors closed behind the last aide, he was already seated again. Then he pushed the closed folder further aside and folded the spectacles into their worn case and buttoned the case into one of his upper tunic pockets, and alone now in the vast splendid room from which even the city's tumult and anguish was fading as the afternoon light died from the ceiling, motionless in the chair whose high carven back topped him like the back of a throne, his hands hidden below the rich tremendous table which concealed most of the rest of him too and apparently not only immobile but immobilised beneath the mass and glitter of his braid and stars and buttons, he resembled a boy, a child, crouching amid the golden debris of the tomb not of a knight or bishop ravished in darkness but (perhaps the mummy itself) of a sultan or pharaoh violated by Christians in broad afternoon.

Then the same leaf of the double door opened again, exactly as before, for exactly six inches and no hand to show for it and making only the slightest of sounds, and even then giving the impression that if it had wanted to, it could have made none and that what it did make was only the absolute minimum to be audible at all, opening for that six inches and then moving no more until the old general said: 'Yes, my child.' Then it began to close, making no sound at all now that sound was no longer necessary, moving on half the distance back to closure with its fellow leaf when it stopped again and with no pause began to open again, still noiseless but quite fast now, so fast that it had opened a good eighteen inches and in another instant who or whatever moved it would of necessity reveal, expose him or itself, before the old general could or did speak. 'No,' he said. The door stopped. It didn't close; it just quit moving at all and seemed to hang like a wheel at balance with neither top nor bottom, hanging so until the old general spoke again: 'Leave them open.'

Then the door closed. It went all the way to this time, and the old general rose and came around the table and went to the nearest window, walking through the official end of day as across a threshold into night, because as he turned the end of the table the scattered bugles began to sound the three assemblies, and as he crossed the room the clash of boots and rifles came up from the courtyard, and when he reached the window the two guards were already facing each other for the first note of the three retreats and the formal exchange to begin. But the old general didn't seem to be watching it. He just stood in the window above the thronged motionless *Place* where the patient mass of people lay against the iron fence; nor did he turn his head when the door opened rapidly this time and the young aide entered, carrying a telephone whose extension flowed behind him across the white rug like the endless tail of a trophy, and went behind the table and with his boot drew up one of the chairs and sat down and set the telephone on the table and lifted the receiver and shot into view the watch on his other wrist and became motionless, the receiver to his ear and his eyes on the watch. Instead, he just stood there, a little back from the window and a little to one side, holding the curtain slightly aside, visible if anyone in the *Place* had thought to look up, while the scattered brazen adjurations died into the clash and stamp as the two guards came to *at ease* and the whole borderline, no longer afternoon yet not quite evening either, lay in unbreathing suspension until the bugles began again, the three this time in measured discordant unison, the three voices in the courtyard barking in unison too yet incorrigibly alien, the two groups of heavily armed men posturing rigidly at each other like a tribal ritual for religious immolation. He could not have heard the telephone, since the aide already had the receiver to his ear and merely spoke an acknowledging word into it, then listened a moment and spoke another word and lowered the receiver and sat waiting too while the bugles chanted and wailed like cocks in the raddled sunset, and died away.

'He has landed,' the aide said. 'He got down from the aeroplane and drew a pistol and called his pilot to attention and shot him through the face. They don't know why.'

'They are Englishmen,' the old general said. 'That will do.'

'Of course,' the aide said. 'I'm surprised they have as little trouble as they do in Continental wars. In any of their wars.' He said: 'Yes sir.' He rose to his feet. 'I had arranged to have this line open at five points between here and Villeneuve Blanche, so you could keep informed of his progress—'

'It is indistinguishable from his destination,' the old general said without moving. 'That will do.' The aide put the receiver back on its hook and took up the telephone and went back around the table, the limber endless line recoiling on to itself across the rug until he flicked the diminishing loop after him through the door, and closed it. At that moment the sunset gun thudded: no sound, but rather a postulation of vacuum, as though back into its blast-vacated womb the regurgitated martial day had poured in one reverberant clap; from just beyond the window came the screak and whisper of the three blocks and the three down-reeling lanyards and the same leaf of the door opened again for that exact six inches, paused, then without any sound opened steadily and unmotived onward and still the old general stood while the thrice-alien voices barked, and beneath the three tenderly borne mystical rags the feet of the three colour guards rang the cobbled courtyard and, in measured iron diminution, the cobbled evening itself.

And now the mass beyond the fence itself began to move, flowing back across the *Place* toward the diverging boulevards, emptying the *Place*, already fading before it was out of the *Place*, as though with one long quiet inhalation evening was effacing the whole meek mist of man; now the old general stood above the city which, already immune to man's enduring, was now even free of this tumult. Or rather, the evening effaced not man from the *Place de Ville* so much as it effaced the *Place de Ville* back into man's enduring anguish and his invincible dust, the city itself not really free of either but simply taller than both. Because they endured, as only endurance can, firmer than rock, more impervious than folly, longer than grief, the darkling and silent city rising out of the darkling and empty twilight to lower like a thunderclap, since it was the effigy and the power, rising tier on inviolate tier out of that mazed chiaroscuro like a tremendous beehive whose crown challenged by day the sun and stemmed aside by night the myriad smore of stars.

First and topmost were the three flags and the three supreme generals who served them: a triumvirate consecrated and anointed, a constellation remote as planets in their immutability, powerful as archbishops in their trinity, splendid as cardinals in their retinues and myriad as Brahmins in their blind followers; next were the three thousand lesser generals who were their deacons and priests and the hierarchate of their households, their acolytes and bearers of monstrance and host and censer: the colonels and majors who were in charge of the portfolios and maps and memoranda, the captains and subalterns who were in charge of the communications and errands which kept the portfolios and maps up to date, and the sergeants and corporals who actually carried the portfolios and mapcases and protected them with their lives and answered the telephone and ran the errands, and the privates who sat at the flickering switchboards at two and three and four o'clock in the morning and rode the motorcycles in the rain and snow and drove the starred and pennoned cars and cooked the food for the generals and colonels and majors and captains and subalterns and made their beds and shaved them and cut their hair and polished their boots and brass; and inferior and nethermost even in that braided inviolate hierarchate: so crowded was the city with generals of high rank and their splendid and shining staffs that not only were subalterns and captains and even majors and colonels nothing, distinguishable from civilians only because they wore uniforms, there was even a nadir among these: men who had actually been in, come out of, the battle zone, as high in rank as majors and even colonels sometime, strayed into the glittering and gunless city through nobody knew what bizarre convulsion of that military metabolism which does everything to a man but lose him, which learns nothing and forgets nothing and loses nothing at all whatever and forever—no scrap of paper, no unfinished record or uncompleted memorandum no matter how inconsequential or trivial; a few of them were always there, not many but enough: platoon or section leaders and company commanders and battalion seconds stained with the filth of front lines who amid that thronged pomp and glitter of stars and crossed batons and braid and brass and scarlet tabs moved diffident and bewildered and ignored with the lost air of oafish peasants smelling of field and stable summoned to the castle, the Great House, for an accounting or a punishment: a wounded man armless, legless or eyeless, was stared at with the same aghast distasteful revoltive pity and shock and outrage as a man in an epileptic seizure at high noon on a busy downtown corner; then the civilians: Antipas his friends and their friends, merchant and prince and bishop, administrator clacquer and absolver to ministrate the attempt and applaud the intention and absolve the failed result, and all the nephews and godsons of Tiberius in far Rome and their friends and the friends of the wives and the husbands of their friends come to dine with the generals and sell to the generals' governments the shells and guns and aircraft and beef and shoes for the generals to expend against the enemy, and their secretaries and couriers and chauffeurs who had got military deferment because the briefcases had to be carried and the motorcars driven, and those who actually dwelled as *paterfamiliae* among the city's boulevards and avenues and even less base streets already before the city entered its four-year apotheosis and while apotheosis obtained and would still (so they hoped) after apotheosis had ceased and been forgotten—mayor and burgher, doctor attorney director inspector and judge who held no particular letter from Tiberius in Rome yet whose contacts were still among generals and colonels and not captains and subalterns even if they were restricted to drawing rooms and dining tables, publican and smith and baker and grocer and wright whose contacts were not with captains nor subalterns nor with sergeants and corporals and privates neither since it was their wives who knitted behind the zinc bars and weighed and exchanged sous for the bread and greens and beat the underwear on the river's margin stones; and the women who were not the wives of directors or bakers, who traded not in war but because of war and who as in a sense two thousand nine hundred and ninety-seven of the generals were just one general were all one woman too whether staff colonels stood when they entered rooms or whether they lived on the same floor in modest *pensions* with Service Corps captains or boiled the soup of communications corporals or, troops themselves, received their partners in what is called love and perhaps even is from a sergeant's roll-call as a soldier receives his iron ration or boots and no need for that partner to put back on his tunic or greatcoat before going on into the lines because the sergeant who checked him into and out of that love which perhaps had never let him take either off, so that as often as not she carried into sleep with her that night a dead man's still warm and living seed; and then and last even anonymity's absolute whose nameless faceless mass cluttered old Jerusalem and old Rome too while from time to time governor and caesar flung them bread or a circus as in the old snowy pantomime the fleeing shepherd casts back to the pursuing wolves fragments of his lunch, a garment, and as a last resort the lamb itself—the labourers who owned today only the spending of what they earned yesterday, the beggars and thieves who did not always understand that what they did was beggary and theft, the lepers beneath city gate and temple door who did not even know they were not whole, who belonged neither to the military nor to the merchants and princes and bishops, who neither derived nor hoped for any benefit from army contracts nor battened by simple existing, breathing coeval with the prodigality and waste concomitant with a nation's mortal agony, that strange and constant few who each time are denied any opportunity whatever to share in the rich carnival of their country's wasting life-blood, whose luck is out always with no kin nor friends who have kin or friends who have powerful kin or friends or patrons, who owned nothing in fact save a reversion in endurance without hope of betterment nor any spur of pride—a capacity for endurance which even after four years of existence as tolerated and rightless aliens on their own land and in their own city still enabled them without hope or pride even in the endurance to endure, asking or expecting no more than permission to exercise it, like a sort of immortality. Out of that enduring and anguished dust it rose, out of the dark Gothic dream, carrying the Gothic dream, arch- and buttress-winged, by knight and bishop, angels and saints and cherubim groined and pilastered upward into soaring spire and pinnacle where goblin and demon, gryphon and gargoyle and hermaphrodite yelped in icy soundless stone against the fading zenith. The old general dropped the curtain and began to turn from the window.

'You may close—' he said. Then he stopped. It was as though he didn't anticipate the sound so much as he simply foreknew it, already motionless when the sound came into the window—an uproar thin and distant across the city, not diffuse now but local-ised and still curiously localised by source even when it began to move as if it were directed at some small specific object no larger than a man and it was not the yelling which moved but the object of it retreating slowly before the yelling—not turning back to the window but simply arrested beside it. Hooves clattered suddenly in the *Place* and a body of cavalry crossed it at trot and entered the boulevard leading toward the old eastern gate, already at canter and went on. Then for a time the sound of the hooves seemed to have dissolved into, been smothered by, the yelling, until suddenly the cavalry had ridden as though into the yelling as into a weightless mass of dead leaves, exploding them, flinging and hurling them, to reappear the next second like centaurs in furious soundless motion intact in an intact visible cloud of swirling frantic screams which continued to swirl and burst in that faint frenetic tossing even after the horses must indubitably have been gone, still swirling and tossing in scattered diminuendo when the other sound began. It came up beneath them, beginning not as sound at all but rather as light, diffused yet steady from across the plain beyond the city: the voices of men alone, choral almost, growing not in volume but in density as dawn itself increases, filling the low horizon beyond the city's black and soaring bulk with a band not of sound but light while above and into it the thin hysteric nearer screams and cries skittered and spun and were extinguished like sparks into water, still filling the horizon even after the voices themselves had ceased with a resonant humming like a fading sunset and heatless as aurora against which the black tremendous city seemed to rush skyward in one fixed iron roar out of the furious career of earth toward its furious dust, upreared and insensate as an iron ship's prow among the fixed insensate stars.

This time the old general turned from it. The single leaf of the door was now open about three feet and there stood beside it an old man, not at all at attention but just standing there. He was hardly larger than a child, not stooped or humped, and shrunken was not the word either. He was condensed, intact and unshrivelled, the long ellipsoid of his life almost home again now, where rosy and blemishless, without memory or grieving flesh, mewling bald and toothless, he would once more possess but three things and would want no more: a stomach, a few surface nerves to seek warmth, a few cells capable of sleep. He was not a soldier. The very fact that he wore not only a heavy regulation infantryman's buttoned-back greatcoat but a steel helmet and a rifle slung across his back merely made him look less like one. He stood there in spectacles, in the faded coat which had been removed perhaps from its first (or last) owner's corpse—it still bore the darker vacancies where an N.C.O.'s chevrons and a regimental number had been removed, and neatly stitched together on the front of it, just above where the skirts folded back, was the suture where something (a bayonet obviously) had entered it, and within the last twenty-four hours it had been brushed carefully and ironed by hand by someone who could not see very well—and processed through a cleansing and delousing plant and then issued to him from a quartermaster's salvage depot, and the polished steel helmet and the clean polished rifle which looked as lovingly-tended and unused as a twelfth-century pike from a private museum, which he had never fired and did not know how to fire and would not have fired nor accepted a live-cartridge for even if there was a single man in all the French armies who would have given him one. He had been the old general's batman for more than fifty years (except for the thirteen years beginning on the day more than forty years ago now when the old general, a captain with a brilliant and almost incredible future, had vanished not only from the army lists but from the ken of all the people who up to that time had thought they knew him also, to reappear thirteen years later in the army lists and the world too with the rank of brigadier and none to know whence nor why either although as regards the rank they did know how; his first official act had been to find his old batman, then a clerk in a commissary's office in Saigon, and have him assigned back to his old position and rating); he stood there healthily pink as an infant, ageless and serene in his aura of indomitable fidelity, invincibly hardheaded, incorrigibly opinionated and convinced, undeflectable in advice suggestion and comment and indomitably contemptuous of war and all its ramifications, constant durable faithful and insubordinate and almost invisible within the clutter and jumble of his martial parody so that he resembled an aged servant of some ancient ducal house dressed in ceremonial regalia for the annual commemoration of some old old event, some ancient defeat or glory of the House so long before his time that he had long ago forgotten the meaning and significance if he ever knew it, while the old general crossed the room and went back around the table and sat down again. Then the old batman turned and went back through the door and reappeared immediately with a tray bearing a single plain soup bowl such as might have come from an N.C.O.'s mess or perhaps from that of troops themselves, and a small stone jug and the heel of a loaf and a battered pewter spoon and an immaculate folded damask napkin, and set the tray on the table before the old marshal and, the beautifully polished rifle gleaming and glinting as he bent and recovered and stood back, watched, fond and domineering and implacable, every move as the old marshal took up the bread and began to crumple it into the bowl.

When he entered St. Cyr at seventeen, except for that fragment of his splendid fate which even here he could not escape, he seemed to have brought nothing of the glittering outside world he had left behind him but a locket—a small object of chased worn gold, obviously valuable or anyway venerable, resembling a hunting-case watch and obviously capable of containing two portraits; only capable of containing such since none of his classmates ever saw it open and in fact they only learned he possessed it through the circumstance that one or two of them happened to see it on a chain about his neck like a crucifix in the barracks bathroom one day. And even that scant knowledge was quickly adumbrated by the significance of that destiny which even these gates were incapable of severing him from—that of being not only the nephew of a Cabinet Minister, but the godson of the board chairman of that gigantic international federation producing munitions which, with a few alterations in the lettering stamped into the head of each cartridge- and shell-case, fitted almost every military rifle and pistol and light field-piece in all the Western Hemisphere and half the Eastern too. Yet despite this, because of his secluded and guarded childhood, until he entered the Academy the world outside the Faubourg St. Germain had scarcely ever seen him, and the world which began at the Paris *banlieu* had never even heard of him except as a male Christian name. He was an orphan, an only child, the last male of his line, who had grown from infancy in the sombre insulate house of his mother's eldest sister in the rue Vaugirard—wife of a Cabinet Minister who was himself a nobody but a man of ruthless and boundless ambition, who had needed only opportunity and got it through his wife's money and connections, and—they were childless—had legally adopted her family by hyphenating its name on to his own, the child growing to the threshold of manhood not only his uncle's heir and heir to the power and wealth of his bachelor godfather, the *Comité de Ferrovie* chairman who had been his father's closest friend, but before any save his aunt's Faubourg St. Germain *salons* and their servants and his tutors could connect his face with his splendid background and his fabulous future.

So when he entered the Academy, none of the classmates with whom he was to spend the next four years (and probably the staff and the professors too) had ever seen him before. And he had been there probably twenty-four hours before any of them except one even connected his face with his great name. This one was not a youth too but instead already a man, twenty-two years old, who had entered the Academy two days before and was to stand Number Two to the other's One on the day of graduation, who on that first afternoon began to believe, and for the next fifteen years would continue, that he had seen at once in that seventeen-year-old face the promise of a destiny which would be the restored (this was 1873, two years after the capitulation and formal occupation of Paris) glory and destiny of France too. As for the rest of them, their first reaction was that of the world outside: surprise and amazement and for the moment downright unbelief, that he, this youth, was here at all. It was not because of his appearance of fragility and indurability; they simply read the face also into that fragility and indurability which, during that first instant when

222

he seemed to be not entering the gates but rather framed immo-
bilely by them, had fixed him as absolutely and irrevocably dis-
crepant to that stone-bastioned iron maw of war's apprenticeship
as a figure out of a stained-glass cathedral window set by incomprehensible chance into the breached wall of a fort. It was because,
to them, his was the golden destiny of an hereditary crown prince
of paradise. To them, he was not even a golden youth: he was *the*
golden youth; to them inside the Academy and to all that world
stretching from the Paris *banlieu* to the outermost rim where the
word Paris faded, he was not even a Parisian but *the* Parisian: a
millionaire and an aristocrat from birth, an orphan and an only
child, not merely heir in his own right to more francs than anyone knew save the lawyers and bankers who guarded and nursed
and incremented them, but to the incalculable weight and influence of the uncle who was the nation's first Cabinet member even
though another did bear the title and precedence, and of that
godfather whose name opened doors which (a *Comité de Ferrovie*
chairman's), because of their implications and commitments, or
(a bachelor's) of their sex, gender, even that of a Cabinet Minister
could not; who had only to reach majority in order to inherit that
matchless of all catastrophes: the privilege of exhausting his life
—or if necessary, shortening it—by that matchless means of all:
being young, male, unmarried, an aristocrat, wealthy, secure by
right of birth, in Paris: that city which was the world too, since
of all cities it was supreme, dreamed after and adored by all men,
and not just when she was supreme in her pride but when—as
now—she was abased from it. Indeed, never more dreamed after
and adored than now, while in abasement; never more so than
now because of what, in any other city, would have been abasement. Never more than now was she, not France's Paris but the
world's, the defilement being not only a part of the adored immortality and the immaculateness and therefore necessary to them,
but since it was the sort of splendid abasement of which only Paris
was capable, being capable of it made her the world's Paris: conquered—or rather, not conquered, since, France's Paris, she was
inviolate and immune to the very iron heel beneath which the rest
of France (and, since she was the world's Paris too, the rest of the
world also) lay supine and abased—impregnable and immune:
the desired, the civilised world's inviolate and forever unchaste,

virgin barren and insatiable: the mistress who renewed her barren virginity in the very act of each barren recordless promiscuity, Eve and Lilith both to every man in his youth so fortunate and blessed as to be permitted within her omnivorous insatiable orbit; the victorious invading hun himself, bemazed not so much by his success as his sudden and incredible whereabouts, shuffling his hobbled boots in the perfumed anteroom, dreaming no less than one born to that priceless fate on whom, herself immortal, she conferred brief immortality's godhead in exchange for no more than his young man's youth.

Yet here he was, just another anonymous one in a class of candidates for professional careers, not merely in the rigid hierarchy of an army but in an army which for the next fifty years would be struggling simply to survive, to emerge from the debacle and debasement of defeat in order not to be feared as a threat but merely respected as a monument. An Anglo-Saxon mind could, and almost any American would, have read into his presence here a young man's dream in which he would see himself, not by some irremediable sacrifice rescuing that adored city Andromeda-like from her brutal rock perhaps, but at least as one of Niobe's or Rachel's children clapping up sword and buckler. But not the Latin, the French mind; to it, that city had nothing to be saved from, who had strangled all man's heart in any one strand of her vagrant Lilith hair; who, barren, had no sons: they were her lovers, and when they went to war, it was for glory to lay before the altar of that unchaste unstale bed.

So only that single classmate ever believed other than that it was not the youth who repudiated paradise but paradise which repudiated its scion and heir; not he but his family which had put him where he was, not disinherited at all but disfranchised, segregated: the family which had compelled him into the army as—for them, their name and position—at best the isolation, quarantine, of whatever was the threat he had become or represented, and at worst the mausoleum of the shame which would be its result, and—for him—a refuge from the consequences. Because he was still who he was, male and solitary and heir; the family would still use the power and the influence, even though they had had to isolate and quarantine his failure to be what he might—should —have been. In fact, his family had not even merely bought absolution for him. On the contrary, they would gain a sort of blinding redundance on the great name's original splendour from the golden braid which his hat and sleeves would some day bear. Because even the single classmate believed that all that class (and presently the three ahead of it too) were eating and sleeping with one who would be a general at forty and—given any sort of opportunity for any kind of a military debacle worthy of the name inside the next thirty years—a marshal of France when the nation buried him.

Only he didn't use the influence, not in the next four years at least. He didn't even need it. He graduated not only at the top of the class but with the highest marks ever made at the Academy; such was his record that not even his classmates, who would not have been offered it no matter what grades they graduated with, were not even jealous of the Quartermaster captaincy which rumour said was waiting for him at the Academy's exit like a hat or a cloak on the arm of a footman at the exit from a theatre or a restaurant. Yet when he next came into their cognizance—which was immediately on the succeeding day, when the rest of the class had barely begun the regulation two weeks' leave before assuming duty—he didn't have the captaincy. He simply appeared at Toulon without it, still looking little different from what he had four years ago: not fragile so much as indurable, with his unblemished paybook for which he would have no more use than would the beggar for the king's farrier's nail or the king for the beggar's almsbox, and his untried spartan subaltern's kit and his virgin copy of the *Manual of War* (and the locket of course; his classmates had not forgot that; in fact they even knew now what the two portraits in it would be: the uncle and the godfather: his crucifix indeed, his talisman, his reliquary) but with no more captaincy than the guest or patron leaving the theatre or restaurant by a fire exit or rear alley would have hat or cloak when he reached the boulevard.

But—save that one—they believed they knew the answer to this. It was a gesture, not the youth's but the family's—one of those gestures of modesty and discretion of the potent and powerful who are powerful and potent enough to afford even discretion and modesty; they and he too were all waiting for the same thing: for the arrival of the great suave hearselike midnight-coloured limousine bringing not the civilian secretary bearing the captaincy like a ducal coronet on a velvet cushion, but rather the uncle-Minister himself, who would walk the nephew back to the Quai d'Orsay and in that privacy fling away the meagre African subaltern's kit with the cold outrage of a cardinal plucking a Baptist hymnal from the robe of a kneeling candidate for conse-cration. But that didn't happen either. The car would have come too late. Because, although the draft to which he would have been posted was not to leave for two weeks yet and its personnel had not even begun to arrive at the depot, he was gone after only one night, to Africa, to immediate field service, quietly, almost surreptitiously, with the same simple sublieutenant's rank and the same meagre equipment which the rest of them would have in their turn.

So now those who might have been jealous of him (not only his St. Cyr coevals, junior and senior, who had no Minister-uncles and chairman-godfathers, but the career men who did have parents and guardians but not Cabinet members and *Comité de Ferrovie* chairmen, who hated him not because he had been offered the captaincy but because he had not accepted it) no longer had to be. Because they knew that they would never overtake him now: who would be removed forever more from envy and hence from hatred and fear both, the three of them, nephew godfather and uncle, going fast now, who had been ruthless even to the long tradition of nepotism, the youth hurried to whatever remote frontier where rampant indeed would be the uncle's and the god-father's power and will, with none save an occasional inspector-general to challenge it; no bounds to the family's ambition nor check to that which furthered it. They would be free, who had bought immunity from envy by simply outlasting it; when he reappeared, say two years from now as a colonel of twenty-three, he would be far beyond the range of any envy and jealousy, let alone theirs. Or perhaps it wouldn't even take two years, one might be enough, so great was their faith in, not just the uncle's and the godfather's power and will, but in rapacity itself: the compas-sionate, the omnipotent, the all-seeing and all-pervading; one day the Quai d'Orsay would gently out-breathe, and against that fierce African foreshore would officially beat a national unanimity loud and long enough not only to obfuscate the mere circumstances of fact, but to distract the mind from all curiosity regarding them; there would remain only the accomplishment and its protagonist juxtaposed without past on a stage without yesterday, like two masques for a pantomime furbished out of the bloodless lumber-room of literature, because by that time he would have escaped not merely from fear and hatred but from the long rigid mosaic of seniority itself, as irrevocably as does a girl from maiden-hood; they would—could—even watch him now, heatless peaceful and immune to any remembered anguish—even see him again passing among the windy bunting and the paraded troops in the cheering Oran street in the Governor General's car, sitting on the right hand of the Governor General himself: the hero of twenty-two or -three who had not at all merely saved some what-ever scrap or fragment of an empire, but had set again against the zenith the fierce similitude of a bird, be though as it was but one more lost feather of the eagles which seventy years ago had stooped at all Europe and Africa and Asia too, they watching without jealousy now or even rancour, but rather with amazed admiration not merely for France but for invincible Man—the hero still girlish-looking even after two years of African sun and solitude, still frail and fragile in the same way that adolescent girls appear incredibly delicate yet at the same time durable, like wisps of mist or vapour drifting checkless and insensate among the thunderous concrete-bedded mastodons inside a foundry; appearing now only the more durable because of the proven— no: reproven—fragility, at once frail yet at the same time intact and inviolable because of what in another had been not merely ruin but destruction too: like the saint in the old tale, the maiden who without hesitation or argument feeds in advance with her maidenhood the ferryman who set her across the stream and into heaven (an Anglo-Saxon fable too, since only an Anglo-Saxon could seriously believe that anything buyable at no more cost than that could really be worth a sainthood)—the hero, the sheep-like acclaiming mass with not one among them all to ask or even wonder what he had done or when or where, nor even against what or whom the victory, as he passed immune even to the uproar, across the cheering city to the quai and the destroyer (a cruiser maybe, a destroyer certainly) which would carry him to his Paris triumph and then return him, chief of a corps and commander of a department, or perhaps even Governor General himself.

But that didn't happen either. He crossed the Mediterranean and disappeared. When they followed in the order of their postings, they learned that he had gone on from the port base too, after even less than one night, to assigned duty somewhere in the interior, exactly where and on exactly what service, nobody at the port base knew either. But they had expected that. They believed they even knew where he would be: no place remote merely because it was far away and impossible to reach, like Brazzaville, say, where the three pale faces—Commandant-governor, new subaltern, and halfbreed interpreter—would slumber hierarchate and superposed, benignant and inscrutable, irascible and hiero-glyph like an American Indian totem pole in ebon Eden innocence; but a place really remote, not even passively isolate but actively and even aggressively private, like an oasis in the desert's heart itself, more blind than cave and circumferenced than safari—a silken tent odorous with burning pastille and murmurous with the dreamy *chock* of the woodcutter's axe and the pad of watercarriers' feet, where on a lion-robed divan he would await untimed destiny's hasteless accouchement. But they were wrong. He had left the port base the same day he arrived, for a station as famous in its circles as the Black Hole of Calcutta—a small outpost not only five hundred kilometres from anything resembling a civilised stronghold or even handhold, but sixty and more from its nearest support—a tiny lost compound manned by a sergeant's platoon out of a foreign legion battalion recruited from the gutter-sweepings of all Europe and South America and the Levant—a well, a flag-staff, a single building of loop-holed clay set in a seared irrecon-cilable waste of sun and sand which few living men had ever seen, to which troops were sent as punishment or, incorrigibles, for segregation until heat and monotony on top of their natural and acquired vices divorced them permanently from mankind. He had gone straight there from the port base three years ago and (the only officer present and, for all practical purposes, the only white man too) had not only served out his own one-year tour of com-mand, but that of his successor too, and was now ten months for-ward in that of what would have been his successor's successor; in the shock of that first second of knowledge it seemed to them—

except that one—that earth itself had faltered, rapacity itself had failed, when regardless of whatever had been the nephew's old defalcation from his family's hope or dream seven or eight or ten years ago, even that uncle and that godfather had been incapable of saving him; this, until that single classmate picked up the whole picture and reversed it.

He was a Norman, son of a Caen doctor whose grandfather, while an art student in Paris, had become the friend and then the fanatic disciple of Camille Desmoulins until Robespierre executed them both, the great-grandson come to Paris to be a painter too but relinquished his dream to the Military Academy for the sake of France as the great-grandfather had done his to the guillotine for the sake of Man: who for all his vast peasant bones had looked at twenty-two even more impermanent and brittle-keyed than ever had his obsession at seventeen—a man with a vast sick flaccid moon of a face and hungry and passionate eyes, who had looked once at that one which to all the world else had been that of any seventeen-year-old youth and relinquished completely to it like a sixty-year-old longtime widower to that of a pubic unconscious girl, who picked up the three figures—uncle, nephew and god-father—like so many paper dolls and turned them around and set them down again in the same positions and attitudes but obversed. Though this would be several years yet, almost ten in fact after that day when they had watched that sunstricken offing behind Oran accept that fragile stride and then close markless behind it like a painted backdrop, not only markless but impenetrable too; and not just a backdrop but a looking-glass through which he had stepped not into unreality but instead carrying unreality with him to establish it where before there had been none: four years from that day and he was still there at his little lost barren sunglared unfutured outpost: who, whether or not he had ever been an actual threat once, was now an enigma burying its ostrich-head from the staff commission which would drag him back to Paris and at least into vulnerable range of his old sybaritic renunciation; five years from that day and beginning the sixth voluntary tour of that duty which should have fallen to every officer in the Army List (every man everywhere) before it came to him, and (so grave the defalcation from which his family had had to bury him that not only was mere seniority confounded, but the immutable rotation of military leave too) not even the cafés of Casablanca or Oran or Algiers, let alone Paris, had ever seen him.

Then six years from that day and he had vanished from Africa too, none knew where except the Norman classmate's passionate and hungry hope, vanished not only from the knowledge of man but from the golden warp and woof of the legend too, leaving behind him only a name in the Army List, still with the old unchanged rank of sublieutenant but with nothing after it: not even dead, not even whereabouts unknown; and even this was another two years, by which time all of them who had feared him once, not only the old St. Cyr class but its successors too, were scattered and diffused about the perimeter where the thrice-barred flag flew, until the afternoon when five of them, including the Norman classmate and a staff captain, met by chance in a Quai d'Orsay anteroom, were now sitting about a sidewalk table in front of the most adjacent café, the staff officer already four years a captain even though only five years out of St. Cyr, descendant of a Napoleonic duchy whose founder or recipient had been a butcher then a republican then an imperialist then a duke, and his son a royalist then a republican again and—still alive and still a duke—then a royalist again: so that three of the four watching and listening to him thought how here was the true golden youth which that other one of eleven years ago whom he was talking about, had refused to be, realising, aware for the first time, not just what the other would have been by now, but—with that family and background and power—what matchless pinnacle he might have reached, since this one had behind him only simple proprietors of banks and manipulators of shares; the staff captain using the anteroom to serve his captaincy in, and three of the other four having reported to it that morning by mutual coincidence after three years on the Asiatic Station, and the fourth one, the junior, having been assigned to it right out of the gates themselves, the five of them coincidental about the cramped table on the crowded terrace while three of them—including the Norman giant who sat not among them so much as above them, immense and sick and apparently insensate as a boulder save for his flaccid and hungry face and the passionate and hungry eyes—listening while the staff captain, burly blunt brutal heavy-witted and assured and so loud that people at the other tables had begun to turn, talked about the almost-forgotten sublieutenant at his tiny lost post in the depths of Never-Never: who should have been the idol pattern and hope not merely for all career officers but for all golden youth everywhere, as was Bonaparte not merely for all soldiers but for every ancestorless Frenchman qualified first in poverty, who was willing to hold life and conscience cheap enough: wondering (the staff captain) what could have been out there in that desert to hold for six years above a quartermaster captaincy, the sublieutenant-command of a stinking well enclosed by eight palm trees and inhabited by sixteen un-nationed cutthroats; what out there that Oran or Casablanca or even Paris couldn't match—what paradise within some camel-odoured tent—what limbs old and weary and cunning with ancient pleasures that Montmartre bagnios (and even St. Germain boudoirs) knew nothing of, yet so ephemeral, so incipient with satiation and at last actual revulsion, that after only six years the sultan-master must vacate it—

'Vacate it?' one of the three said. 'You mean he's gone? He actually left that place at last?'

'Not quite gone,' the staff captain said. 'Not until his relief arrives. After all, he accepted an oath to France, even he, even if he does hold from the *Comité de Ferrovie*. He failed. He lost a camel. There was a man too, even if he had spent most of his five enlistments in clink—' telling it: the soldier spawned by a Marseilles cesspool to be the ultimate and fatal nemesis of a woman a girl whom eighteen years ago he had corrupted and diseased and then betrayed into prostitution and at last murdered and had spent the eighteen years since as member of lost frontier garrisons such as this because this—the rim of oblivion—was the one place on earth where he could continue to walk and breathe and be fed and clothed whose one fear now was that he might do something which would prompt someone to make him a corporal or a sergeant and so compel him back to some post within a day's walk of any community large enough to possess one civilian policeman, where not he would see a strange face but where some strange face would see him; he—the soldier, the trooper, had vanished along with the camel, obviously into the hands of a adjacent band or tribe of the Riffs who were the excuse for the garrison being where it was and the reason for its being armed. And though the man was a piece of government property too, even

231

if not a very valuable one, that camel was a camel. Yet the commander of the post had apparently made no effort whatever to recover them; whereupon they—his listeners—might say that the commander's only failure in the matter had been that he had prevented a local war. Which was wrong. He had not stopped a war: he had simply failed to start one. Which was not his purpose there, not why he had been tested and found competent for that command: not to fail to start wars, but to preserve government property. So he had failed, and yesterday his official request to be relieved had been forwarded to the Adjutant-General's desk—

The Norman was already on his feet while the staff captain was still talking; at least four of them knew how he heard of the command's vacancy but not even these knew how he managed to get the succession to it—a man without family or influence or money at all, with nothing in fact to front or fend for him in his profession save the dubious capacity of his vast ill body to endure, and the rating of Two in his St. Cyr class; already, because of the rating, a sublieutenant of engineers and, because of the rating and his sick body both, in addition to the fact that he had just completed a tour of field service in Indo-China, secure for a Home Establishment post probably in Paris itself, from now on until retirement age overtook him. Yet within an hour he was in the office of the Quartermaster General himself, using, having deliberately used the Number Two rating for the first (and probably the last) time in his life for the chance to stand facing the desk which he could not know or dream that some day he himself would sit behind, himself in his turn sole unchallengeable arbiter over the whereabouts and maintenance of every man wearing a French uniform.

'You? An Engineer?' the man facing him said.

'So was he'—the voice eager, serene, not importunate so much as simply not to be denied: 'That's why, you see. Remember, I was Number Two to him in our class. When he leaves it, it belongs to me.'

'Then you remember this,' the other said, tapping the medical survey on the desk before him. 'This is why you are not going back to Saigon after your leave, why you are going on Home Establishment from now on. As for that, you wouldn't live a year out there in that—'

'You were about to say "hole",' he said. 'Isn't that its purpose: for the honourable disposal of that which is self-proven to have no place in the Establishment of Man?'

'Man?'

'France, then,' he said; and thirteen days later looked from the back of the camel across the glaring markless intervening miles, as a thousand years later the first pilgrim must have looked at the barely distinguishable midden which the native guide assured him had been, not Golgotha of course but Gethsemane, at the flagstaff and the sun-blanched walls in a nest of ragged and meagre palms; at sunset he stood inside them, rigid and abnegant while the horn chanted and there descended on him in his turn that fringy ravelling of empire's carapace; at first dark, the two camels rumbling and gurgling just beyond earshot above the waiting orderly, he stood at the gate beside the man who had been One to his Two in the old class six years ago, the two of them barely visible to each other, leaving only the voice serene and tender, passionate for suffering, sick with hope:

'I know. They thought you were hiding. They were afraid of you at first. Then they decided you were just a fool who insisted on becoming a marshal of France at fifty instead of forty-five, using the power and influence at twenty-one and -two and -three and -four and -five to evade at forty-five the baton you would have nothing left to fend off at fifty; the power and the influence to escape the power and influence, the world to escape the world; to free yourself of flesh without having to die, without having to lose the awareness that you were free of flesh: not to escape from it and you could not be immune to it nor did you want to be: only to be free of it, to be conscious always that you were merely at armistice with it at the price of constant and unflagging vigilance, because without that consciousness, flesh would not exist for you to be free of it and so there would be nothing anywhere for you to be free of. Oh yes, I knew: the English poet Byron's dream or wish or cry that all living women had but one single mouth for his kiss: the supreme golden youth who encompassed all flesh by putting, still virgin to it, all flesh away. But I knew better: who sought a desert not as Simeon did but as Anthony, using Mithridates and Heliogabalus not merely to acquire a roosting-place for contempt and scorn, but for fee to the cave where the lion itself lay down: who—the ones who feared you once—believed that they had seen ambition and greed themselves default before one seventeen-year-old child—had seen the whole vast hitherto invulnerable hegemony of ruthlessness and rapacity reveal itself unfearsome and hollow when even that uncle and that godfather could not cope with your crime or defalcation, as though so poor and thin was the ambition and greed to which even that uncle and that godfather were dedicant, that voracity itself had repudiated them who had been its primest pillars and its supremest crown and glory.

'Which could not be. That was not merely incredible, it was unbearable. Rapacity does not fail, else man must deny he breathes. Not rapacity: its whole vast glorious history repudiates that. It does not, cannot, must not fail. Not just one family in one nation privileged to soar cometlike into splendid zenith through and because of it, not just one nation among all the nations selected as heir to that vast splendid heritage; not just France, but all governments and nations which ever rose and endured long enough to leave their mark as such, had sprung from it and in and upon and by means of it became forever fixed in the amazement of man's present and the glory of his past; civilisation itself is its password and Christianity its masterpiece, Chartres and the Sistine Chapel, the pyramids and the rock-wombed powder-magazines under the Gates of Hercules its altars and monuments, Michelangelo and Phidias and Newton and Ericsson and Archimedes and Krupp its priests and popes and bishops; the long deathless roster of its glory —Caesar and the Barcas and the two Macedonians, our own Bonaparte and the great Russian and the giants who strode nimbused in red hair like fire across the Aurora Borealis, and all the lesser nameless who were not heroes but, glorious in anonymity, at least served the destiny of heroes—the generals and admirals, the corporals and ratings of glory, the batmen and orderlies of renown, and the chairmen of boards and the presidents of federations, the doctors and lawyers and educators and churchmen who after nineteen centuries have rescued the son of heaven from oblivion and translated him from mere meek heir to earth to chairman of its board of trade; and those who did not even have names and designations to be anonymous from—the hands and the backs which carved and sweated aloft the stone blocks and painted the ceilings and invented the printing presses and grooved the barrels, down to the last indestructible voice which asked nothing but the right to speak of hope in Roman lion-pits and murmur the name of God from the Indian-anticked pyres in Canadian forests—stretching immutable and enduring further back than man's simple remembering recorded it. Not rapacity: it does not fail; suppose Mithridates' and Heliogabalus' heir had used his heritage in order to escape his inheritees: Mithridates and Heliogabalus were Heliogabalus and Mithridates still and that scurry from Oran was still only a mouse's, since one of Grimalkin's parents was patience too and that whole St. Cyr-Toulon-Africa business merely flight, as when the maiden flees the ravisher not toward sanctuary but privacy, and just enough of it to make the victory memorable and its trophy a prize. Not rapacity, which, like poverty, takes care of its own. Because it endures, not even because it is rapacity but because man is man, enduring and immortal; enduring not because he is immortal but immortal because he endures: and so with rapacity, which immortal man never fails, since it is in and from rapacity that he gets, holds, his immortality—the vast, the all-being, the compassionate, which says to him only, Believe in Me; though ye doubt seventy times seven, ye need only believe again.

'But I know. I was there. I saw: that day eleven years ago: paused in that iron maw of war, not fragile actually: just fixed and immune in fragility like the figure in the stained window; not through any looking-glass into unreality, but just immune, moral opposed and invincibly apostate; if there still existed for you even in dream the splendid and glittering boulevards and faubourgs of your old cradle and your lost estate, it was merely as dream forever inextricable from your past and forever interdict from your destiny; inextricable the dream, yourself and the dream one, yourself interdict and free from that pain and that longing forever more; inextricable from that youth who is this man now, as is this little lost barren spot here inextricable forever from that destiny—never that uncle's and that godfather's private donjon but rather the figment of that consecration's necessary tarryment for this time, this space, somewhere in time and space—not the youth: the fragility; not to test the youth but to test the fragility: to measure and gauge and test; never an intractable and perverse child who fled, never an uncle and godfather coercing and compelling by attrition, starvation, but all of them, the trinity still intact because it had never been otherwise, testing as one the fragility's capacity for the destiny and the consecration, using the desert for yardstick as when in the old days the cadet would spend that last night of his maiden squiredom on his knees on the lonely chapel's stone floor before the cushion bearing the virgin spurs of his tomorrow's knighthood.

'That's what they think: not that man failed rapacity, but that man failed man; his own frail flesh and blood lets him down: the blood still runs but cooling now, into the second phase of his brief and furious span when the filling of his belly is better than glory or a throne, then on into the third and last one where anticipation of the latrine is more moving than even the spread of a girl's hair on the pillow. That's what they believe is to be your destiny and end. And ten years from now they will still know no better. Because your time, your moment, will not have come even in ten years. It will take longer than that. It will need a new time, a new age, a new century which doesn't even remember our old passions and failures; a new century from that one when man discovered God for a second and then lost Him, postulated by a new digit in the record of his hope and need; it will be more than twenty years even before the day, the moment when you will appear again, without past, as if you had never been. Because by that time you will no longer exist for them except in mutual remembering: a lay figure not only without life but integrated as myth only in mutual confederation: the property of no one of them because you will be the property of all, possessing unity and integration only when your custodians happen to meet from the ends of the earth (which is the French empire) and match fragments and make you whole for a moment; you will lie weightless across the face of France from Mozambique to Miquelon, and Devil's Island to the Treaty Ports like a barely remembered odour, a fading word, a habit, a legend—an effigy cut by a jigsaw for souvenirs, becoming whole only over a café or mess table in Brazzaville or Saigon or Cayenne or Tananarive, dovetailed for a moment or an hour as when boys match and exchange the pictures of the actresses and generals and presidents from the packets of cigarettes; not even the shadow of a breathing man but instead something synthetic and contrived like the composite one of the homely domestic objects contrived by the nurse's hand between the nursery lamp and the wall for the child to take into slumber with it: a balloon: a duck: Punchinello: *la gloire:* the head of a cat—a shadow cast backward on that arid curtain behind Oran beyond which you disappeared, not by the sun but by that quartermaster captain's commission the refusal of which first struck them with terror and rage, until after twenty years not you nor even your two powerful kinsmen will be real, but only that old fading parchment, and it real only because your refusal of it incorporated it on to your legend—the shopworn and now harmless vellum vainly dangling its fading seals and ribbons beside the rent through which you vanished in the oldest of comedies: the youth fleeing, the forsaken aging yet indomitable betrothed pursuing, abject, constant, undismayable, undeflectable, terrifying not in threat but in fidelity, until at last those who feared you once will have watched you pass out of enmity to amazement: to contempt: to unreality, and at last out of your race and kind altogether, into the dusty lumber room of literature.

'But not I,' he said, looming, visible only as a gaunt gigantic shape, sick, furious, murmuring: 'Because I know better. I knew that first moment eleven years ago when I looked and saw you standing there in that gate. I knew. I won't be here to see it of course (my last medical survey, you know: that marvellous and amazing thing, a human life, spanned and then—what's the Boer word?—outspanned by one dry and dusty page of doctor's jargon. They are wrong of course. I mean in the Quai d'Orsay. They didn't want to post me here at all, since in doing it they would in their opinion simply double the work of whatever clerk would not only have to relieve me but discharge me from the army list also and then post my successor before my tour here was even completed) and at first I grieved a little because once I thought that you might need me. I mean, need me other than for my simple seniority of hope in the condition of man. —That's right,' he said, though the other had made no sound: 'Laugh, at that dream, that vain hope too. Because you will not need anybody wherever it is you are going now in order to return from it. Mind you, I don't ask where. I was about to say "to find whom or what you will need to be your instrument" but I refrained from that in time too. So at least you don't need to laugh at that, since I know that you are going wherever it is you are going, in order to return from it when the time, the moment comes, in the shape of man's living hope. May I embrace you?'

'Must you?' the other said. Then: 'Should you?' Then quickly: 'Of course.' But before he moved the taller one had stooped, loomed downward from his vast and depthless height and took the smaller man's hand and kissed it and released it and, erect again, took the other's face between his two hands almost like a parent, a mother, and held it for a moment, then released it.

'With Christ in God,' he said. 'Go now.'

'So I'm to save France,' the other said.

'France,' he said, not even brusquely, not even contemptuously. 'You will save man. Farewell.'

And he was right for almost two years. That is, he was almost wrong. He did not remember the camel or litter—whatever it had been—at all; only a moment—probably, without doubt, in the base hospital in Oran—a face, a voice, probably a doctor's, marvelling not that he had failed to keep consciousness over that fierce and empty distance, but that he had kept life at all; then not much again, only motion: the Mediterranean: then he knew peacefully, not with joy or exultation: just peacefully, almost unattentively, unable yet (nor did that matter either) to raise his own head to look, that this was France, Europe, home. Then he could move his head and lift his hands too, even if the vast peasant Norman frame did seem still to lie outside its transparent envelope; he said weakly but aloud, with a sort of peaceful amazement, weakly, but at least aloud: 'I had forgot what winter looks like,' lying half-propped all day now on the glassed veranda above Zermatt watching the Matterhorn, watching not the ordered and nameless progression of days fade but rather the lesser earth, since always the great peak carried into the next one, as in a gigantic hand, one clutch of light. But that was only the body and it was mending too; soon it would be as strong, not perhaps as it ever was nor even as it ever would but rather as it would ever need to be, since they were the same—only the body: not the memory because it had forgotten nothing, not even for one second the face which had been the junior that afternoon two years ago around the table on the Quai d'Orsay terrace, come all the way from Paris just to see him—

'Not Paris,' the other said. 'Verdun. We're building fortifications there now which they will never pass again.'

'They?' he said peacefully. 'It's too late now.'

'Too late? Nonsense. The fever and the fury are still there, I grant you. It seems to be born in them; they probably can't help it. But it will be decades, perhaps a whole generation, before it reaches convulsion again.'

'Not for us,' he said. 'Too late for them.'

'Oh,' the other said, who did not see at all; he knew that. Then the other said: 'I brought this. It came out just after you left for Africa. You probably haven't seen it yet.' It was a page from the Gazette, yellowed, faded, almost three years old now, the other holding it spread while he looked at the rigid epitaph:

> To Lieutenant-Colonel:
> Sous-Lieutenant (and the name)
> March 29, 1885

> Relieved and Retired:
> Lieutenant-Colonel (and the name)
> March 29, 1885

'He never came back to Paris,' the other said. 'Not even to France—'

'No,' he said peacefully.

'So you were probably the last to see him.—You did see him, didn't you?'

'Yes,' he said.

'Then maybe you even know where he went. Where he is.'

'Yes,' he said peacefully.

'You mean he told you himself? I don't believe it.'

'Yes,' he said, 'it is nonsense, isn't it? Not for me to claim that he told me, but that he should have to have told anyone. He's in a Tibetan lamasery.'

'A what?'

'Yes. The east, the morning, which even the dead, even the pagan dead, lie facing, so that the first faint fall of shadow of the risen sun of it can break their sleep.' Now he could feel the other watching him and there was something in the face but he would not bother about it yet, and when the other spoke there was something in the voice too but he would not bother about that yet either.

'They gave him a ribbon too,' the other said. 'It was the red one. He not only saved your post and garrison for you, he probably saved Africa. He prevented a war. Of course, they had to get rid of him afterward—ask for his resignation.'

'All right,' he said peacefully. Then he said, 'What?'

'The camel and the soldier he lost: the murderer—don't you remember? Surely, if he told you where he was going, he told you about that too.' Now the other was looking at him, watching him. 'There was a woman in it—not his, of course. You mean he didn't tell you?'

'Yes,' he said. 'He told me.'

'Then of course I won't have to.'

'Yes,' he said again. 'He told me.'

'She was a Riff, a native, belonging to the village, tribe, settlement, whatever it was, which was the reason for the post and the garrison being there; you must have seen that anyway while you were there—a slave, valuable; nobody's wife or daughter or favourite it appeared, or anyway was reported: just simply merchantable. She died too, like the other one back in Marseilles eighteen years ago; the man's power over women was indeed a fatal one. Whereupon the next morning the camel—it was his—the commandant's—private mount: possibly a pet if you can—want to—pet a camel—and its groom, driver, mahout, whatever they are, had vanished and two dawns later the groom returned, on foot and thoroughly terrified, with the ultimatum from the chief, headman to the commandant, giving the commandant until the next dawn to send him the man (there were three involved but the chief would be content with the principal one) responsible for the woman's death and her spoliation as merchandise; else the chief and his men would invest the post and obliterate it and its garrison, which they could probably have done, if not immediately, certainly in the almost twelve months before the next inspector-general would turn up to look at it. So the commandant asked for a volunteer to slip away that night, before the ultimatum went into effect at dawn and the place was surrounded, and go to the next post and bring back a relieving force.—I beg your pardon?' But he had not spoken, rigid, himself the fragile one now, who was yet only barely erect from death.

'I thought you said "chose one," ' the other said. 'He didn't need to choose. Because this was the man's one chance. He could have escaped at any time—hoarded food and water and stolen away on almost any night during the whole eighteen years, possibly reached the coast and perhaps even France. But where would he go then, who could have escaped only from Africa: never from himself, from the old sentence, from which all that saved him was his uniform, and that only while he wore it in the light of day. But now he could go. He was not even escaping, he was not even entering mere amnesty but absolution; from now on, the whole edifice of France would be his sponsor and his purification, even though he got back with the relief too late, because he not only had the commandant's word, but a signed paper also to avouch his deed and command all men by these presents to make good its reward.

'So the commandant didn't need to choose him: only accept him; and at sunset the garrison paraded and the man stepped out of ranks; and now the commandant should have taken the decoration from his own breast and pinned it on that of the sacrifice, except that the commandant had not got the ribbon yet (oh yes, I've thought of the locket too: to remove the chain from his own neck and cast it about the condemned's, but that is reserved for some finer, more durable instant in that rocket's course than the abolishment of a blackguard or the preservation of a flyspeck). So without doubt that would be the moment when he gave him the signed paper setting him free of his past, the man not knowing then that that first step out of ranks had already set him free of whatever else breathing could do to him more; and the man saluted and about faced and marched out the gate into darkness. Into death. And I thought for a moment you had spoken again, were about to ask how, if the ultimatum would not take effect until dawn tomorrow, did the Riff chief discover that a scout would attempt to get out that night, and so have an ambush ready at the mouth of the wadi through which the scout would pass. Yes, how: the man himself probably asking that in the one last choked cry or scream remaining to him of indictment and repudiation, because he didn't know about the ribbon then either.

'Into darkness: night: the wadi. Into hell; even Hugo didn't think of that. Because from the looks of what remained of him, it took him most of that night to die; the sentry above the gate

241

challenged at dawn the next morning, then the camel (not the plump missing one of course but an old mangy one, because the dead woman was valuable; and besides, one camel looks just like another in a Transport Office return) cantered in with the body tied on it, stripped of clothing and most of the flesh too. So the siege, the investment, was lifted; the enemy retired and that sunset the commandant buried its lone casualty (except for the better camel: and after all, the woman had been valuable) with a bugle and a firing squad, and you relieved him and he departed, a lieutenant-colonel with the rosette in a Himalayan lamasery, leaving nothing behind him but that little corner of France which he saved, to be mausoleum and cenotaph of the man whom he tricked into saving it. A man,' the other said, watching him. 'A human being.'

'A murderer,' he said. 'A murderer twice—'

'Spawned into murder by a French cesspool.'

'But repudiated by all the world's cesspools: nationless twice, without fatherland twice since he had forfeited life, worldless twice since he was already forfeit to death, belonging to no man since he was not even his own—'

'But a man,' the other said.

'—speaking, thinking in French only because, nationless, he must of necessity use that tongue which of all is international; wearing that French uniform because inside a French uniform was the only place on earth where a murderer could be safe from his murder—'

'But bearing it, bearing at least without complaint his rewardless share of the vast glorious burden of empire where few other men dared or could; even behaving himself in his fashion: nothing in his record but a little drunkenness, a little thievery—'

'Until now,' he cried. '—only thievery, buggery, sodomy—until now.'

'—which were his sole defence against the corporal's or sergeant's warrant which would have been his death sentence. Asking nothing of none until his blind and valueless fate tangled with that of him who had already exhausted the *Comité de Ferrovie* and the French Army, and was now reduced to rooting about among the hog-wallows and cesspools of the human race itself; who, already forfeit of life, owed nothing to France save the uniform he wore and the rifle he oiled and tended, who in return for filling on demand a man's width of space in a platoon front, asked and expected nothing save the right to hope to die in a barracks-bed, still unregenerate, yet who had been tricked into giving his life, without even the chance to prepare himself, for that country which would guillotine him within fifteen minutes of putting its civilian hand on him.'

'He was a man,' the other said. 'Even dead, angels—justice itself —still fought for him. You were away at the time, so you have not heard this either. It was at the signing of the citation for that rosette. While bearing the parchment across to the desk for the Grand Commander's signature, the clerk (in private life an amateur Alpinist) stumbled and overturned a litre bottle of ink on to it, blotting out not merely the recipient's name but the entire record of the achievement. So they produced a new parchment. It reached the desk, but even as the Grand Commander extended his hand for the pen, a draft of air came from nowhere (if you know General Martel, you know that any room he stops in long enough to remove his hat, must be hermetically sealed)—came from nowhere and wafted the parchment twenty metres across the room and into the fire, where it vanished pouf! like celluloid. But to what avail, between them armed only with the flaming swords of clumsy mythology, and the *Comité de Ferrovie* snoring with revolving pistols and the rattling belch of Maxim guns? So now he has gone to a Tibetan lamasery. To repent.'

'To wait!' he cried. 'To prepare!'

'Yes,' the other said. 'That's what they call it too: *Der Tag*. So maybe I'd better hurry on back to Verdun and get on with our preparing and waiting too, since we are warned now that we shall need them both. Oh, I know. I was not there that day to see his face in that gate as you saw it. But at least I inherited it. We all did: not just that class, but all the others which came after yours and his. And at least we know now what we inherited: only fear, not anguish. A prophet discharged us of that by giving us a warning of it. So only the respect for the other need remain.'

'A murderer,' he said.

'But a man,' the other said, and was gone, leaving him not quite erect from death perhaps but at least with his back once more toward it; erect enough to be aware of the steadily diminishing numbers of his seniority: that diminishing reservoir on which the bark of his career floated, to be aground soon at this rate. In fact, that day would come when he would know that it was aground, revocable never more by any tide or wave or flood: who had believed all his life, if not in his durability, at least in the vast frame which the indurability clothed: whereupon in the next moment he would know that, aground or not, it—he—would never be abandoned; that that edifice which had accepted the gaunt frame's dedication would see always that there was at least one number between him and zero, even if it were only his own; so that the day came, *Der Tag*, the enemy poured, not through Verdun because his caller of that morning twenty-five years back had been right and they would not pass there, but through Flanders so fast and so far that a desperate rag-tag met them in Paris taxi-cabs and held them for the necessary desperate moment, and still behind his glassed veranda he heard how that Number One to his Two in the old St. Cyr class was now Number One among all the desperate and allied peoples in Western Europe, and he said, *Even from here I will have seen the beginning of it*. Then two months later he stood across a desk from the face which he had not seen in thirty years, which he had seen the first time in the St. Cyr gate forty years ago and had been marked forever with it, looking not much older, still calm, composed, the body, the shoulders beneath it still frail and delicate yet doomed—no: not doomed: potent—to bear the fearful burden of man's anguish and terror and at last his hope, looking at him for a moment, then saying: 'The appointment of Quartermaster General is within my gift. Will you accept the office?' and he said to himself, with a sort of peaceful vindication not even of great and desperate hope now but of simple reason, logic: *I will even see the end, accomplishment of it too. I will even be present there.*

But that was a quarter of a century away yet, as the caller of ten minutes ago had prophesied; now he lay beneath his own peaceful tears while the nurse bent over him with a folded cloth, saying, weak but indomitable still, obdurate, incurable and doomed with hope, using the two 'he's' indiscriminately, as though the nurse too knew: 'Yes, he was a man. But he was young then, not much more than a child. These tears are not anguish: only grief.'

The room was now lighted, candelabrum, sconce and girandole.
The windows were closed now, curtain and casement; the room
seemed now to hang insulate as a diving bell above the city's
murmur where the people had already begun to gather again in
the *Place* below. The jug and bowl were gone and the old general
sat once more flanked by his two confreres behind the bare table,
though among them now was a fourth figure as incongruous and
paradoxical as a magpie in a bowl of goldfish—a bearded civilian
sitting between the old generalissimo and the American in that
black-and-white costume which to the Anglo-Saxon is the formal
regalia for eating or seduction or other diversions of the dark, and
to the Continental European and South American the rigid
uniform for partitioning other governments or overthrowing his
own. The young aide stood facing them. He said rapid and glib in
French: 'The prisoners are here. The motorcar from Villeneuve
Blanche will arrive at twenty-two hours. The woman about the
spoon.'

'Spoon?' the old general said. 'Did we take her spoon? Return it.'

'No sir,' the aide said. 'Not this time. The three strange women.
The foreigners. His Honour the Mayor's business.' For a moment
the old general sat perfectly still. But there was nothing in his voice.

'They stole the spoon?'

Nor was there anything in the aide's either: rigid, inflectionless:
'She threw the spoon at them. It disappeared. She has witnesses.'

'Who saw one of them pick up the spoon and hide it,' the old
general said.

The aide stood rigid, looking at nothing. 'She threw a basket
too. It was full of food. The same one caught it in the air without
spilling it.'

'I see,' the old general said. 'Does she come here to protest a
miracle, or merely affirm one?'

'Yes sir,' the aide said 'Do you want the witnesses too?'

'Let the strangers wait,' the old general said. 'Just the plaintiff.'

'Yes sir,' the aide said. He went out again by the smaller door at
the end of the room. Though when in the next second almost he
reappeared, he had not had time to get out of anyone's way. He
returned not swept but tumbled, not in but rather on because he
rose, loomed not half a head nor even a whole head but half a
human being above a tight clump of shawled or kerchiefed women

led by one of a short broad strong fifty-ish who stopped just at the edge of the white rug as if it were water and gave the room one rapid comprehensive look, then another rapid one at the three old men behind the table, then moved again unerringly toward the old generalissimo, leading her group, save the aide who had at last extricated himself beside the door, firmly out on to the blanched surface of the rug, saying in a strong immediate voice:

'That's right. Don't hope to conceal yourself—not behind a mayor anyway; there are too many of you for that. Once I would have said that the curse of this country is its forest of mayorial sashes and swords; I know better now. And after four years of this harassment, even the children can tell a general on sight— provided you can ever see one when you need him.'

'A third miracle then,' the old general said. 'Since your first postulate is proved by the confounding of your second.'

'Miracle?' the woman said. 'Bah. The miracle is that we have anything left after four years of being overrun by foreigners. And now, even Americans. Has France come to that sorry pass where you must not only rob us of our kitchen utensils but even import Americans in order to fight your battles? War, war, war. Don't you ever get tired of it?'

'Indubitably, Madame,' the old general said. 'Your spoon—'

'It vanished. Don't ask me where. Ask them. Or better: have some of your corporals and sergeants search them. It's true there are two of them beneath whose garments even a sergeant would not want to fumble. But none of them would object.'

'No,' the old general said. 'More should not be demanded of corporals and sergeants beyond the simple hazard of military life.' He spoke the aide's name.

'Sir,' the aide said.

'Go to the scene. Find the gentlewoman's spoon and return it to her.'

'I, sir?' the aide cried.

'Take a full company. On your way out, let the prisoners come in. —No: first, the three officers. They are here?'

'Yes sir,' the aide said.

'Good,' the old general said. He turned to the civilian; when he did so, the civilian began to rise from his seat with a sort of startled and diffuse alacrity. 'That should take care of the spoon,' the old general said. 'I believe the rest of your problem was the complaint of the three strange women that they have no place to sleep tonight.'

'That; and—' the mayor said.

'Yes,' the old general said. 'I will see them presently. Meanwhile, will you take care of finding quarters for them, or shall—'

'But certainly, General,' the mayor said.

'Thank you. Then, good night.' He turned to the woman. 'And to you also. And in peace; your spoon will be restored.' Now it was the mayor who was swept, carried—the magpie this time in a flock of pigeons or perhaps hens or maybe geese—back toward the door which the aide held open, and through it, the aide still looking back at the old general with his expression of shocked disbelief.

'A spoon,' the aide said. 'A company. I've never commanded one man, let alone a company of them. And even if I could, knew how, how can I find that spoon?'

'Of course you will find it,' the old general said. 'That will be the fourth miracle. Now, the three officers. But first take the three strange ladies to your office and ask them to wait there for me.'

'Yes sir,' the aide said. He went out and closed the door. It opened again; three men entered: a British colonel, a French major, an American captain, the two juniors flanking the colonel rigidly down the rug and to rigid attention facing the table while the colonel saluted.

'Gentlemen,' the old general said. 'This is not a parade. It is not even an inquiry: merely an identification.—Chairs, please,' he said without turning his head to the galaxy of staff behind him. 'Then the prisoners.' Three of the aides brought chairs around; now that end of the room resembled one end of an amphitheatre or a section of an American bleachers, the three generals and the three newcomers sitting in the beginning of a semi-circle against the bank of aides and staff as one of the aides who had fetched the chairs went on to the smaller door and opened it and stood aside. And now they could smell the men before they even entered—that thin strong ineradicable stink of front lines: of foul mud and burnt cordite and tobacco and ammonia and human filth. Then the thirteen men entered, led by the sergeant with his slung rifle and closed by another armed private, bareheaded, unshaven, alien, stained still with battle, bringing with them still another compounding of the smell—wariness, alertness, just a little of fear too but mostly just watchfulness, deploying a little clumsily as the sergeant spoke two rapid commands in French and halted them into line. The old general turned to the British colonel. 'Colonel?' he said.

'Yes sir,' the colonel said immediately. 'The corporal.' The old general turned to the American.

'Captain?' he said.

'Yes sir,' the American said. 'That's him. Colonel Beale's right —I mean, he can't be right—' But the old general was already speaking to the sergeant.

'Let the corporal remain,' he said. 'Take the others back to the anteroom and wait there.' The sergeant wheeled and barked, but the corporal had already paced once out of ranks, to stand not quite at attention but almost, while the other twelve wheeled into file, the armed private now leading and the sergeant last, up the room to the door, not through it yet but to it, because the head of the file faltered and fell back on itself for a moment and then gave way as the old general's personal aide entered and passed them and then himself gave way aside until the file had passed him, the sergeant following last and drawing the door after him, leaving the aide once more solus before it, boneless, tall, baffled still and incredulous still but not outraged now: merely disorganised. The British colonel said:

'Sir.' But the old general was looking at the aide at the door. He said in French:

'My child?'

'The three women,' the aide said. 'In my office now. While we have our hands on them, why don't—'

'Oh yes,' the old general said. 'Your authority for detached duty. Tell the Chief-of-Staff to let it be a reconnaissance, of—say —four hours. That should be enough.' He turned to the British colonel. 'Certainly, Colonel,' he said.

The colonel rose quickly, staring at the corporal—the high calm composed, not wary but merely watchful, mountain face looking, courteous and merely watchful, back at him. 'Boggan,' the colonel said. 'Don't you remember me? Lieutenant Beale?' But still the face only looked at him, courteous, interrogatory, not baffled: just blank, just waiting. 'We thought you were dead,' the colonel said. 'I—saw you—'

'I did more than that,' the American captain said. 'I buried him.' The old general raised one hand slightly at the captain. He said to the Briton:

'Yes, Colonel?'

'It was at Mons, four years ago. I was a subaltern. This man was in my platoon that afternoon when they . . . caught us. He went down before a lance. I . . . saw the point come through his back before the shaft broke. The next two horses galloped over him. On him. I saw that too, afterward. I mean, just for a second or two, how his face looked after the last horse, before I—I mean, what had used to be his face—' He said, still staring at the corporal, his voice if anything even more urgent because of what its owner had now to cope with: 'Boggan!' But still the corporal only looked at him, courteous, attentive, quite blank. Then the corporal turned and said to the old general in French:

'I'm sorry. I understand only French.'

'I know that,' the old general said also in French. He said in English to the Briton: 'Then this is not the man.'

'It can't be, sir,' the colonel said. 'I saw the head of that lance. I saw his face after the horses—Besides, I—I saw—' He stopped and sat there, martial and glittering in his red tabs and badges of rank and the chain-wisps symbolising the mail in which the regiment had fought at Crécy and Agincourt seven and eight hundred years ago, with his face above them like death itself.

'Tell me,' the old general said gently. 'You saw what? You saw him again later, afterward? Perhaps I know already—the ghosts of your ancient English bowmen there at Mons?—in leather jerkins and hose and crossbows, and he among them in khaki and a steel helmet and an Enfield rifle? Was that what you saw?'

'Yes sir,' the colonel said. Then he sat erect; he said quite loudly: 'Yes sir.'

'But if this could be the same man,' the old general said.

'I'm sorry, sir,' the colonel said.

'You won't say either way: that he is or is not that man?'

'I'm sorry, sir,' the colonel said. 'I've got to believe in something.'

'Even if only death?'

'I'm sorry, sir,' the colonel said. The old general turned to the American.

'Captain?' he said.

'That puts us all in a fix, doesn't it?' the American captain said. 'All three of us; I don't know who's worst off. Because I didn't just see him dead: I buried him, in the middle of the Atlantic Ocean. His name is—was—no, it can't be because I'm looking at him— wasn't Brzonyi. At least it wasn't last year. It was—damn it—I'm sorry sir—is Brzewski. He's from one of the coal towns back of Pittsburgh. I was the one that buried him. I mean, I commanded the burial party read the service: you know. We were National Guard; you probably don't know what that means—'

'I know,' the old general said.

'Sir?' the captain said.

'I know what you mean,' the old general said. 'Continue.'

'Yes sir.—Civilians, organised our own company ourselves, to go out and die for dear old Rutgers—that sort of thing; elected our officers, notified the Government who was to get what commission and then got hold of the Articles of War and tried to memorise as much of it as we could before the commission came back. So when the flu hit us, we were in the transport coming over last October, and when the first one died—it was Brzewski—we found out that none of us had got far enough in the manual to find out how to bury a dead soldier except me—I was a sha—second lieutenant then—and I just happened to have found out by accident the last night before we left because a girl had stood me up and I thought I knew why. I mean, who it was, who the guy was. And you know how it is: you think of all the things to do to get even, make her sorry; you lying dead right there where she's got to step over you to pass, and it's too late now and boy, won't that fix her—'

'Yes,' the old general said. 'I know.'

'Sir?' the captain said.

'I know that too,' the old general said.

'Of course you do—remember, anyway,' the captain said. Nobody's really that old, I don't care how—' going that far before he managed to stop himself. 'I'm sorry, sir,' he said.

'Don't be,' the old general said. 'Continue. So you buried him.'

'So that night just by chance or curiosity or maybe it was personal interest, I was reading up on what somebody would have to do to get rid of me afterward and make Uncle Sam's books balance, and so when Br—' he paused and glanced rapidly at the corporal but only for a second, even less than that: barely a falter even: '—the first one died, I was elected, to certify personally with the M.O. that the body was a dead body and sign the certificate and drill the firing squad and then give the command to dump him overboard. Though by the time we got to Brest two weeks later, all the rest of them had had plenty of practice at it. So you see where that leaves us. I mean, him; he's the one in the fix: if I buried him in the middle of the Atlantic Ocean in October last year, then Colonel Beale couldn't have seen him killed at Mons in 1914. And if Colonel Beale saw him killed in 1914, he can't be standing here now waiting for you to shoot him tomor—' He stopped completely. He said quickly: 'I'm sorry, sir. I didn't—'

'Yes,' the old general said in his courteous and bland and inflectionless voice. 'Then Colonel Beale was wrong.'

'No sir,' the captain said.

'Then you wish to retract your statement that this is the man whose death you personally certified and whose body you saw sink into the Atlantic Ocean?'

'No sir,' the captian said.

'So you believe Colonel Beale.'

'If he says so, sir.'

'That's not quite an answer. Do you believe him?' He watched the captain. The captain looked as steadily back at him. Then the captain said:

'And that I certified him dead and buried him.' He said to the corporal, even in a sort of French: 'So you came back. I'm glad to see you and I hope you had a nice trip,' and looked back at the old general again as steadily as he, as courteously and as firm, a good moment this time until the old general said in French:

'You speak my tongue also.'

'Thank you, sir,' the captain answered him. 'No other French-man ever called it that.'

'Do not demean yourself. You speak it well. What is your name?'

'Middleton, sir.'

'You have—twenty-five years, perhaps?'

'Twenty-four, sir.'

'Twenty-four. Some day you are going to be a very dangerous man, if you are not already so': and said to the corporal: 'Thank you, my child. You may return to your squad,' and spoke a name

251

over his shoulder without turning his head, though the aide had already come around the table as the corporal about-faced, the aide flanking him back to the door and through it and out, the American captain turning his head back in time to meet for another second the quiet and inscrutable eyes, the courteous, bland, almost gentle voice: 'Because his name is Brzewski here too.' He sat back in the chair; again he looked like a masquerading child beneath the illusion of crushing and glittering weight of his blue-and-scarlet and gold and brass and leather, until even the five who were still sitting had the appearance of standing too, surrounding and enclosing him. He said in English: 'I must leave you for a short time. But Major Blum speaks English. It is not as good as yours of course, nor as good as Captain Middleton's French, but it should do; one of our allies—Colonel Beale—saw him slain, and the other—Captain Middleton—buried him, so all that remains for us is to witness to his resurrection, and none more competent for that than Major Blum, who was graduated from the Academy into the regiment in 1913 and so was in it before and has been in it ever since the day when this ubiquitous corporal reached it. So the only question is—' he paused a second; it was as though he had even glanced about at them without even moving: the delicate and fragile body, the delicate face beautiful, serene, and terrifying '—who knew him first: Colonel Beale at Mons in August, 1914, or Major Blum at Chalons in that same month—before of course Captain Middleton buried him at sea in 1917. But that is merely academic: identity—if there is such—has been established (indeed, it was never disputed): there remains only recapitulation, and Major Blum will do that.' He stood up; except for the two generals, the others rose quickly too and although he said rapidly: 'No no, sit down, sit down,' the three newcomers continued to stand. He turned to the French major. 'Colonel Beale has his ghostly bowmen in Belgium; at least we can match that with our archangels on the Aisne. Surely you can match that for us—the tremendous aerial shapes patrolling our front, and each time they are thickest, heaviest, densest, most archangelic, our corporal is there too perhaps, pacing with them—the usual night firing going on, just enough to make a sane man keep his head below the trench and be glad he has a trench to keep his head below, yet this corporal is outside the trench, between the parapet and the wire, pacing along as peacefully as a monk in his cloister while the great bright formless shapes pace the dark air beside and above him? Or perhaps not even pacing but simply leaning on the wire contemplating that desolation like a farmer his turnip-field? Come, Major.'

'My imagination wears only a majority, sir,' the major said. 'It cannot compete with yours.'

'Nonsense,' the old general said. 'The crime—if any—is already established. If any? Established? We did not even need to establish it; he did not even merely accept it in advance: he abrogated it. All that remains now is to find extenuation—pity, if we can persuade him to accept pity. Come, tell them.'

'There was the girl,' the major said.

'Yes,' the old general said. 'The wedding and the wine.'

'No sir,' the major said. 'Not quite now. You see, I can—how do you say?—*démentir—contredire*—say against—'

'Contradict,' the American captain said.

'Thank you,' the major said. '—contradict you here; my majority can cope with simple regimental gossip.'

'Tell them,' the old general said. So the major did, though that was after the old general had left the room—a little girl, a child going blind in one of the Aisne towns for lack of an operation which a certain famous Paris surgeon could perform, the corporal levying upon the troops of two nearby divisions, a franc here and two francs there until the surgeon's fee was raised and the child sent to him. And an old man; he had a wife, daughter and grandson and a little farm in 1914 but waited too long to evacuate it, unable until too late to tear himself away from what he possessed; his daughter and grandson vanished in the confusion which ended at the first Marne battle, his old wife died of exposure on the roadside, the old man returning alone to the village when it was freed again and he could, where, an idiot, name forgotten, grief and all forgotten, only moaning a little, drooling, grubbing for food in the refuse of army kitchens, sleeping in ditches and hedgerows on the spot of earth which he had owned once, until the corporal used one of his leaves to hunt out a remote kinsman of the old man's in a distant Midi village and levied again on the regiment for enough to send him there.

'And now,' the major said. He turned to the American captain. 'How to say, *touché?*'

'You're out,' the captain said. 'And I wish he was still present so I could hear you say it to him.'

'Bah,' the major said. 'He is a Frenchman. It is only a boche marshal that no man can speak to. And now, you're out, from him to me. Because now the wedding and the wine—' and told that—a village behind Montfaucon and only this past winter because they were American troops; they had just been paid, a dice game was going on, the floor littered with franc notes and half the American company crowded around them when the French corporal entered and without a word began to gather up the scattered money; for a time a true international incident was in the making until the corporal finally managed to communicate, explain, what it was about: a wedding: one of the young American soldiers, and a girl, an orphan refugee from somewhere beyond Rheims, who was now a sort of slavey in the local estaminet; she and the young American had—had—

'The rest of his company would say he had knocked her up,' the American captain said. 'But we know what you mean. Go on.' So the major did: the matter ending with the entire company not only attending the wedding but adopting it, taking charge of it, buying up all the wine in the village for the supper and inviting the whole countryside; adopting the marriage too: endowing the bride with a wedding gift sufficient to set up as a lady in her own right, to wait in her own single rented room until—if—her husband returned from his next tour in the lines. But that would be after the old general had left the room; now the three newcomers made way for him as he came around the table and paused and said:

'Tell them. Tell them how he got the medal too. What we seek now is not even extenuation, not even pity, but mercy—if there is such—if he will accept that either,' and turned and went on toward the small door: at which moment it opened and the aide who had taken the prisoner out stood at attention beside it for the old general to pass, then followed and closed the door behind them. 'Yes?' the old general said.

'They are in De Montigny's office,' the aide said. 'The youngest one, the girl, is a Frenchwoman. One of the older ones is the wife of a Frenchman, a farmer—'

'I know,' the old general said. 'Where is the farm?'

'Was, sir,' the aide said. 'It was near a village called Vienne-la-pucelle, north of St. Mihiel. That country was all evacuated in 1914. On Monday morning Vienne-la-pucelle was under the enemy's front line.'

'Then she and her husband don't know whether they have a farm or not,' the old general said.

'No sir,' the aide said.

'Ah,' the old general said. Then he said again: 'Yes?'

'The motorcar from Villeneuve Blanche has just entered the courtyard.'

'Good,' the old general said. 'My compliments to our guest, and conduct him to my study. Serve his dinner there, and request his permission to receive us in one hour.'

The aide's office had been contrived three years ago by carpenters out of—or into—a corner of what had been a ballroom and then a courtroom. The aide saw it each twenty-four hours and obviously even entered it at least once during those periods because on a rack in the corner hung his hat and topcoat and a very fine beautifully-furled London umbrella, in juxtaposition to that hat and that coat as bizarre and paradox as a domino or a fan, until you realised that it could quite well have owed its presence there to the same thing which the only other two objects of any note in the room did: two bronzes which sat at either end of the otherwise completely bare desk—a delicate and furious horse poised weightless and epicene on one leg, and a savage and slumbrous head not cast, molded but cut by hand out of the amalgam by Gaudier-Brzeska. Otherwise the cubicle was empty save for a wooden bench against the wall facing the desk.

When the old general entered, the three women were sitting on it, the two older ones on the outside and the younger one between them; as he crossed to the desk without yet looking at them, the young one gave a quick, almost convulsive start, as though to get up, until one of the others stopped her with one hand. Then they sat again, immobile, watching him while he went around the desk and sat down behind the two bronzes and looked at them—the harsh high mountain face which might have been a twin of the corporal's except for the difference in age, the serene and peaceful one which showed no age at all or perhaps all ages, and between them the strained and anguished one of the girl. Then, as though on a signal, as if she had waited for him to complete the social amenity of sitting too, the peaceful one—she held on her lap a wicker basket neatly covered by an immaculate tucked-in cloth—spoke.

'I'm glad to see you, anyway,' she said. 'You look so exactly like what you are.'

'Marya,' the other older one said.

'Don't be ashamed,' the first one said. 'You can't help it. You should be pleased, because so many don't.' She was already rising. The other said again:

'Marya,' and even raised her hand again, but the first one came on to the desk, carrying the basket, beginning to raise her other hand as though to approach the basket with it as she reached the desk, then extending the hand until it lay on the desk. It now held a long-handled iron spoon.

'That nice young man,' she said. 'At least you should be ashamed of that. Sending him out to tramp about the city at night with all those soldiers.'

'The fresh air will be good for him,' the old general said. 'He doesn't get much of it in here.'

'You could have told him.'

'I never said you had it. I only said I believed you could produce it when it was needed.'

'Here it is.' She released the spoon and laid that hand lightly on the one which held the tucked-in and undisturbed basket. Then immediately and peacefully but without haste she smiled at him, serene and uncritical. 'You really can't help it, can you? You really can't.'

'Marya,' the woman on the bench said. Again immediately but without haste, the smile went away. It was not replaced by any-thing: it just went away, leaving the face unchanged, uncritical, serene.

'Yes, sister,' she said. She turned and went back to the bench where the other woman had risen now; again the girl had made that convulsive start to rise too; this time the tall woman's hard thin peasant hand was gripping her shoulder, holding her down.

'This is—' the old general said.

'His wife,' the tall woman said harshly. 'Who did you expect it to be?'

'Ah yes,' the old general said, looking at the girl; he said, in that gentle inflectionless voice: 'Marseille? Toulon perhaps?' then named the street, the district, pronouncing the street name which was its by-word. The woman started to answer but the old general raised his hand at her. 'Let her answer,' he said, then to the girl: 'My child? A little louder.'

'Yes sir,' the girl said.

'Oh yes,' the woman said. 'A whore. How else do you think she got here—got the papers to come this far, to this place, except to serve France also?'

'But his wife too,' the old general said.

'His wife now,' the woman corrected. 'Accept that, whether you believe it or not.'

'I do both,' the old general said. 'Accept that from me too.'

Then she moved, released the girl's shoulder and came toward the desk, almost to it in fact, then stopping as though at the exact spot from which her voice would be only a murmur to the two still on the bench when she spoke: 'Do you want to send them out first?'

'Why?' the old general said. 'So you are Magda.'

'Yes,' she said. 'Not Marthe: Magda. I wasn't Marthe until after I had a brother and had to cross half of Europe to face thirty years later the French general who would hold the refusal of his life. Not gift: refusal; and even that's wrong: the taking back of it.' She stood, tall, still, looking down at him. 'So you even knew us. I was about to say "Not remembered us," because you never saw us. But maybe that's wrong too and you did see us then. If you did, you would remember us even if I wasn't but nine then and Marya eleven, because as soon as I saw your face tonight I knew that it would never need to flee, hide from, fear or dread or grieve at having to remember anything it ever looked at. Marya might fail to see that maybe—Marya now too, since she also had to come all the way to France to watch the refusal of her half-brother's life, even if she doesn't need to fear or dread or grieve at having to remember either—but not I. Maybe Marya is why you remember us if you saw us then: because she was eleven then and in our country girls at eleven are not girls any more, but women. But I won't

257

say that, not because of the insult that would be even to our
mother, let alone to you—our mother who had something in her—
I don't mean her face—which did not belong in that village—that
village? in all our mountains, all that country while what you
must have had—had? have—in you is something which all the
earth had better beware and dread and be afraid of. The insult
would have been to evil itself. I don't mean just that evil. I mean
Evil, as if there was a purity in it, a severity, a jealousy like in God
—a strictness of untruth incapable of compromise or second-best
or substitute. A purpose, an aim in it, as though not just our
mother but you neither could help yourselves; and not just you
but our—mine and Marya's—father too: not two of you but three
of you doing not what you would but what you must. That people,
men and women, don't choose evil and accept it and enter it, but
evil chooses the men and women by test and trial, proves and tests
them and then accepts them forever until the time comes when
they are consumed and empty and at last fail evil because they no
longer have anything that evil can want or use; then it destroys
them. So it wasn't just you, a stranger happened by accident into
a country so far away and hard to get to that whole generations of
us are born and live and die in it without even knowing or wondering or caring what might be on the other side of our mountains
or even if the earth extends there. Not just a man come there by
chance, having already whatever he would need to charm, trance,
bewitch a weak and vulnerable woman, then finding a woman
who was not only weak and vulnerable but beautiful too—oh yes,
beautiful; if that was what you had to plead, her beauty and your
love, my face would have been the first to forgive you, since the
jealousy would be not yours but hers—just to destroy her home,
her husband's faith, her children's peace, and at last her life—to
drive her husband to repudiate her just to leave her children father-
less, then her to die in childbirth in a cow-byre behind a roadside
inn just to leave them orphans, then at last have the right—
privilege—duty, whatever you want to call it—to condemn that
last and only male child to death just that the name which she
betrayed shall be no more. Because that's not enough. It's nowhere
near enough. It must be something much bigger than that, much
more splendid, much more terrible: not our father gone all that
long distance from our valley to seek a beautiful face to be the

mother of his name's succession, then finding instead the fatal and calamitous one which would end it; not you blundered there by chance, but sent there to meet that beautiful and fatal face; not her so weak in pride and virtue, but rather doomed by that face from them—not the three of you compelled there just to efface a name from man's history, because who on earth outside our valley ever heard that name, or cared? But instead to create a son for one of you to condemn to death as though to save the earth, save the world, save man's history, save mankind.'

She brought both hands up in front of her and let them rest there, the fist of one lying in the other palm. 'Of course you knew us. My folly was in even thinking I would need to bring you proof. So now I don't know just what to do with it, when to use it, like a knife capable of only one stroke or a pistol with just one bullet, which I can't afford to risk too soon and dare not wait too late. Maybe you even know the rest of it already too; I remember how wrong I was that you would not know who we are. Maybe your face is telling me now that you already know the rest of it, end of it, even if you weren't there, had served your destiny—or anyway hers—and gone away.'

'Tell me then,' the old general said.

'—if I must? Is that it? The ribbons and stars and braid that turned forty years of spears and bullets, yet not one of them to stop a woman's tongue?—Or try to tell you, that is, because I don't know; I was only nine then, I only saw and remembered; Marya too, even if she was eleven, because even then she already didn't need to dread or grieve for anything just because her face had looked at it. Not that we needed to look at this because it had been there all our lives, most of the valley's too. It was already ours, our—the valley's—pride (with a little awe in it) as another one might have a peak or glacier or waterfall—that speck, that blank white wall or dome or tower—whatever it was—which was first in all our valley that the sun touched and the last that lost it, still holding light long after the gulch we crouched in had lost what little it had ever snared. Yet it wasn't high either; high wasn't the right word either; you couldn't—we didn't—measure where it was that way. It was just higher than any of our men, even herdsmen and hunters, ever went. Not higher than they could but than they did, dared; no shrine or holy place because we knew them too and even the kind of men that lived in, haunted, served them; mountain men too before they were priests because we knew their fathers and our fathers had known their grandfathers, so they would be priests only afterward with what was left. Instead, it was an eyrie like where eagles nested, where people—men—came as if through the air itself (you), leaving no more trace of coming or arriving (yes, you) or departing (oh yes, you) than eagles would (oh yes, you too; if Marya and I ever saw you then, we did not remember it, nor when you saw us if you ever did except for our mother's telling; I almost said If our father himself ever saw you in the flesh because of course he did, you would have seen to that yourself: a gentleman honourable in gentleman fashion and brave too since it would have taken courage, our father having already lost too much for that little else to be dear spending), come there not to tremble on their knees on stone floors, but to think. To think: not that dreamy hoping and wishing and believing (but mainly just waiting) that we would think is thinking, but some fierce and rigid concentration that at any time—tomorrow, today, next moment, this one—will change the shape of the earth.

'Not high, just high enough to stand between us and the sky like a way-station to heaven, so no wonder when we died the rest of us believed the soul hadn't stopped there maybe but at least had paused to surrender half the coupon; no wonder when our mother was gone for that week in the spring, Marya and I knew where she had gone to; not dead: we had buried nothing, so she wouldn't have to pass it. But certainly there, since where else could she be—that face which had never belonged to, had no place in, our valley from the beginning, not to mention what we, even her children, had felt, sensed, behind that face which had no place in our mountains, among our kind of people anywhere; where else but there? not to think, to be accepted into that awesome and tremendous condition, because even her face and what was behind it could not match that, but at least to breathe, bathe in the lambence of that furious meditation. The wonder was that she came back. Not the valley's wonder but mine and Marya's too. Because we were children, we didn't know: we only watched and saw and knitted, knotted, tried to, what simple threads we had of implication; to us it was simply that the face, that something— whatever it was—in her that had never been ours and our father's

260

anyway even if it had been wife to one and mother to the others, had at last simply done what from the beginning it had been doomed to do. Yet she came back. She didn't change forever that house, home, life and all, she had already done that by leaving as she did and coming back to it only compounded what she had already left there; she had been alien and a passing guest always anyhow, she couldn't possibly come back any more so. So Marya and I, even children, knew even more than the valley did that it couldn't last. The child, another child, a new brother or sister or whichever it would be next winter, meant nothing to us. Even if we were children, we knew about babies; who so young in our country as not to know, since in our country, our hard and unpiteous mountains, people used, had to use, needed, required, had nothing else to use, children as people in lands savage with dangerous animals used guns and bullets: to defend, preserve themselves, endure; we didn't see, as our father did, that child not the brand of sin but incontrovertible proof of something which otherwise he might have schooled himself to bear. He didn't turn her out of his house. Don't think that. It was us—she. He was just going to leave himself, put home, past, all the dreams and hopes that people call home; the rage, the impotence, the out-raged masculinity—oh yes, heartbreak too: why not?—all behind him. It was she who cut that cord and left, swollen belly and all because it could not be long now, it was already winter and maybe we couldn't compute gestation but we had seen enough swelled female bellies to guess approximations.

'So we left. It was at night, after dark. He had left right after supper, we didn't know where, and now I would say, maybe just hunting dark and solitude and space and silence for what wasn't there or anywhere else for him either. And I know now why the direction we—she—took was west too, and where the money came from that we had for a while too until we couldn't pay for riding any more and had to walk, because she—we—took nothing from that house except the clothes we wore and our shawls and a little food which Marya carried in that same basket yonder. And I could say here also: "But you were safe, it was not enough" except that I don't, not to you who have in you what all heaven too might do well to blench at. So we walked then and still westward: who might not have learned to think in that place during that week

261

but at least she had memorised something of geography. Then there was no more food except what we could beg, but it would not be long now even if we had money left to ride with too. Then that night, it was already winter when we left home and now it was Christmas, the eve before; and now I don't remember if we were driven from the inn itself or just turned away or maybe perhaps it was our mother still who would cut even that cord too with man. I remember only the straw, the dark stable and the cold, nor whether it was Marya or I who ran back through the snow to beat on the closed kitchen door until someone came—only the light at last, the lantern, the strange and alien faces crowding downward above us, then the blood and lymph and wet: I, a child of nine and an eleven-year-old idiot sister trying to hide into what privacy we could that outraged betrayed abandon and forsaken nakedness while her closed hand fumbled at mine and she tried to speak, the hand still gripping, holding on to it even after I had given my word, my promise, my oath—'

She stood looking down at him, the closed fist of the one hand lying in the palm of the other. 'Not for you: for him. No, that's wrong; it was already for you, for this moment, that night thirty-three years ago when she first gripped it into my hand and tried to speak; I must have known even at nine that I would cross half of Europe to bring it to you some day, just as I must have known even at nine how vain the bringing it would be. A fate, a doom communicated, imposed on me by the mere touch of it against my flesh, before I even opened it to look inside and divine, surmise who the face belonged to, even before I—we—found the purse, the money which was to bring us here. Oh you were generous; nobody denied that. Because how could you have known that the money which was to have brought you immunity from the consequence of your youthful folly—a dowry if the child should be a girl, a tilted scrap of pasture and a flock to graze it if a boy, and a wife for him in time and so even the same grandchildren to immobilise your folly's partner forever beyond the geographic range of your vulnerability—would instead accomplish the exact opposite by paying our passage to Beirut and—with what was left over—becoming what was its original intent: a dowry?

'Because we could have stayed there, in our mountains, our country, among people whose kind we knew and whose kind knew us. We could have stayed right there at the inn, the village where we were because people are really kind, they really are capable of pity and compassion for the weak and orphaned and helpless because it is pity and compassion and they are weak and helpless and orphaned and people though of course you cannot, dare not believe that: who dare believe only that people are to be bought and used empty and then thrown away. In fact we did stay there for almost ten years. We worked of course, at the inn—in the kitchen, with the milk cows; in—for—the village too; being witless Marya had a way with simple unmartial creatures like cows and geese which were content to be simple cows and geese instead of lions and stags: but then so would we have worked back home, which was where for all their kindness, perhaps because of their kindness, they tried at first to persuade us to return.

'But not I. The doom might have been his, but the curse to hurry it, consummate it, at least was mine; I was the one now wearing the secret talisman, token, not to remember, cherish; no tender memento of devoted troth nor plighted desertion either: but lying instead against my flesh beneath my dress like a brand a fever a coal a goad driving me (I was his mother now; the doom that moved him would have to move me first; already at nine and ten and eleven I was the mother of two—the infant brother and the idiot sister two years my senior too—until at Beirut I found a father for them both) toward the day the hour the moment the instant when with his same blood he would discharge the one and expiate the other. Yes, the doom was his but at least I was its hand-maiden: to bring you this. I must bring you the reason for its need too; to bring you this I must bring with me into your orbit the very object which would constitute and make imperative that need Worse: by bringing it into your orbit, I myself created the need which the token, the last desperate cast remaining to me, would be incapable of discharging.

'A curse and doom which in time was to corrupt the very kindly circumambience which harboured us because already you are trying to ask how we managed to have to pass through Asia Minor in order to reach Western Europe, and I will tell you. It was not us. It was the village. No: it was all of us together: a confederation. France: a word a name a designation significant yet foundationless like the ones for grace or Tuesday or quarantine, esoteric and infrequent not just to us but to the ignorant and kindly people among whom we had found orphaned and homeless haven: who had barely heard of France either and did not care until our advent among them: whereupon it was as though they had established a living rapport with it through, by means of us who did not even know where it was except west and that we—I, dragging the other two with me—must go there: until presently we were known to the whole village—valley, district—as the little Franchini: the three who were going to—bound for—dedicated for—France as others might be for some distant and irrevocable state or condition like a nunnery or the top of Mount Everest—not heaven; everybody believes he will be on his way there just as soon as he finds time to really concentrate on it—but some peculiar and individual esoteric place to which no one really wants to go save in idle speculation yet which reflects a certain communal glory on the place which was host to the departure and witnessed the preparations.

'Because we had never heard of Beirut at all; it required older and more worldly people than us to have known that Beirut even was, let alone that there was a French colony there, a garrison, official—in effect France, the nearest France to where we were. That is, the real France might have been nearer but that was over-land and therefore expensive and we were poor; what we had to travel on was time and leisure. There was the purse of course which probably wouldn't have taken all three of us to France the quickest route anyway, even if there had not been a better reason than that to save the purse. So we spent what we had the most of, travelling as only the very poor or the very rich can; only they travel rapidly who are too rich to have time and too poor to have leisure: by sea, spending only enough of the purse to set the three of us in the nearest available official authentic fringe of France and still leave as much as possible over. Because I was nineteen now and in me we had now something even more mutually compoundable than the purse, of which we needed only enough to set me, not empty-handed, into the quickest marriage-range of the French husband who would be the passport of all three of us into the country where our brother's destiny waited for him.

'That was why Beirut. I had never heard of it but why should I have doubted when the village didn't? Any more that in its or

God's good time Beirut would appear at the end of the ship, the voyage, than that the French husband would be waiting for me there. Which he was. I had never even heard his name before and I don't even recall all the circumstances of our meeting: only that it was not long and he was—is—a good man and has been a good husband to me and brother to Marya and father to him of whom I am apparently to have all the anguishes save the initial one of having borne him, and I have tried—will still try—to be a good wife to him. He was a soldier in the garrison. That is, doing his military service because he was bred a farmer and his time was just up; oh yes, it was that close; one more day and I would have missed him, which should have told me, warned me that what faced us was doom, not destiny, since only destiny is clumsy, inefficient, procrastinative, while doom never is. But I didn't know that then. I knew only that we must reach France, which we did: the farm—I won't even bother to tell you where it is—'

'I know where it is,' the old general said. She had been immobile all the while so she couldn't become stiller—a tall figure breathing so quietly that she didn't seem to be doing that either, clasping the closed fist into the other motionless palm, looking down at him.

'So we have already come to that,' she said. 'Of course you have learned where the farm is; how else could you know what spot to hesitate to give me permission in which to bury the flesh and bone of the flesh and bone you loved once—lusted after once at least. You even know already in advance the request I'll finally demand of you, since we both know now that this—' without uncrossing her hands she moved the closed one slightly then returned it to the other palm '—will be in vain.'

'Yes,' the old general said. 'I know that too.'

'And granted in advance too, since by that time he'll be no more a threat? No no, don't answer yet; let me believe a little longer that I could never have believed that anyone, not even you, could any more control the flux of the bowels of natural compassion than he could his physical ones. Where was I? Oh yes, the farm. In that ship to Beirut I had heard them talk of landfall and harbour; by Beirut I even knew what haven meant and now at last in France I believed that we—he—had found them. Home: who had never known one before: four walls and a hearth to come back to at the end of day because they were mutually his walls and hearth; work to be done not for pay or the privilege of sleeping in a hayloft or left-over food at a kitchen door but because the finished task was mutually his too to choose between its neglect and its completion. Because already he was not just a natural farmer: he was a good one, as though that half of his blood and background and heritage which was peasant had slept in untimed suspension until his destiny found and matched him with land, earth good and broad and rich and deep enough, so that by the end of the second year he was my husband's heir and would still be co-heir even if we had children of our own. And not just home but fatherland too; he was already a French subject; in ten more years he would be a French citizen too, a citizen of France, a Frenchman to all effect and purpose, and his very nameless origin would be as though it had never been.

'So now at last we—I, he—could forget you. No, not that: we couldn't forget you because you were why we were where we were, had at last found the harbour, haven where, as they said in the ship, we could drop anchor and make fast and secure. Besides, he couldn't very well forget you because he had never heard of you yet. It was rather that I forgave you. Now at last I could stop seeking you, harrying, dragging two other people over the earth in order to find and face and reproach, compel, whatever it would be; remember, I was a child still, even if I had been the mother of two since I was nine years old. It was as though it had been I in my ignorance who had misread you and owed you the apology and the shame where you in your wisdom had known all the time the one restitution for which he was fitted; that, because of that ineradicable peasant other half of his origin, any other relationship, juxtaposition, with you would have brought him only disaster, perhaps even to the point of destroying him. Oh yes, I believed now that you already knew this history, not only where we were but how and what we were doing there, hoped—yes, believed— that you had deliberately arranged and planned it to be even if you may not quite have anticipated that I should establish it intact on your own doorstep—haven and harbour and home not just for him but us too, Marya and me too: all four of us, not just yourself and the one you had begot but the other two whose origin you had had no part in, all branded forever more into one irremediable kinship by that one same passion which had created three of our lives and altered forever the course or anyway the pattern of your own; the four of us together even obliterating that passion's irremediable past in which you had not participated: in your own get you dispossessed your predecessor; in Marya and me you effaced even his seniority; and in Marya, her first child, you even affirmed to yourself the trophy of its virginity. More: in the two of us—not Marya this time because, unrational and witless, she was incapable of threatening you and, herself innocent of harm, was herself invulnerable even to you since the witless know only loss and absence: never bereavement—but he and I were not only your absolution but even your expiation too, as though in your design's first completion you had even foreseen this moment here now and had decreed already to me in proxy the last right and privilege of your dead abandoned paramour: to vaunt her virtue for constancy at the same time she heaped on you the reproach of her fall.

'So I didn't even need to forgive you either: we were all four one now in that workable mutual, neither compassionate nor uncompassionate, armistice and none of us neither needed or had the time to waste forgiving or reproaching one another because we would all be busy enough in supporting, balancing that condition of your expiation and our—his—reparations whose instrument you had been. Nor had I ever seen your face to remember either and now I began to believe that I never would, never would have to: that even when—if—the moment ever came when you would have, could no longer evade having, to face one another, he alone would be enough and he would not require my ratification or support. No, it was the past itself which I had forgiven, could at last forgive: swapped all that bitter and outraged impotence for the home—harbour—haven which was within the range of his capacities, which he was fitted and equipped for—more: would have chosen himself if he had had the choice—whose instrument you in your anonymity had been whether you actually intended for it to be in France or not, where, since he was free of you, the two others of us could be also. Then his military class was called. He went almost eagerly—not that he could have done else, as I know, but then so do you know that there are ways and still ways of accepting what you have no choice of refusing. But he went almost eagerly and served his tour—I almost said time, but didn't I just say he went almost eagerly?—and came back home and then I believed that he was free of you—that you and he also had struck a balance, an armistice in liability and threat; he was a French citizen and a Frenchman now not only legally but morally too since the date of his birth proved his right to the one and he had just doffed the uniform in which he himself had proved his right and worthiness to the other; not only was he free of you but each of you was free now of the other: you absolved of the liability since, having given him life, you had now created for him security and dignity in which to end it and so you owed him nothing; he absolved of threat since you no longer harmed him now and so you didn't need to fear him any more.

'Yes, free of you at last, or so I thought. Or you were free of him, that is, since he was the one who had better be afraid. If any minuscule of danger still remained for you in him, he himself would eradicate it now by the surest means of all: marriage, a wife and family; so many economic responsibilities to bear and discharge that he would have no time over to dream of his moral rights; a family, children: that strongest and most indissoluble bond of al to mesh him harmless forever more into his present and commit him irrevocably to his future and insulate him for good and always from the griefs and anguishes (he had none of course in the sense I mean because he still had never heard of you) of his past.

'But it seems that I was wrong. Wrong always in regard to you, wrong every time in what I thought you thought or felt or feared from him. Never more wrong than now, when apparently you had come to believe that bribing him with independence of you had merely scotched the snake, not killed it, and marriage would compound his threat to you in children, any one of which might prove impervious to the bribe of a farm. Any marriage, even this one. And at first it looked as if your own blood was trying to fend and shield you from this threat as though in a sort of instinctive filial loyalty. We had long ago designed marriage for him and, now that he was free, grown, a man, a citizen, heir to the farm because we —my husband and I—knew now that we would have no children, his military service forever (so we thought then) behind him, we began to plan one. Except that he refused twice, declined twice the candidates virtuous and solvent and suitable which we picked for him, and still in such a way that we could never tell if it was the girl he said no to or the institution. Perhaps both, being your son though as far as I know he still didn't know you even existed; perhaps both, having inherited both from you: the repudiation of the institution since his own origin had done without it; the finicky choosing of a partner, since with him once passion had had to be enough because it was all and he in his turn felt, desired, believed that he deserved, no less to match his own inheritance.

'Or was it even worse than that to you: your own son truly, demanding not even revenge on you but vengeance: refusing the two we picked who were not only solvent but virtuous too, for that one who had not even sold the one for the other but in bartering one had trafficked them both away? I didn't know, we didn't know: only that he had refused, declined, and still in that way I told you of, less of refusal than negation, so that we just thought he wasn't ready yet, that he still wanted a little more of that young man's bachelor and tieless freedom which he had only regained— regained? found—yesterday when he doffed the uniform. So we could wait too and we did; more time passed but we still thought there was enough of it, since marriage is long enough to have plenty of room for time behind it. Then—suddenly, with no warning to us who knew only work and bread, not politics and glory—it was 1914 and whether there had been time enough or not or he had been right to wait or not didn't matter. Because he didn't wait now either; he was gone that first week in the old uniform still stinking of the mothballs from the garret trunk but even that was no quicker nor faster than we were; you know where the farm is—was (no: still is since it will have to still be there in order to be a basis for what you will finally grant us) so I don't need to tell you how we left it either, since a part of your trade is coping with the confused and anguished mass of the civilian homeless in order to make room for your victories.

'He didn't even wait to be called by his class. A stranger might have guessed it to be a young bachelor accepting even war as a last desperate cast to escape matrimony, but that stranger would be wrong of course, as he himself proved two years later. But we knew better. He was a Frenchman now. All France asked of him in return for that dignity and right and that security and independence was his willingness to defend it and them, and he had gone to do that. Then suddenly all France (all Western Europe too for that matter) was loud with your name; every child even in France knew your face because you would save us—you, to be supreme of all, not to command our armies and the armies of our allies because they did not need to be commanded, since the terror and the threat was their terror and threat too and all they needed was to be led, comforted, reassured and you were the one to do that because they had faith in you, believed in you. But I knew more. Not better: just more; I had only to match almost any newspaper with this—' again she moved slightly the closed hand lying in the other palm '—and now I knew not only who you were but what you were and where you were. No no, you didn't start this war just to further prove him as your son and a Frenchman, but rather since this war had to be, his own destiny, fate would use it to prove him to his father. You see? You and he together to be one in the saving of France, he in his humble place and you in your high and matchless one and victory itself would be that day when at last you would see one another face to face, he rankless still save for the proven bravery and constancy and devotion which the medal you would fasten to his breast would symbolise and affirm.

'It was the girl of course; his revenge and vengeance on you which you feared: a whore, a Marseille whore to mother the grandchildren of your high and exalted blood. He told us of her on his leave in the second year. We—I—said no of course too, but then he had that of you also; the capacity to follow his will always. Oh yes, he told us of her: a good girl, he said, leading through her own fate, necessity, compulsions (there is an old grandmother) a life which was not her life. And he was right. We saw that as soon as he brought her to us. She is a good girl, now anyway, since then anyway, maybe always a good girl as he believed or maybe only since she loved him. Anyway, who are we to challenge him and her, if what this proves is what love can do: save a woman as well as doom her? But no matter now. You will never believe, perhaps you dare not risk it, chance it, that he would never have made any claim on you: that this whore's children would bear not his father's name but my father's. You would never believe that they would never any more know whose blood they carried than he would have known except for this. But it's too late now. That's all over now; I had imagined you facing him for the first time on that last victorious field while you fastened a medal to his coat; instead you will see him for the first time—no, you won't even see him; you won't even be there—tied to a post, you to see him—if you were to see him, which you will not—over the shoulders and the aimed rifles of a firing-squad.'

The hand, the closed one, flicked, jerked, so fast that the eye almost failed to register it and the object seemed to gleam once in the air before it even appeared, already tumbling across the vacant top of the desk until it sprang open as though of its own accord and came to rest—a small locket of chased worn gold, opening like a hunting-case watch upon twin medallions, miniatures painted on ivory. 'So you actually had a mother. You really did. When I first saw the second face inside it that night, I thought it was your wife or sweetheart or mistress, and I hated you. But I know better now and I apologise for imputing to your character a capacity so weak as to have earned the human warmth of hatred.' She looked down at him. 'So I did wait too late to produce it, after all. No, that's wrong too. Any moment would have been too late; any moment I might have chosen to use it as a weapon, the pistol would have misfired, the knife-blade shattered at the stroke. So of course you know what my next request will be.'

'I know it,' the old general said.

'And granted in advance of course, since then he can no longer threaten you. But at least it's not too late for him to receive the locket, even though it cannot save him. At least you can tell me that. Come. Say it: At least it's not too late for him to receive it.'

'It's not too late,' the old general said. 'He will receive it.'

'So he must die.' They looked at each other. 'Your own son.'

'Then will he not merely inherit from me at thirty-three what I had already bequeathed to him at birth?'

By its size and location, the room which the old general called his study had probably been the chamber, cell of the old marquise's favourite lady-in-waiting or perhaps tiring-woman, though by its appearance now it might have been a library lifted bodily from an English country home and then reft of the books and furnishings. The shelves were empty now except for one wall, and those empty too save for a brief row of the text-books and manuals of the old general's trade, stacked neatly at one end of one shelf. Beneath this, against the wall, was a single narrow army cot pillowless beneath a neatly and immaculately drawn grey army blanket; at the foot of it sat the old general's battered field desk. Otherwise the room contained a heavyish, Victorian-looking, almost American-looking table surrounded by four chairs in which the four generals were sitting. The table had been cleared of the remains of the German general's meal; an orderly was just going out with the final tray of soiled dishes. Before the old general were a coffee service and a tray of decanters and glasses. The old general filled the cups and passed them. Then he took up one of the decanters.

'Schnapps, General, of course,' he said to the German general.

'Thanks,' the German general said. The old general filled and passed the glass. The old general didn't speak to the British general at all; he simply passed the port decanter and an empty glass to him, then a second empty glass.

'Since General (he called the American general's name) is already on your left.' He said to no one directly, calling the American general's name again: '—doesn't drink after dinner, as a rule. Though without doubt he will void it tonight.' Then to the American: 'Unless you will have brandy too?'

'Port, thank you, General,' the American said. 'Since we are only recessing an alliance: not abrogating it.'

'Bah,' the German general said. He sat rigid, bright with medals, the ground glass monocle (it had neither cord nor ribbon; it was not on his face, his head, like an ear, but set as though inevictably into the socket of his right eye like an eyeball itself) fixed in a rigid opaque glare at the American general. 'Alliances. That is what is wrong each time. The mistake we—us and you—and you—and you—' his hard and rigid stare jerking from face to face as he spoke '—have made always each time as though we will never learn. And this time, we are going to pay for it. Oh yes, we. Don't you realise that we know as well as you do what is happening, what is going to be the end of this by another twelve months? Twelve months? Bah. It won't last twelve months; another winter will see it. We know better than you do—' to the British general '—because you are on the run now and do not have time to do anything else. Even if you were not running, you probably would not realise it, because you are not a martial people. But we are. Our national destiny is for glory and war; they are not mysteries to us and so we know what we are looking at. So we will pay for that mistake. And since we will, you—and you—and you—' the cold and lifeless glare stopping again at the American '—who only think you came in late enough to gain at little risk—must pay also.' Then he was looking at none of them; it was almost as though he had drawn one rapid quiet and calming inhalation, still rigid though and still composed. 'But you will excuse me, please. It is too late for that now —this time. Our problem now is the immediate one. Also, first—' He rose, tossing his crumpled napkin on to the table and picking up the filled brandy glass, so rapidly that his chair scraped back across the floor and would have crashed over had not the American general put out a quick hand and saved it, the German general standing rigid, the brandy glass raised, his close uniform as unwrinkable as mail against the easy coat of the Briton like the comfortable jacket of a game-keeper, and the American's like a tailor-made costume for a masquerade in which he would represent the soldier of fifty years ago, and the old general's which looked as if a wife had got it out of a moth-balled attic trunk and cut some of it off and stitched some braid and ribbons and buttons on what remained. '*Hoch!*' the German general said and tossed the brandy down and with the same motion flung the empty glass over his shoulder.

'*Hoch,*' the old general said courteously. He drank too but he set his empty glass back on the table. 'You must excuse us,' he said. 'We are not situated as you are; we cannot afford to break French glasses.' He took another brandy glass from the tray and began to fill it. 'Be seated, General,' he said. The German general didn't move.

'And whose fault is that,' the German general said. 'That we have been—ja, twice—compelled to destroy French property? Not yours and mine, not ours here, not the fault of any of us, all of us who have to spend the four years straining at each other from behind two wire fences. It's the politicians, the civilian imbeciles who compel us every generation to have to rectify the blunders of their damned international horse-trading—'

'Be seated, General,' the old general said.

'As you were!' the German general said. Then he caught himself. He made a rigid quarter-turn and clapped his heels to face the old general. 'I forgot myself for a moment. You will please to pardon it.' He reversed the quarter-turn, but without the heel-clap this

S

time. His voice was milder now, quieter anyway. 'The same blunder because it is always the same alliance: only the pieces moved and swapped about. Perhaps they have to keep on doing, making the same mistake; being civilians and politicians, perhaps they can't help themselves. Or, being civilians and politicians, perhaps they dare not. Because they would be the first to vanish under that alliance which *we* would establish. Think of it, if you have not already: the alliance which would dominate all Europe. Europe? Bah. The world—Us, with you, France, and you, England—' he seemed to catch himself again for a second, turning to the American general. '—with you for—with your good wishes—'

'A minority stockholder,' the American said.

'Thank you,' the German general said. '—An alliance, the alliance which will conquer the whole earth—Europe, Asia, Africa, the islands—to accomplish where Bonaparte failed, what Caesar dreamed of, what Hannibal didn't live long enough to do—'

'Who will be emperor?' the old general said. It was so courteous and mild that for a moment it didn't seem to register. The German general looked at him.

'Yes,' the British general said as mildly: 'Who?' The German general looked at him. There was no movement of the face at all: the monocle simply descended from the eye, down the face and then the tunic, glinting once or twice as it turned in the air, into the palm lifted to receive it, the hand shutting on it then opening again, the monocle already in position between the thumb and the first finger, to be inserted again; and in fact there was no eyeball behind it: no scar nor healed suture even: only the lidless and empty socket glaring down at the British general.

'Perhaps now, General?' the old general said.

'Thanks,' the German general said. But still he didn't move. The old general set the filled brandy glass in front of his still-vacant place. 'Thanks,' the German general said. Still staring at the British general, he drew a handkerchief from his cuff and wiped the monocle and set it back into the socket; now the opaque oval stared down at the British general. 'You see why we have to hate you English,' he said. 'You are not soldiers. Perhaps you can't be. Which is all right; if true, you can't help it; we don't hate you for that. We don't even hate you because you don't try to be. What we hate you for is because you won't even bother to try. You are in a war; you blunder through it some-how and even survive. Because of your little island you can't possibly get any bigger, and you know it. And because of that, you know that sooner or later you will be in another war, yet this time too you will not even prepare for it. Oh, you send a few of your young men to your military college, where they will be taught perfectly how to sit a horse and change a palace guard; they will even get some practical experience by transferring this ritual intact to little outposts beside rice-paddies or tea-plantations or Himal-ayan goat-paths. But that is all. You will wait until an enemy is actually beating at your front gate. Then you will turn out to repel him exactly like a village being turned out cursing and swearing on a winter night to salvage a burning hayrick—gather up your gutter-sweepings, the scum of your slums and stables and paddocks; they will not even be dressed to look like soldiers, but in the garments of ploughmen and ditchers and carters; your officers look like a country-house party going out to the butts for a pheasant drive. Do you see? Getting out in front armed with nothing but walking sticks, saying, "Come along, lads. That seems to be the enemy yonder and there appear to be a goodish number of them but I dare say not too many"—and then walking, strolling on, not even looking back to see if they are followed or not because they don't need to because they are followed, do follow, cursing and grumbling still and unprepared still, but they follow and die, still cursing and grumbling, still civilians. We have to hate you. There is an immor-ality, an outrageous immorality; you are not even contemptuous of glory: you are simply not interested in it: only in solvency.' He stood, rigid and composed, staring down at the British general; he said calmly, in a voice of composed and boundless despair: 'You are swine, you know.' Then he said, 'No,' and now in his voice there was a kind of incredulous outrage too. 'You are worse. You are unbelievable. When we are on the same side, we win—always; and the whole world gives you the credit for the victory: Waterloo. When we are against you, you lose—always: Passchendaele, Mons, Cambrai and tomorrow Amiens—and you don't even know it—'

'If you please, General,' the old general said in his mild voice. The German general didn't even pause. He turned to the American.

'You also.'

'Swine?' the American said.

'Soldiers,' the German said. 'You are no better.'

'You mean, no worse, don't you?' the American said. 'I just got back from St. Mihiel last night.'

'Then perhaps you can visit Amiens tomorrow,' the German said. 'I will conduct you.'

'General,' the old general said. This time the German general stopped and even looked at the old general. He said:

'Not yet. I am—how you say?—supplicant.' He said again: 'Supplicant.' Then he began to laugh, that is, up to the dead indomitable unregenerate eye, speaking not even to anyone, not even to himself: only to outraged and unregenerate incredulity: 'I, a German lieutenant general, come eighty-seven kilometres to request of—ja, insist on—an Englishman and a Frenchman the defeat of my nation. We—I—could have saved it by simply refusing to meet you here. I could save it now simply by walking out. I could have done it at your aerodrome this afternoon by using on myself the pistol which I employed to preserve even in defeat the integrity of what this—' he made a brief rapid gesture with one hand; with barely a motion of it he indicated his entire uniform— belts brass braid insigne and all '—represents, has won the right to stand for, preserves still that for which those of us who have died in it died for. Then this one, this blunder of the priests and politicians and civilian time-servers, would stop now, since in fact it already has, three days ago now. But I did not. I do not, as a result of which inside another year we—not us—' again without moving he indicated his uniform '—but they whose blunder we tried to rectify, will be done, finished; and with them, us too since now we are no longer extricable from them—oh yes, us too, let the Americans annoy our flank as much as they like: they will not pass Verdun either; by tomorrow we will have run you—' to the Briton '—out of Amiens and possibly even into what you call your ditch, and by next month your people—' to the old general now '—in Paris will be cramming your official sacred talismans into brief-cases on the way to Spain or Portugal. But it will be too late, it will be over, finished; twelve months from now and we—not they for this but we, us—will have to plead with you on your terms for their survival, since already it is impossible to extricate theirs from ours. Because I am a soldier first, then a German, then—or hope to be—a victorious German. But that is not even second, but only third.

Because this—' again he indicated the uniform '—is more important than any German or even any victory.' Now he was looking at all of them; his voice was quite calm, almost conversational now: 'That is our sacrifice: the whole German army against your one French regiment. But you are right. We waste time.' He looked at them, rapidly, erect still but not quite rigid. 'You are here. I am . . .' He looked at them again; he said again, 'Bah. For a little time anyway we don't need secrets. I am eighty-seven kilometres from here. I must return. As you say—' he faced the American general; his heels clapped again, a sound very loud in the quiet and insulate room '—this is only a recess: not an armistice.' Still without moving, he looked rapidly from the American to the Briton then back again. 'You are admirable. But you are not soldiers—'

'All young men are brave,' the American said.

'Continue,' the German general said. 'Say it. Even Germans.'

'Even Frenchmen,' the old general said in his mild voice. 'Wouldn't we all be more comfortable if you would sit down?'

'A moment,' the German general said. He did not even look at the old general. 'We—' again without moving he looked rapidly from one to the other '—you two and I discussed this business thoroughly while your—what do I say: formal or mutual?— Commander-in-Chief was detained from us. We are agreed on what must be done; that was never any question. Now we need only to agree to do it in this little time we have out of the four years of holding one another off—we, Germans on one side, and you, English and French—' he turned to the American; again the heels clapped '—you Americans too; I have not forgot you—on the other, engaging each the other with half a hand because the other hand and a half was required to defend our back areas from our own politicians and priests. During that discussion before your Commander-in-Chief joined us, something was said about decision.' He said again, 'Decision.' He didn't even say 'bah' now. He looked rapidly again from the American to the Briton, to the American again. 'You,' he said.

'Yes,' the American general said. 'Decision implies choice.'

The German general looked at the Briton. 'You,' he said.

'Yes,' the British general said. 'God help us.'

The German general paused. 'Pardon?'

'Sorry,' the British general said. 'Let it be just yes then.'

'He said, God help us,' the American general said. 'Why?'

'Why?' the German general said. 'The why is to me?'

'We're both right this time,' the American general said. 'At least we don't have to cope with that.'

'So,' the German general said. 'That is both of you. Three of us.' He sat down, picked up the crumpled napkin and drew his chair up, and took up the filled brandy glass and sat back and erect again, into that same rigidity of formal attention as when he had been standing to toast his master, so that even sitting the rigidity had a sort of visible inaudibility like a soundless clap of heels, the filled glass at level with the fixed rigid glare of the opaque monocle; again without moving he seemed to glance rapidly at the other glasses. 'Be pleased to fill, gentlemen,' he said. But neither the Briton nor the American moved. They just sat there while across the table from them the German general sat with his lifted and rigid glass; he said, indomitable and composed, not even contemptuous: 'So then. All that remains is to acquaint your Commander-in-Chief with what part of our earlier discussion he might be inclined to hear. Then the formal ratification of our agreement.'

'Formal ratification of what agreement?' the old general said.

'Mutual ratification then,' the German general said.

'Of what?' the old general said.

'The agreement,' the German general said.

'What agreement?' the old general said. 'Do we need an agreement? Has anyone missed one?—The port is with you, General,' he said to the Briton. 'Fill and pass.'

THIS time it was a bedroom. The grave and noble face was framed by a pillow, looking at the runner from beneath a flannel nightcap tied under the chin. The nightshirt was flannel too, open at the throat to reveal a small cloth bag, not new and not very clean and apparently containing something which smelled like asafoetida, on a soiled string like a necklace. The youth stood beside the bed in a brocade dressing gown.

'They were blank shells,' the runner said in his light dry voice. 'The aeroplane—all four of them—flew right through the bursts. The German one never even deviated, not even going fast, even when one of ours hung right on its tail from about fifty feet for more than a minute while I could actually see the tracer going into it. The same one—aeroplane—ours—dove at us, at me; I even felt one of whatever it was coming out of the gun hit me on the leg here. It was like when a child blows a garden pea at you through a tube except for the smell, the stink, the burning phosphorus. There was a German general in it, you see. I mean in the German one. There had to be; either we had to send someone there or they had to send someone here. And since we—or the French—were the ones who started it, thought of it first, obviously it would be our right—privilege—duty to be host. Only it would have to look all right from beneath; they couldn't—couldn't dare anyway—issue a synchronised simultaneous order for every man on both sides to shut his eyes and count a hundred so they had to do the next best thing to make it look all regular, all orthodox to anyone they couldn't hide it from—'

'What?' the old Negro said.

'Don't you see yet? It's because they can't afford to let it stop like this. I mean, let us stop it. They don't dare. If they ever let us find out that we can stop a war as simply as men tired of digging a ditch decide calmly and quietly to stop digging the ditch—'

'I mean that suit,' the old Negro said. 'That policeman's suit. You just took it, didn't you?'

'I had to,' the runner said with that peaceful and terrible patience. 'I had to get out. To get back in too. At least back to where I hid my uniform. It used to be difficult enough to pass either way, in or out. But now it will be almost impossible to get back in. But don't worry about that; all I need—'

'Is he dead?' the old Negro said.

'What?' the runner said. 'Oh, the policeman. I don't know. Probably not.' He said with a sort of amazement: 'I hope not.' He said: 'I knew night before last—two nights ago, Tuesday night— what they were planning to do, though of course I had no proof then. I tried to tell him. But you know him; you've probably tried yourself to tell him something you couldn't prove or that he didn't want to believe. So I'll need something else. Not to prove it to him, make him believe it: there's not time enough left to waste that way. That's why I came here. I want you to make me a Mason too. Or maybe there's not even time for that either. So just show me the sign—like this—' He jerked, flicked his hand low against his flank, as near as he had been able to divine at the time or anyway remember now from the man two years ago on the day he joined the battalion. 'That will be enough. It will have to be; I'll bluff the rest of it through—'

'Wait,' the old Negro said. 'Tell me slow.'

'I'm trying to,' the runner said with that terrible patience. 'Every man in the battalion owes him his pay for weeks ahead, provided they live long enough to earn it and he lives long enough to collect it from them. He did it by making them all Masons or anyway making them believe they are Masons. He owns them, you see. They can't refuse him. All he will need to do is—'

'Wait,' the old Negro said. 'Wait.'

'Don't you see?' the runner said. 'If all of us, the whole battalion, at least one battalion, one unit out of the whole line to start it, to lead the way—leave the rifles and grenades and all behind us in the trench: simply climb barehanded out over the parapet and through the wire and then just walk on barehanded, not with our hands up for surrender but just open to show that we had nothing to hurt, harm anyone; not running, stumbling: just walking forward like free men—just one of us, one man; suppose just one man, then multiply him by a battalion; suppose a whole battalion of us, who want nothing except just to go home and get themselves into clean clothes and work and drink a little beer in the evening and talk and then lie down and sleep and not be afraid. And maybe, just maybe that many Germans who don't want anything more too, or maybe just one German who doesn't want more than that, to put his or their rifles and grenades down and climb out too with their hands empty too not for surrender but just so every man could see there is nothing in them to hurt or harm either—'

'Suppose they don't,' the old Negro said. 'Suppose they shoot at us.' But the runner didn't even hear the 'us.' He was still talking.

'Won't they shoot at us tomorrow anyway, as soon as they have recovered from the fright? As soon as the people at Chaulnesmont and Paris and Poperinghe and whoever it was in that German aeroplane this afternoon have had time to meet and compare notes and decide exactly where the threat, danger is, and eradicate it and then start the war again: tomorrow and tomorrow and tomorrow until the last formal rule of the game has been fulfilled and discharged and the last ruined player removed from sight and the victory immolated like a football trophy in a club-house showcase. That's all I want. That's all I'm trying to do. But you may be right. So you tell me.'

The old Negro groaned. He groaned peacefully. One hand came out from beneath the covers and turned them back and he swung his legs toward the edge of the bed and said to the youth in the dressing gown: 'Hand me my shoes and britches.'

'Listen to me,' the runner said. 'There's not time. It will be daylight in two hours and I've got to get back. Just show me how to make the sign, the signal.'

'You can't learn it right in that time,' the old Negro said. 'And even if you could, I'm going too. Maybe this is what I been hunting for too.'

'Didn't you just say the Germans might shoot at us?' the runner said. 'Don't you see? That's it, that's the risk: if some of the Germans do come out. Then they will shoot at us, both of them, their side and ours too—put a barrage down on all of us. They'll have to. There won't be anything else for them to do.'

'So your mind done changed about it,' the old Negro said.

'Just show me the sign, the signal,' the runner said. Again the old

Negro groaned, peaceful, almost inattentive, swinging his legs on out of the bed. The innocent and unblemished corporal's uniform was hanging neatly on a chair, the shoes and the socks were placed neatly beneath it. The youth had picked them up and he now knelt beside the bed, holding one of the socks open for the old Negro's foot. 'Aren't you afraid?' the runner said.

'Ain't we already got enough ahead of us without bringing that up?' the old Negro said pettishly. 'And I know what you're fixing to say next: How am I going to get up there? And I can answer that: I never had no trouble getting here to France; I reckon I can make them other just sixty miles. And I know what you are fixing to say after that one too: I can't wear this French suit up there neither without no general with me. Only I don't need to answer that one because you done already answered it.'

'Kill a British soldier this time?' the runner said.

'You said he wasn't dead.'

'I said maybe he wasn't.'

'You said you hoped he wasn't. Don't never forget that.'

The runner was the last thing which the sentry would ever see. In fact, he was the first thing the sentry saw that morning except for the relief guard who had brought his breakfast and who now sat, his rifle leaning beside him against the dugout's opposite earthen shelf.

He had been under arrest for almost thirty hours now. That was all: just under arrest, as though the furious blows of the rifle-butt two nights ago had not simply hushed a voice which he could bear no longer but had somehow separated him from mankind; as if that aghast reversal, that cessation of four years of mud and blood and its accompanying convulsion of silence had cast him up on this buried dirt ledge with no other sign of man at all save the rotation of guards who brought him food and then sat opposite him until the time came for their relief. Yesterday and this morning too in ordained rote the Orderly Officer's sergeant satellite had appeared suddenly in the orifice, crying 'Shun!' and he had stood bareheaded while the guard saluted and the Orderly Officer himself entered and said, rapid and glib out of the glib and routine book: 'Any complaints?' and was gone again before he could have made any answer he did not intend to make. But that was all. Yesterday he had tried for a little while to talk to one of the rotated guards and since then some of them had tried to talk to him, but that was all of that too, so that in effect for over thirty hours now he had sat or sprawled and lay asleep on his dirt shelf, morose, sullen, incorrigible, foul-mouthed and snarling, not even waiting but just biding, pending whatever it was they would finally decide to do with him or with the silence, both or either, if and when they did make up their minds.

Then he saw the runner. At the same moment he saw the pistol already in motion as the runner struck the guard between the ear and the rim of the helmet and caught him as he toppled and tumbled him on to the ledge and turned and the sentry saw the burlesque of a soldier entering behind him—the travesty of the wrapped puttees, the tunic whose lower buttons would not even meet across the paunch not of sedentariness but of age and above it, beneath the helmet, the chocolate face which four years ago he had tried to relegate and repudiate into the closed book of his past.

'That makes five,' the old Negro said.

'All right, all right,' the runner answered, rapidly and harshly. 'He's not dead either. Don't you think that by this time I have learned how to do it?' He said rapidly to the sentry: 'You don't need to worry either now. All we need from you now is inertia.' But the sentry was not even looking at him. He was looking at the old Negro.

'I told you to leave me alone,' he said. And it was the runner who answered him, in that same rapid and brittle voice:

'It's too late for that now. Because I am wrong, we don't want inertia from you: what we want is silence. Come along. Notice, I have the pistol. If I must, I shall use it. I've already used it six times, but only the flat of it. This time I'll use the trigger.' He said to the old Negro, in the rapid brittle and almost despairing voice: 'All right, this one will be dead. Then you suggest something.'

'You can't get away with this,' the sentry said.

'Who expects to?' the runner said. 'That's why we have no time to waste. Come along. You've got your investments to protect, you know; after a breathing spell like this and the fresh start it will give them, let alone the discovery of what can happen simply by letting the same men hang around in uniforms too long, the whole battalion will probably be wiped out as soon as they can get us up in gun-range again. Which may be this afternoon. They flew a

German general over yesterday; without doubt he was at Chaulnesmont by late dinner last night, with our pooh-bahs and the American ones too already waiting for him and the whole affair settled and over with by the time the port passed (if German generals drink port, though why not, since we have had four years to prove to us, even if all history had not already done it, that the biped successful enough to become a general had ceased to be a German or British or American or Italian or French one almost as soon as it never was a human one) and without doubt he is already on his way back and both sides are merely waiting until he is out of the way as you hold up a polo game while one of the visiting rajahs rides off the field—'

The sentry—in what time he had left—would remember it. He knew at once that the runner meant exactly what he said about the pistol; he had proof of that at once—of the flat side of it anyway—when he almost stumbled over the sprawled bodies of the orderly officer and his sergeant in the tunnel before he saw them. But it would seem to him that it was not the hard muzzle of the pistol in the small of his back, but the voice itself—the glib calm rapid desperate and despairing voice carrying, sweeping them into the next dugout where an entire platoon lay or sat along the earthen shelf, the faces turning as one to look at them as the runner thrust him in with the muzzle of the pistol and then thrust the old Negro forward too, saying:

'Make the sign. Go on. Make it.' The tense calm desperate voice not even stopping then, as it seemed to the sentry that it never had: 'That's right, of course he doesn't need to make the sign. He has enough without. He has come from outside. So have I, for that matter but you won't even need to doubt me now, you need only look at him; some of you may even recognise Horn's D.C.M. on that tunic. But don't worry; Horn isn't dead any more than Mr. Smith and Sergeant Bledsoe; I have learned to use the flat of this—' he raised the pistol for an instant into sight '—quite neatly now. Because here is our chance to have done with it, be finished with it, quit of it, not just the killing, the getting dead, because that's only a part of the nightmare, of the rot and the stinking and the waste—'

The sentry would remember it, incorrigible still, merely acquiescent, believing still that he was waiting, biding the moment when he or perhaps two or three of them at once would take the runner off guard and smother him, listening to the glib staccato voice, watching the turned faces listening to it too, believing still that he saw in them only astonishment, surprise, presently to fade into one concert which he would match: 'And neither of us would have got back in if it had not been for his pass from the Ministry of War in Paris. So you don't even know yet what they have done to you. They've sealed you up in here—the whole front from the Channel to Switzerland. Though from what I saw in Paris last night—not only military police, the French and American and ours, but the civilian police too—I wouldn't have thought they'd have enough left to seal anything with. But they have; the Colonel himself could not have got back in this morning unless the pass bore the signature of that old man in the castle at Chaulnesmont. It's like another front, manned by all the troops in the three forces who can't speak the language belonging to the coat they came up from under the equator and half around the world to die in, in the cold and the wet—Senegalese and Moroccans and Kurds and Chinese and Malays and Indians—Polynesian Melanesian Mongol and Negro who couldn't understand the password nor read the pass either: only to recognise perhaps by memorised rote that one cryptic hieroglyph. But not you. You can't even get out now, to try to come back in. No-man's Land is no longer in front of us. It's behind us now. Before, the faces behind the machine guns and the rifles at least thought Caucasian thoughts even if they didn't speak English or French or American; now they don't even think Caucasian thoughts. They're alien. They don't even have to care. They have tried for four years to get out of the white man's cold and mud and rain just by killing Germans, and failed. Who knows? by killing off the Frenchmen and Englishmen and Americans whom they have bottled up here, they might all be on the way home tomorrow. So there is nowhere for us to go now but east—'

Now the sentry moved. That is, he did not move yet, he dared not: he simply made a single infinitesimal transition into a more convulsive rigidity, speaking now, harsh and obscene, cursing the rapt immobilised faces: 'Are you going to let them get away with this? Don't you know we're all going to be for it? They have already killed Lieutenant Smith and Sergeant Bledsoe—'

'Nonsense,' the runner said. 'They aren't dead. Didn't I just tell you I have learned how to use the flat of a pistol? It's his money. That's all. Everyone in the battalion owes him. He wants us to sit here and do nothing until he has earned his month's profit. Then he wants them to start it up again so we will be willing to bet him twenty shillings a month that we will be dead in thirty days. Which is what they are going to do—start it up again. You all saw those four aeroplanes yesterday, and all that archie. The archie were blank shells. There was a German general in the hun aeroplane. Last night he was at Chaulnesmont. He would have to have been; else, why did he come at all? Why else wafted across on a cloud of blank archie shell, with three S.E.5's going through the motion of shooting him down with blank ammunition? Oh yes, I was there; I saw the lorries fetching up the shells night before last, and yesterday I stood behind one of the batteries firing them when one of the S.E.'s—that pilot would have been a child of course, too young for them to have dared inform him in advance, too young to be risked with the knowledge that fact and truth are not the same—dived and put a burst right into the battery and shot me in the skirt of my tunic with something—whatever it was —which actually stung a little for a moment. What else, except to allow a German general to visit the French and the British and the American ones in the Allied Commandery-in-Chief without alarming the rest of us bipeds who were not born generals but simply human beings? And since they—all four of them—would speak the same language, no matter what clumsy isolated national tongues they were compelled by circumstance to do it in, the matter probably took them no time at all and very likely the German one is already on his way back home at this moment, not even needing the blank shells now because the guns will be already loaded with live ones, merely waiting for him to get out of the way in order to resume, efface, obliterate forever this ghastly and incredible contretemps. So we have no time, you see. We may not even have an hour. But an hour will be enough, if only it is all of us, the whole battalion. Not to kill the officers; they themselves have abolished killing for a recess of three days. Besides, we won't need to, with all of us. If we had time, we could even draw lots: one man to each officer, simply to hold his hands while the rest of us go over. But the flat of a pistol is quicker and no more harmful really, as Mr. Smith and Sergeant Bledsoe and Horn will tell you when they awake. Then never to touch pistol or rifle or grenade or machine gun again, to climb out of ditches forever and pass through the wire and then advance with nothing but our bare hands, to dare, defy the Germans not to come out too and meet us.' He said quickly, in the desperate and calmly despairing voice: 'All right: meet us with machine-gun fire, you will say. But the hun archie yesterday was blank too.' He said to the old Negro: 'Now, make them the sign. Have not you already proved that, if anything, it means brotherhood and peace?'

'You fools!' the sentry cried, except that he did not say fools: virulent and obscene out of his almost inarticulate paucity, struggling now, having defied the pistol in one outraged revulsion of repudiation before he realised that the hard little iron ring was gone from his spine and that the runner was merely holding him, he (the sentry) watching, glaring at the faces which he had thought were merely fixed in a surprise precursive to outrage too, looming, bearing down on him, identical and alien and concerted, until so many hard hands held him that he could not even struggle, the runner facing him now, the pistol poised flat on one raised palm, shouting at him:

'Stop it! Stop it! Make your choice, but hurry. You can come with us, or you can have the pistol. But decide.'

He would remember; they were topside now, in the trench, he could see a silent and moiling group within which or beneath which the major and two company commanders and three or four sergeants had vanished (they had taken the adjutant and the sergeant-major and the corporal signalman in the orderly dugout and the colonel still in bed) and in both directions along the trench he could see men coming up out of their holes and warrens, blinking in the light, dazed still yet already wearing on their faces that look of amazed incredulity fading with one amazed concert into dawning and incredulous hope. The hard hands still grasped him; as they lifted, flung him up on to the firestep and then over the lip of the parapet, he already saw the runner spring up and turn and reach down and pull the old Negro up beside him while other hands boosted from beneath, the two of them now standing on the parapet facing the trench, the runner's voice thin and high now with that desperate and indomitable despair:

'The sign! The sign! Give it us! Come on, men! If this is what they call staying alive, do you want that on these terms forever either?'

Then he was struggling again. He didn't even know he was about to, when he found himself jerking and thrashing, cursing, flinging, beating away the hands, not even realising then why, for what, until he found himself in the wire, striking, hitting backward at the crowding bodies at the entrance to the labyrinthine passageway which the night patrols used, hearing his own voice in one last repudiation: 'F . . . them all! Bugger all of you!' crawling now, not the first one through because when he rose to his feet, running, the old Negro was panting beside him, while he shouted at the old Negro: 'Serve you f . . . ing well right! Didn't I warn you two years ago to stay away from me? Didn't I?'

Then the runner was beside him, grasping his arm and stopping him and turning him about, shouting: 'Look at them!' He did so and saw them, watched them, crawling on their hands and knees through the gaps in the wire as though up out of hell itself, faces clothes hands and all stained as though forever one single nameless and identical colour from the mud in which they had lived like animals for four years, then rising to their feet as though in that four years they had not stood on earth, but had this moment returned to light and air from purgatory as ghosts stained forever to the nameless single colour of purgatory. 'Over there too!' the runner cried, turning him again until he saw that also: the distant German wire one faint moil and pulse of motion, indistinguishable until it too broke into men rising erect; whereupon a dreadful haste came over him, along with something else which he had not yet time to assimilate, recognise, knowing, aware of only the haste; and not his haste but one haste, not only the battalion but the German one or regiment or whatever it was, the two of them running toward each other now, empty-handed, approaching until he could see, distinguish the individual faces but still all one face, one expression, and then he knew suddenly that his too looked like that, all of them did: tentative, amazed, defenceless, and then he heard the voices too and knew that his was one also—a thin murmuring sound rising into the incredible silence like a chirping of lost birds, forlorn and defenceless too; and then he knew what the other thing was even before the frantic uprush of the rockets from behind the two wires, German and British too.

'No!' he cried, 'no! Not to us!' not even realising that he had said 'we' and not 'I' for the first time in his life probably, certainly for the first time in four years, not even realising that in the next moment he had said 'I' again, shouting to the old Negro as he whirled about: 'What did I tell you? Didn't I tell you to let me alone?' Only it was not the old Negro, it was the runner, standing facing him as the first ranging burst of shells bracketed in. He never heard them, nor the wailing rumble of the two barrages either, nor saw nor heard little more of anything in that last second except the runner's voice crying out of the soundless rush of flame which enveloped half his body neatly from heel through navel through chin:

'They can't kill us! They can't! Not dare not: they can't!'

Except of course that he couldn't sit here save for a definitely physically limited length of time because after a while it would be daylight. Unless of course the sun really failed to rise tomorrow, which as they taught you in that subsection of philosophy they called dialectics which you were trying to swot through in order to try to swot through that secton of being educated they called philosophy, was for the sake of argument possible. Only why shouldn't he be sitting here after daylight or for the rest of the day itself for that matter, since the only physical limitation to that would be when someone with the authority and compulsion to resist the condition of a young man in a second lieutenant's uniform sitting on the ground against the wall of a Nissen hut, had his attention called to it by a horn or whistle; and that greater condition which yesterday had sent three fairly expensive aeroplanes jinking up and down the sky with their Vickerses full of blank ammunition, might well invalidate that one too.

Then the first limitation had been discharged, because now it was day and none to know where the night had gone: not a dialectic this time, but he who didn't know where night had gone this soon, this quick. Or maybe it was a dialectic since as far as he knew only he had watched it out and since only he in waking had watched it out, to all the others still in slumber it still obtained,

like the tree in darkness being no longer green, and since he who
had watched it out still didn't know where it had gone, for him it
was still night too. Then almost before he had had time to begin
to bother to think that out and so have done with it, a bugle
blowing *reveille* confounded him, the sound (that sound: who had
never heard it before or even heard of it: a horn blowing at day-
break on a forward aerodrome where people did not even have
guns but were armed only with maps and what Monaghan called
monkey-wrenches) even getting him up on to his feet: that greater
condition's abrogation which had now reabrogated. In fact, if he
had been a cadet still, he would even know what crime whoever
found him sitting there would charge him with: not shaving: and,
standing now, he realised that he had even forgot his problem too,
who had sat there all night thinking that he had none evermore,
as though sitting so long within that peaceful stink had robbed
olfactory of its single sense or perhaps the Sidcott of its smell and
only getting up restored them both. In fact, for a moment he
toyed with the idea of unrolling the Sidcott to see how far the
burning had spread, except that if he did that and let the air in,
the burning might spread faster, thinking, with a sort of peaceful
amazement hearing himself: *Because it's got to last;* no more: not
last until, just *last*.

At least he wouldn't take it inside with him, so he left it against
the wall and went around the hut and inside it—Burk and Hanley
and De Marchi had not stirred, so the tree was not green yet for
some anyway—and got his shaving tackle and then picked up the
Sidcott again and went to the wash-room; nor would the tree be
quite green yet here either, and if not here, certainly not in the
latrines. Though now it would because the sun was well up now
and, once more smooth of face, the Sidcott stinking peacefully
under his arm, he could see movement about the mess, remembering suddenly that he had not eaten since lunch yesterday. But then
there was the Sidcott, when suddenly he realised that the Sidcott
would serve that too, turning and already walking. They—someone—had brought his bus back and rolled it in, so he trod his long
shadow toward only the petrol tin and put the Sidcott into it and
stood peaceful and empty while the day incremented, the infinitesimal ineluctable shortening of the shadows. It was going to rain
probably, but then it always was anyway; that is, it always did on

days-off from patrols, he didn't know why yet, he was too new. 'You will though,' Monaghan told him. 'Just wait till after the first time you've been good and scared'—pronouncing it 'skeered.'

So it would be all right now, the ones who were going to get up would have already had breakfast and the others would sleep on through till lunch; he could even take his shaving kit on to the mess without going to the hut at all: and stopped, he could not even remember when he had heard it last, that alien and divorced —that thick dense mute furious murmur to the north and east; he knew exactly where it would be because he had flown over the spot yesterday afternoon, thinking peacefully *I came home too soon. If I had only sat up there all night instead I could have seen it start again*—listening, motionless in midstride, hearing it murmur toward and into its crescendo and sustain a time, a while and then cut short off, murmuring in his ears for a little time still until he discovered that what he was actually listening to was a lark: and he had been right, the Sidcott had served even better than it knew even or even perhaps intended, carrying him still intact across lunch too, since it was after ten now. Provided he could eat enough of course, the food—the eggs and bacon and the marmalade— having no taste to speak of, so that only in that had he been wrong; then presently he was wrong there too, eating steadily on in the empty mess until at last the orderly told him there was simply no more toast.

Much better than the Sidcott could have known to plan or even dream because during lunch the hut itself would be empty and for that while he could use his cot to do some of the reading he had imagined himself doing between patrols—the hero living by proxy the lives of heroes between the monotonous peaks of his own heroic derring: which he was doing for another moment or two while Bridesman stood in the door, until he looked up. 'Lunch?' Bridesman said.

'Late breakfast, thanks,' he said.

'Drink?' Bridesman said.

'Later, thanks,' he said: and moved in time, taking the book with him; there was a tree, he had discovered it in the first week— an old tree with two big roots like the arms of a chair on the bank above the cut through which the road ran past the aerodrome to Villeneuve Blanche so that you could sit as in a chair with the roots to prop the elbows which propped in turn the book, secure from war yet still of it, not that remote, in those days when they had called it war: who apparently were not decided yet what to call this now. And so now there would have been time enough; Bridesman would know by now what that had been this morning: thinking peacefully, the open book still propped before he began to move: *Yes, he will know by now. He will have to make the decision to tell me or not, but he will make it.*

Nor was there any reason to take the book to the hut because he might even read some more, entering and then leaving Bridesman's hut with the book still closed on one finger to mark his place, still strolling; he had never been walking fast anyway and finally stopping, empty and peaceful, only blinking a little, looking out across the empty field, the line of closed hangars, the mess and the office where a few people came and went. Not too many though; apparently Collyer had lifted the ban on Villeneuve Blanche; soon he would be looking at evening too and suddenly he thought of Conventicle but for an instant only and then no more because what could he say to Conventicle or they to each other? 'Well, Flight Captain Bridesman tells me one of our battalions put their guns down this morning and climbed out of the trench and through the wire and met a similar unarmed German one until both sides could get a barrage down on them. So all we need now is just to stand by until time to take that Jerry general home.' And then Conventicle: 'Yes sir. So I heard.'

And now he was looking at evening, the aftermath of sun, treading no shadow at all now to the petrol tin. Though almost at once he began to hurry a little, remembering not the Sidcott but the burning; it had been more than twelve hours now since he left it in the tin and there might not be anything left of it. But he was in time: just the tin itself too hot to touch so that he kicked it over and tumbled the Sidcott out, which would have to cool a little too. Which it did: not evening incrementing now but actual night itself, almost summer night this time at home in May; and in the latrine the tree once more was no longer green; only the stink of the Sidcott which had lasted, he had wasted that concern dropping it into the sink where it unfolded as of its own accord into visibility, into one last repudiation—the slow thick smell of the burning itself visible now in creeping overlaps, almost gone now—only a beggar's crumb but perhaps there had been an instant in the beginning when only a crumb of fire lay on the face of darkness and the falling waters, and he moved again; one of the cubicles had a wooden latch inside the door if you were there first and he was and latched the invisible door and drew the invisible pistol from his tunic pocket and thumbed the safety off.

Again the room was lighted, candelabrum, sconce and girandole, curtain and casement once more closed against the swarm-dense city's unsleeping and anguished murmur; again the old general looked like a gaudy toy in his blanched and glittering solitude, just beginning to crumble the heel of bread into the waiting bowl as the smaller door opened and the youthful aide stood in it. 'He is here?' the old general said.

'Yes sir,' the aide said.

'Let him come in,' the old general said. 'Then let nobody else.'

'Yes sir,' the aide said and went out and closed the door and in a time opened it again; the old general had not moved except to put quietly down beside the bowl the uncrumbled bread; the aide entering and turning stiffly to attention beside the door as the Quartermaster General entered and came on a pace or two and then stopped, paused, the aide going back out the door and drawing it to behind him, the Quartermaster General standing for a moment longer—the gaunt gigantic peasant with his sick face and his hungry and stricken eyes, the two old men looking at each other for another moment, then the Quartermaster General partly raised one hand and dropped it and came on until he faced the table.

'Have you dined?' the old general said.

The other didn't even answer. 'I know what happened,' he said. 'I authorised it, permitted it, otherwise it couldn't have. But I want you to tell me. Not admit, confess: affirm it, tell me to my face that we did this. Yesterday afternoon a German general was brought across the lines and here, to this house, into this house.'

'Yes,' the old general said. But the other still waited, inexorable. 'We did it then,' the old general said.

'Then this morning an unarmed British battalion met an unarmed German force between the lines until artillery from both sides was able to destroy them both.'

'We did it then,' the old general said.

'We did it,' the Quartermaster General said. 'We. Not British and American and French we against German them nor German they against American and British and French us, but We against all because we no longer belong to us. A subterfuge not of ours to confuse and mislead the enemy nor of the enemy to mislead and confuse us, but of We to betray all, since all has had to repudiate us in simple defensive horror; no barrage by us or vice versa to prevent an enemy running over us with bayonets and hand grenades or vice versa, but a barrage by both of We to prevent naked and weaponless hand touching opposite naked and weaponless hand. We, you and I and our whole unregenerate and unregenerable kind; not only you and I and our tight close jealous unchallengeable hierarchy behind this wire and our opposite German one behind that one, but more, worse: our whole small repudiated and homeless species about the earth who not only no longer belong to man, but even to earth itself, since we have had to make this last base desperate cast in order to hold our last desperate and precarious place on it.'

'Sit down,' the old general said.

'No,' the other said. 'I was standing when I accepted this appointment. I can stand to divest myself of it.' He thrust one big fleshless hand rapidly inside his tunic then out again, though once more he stood just holding the folded paper in it, looking down at the old general. 'Because I didn't just believe in you. I loved you. I believed from that first moment when I saw you in that gate that day forty-seven years ago that you had been destined to save us. That you were chosen by destiny out of the paradox of your background, to be a paradox to your past in order to be free of human past to be the one out of all earth to be free of the compulsions of fear and weakness and doubt which render the rest of us incapable of what you were competent for; that you in your strength would even absolve us of our failure due to our weakness and fears. I don't mean the men out there tonight—' This time the vast hand holding the folded paper made a single rapid clumsy gesture which indicated, seemed to shape somehow in the brilliant insulate room the whole scope of the murmurous and anguished darkness outside and even as far away as the lines themselves—the wire, the ditches dense and, for this time anyway, silent with dormant guns and amazed and incredulous men, waiting, alerted, confused and incredulous with hope '—they don't need you, they are capable of saving themselves, as three thousand of them proved four days ago. They only needed to be defended, protected from you. Not expected to be nor even hope to be: just should have been, except that we failed them. Not you this time, who did not even what you would but what you must, since you are you. But I and my few kind, who had rank enough and authority and position enough, as if God Himself had put this warrant in my hand that day against this one three years later, until I failed them and Him and brought it back.' His hand also jerked, flicked, and tossed the folded paper on to the desk in front of the bowl and jug and the still intact morsel, on either side of which the old general's veined and mottled hands lay faintly curled at rest. 'Back to you by hand, as I received it from you. I will have no more of it. I know: by my own token I am too late in returning what I should never have accepted to begin with because even at first I would have known myself incapable of coping with what it was going to entail, if I had only known then what that entailment was going to be. I am responsible. I am responsible, mine is the blame and solely mine; without me and this warrant which you gave me that day three years ago, you could not have done this. By this authority I could have prevented you then, and even afterward I could have stopped it, remanded it. As you—the Commander-in-Chief of all the Allied Armies in France—as Quartermaster General over all embattled Europe west of our and the British and the American wire, I could have decreed that whole zone containing Villeneuve Blanche (or arbitrarily any other point which you might have threatened) at one hundred point one of saturation and forbidden whatever number of men it took to drive those lorries of blank anti-aircraft shells to enter it and even at one hundred absolute of saturation and so forbidden that single supernumerary German one to come out of it. But I didn't. So I was responsible even more than you because you had no choice. You didn't even do what you would but only what you could, since you were incapable of else, born and doomed incapable of else. While I did have a choice between could and would, between shall and must and cannot, between must and dare not, between *will do* and *I am afraid to do:* had that choice, and found myself afraid. Oh yes, afraid. But then why shouldn't I be afraid of you, since you are afraid of man?'

'I am not afraid of man,' the old general said. 'Fear implies ignorance. Where ignorance is not, you do not need to fear: only respect. I don't fear man's capacities, I merely respect them.'

'And use them,' the Quartermaster General said.

'Beware of them,' the old general said.

'Which, fear them or not, you should. You some day will. Not I, of course. I'm an old man, finished; I had my chance and failed; who—what—wants or needs me further now? What midden or rubbish heap, least of all that one beside the Seine yonder with its gold hemisphere ravaged from across all of Europe by a lesser one than you, since he embroiled himself with all the armies of Europe in order to lose a petty political empire, where you have allied all the armies of both hemispheres and finally even the German one too, to lose the world to man.'

'Will you let me speak a moment?' the old general said.

'Of course,' the other said. 'Didn't I tell you I loved you once? Who can control that? All you dare assume mandate over is oath, contract.'

'You say they do not need me to save themselves from me and us since they themselves will save themselves if they are only let alone, only defended and preserved that long from me and us. How do you think we coped with this in time at time and place—at this particular moment in four whole years of moments, at this particular point in that thousand kilometres of regimental fronts between the Alps and the Channel? Just by being alert? Not only alert at this specific spot and moment but prepared to cope and concentrate and nullify at this specific spot and moment with that which every trained soldier has been trained and taught to accept as a factor in war and battle as he must logistics and climate and failure of ammunition; this, in four long years offateful and vulnerable moments and ten hundred kilometres offateful and vulnerable spots—spots and moments fateful and vulnerable because as yet we have found nothing better to man them with than man? How do you think we knew in time? Don't you know how? Who, since you believe in man's capacities, must certainly know them?'

Now the other had stopped, immobile, looming, vast, his sick and hungry face as though sick anew with foreknowledge and despair. Though his voice was quiet, almost gentle. 'How?' he said.

'One of them told us. One of his own squad. One of his close and familiar own—as always. As that or them or at least one among them for whom man sets in jeopardy what he believes to be his life and assumes to be his liberty or his honour, always does. His name was Polchek. He went on sick parade that Sunday midnight and we should have known about it inside an hour except that apparently a traitor too (by all means call him that if you like) had to outface regimental tape. So we might not have learned in time at all until too late, the Division Commander being himself already an hour before dawn in a forward observation post where he likewise had no business being, except for a lieutenant (a blatant and unregenerate eccentric whose career very probably ended there also since he held the sanctity of his native soil above that of his divisional channels; he will get a decoration of course but no more, the utmost venerability of his beard can only expose that same lieutenant's insigne) who rang directly through to, and insisted on speaking to someone in authority at, his Army Headquarters. That was how we knew, had even that little time to nullify, get in touch with the enemy and offer him too an alternate to chaos.'

'So I was right,' the other said. 'You were afraid.'

'I respected him as an articulated creature capable of locomotion and vulnerable to self-interest.'

'You were afraid,' the Quartermaster General said. 'Who with two armies which had already been beaten once and a third one not yet blooded to where it was a calculable quantity had nevertheless managed to stalemate the most powerful and skillful and dedicated force in Europe, yet had had to call upon that enemy for help against the simple unified hope and dream of simple man. No, you are afraid. And so I am well to be. That's why I brought it back. There it lies. Touch it, put your hand on it. Or take my word for it that it's real, the same one, not defiled since the defilement was mine who shirked it in the middle of a battle, and a concomitant of your rank is the right and privilege to obliterate the human instrument of a failure.'

'But can you bring it back here? To me?' the old general said mildly.

'Why not? Weren't you the one who gave it to me?'

'But can you?' the old general said. 'Dare you ask me to grant you a favour, let along accept it from me? This favour,' the old general said in that gentle and almost inflectionless voice. 'A man is to die what the world will call the basest and most ignominious of deaths: execution for cowardice while defending his native—anyway adopted—land. That's what the ignorant world will call it, who will not know that he was murdered for that principle which, by your own bitter self-flagellation, you were incapable of risking death and honour for. Yet you don't demand that life. You demand instead merely to be relieved of a commission. A gesture. A martyrdom. Does it match his?' 'He won't accept that life!' the other cried. 'If he does—' and stopped, amazed, aghast, foreknowing and despaired while the gentle voice went on:

'If he does, if he accepts his life, keeps his life, he will have abrogated his own gesture and martyrdom. If I gave him his life tonight, I myself could render null and void what you call the hope and the dream of his sacrifice. By destroying his life tomorrow morning, I will establish forever that he didn't even live in vain, let alone die so. Now tell me who's afraid?'

Now the other began to turn, slowly, a little jerkily, as though he were blind, turning on until he faced the small door again and stopping not as though he saw it but as if he had located its position and direction by some other and lesser and less exact sense, like smell, the old general watching him until he had completely turned before he spoke:

'You've forgotten your paper.'

'Of course,' the other said. 'So I have.' He turned back, jerkily, blinking rapidly; his hand fumbled on the table top for a moment, then it found the folded paper and put it back inside the tunic, and he stood again, blinking rapidly. 'Yes,' he said. 'So I did.' Then he turned again, a little stiffly still but moving almost quickly now, directly anyhow, and went on across the blanched rug, toward the door; at once it opened and the aide entered, carrying the door with him and already turning into rigid attention, holding it while the Quartermaster General walked toward it, a little stiffly and awkwardly, too big too gaunt too alien, then stopped and half-turned his head and said: 'Good-bye.'

'Good-bye,' the old general said. The other went on, to the door now, almost into it, beginning to bow his head a little as though from long habit already too tall for most doors, stopping almost in the door now, his head still bowed a little even after he turned it not quite toward where the old general sat immobile and gaudy as a child's toy behind the untouched bowl and jug and the still uncrumbled bread.

'And something else,' the Quartermaster General said. 'To say. Something else—'

'With God,' the old general said.

'Of course,' the Quartermaster General said. 'That was it. I almost said it.'

The door clashed open; the sergeant with his slung rifle entered first, followed by a private carrying his unslung one, unbelievably long now with the fixed bayonet, like a hunter dodging through a gap in a fence. They took position one on either side of the door, the thirteen prisoners turning their thirteen heads as one to watch quietly while two more men carried in a long wooden bench-attached mess table and set it in the centre of the cell and went back out.

'Going to fatten us up first, huh?' one of the prisoners said. The sergeant didn't answer; he was now working at his front teeth with a gold toothpick.

'If the next thing they bring is a tablecloth, the third will be a priest,' another prisoner said. But he was wrong, although the number of casseroles and pots and dishes (including a small caldron obviously soup) which did come next, followed by a third man carrying a whole basket of bottles and a jumble of utensils and cutlery, was almost as unnerving, the sergeant speaking now though still around, past the toothpick:

'Hold it now. At least let them get their hands and arms out of the way.' Though the prisoners had really not moved yet to rush upon the table, the food: it was merely a shift, semicircular, poised while the third orderly set the wine (there were seven bottles) on the table and then began to place the cups, vessels, whatever anyone wanted to call them—tin cups, pannikins from mess kits, two or three cracked tumblers, two flagons contrived by bisecting laterally one canteen.

'Don't apologise garçon,' the wit said. 'Just so it's got a bottom at one end and a hole at the other.' Then the one who had brought the wine scuttled back to the door after the two others, and out of it; the private with the bayonet dodged his seven-foot-long implement through it again and turned, holding the door half closed for the sergeant.

'All right, you bastards,' the sergeant said. 'Be pigs.'

'Speak for yourself, *maître*,' the wit said. 'If we must dine in stink, we prefer it to be our own.' Then suddenly, in unpremeditated concert as though they had not even planned it or instigated it, they had not even been warned of it but instead had been overtaken from behind by it like wind, they had all turned on the sergeant, or perhaps not even the sergeant, the human guards, but just the rifles and the bayonets and the steel lockable door, not moving, rushing toward them but just yelling at them—a sound hoarse, loud, without language, not of threat or indictment either: just a hoarse concerted affirmation or repudiation which continued for another moment or so even after the sergeant had passed through the door and it had clashed shut again. Then they stopped. Yet they still didn't rush at the table, still hovering, semicircular, almost diffidently, merely enclosing it, their noses trembling questing like those of rabbits at the odours from it, grimed, filthy, reeking still of the front lines and uncertainty and perhaps despair; unshaven, faces not alarming nor even embittered but harassed— faces of men who had already borne not only more than they expected but than they believed they could and who knew that it was still not over and—with a sort of amazement, even terror— that no matter how much more there would be, they would still bear that too.

'Come on, Corp,' a voice said. 'Let's go.'

'All right,' the corporal said. 'Watch it now.' But still there was no stampede, rush. It was just a crowding, a concentration, a jostling itself almost inattentive, not of famishment, hunger but rather of the watchful non-committance of people still—so far at least—keeping pace with, holding their own still within the fringe of a fading fairy-tale, the cursing itself inattentive and impersonal, not eager: just pressed as they crowded in on to both the fixed benches, five on one side and six on the other facing them until the twelfth man dragged up the cell's one stool to the head of the table for the corporal and then himself took the remaining place at the foot end of the unfilled bench like the Vice to the Chair in a Dickensian tavern's back room—a squat powerful weathered man with the blue eyes and reddish hair and beard of a Breton fisherman, captain, say, of his own small tough and dauntless boat—laden doubtless with contraband. The corporal filled the bowls while they passed them hand to hand. But still there was no voracity. A leashed quality, but even, almost unimpatient as they sat holding each his upended unsoiled spoon like a boat-crew.

'This looks bad,' one said.

'It's worse,' another said. 'It's serious.'

'It's a reprieve,' a third said. 'Somebody besides a garage mechanic cooked this. So if they went to all that trouble—' a third began.

'Hold it,' the Breton said. The man opposite him was short and very dark, his jaw wrenched by an old healed wound. He was saying something rapidly in an almost unintelligible Mediterranean dialect—Midi or perhaps Basque. They looked at one another. Suddenly still another spoke. He looked like a scholar, almost like a professor.

'He wants someone to say grace,' he said.

The corporal looked at the Midian. 'Say it then.' Again the other said something rapid and incomprehensible. Again the one who resembled a scholar translated.

'He says he doesn't know one.'

'Does anybody know one?' the corporal said. Again they looked at one another. Then one said to the fourth one:

'You've been to school. Say one.'

'Maybe he went too fast and passed it,' another said.

'Say it then,' the corporal said to the fourth one. The other said rapidly:

'Benedictus. Benedicte Benedictissimus. Will that do?'

'Will that do, Luluque?' the corporal said to the Midian.

'Yes yes,' the Midian said. They began to eat now. The Breton lifted one of the bottles slightly toward the corporal.

'Now?' he said.

'All right,' the corporal said. Six other hands took up the other bottles; they ate and poured and passed the bottles too.

'A reprieve,' the third said. 'They wouldn't dare execute us until we have finished eating this cooking. Our whole nation would rise at that insult to what we consider the first of the arts. How's this for an idea? We stagger this, eat one at a time, one man to each hour, thirteen hours; we'll still be alive at ... almost noon tomorrow—'

'—when they'll serve us another meal,' another said, 'and we'll stagger that one into dinner and then stagger dinner on through tomorrow night—'

'—and in the end eat ourselves into old age when we can't eat any more—'

'Let them shoot us then. Who cares?' the third said. 'No. That bastard sergeant will be in here with his firing squad right after the coffee. You watch.'

'Not that quick,' the first said. 'You have forgot what we consider the first of the virtues too. Thrift. They will wait until we have digested this and defecated it.'

'What will they want with that?' the fourth said.

'Fertiliser,' the first said. 'Imagine that corner, that garden-plot manured with the concentrate of this meal—'

'The manure of traitors,' the fourth said. He had the dreamy and furious face of a martyr.

'In that case, wouldn't the maize, the bean, the potato grow upside down, or anyway hide its head even if it couldn't bury it?' the second said.

'Stop it!' the corporal said.

'Or more than just the corner of a plot,' the third said. 'The carrion we'll bequeath France tomorrow—'

'Stop it!' the corporal said.

'Christ assoil us,' the fourth said.

'Aiyiyi,' the third said. 'We can call on him then. He need not fear cadavers.'

'Do you want me to make them shut up, Corp?' the Breton said.

'Come on now,' the corporal said. 'Eat. You'll spend the rest of the night wishing you did have something to clap your jaws on. Save the philosophy for then.'

'The wit too,' the third said.

'Then we will starve,' the first said.

'Or indigest,' the third said. 'If much of what we've heard tonight is wit.'

THURSDAY NIGHT

'Come on now,' the corporal said. 'I've told you twice. Do you want your bellies to say you've had enough, or that sergeant to come back in and say you've finished?' So they ate again, except the man on the corporal's left, who once more stopped his laden knife blade halfway to his mouth.

'Polchek's not eating,' he said suddenly. 'He's not even drinking. What's the matter, Polchek? Afraid yours won't produce anything but nettles and you won't make it to the latrine in time and we'll have to sleep in them?' The man addressed was on the corporal's immediate right. He had a knowing, almost handsome metropolitan face, bold but not at all arrogant, masked, composed, and only when you caught his eyes unawares did you realise how alert.

'A day of rest at Chaulnesmont wasn't the right pill for that belly of his maybe,' the first said.

'The sergeant-major's *coup de grace* tomorrow morning will be though,' the fourth said.

'Maybe it'll cure all of you of having to run a fever over what I don't eat and drink,' Polchek said.

'What's the matter?' the corporal said to him. 'You went on sick parade Sunday night before we came out. Haven't you got over it yet?'

'So what?' Polchek said. 'Is it an issue? I had a bad belly Sunday night. I've still got it but it's still mine. I was just sitting here with it, not worrying half as much about what I don't put in it as some innocent bystanders do because I don't.'

'Do you want to make an issue of it?' the fourth said.

'Bang on the door,' the corporal said to the Breton. 'Tell the sergeant we want to report a sick man.'

'Who's making an issue of it now?' Polchek said to the corporal before the Breton could move. He picked up his filled glass. 'Come on,' he said to the corporal. 'No heel taps. If my belly don't like wine tonight, as Jean says, that sergeant-major's pistol will pump it all out tomorrow morning.' He said to all of them: 'Come on. To peace. Haven't we finally got what we've all been working for for four years now? Come on, up with them!' he said, louder and sharply, with something momentary and almost fierce in his voice, face, look. At once the same excitement, restrained fierceness, seemed to pass through all of them; they raised their glasses too except one—the fourth one of the mountain faces, not quite as tall as the others and with something momentary and anguished in it almost like despair, who suddenly half raised his glass and stopped it and did not drink when the others did and banged the bizarre and incongruous vessels down and reached for the bottles again as, preceded by the sound of the heavy boots, the door clashed open again and the sergeant and his private entered; he now held an unfolded paper in his hand.

'Polchek,' he said. For a second Polchek didn't stir. Then the man who had not drunk gave a convulsive start and although he arrested it at once, when Polchek stood quietly up they both for a moment were in motion, so that the sergeant, about to address Polchek again, paused and looked from one to the other. 'Well?' the sergeant said. 'Which? Don't you even know who you are?' Nobody answered. As one, the others except Polchek were looking at the man who had not drunk. 'You,' the sergeant said to the corporal. 'Don't you know your own men?'

'This is Polchek,' the corporal said, indicating Polchek.

'Then what's wrong with him?' the sergeant said. He said to the other man: 'What's your name?'

'I—' the man said; again he glanced rapidly about, at nothing, no one, anguished and despairing.

'His name is—' the corporal said. 'I've got his papers—' He reached inside his tunic and produced a soiled dog-eared paper, obviously a regimental posting order. 'Pierre Bouc.' He rattled off a number.

'There's no Bouc on this list,' the sergeant said. 'What's he doing here?'

'You tell me,' the corporal said. 'He got mixed in with us somehow Monday morning. None of us know any Pierre Bouc either.'

'Why didn't he say something before this?'

'Who would have listened?' the corporal said.

'Is that right?' the sergeant said to the man. 'You don't belong in this squad?' The man didn't answer.

'Tell him,' the corporal said.

'No,' the man whispered. Then he said loudly: 'No!' He blundered up. 'I don't know them!' he said, blundering, stumbling half-falling backward over the bench almost as though in flight until the sergeant checked him.

'The major will have to settle this,' the sergeant said. 'Give me that order.' The corporal passed it to him. 'Out with you,' the sergeant said. 'Both of you.' Now those inside the room could see beyond the door another file of armed men, apparently a new one, waiting. The two prisoners passed on through the door and into it, the sergeant, then the orderly following; the iron door clashed behind them, against that room and all it contained, signified, portended; beyond it Polchek didn't even lower his voice:

'They promised me brandy. Where is it?'

'Shut up,' the sergeant's voice said. 'You'll get what's coming to you, no bloody fear.'

'I'd better,' Polchek said. 'If I don't, I might know what to do about it.'

'I've told him once,' the sergeant's voice said. 'If he don't shut up this time, shut him up.'

'With pleasure, sergeant,' another voice said. 'Can do.'

'Take them on,' the sergeant's voice said. Though before the iron clash of the door had ceased the corporal was already speaking, not loud: just prompt, still mild, not peremptory: just firm:

'Eat.' The same man essayed to speak again but again the corporal forestalled him. 'Eat,' he said. 'Next time he will take it out.' But they were spared that. The door opened almost immediately, but this time it was only the sergeant, alone, the eleven heads which remained turning as one to look at him where he faced the corporal down the length of the littered table.

'You,' the sergeant said.

'Me?' the corporal said.

'Yes,' the sergeant said. Still the corporal didn't move. He said again:

'You mean me?'

'Yes,' the sergeant said. 'Come on.' The corporal rose then. He gave one rapid look about at the ten faces now turning from the sergeant to look at him—faces dirty, unshaven, strained, which had slept too litttle in too long, harassed, but absolute, one in whatever it was—not trust exactly, not dependence: perhaps just one-ness, singleness.

'You're in charge, Paul,' he said to the Breton.

'Right,' the Breton said. 'Till you get back.' But this time the corridor was empty; it was the sergeant himself who closed the door behind them and turned the heavy key and pocketed it. There was no one in sight at all where he—the corporal—had expected to find armed men bristling until the moment when they in the white glittering room in the *Hôtel de Ville* sent for them for the last time. Then the sergeant turned from the door and now he—the corporal —realised that they were even hurrying a little: not at all furtive nor even surreptitious: just expedite, walking rapidly back up the corridor which he had already traversed three times—once yesterday morning when the guards had brought them from the lorry to the cell, and twice last night when the guards had taken them to the *Hôtel de Ville* and brought them back, their—his and the sergeant's—heavy boots not ringing because (so recent the factory —when it had been a factory—was) these were not stone but brick, but making instead a dull and heavy sound seeming only the louder because there were only four now instead of twenty-six plus the guards. So to him it was as though there was no other way out of it save that one exit, no direction to go in it except on, so that he had already begun to pass the small arch with its locked iron gate when the sergeant checked and turned him, nor any other life in or near it so that he didn't even recognise the silhouette of the helmet and the rifle until the man was in the act of unlocking the gate from the outside and swinging it back for them to pass through.

Nor did he see the car at once, the sergeant not quite touching him, just keeping him at that same pace, rapidity, as though by simple juxtaposition, on through the gate into an alley, a blank wall opposite and at the kerb-edge the big dark motionless car which he had not noticed yet because of the silence—not the cavernous emptiness in which their boots had echoed a moment back but a *cul-de-sac* of it, himself and the sergeant and the two sentries—the one who had unlocked the gate for them and then locked it after them, and his opposite flanking the other side of the gate—not even at parade rest but at ease, their rifles grounded, immobile and remote, as though oblivious to that to which they in their turn were invisible, the four of them set down in a vacuum of silence within the city's distant and indefatigable murmur. Then he saw the car. He didn't stop, it was barely a falter, the sergeant's shoulder barely nudged him before he went on. The driver didn't even move to descend; it was the sergeant who opened the door, the shoulder, a hand too now, firm and urgent against his back because he had stopped now, erect, immobile and immovable even after the voice inside the car said, 'Get in, my child'; then immovable for another second yet before he stooped and entered it, seeing as he did so the pallid glint of braid, a single plane of face above the dark enveloping cloak.

Then the sergeant shut the door, the car already in motion and that was all; only the three of them: the old man who bore far too much rank to carry a lethal weapon even if he were not already too old to use it, and the driver whose hands were full with managing the car even if he had not had his back to him who could not remember in four days anyhow when there had not been one arm or two but from twenty to a thousand already cocked and triggered for his life: out of the alley and still no word—direction or command—from the old man in the braided hat and the night-coloured cloak in the corner opposite him, not back to the city but skirting through the fringe of it, faster and faster, pacing its cavernous echoes through the narrow ways of the deserted purlieus, taking the rapid turnings as if the mechanism itself knew their destination, making a long concentric through the city's edge, the ground rising now so that even he began to know where they were probably going, the city itself beginning to tilt toward them as it sank away beneath; nor any word from the old man this time either: the car just stopped, and looking past the fine and delicate profile beneath what should have been the insuperable weight of the barred and braided hat, he could see not the *Place de Ville* itself, they were not that high above the city yet, but rather as though the concentration of its unwearyable and sleepless anxiety had taken on the glow and glare of light.

'Now, my child,' the old general said: not to him this time but to the driver. The car went on and now he did know where they were going because there was nothing else up here but the old Roman citadel. But if he felt any first shock of instinctive and purely physical terror, he didn't show it. And if at the same instant reason was also telling him, *Nonsense. To execute you secretly in a dungeon would undo the very thing which they stopped the war and brought all thirteen of you here to accomplish*, nobody heard that either: he just sat there, erect, a little stiffly who never had sat completely back in the seat, alert but quite calm, watchful and composed, the

car in second gear now but still going fast around the final convoluted hairpin turns until at last the stone weight of the citadel
itself seemed to lean down and rest upon them like a ponderable
shadow, the car making the last *renversement* because now it could
go no farther, stopping at last and not he nor the driver but the old
general himself who opened the door and got out and held the
door until he was out and erect again and had begun to turn his
head to look until the old general said, 'No, not yet,' and turned
on himself, he following, up the final steep and rocky pitch where
they would have to walk, the old citadel not looming above them
but squatting, not Gothic but Roman: not soaring to the stars out
of the aspiration of man's past but a gesture against them of his
mortality like a clenched fist or a shield.

'Now turn and look at it,' the old general said. But he already
had, was—down the declivity's black pitch to where the city lay
trembling and myriad with lights in its bowl of night like a scatter
of smouldering autumn leaves in the windy darkness, thicker and
denser than the stars in its concentration of anguish and unrepose,
as if all of darkness and terror had poured down in one wash, one
wave, to lie palpatant and unassuageable in the *Place de Ville*.
'Look at it. Listen to it. Remember it. A moment: then close the
window on it. Disregard that anguish. You caused them to fear and
suffer, but tomorrow you will have discharged them of both and
they will only hate you: once for the rage they owe you for giving
them the terror, once for the gratitude they will owe you for taking
it away, and once for the fact that you are beyond the range of
either. So close the window on that, and be yourself discharged.
Now look beyond it. The earth, or half of it, full half the earth as
far as horizon bounds it. It is dark of course, but only dark from
here; its darkness is only that anonymity which a man can close
behind him like a curtain on his past, not even when he must in his
desperation but when he will for his comfort and simple privacy.
Of course he can go only in one direction in it now: west; only one
hemisphere of it—the Western—is available to him now. But that
is large enough for his privacy for a year because this condition
will only last another year, then all earth will be free to him. They
will ask for a formal meeting, for terms, some time this winter; by
next year we will even have what we will call peace—for a little
while. Not we will request it: they will—the Germans, the best

soldiers on earth today or in two thousand years, for that matter, since even the Romans could not conquer them—the one people out of all the earth who have a passion and dedication not even for glory but for war, who make war not even for conquest and aggrandisement but as an occupation, a vocation, and who will lose this one for that very reason: that they are the best soldiers on earth; not we French and British, who accept war only as a last resort when everything else has failed, and even enter that final one with no confidence in it either; but they, the Germans, who have not receded one foot since they crossed the Belgian frontier almost four years ago and every decision since has been either nil or theirs and who will not stop now even though they themselves know that one more victory will destroy them; who will win perhaps two or even three more (the number will not matter) and then will have to surrender because the phenomenon of war is its hermaphroditism: the principles of victory and of defeat inhabit the same body and the necessary opponent, enemy, is merely the bed they self-exhaust each other on: a vice only the more terrible and fatal because there is no intervening breast or division between to frustrate them into health by simple normal distance and lack of opportunity for the copulation from which even orgasm cannot free them; the most expensive and fatal vice which man has invented yet, to which the normal ones of lechery and drink and gambling which man fatuously believes are capable of destroying him, stand as does the child's lollypop to the bottle, the courtesan and the playing-card. A vice so long ingrained in man as to have become an honourable tenet of his behaviour and the national altar for his love of bloodshed and glorious sacrifice. More than that even: a pillar not of his nation's supremacy but of his national survival; you and I have seen war as the last recourse of politics; I shan't of course but you will—can—see it become the last refuge from bankruptcy; you will—can, provided you will—see the day when a nation insolvent from over-population will declare war on whatever richest and most sentimental opponent it can persuade to defeat it quickest, in order to feed its people out of the conqueror's quartermaster stores. But that is not our problem today; and even if it were, by simply being in alliance with the ultimate victor, we—France and Britain—would find ourselves in the happy situation of gaining almost as much from our victory as the

German will through his defeat. Our—call it mine if you like—problem is more immediate. There is the earth. You will have half of it now; by New Year's you will very probably have all of it, all the vast scope of it except this minuscule suppuration which men call Europe—and who knows? in time and with a little discretion and care, even that again if you like. Take my car—you can drive one, can't you?'

'Yes,' the corporal said. 'Go?'

'Now,' the old general said. 'Take my car. If you can drive at all, the pennon on its bonnet will carry you anywhere in Europe west of the German wire; if you can drive well, the engine beneath it will take you to the coast—Brest or Marseille either—in two days; I have papers ready to pass you aboard any ship you choose there and command its captain. Then South America—Asia—the Pacific islands; close that window fast; lock it forever on that aberrant and futile dream. No no,' he said quickly, 'don't for one second suspect me of that base misreading of your character—you who in five minutes Monday voided that war which the German himself, the best soldier in Europe, in almost four years has never quite nudged from stalemate. Of course you will have money, but only that balance exactly matched to freedom as the eagle or the bandit carry theirs. I don't bribe you with money. I give you liberty.'

'To desert them,' the corporal said.

'Desert whom? Look again.' His hand appeared in a brief rapid gesture toward the wan city unsleeping below them—a gesture not even contemptuous, not anything: just a flick, then gone, already vanished again within the midnight-coloured cloak. 'Not them. Where have they been since Monday? Why with their bare hands, since they have enough of them, have they not torn down brick by brick the walls which far fewer hands than theirs sufficed to raise, or torn from its hinges that one door which only one hand sufficed to lock, and set all of you free who had essayed to die for them? Where are the two thousand nine hundred and eighty-seven others you had—or thought you had—at dawn Monday? Why, as soon as you were through the wire, didn't all of them cast down their arms too and simply follow you, if they too believed you were all weaponed and bucklered out of the arsenal of invulnerable human aspiration and hope and belief? Why didn't even that mere three thousand then—they would have been enough—erase the bricks and wrench away that door, who believed in you for five minutes anyway enough to risk what you anyway knew you risked—the three thousand that is lacking the twelve who have been locked inside the same incommunicant bricks with you ever since? Where are they even? One of them, your own countryman, blood brother, kinsman probably since you were all blood kin at some time there —one Zsettlani who has denied you, and the other, whether Zsettlani or not or blood kin or not, at least was—or anyway had been accepted into—the brotherhood of your faith and hope— Polchek, who had already betrayed you by midnight Sunday. Do you see? You even have a substitute to your need as on that after-noon God produced the lamb which saved Isaac—if you could call Polchek a lamb. I will take Polchek tomorrow, execute him with rote and fanfare; you will not only have your revenge and discharge the vengeance of the rest of those three thousand whom he betrayed, you will repossess the opprobrium from all that voice down there which cannot even go to bed because of the frantic need to anathemise you. Give me Polchek, and take freedom.'

'There are still ten,' the corporal said.

'Let's try it. We will remain here; I will send the car back with orders to unlock and open that door and then for every man in that building to vanish from it, oblivious of all to which they them-selves will be invisible—quietly unlock that door, unlock that gate, and vanish. How long before that ten will have denied you too— betrayed you too, if you can call that choice betrayal?'

'And you see too,' the corporal said. 'In ten minutes there would not be ten but a hundred. In ten hours there would not be ten hundred but ten thousand. And in ten days—'

'Yes,' the old general said. 'I have seen that. Have I not said I don't so basely misread your character? Oh yes, let us say it: your threat. Why else have I offered to buy my—our—security with things which most men not only do not want but on the contrary do well to fear and flee from, like liberty and freedom? Oh yes, I can destroy you tomorrow morning and save us—for the time. For the length of my life, in fact. But only for the time. And if I must, I will. Because I believe in man within his capacities and limitations. I not only believe he is capable of enduring and will endure, but that he must endure, at least until he himself invents evolves produces a better tool than he to substitute for himself. Take my car and freedom, and I will give you Polchek. Take the highest of all the ecstasies: compassion, pity: the orgasm of forgiving him who barely escaped doing you a mortal hurt—that glue, that catalyst which your philosophers have trained you to believe holds the earth together. Take the earth.'

'There are still ten,' the corporal said.

'Have I forgotten them?' the old general said. 'Have I not said twice that I have never misread you? You don't need to threaten me; I know that they, not you, are the problem; not you but they are what we are bargaining for. Because for your profit, I must destroy all eleven of you and so compound tenfold the value of your threat and sacrifice. For my profit, I must let them go too, to be witnesses to all the earth that you forsook them; for, talk as much and as loudly and as long as they will, who to believe in the value—value? validity—of the faith they preach when you, its prophet and instigator, elected your liberty to its martyrdom? No no, we are not two Greek or Armenian or Jewish—or for that matter, Norman—peasants swapping a horse: we are two articulations, self-elected possibly, anyway elected, anyway postulated, not so much to defend as to test two inimical conditions which, through no fault of ours but through the simple paucity and restrictions of the arena where they meet, must contend and—one of them—perish: I champion of this mundane earth which, whether I like it or not, is, and to which I did not ask to come, yet since I am here, not only must stop but intend to stop during my allotted while; you champion of an esoteric realm of man's baseless hopes and his infinite capacity—no: passion—for unfact. No, they are not inimical really, there is no contest actually; they can even exist side by side together in this one restricted arena, and could and would, had yours not interfered with mine. So once more: take the earth. Now, answer as I know you will: There are still ten.'

'There are still that ten,' the corporal said.

'Then take the world,' the old general said. 'I will acknowledge you as my son; together we will close the window on this aberration and lock it forever. Then I will open another for you on a world such as caesar nor sultan nor khan ever saw, Tiberius nor Kubla nor all the emperors of the East ever dreamed of—no Rome and Baiae: mere depot for the rapine of ravagers and bagnio for one last exhaustion of the nerve-ends before returning to their gloomy deserts to wrest more of the one or face at home the hired knives of their immediate underlings thirsting to cure them of the need for both; no Cathay: chimera of poets bearing the same relation to the reality of attainment as the Mahometan's paradise —a symbol of his escape and a justification of its need, from the stinking alleys or fierce sand of his inescapable cradle; nor Kubla's Xanadu which was not even a poet's rounded and completed dream but a drug-sodden English one's lightning-bolt which electrocuted him with the splendour he could not even face long enough to get it down—none of these which were but random and momentary constellations in the empyrean of the world's history: but Paris, which is the world as empyrean is the sum of its constellations—not that Paris in which any man can have all of these—Rome, Cathay and Xanadu—provided he is connected a little and does not need to count his money, because you do not want these: have I not said twice now that I have not misread you? But that Paris which only my son can inherit from me— that Paris which I did not at all reject at seventeen but simply held in abeyance for compounding against the day when I should be a father to bequeath it to an heir worthy of that vast and that terrible heritage. A fate, a destiny in it: mine and yours, one and inextricable. Power, matchless and immeasurable; oh no, I have not misread you—I, already born heir to that power as it stood then, holding that inheritance in escrow to become unchallenged and unchallengeable chief of that confederation which would defeat and subjugate and so destroy the only factor on earth which threatened it; you with the power and gift to persuade three thousand men to accept a sure and immediate death in preference to a problematical one based on tried mathematical percentage, when you had at most only a division of fifteen thousand to work on and your empty hands to work with. What can you not—will you not—do with all the world to work on and the heritage I can give you to work with? A king, an emperor, retaining his light and untensile hold on mankind only until another appears capable of giving them more and bloodier circuses and more and sweeter bread? You will be God, holding him forever through a far, far stronger ingredient than his simple lusts and appetites: by his triumphant and ineradicable folly, his deathless passion for being led, mystified, and deceived.'

'So we ally—confederate,' the corporal said. 'Are you that afraid of me?'

'I already respect you; I don't need to fear you. I can do without you. I shall; I intend to. Of course, in that case you will not see it—and how sad that commentary: that one last bitterest pill of martyrdom, without which the martyrdom itself could not be, since then it would not be martyrdom: even if by some incredible chance you shall have been right, you will not even know it—and paradox: only the act of voluntarily relinquishing the privilege of ever knowing you were right, can possible make you right.—I know, don't say it: if I can do without you, then so can you yourself; to me, your death is but an ace to be finessed, while to you it is the actual ace of trumps. Nor this either: I mentioned the word bribe once; now I have offered it: I am an old man, you a young one; I will be dead in a few years and you can use your inheritance to win the trick tomorrow which today my deuce finessed you of. Because I will take that risk too. Don't even say—' and stopped and raised the hand quickly this time from inside the cloak and said: 'Wait. Don't say it yet.—Then take life. And think well before you answer that. Because the purse is empty now; only one thing else remains in it. Take life. You are young; even after four years of war, the young can still believe in their own invulnerability: that all else may die, but not they. So they don't need to treasure life too highly since they cannot conceive, accept, the possible end of it. But in time you become old, you see death then. Then you realise that nothing—nothing—nothing—not power nor glory nor wealth nor pleasure nor even freedom from pain, is as valuable as simple breathing, simply being alive even with all the regret of having to remember and the anguish of an irreparable worn-out body; merely knowing that you are alive—Listen to this. It happened in America, at a remote place called by an Indian name I think: Mississippi: a man who had committed a brutal murder for some base reason—gain or revenge perhaps or perhaps simply to free himself of one woman in order to espouse another; it doesn't matter—who went to his trial still crying his innocence and was convicted and sentenced still crying it and even in the death cell beneath the gallows still crying it, until a priest came to him; not the first time of course nor the second nor perhaps even the third, but presently and in time: the murderer at last confessed his crime against man and so making his peace with God, until presently it was almost as though the murderer and the priest had exchanged places and offices: not the priest now but the murderer the strong one, the calm one, the strong calm steadfast rock not even of tremulous hope but of conviction and unshakable faith, on which the priest himself could now lean for strength and courage; this right up to the very morning of the execution, toward which the murderer now looked with a sort of impatience almost, as though actually fretting a little for the moment when he could doff the sorry ephemeral world which had brought him to this and demanded this expiation and accepted his forgiveness; right up to the gallows itself: which at Mississippi I understand is out-of-doors in the yard of the jail, enclosed temporarily in a high stockade of planks to shield the principal's departure from earth from the merely morbid and curious anyway; though they would come: in their carts and carriages for miles, bringing box lunches: men women children and grandparents, to stand along the tall fence until the bell, clock, whatever it was to mark the passing of the soul, struck and released them to go back home; indeed, able to see even less than the man who stood beneath the noose, already free this whole week now of that sorry and mortal body which was the sorry all which penance could rob him of, standing calm composed and at peace, the trivial noose already fitted to his neck and in his vision one last segment of the sky beyond which his theology had taught him he would presently be translated, and one single branch of an adjacent tree extending over the stockade as though in benison, one last gesture of earth's absolution, with which he had long since severed any frail remaining thread; when suddenly a bird flew on to that bough and stopped and opened its tiny throat and sang—whereupon he who less than a second before had his very foot lifted to step from earth's grief and anguish into eternal peace, cast away heaven, salvation, immortal soul and all, struggling to free his bound hands in order to snatch away the noose, crying, 'Innocent! Innocent! I didn't do it!' even as the trap earth, world and all, fell from under him—all because of one bird, one weightless and ephemeral creature which hawk might stoop at or snare or lime or random pellet of some idle boy destroy before the sun set—except that tomorrow, next year, there would be another bird, another spring, the same bough leafed again and another bird to sing on it, if he is only here to hear it, can only remain—Do you follow me?'

'Yes,' the corporal said.

'Then take that bird. Recant, confess, say you were wrong; that what you led was—led? you led nothing: you simply participated —an attack which failed to advance. Take life from me; ask mercy and accept it. I can give it, even for a military failure. The general commanding your division will—he already has—demand a sacrifice, not in the name of France or of victory, but in that of his blemished record. But it's not he, it's I who wear this hat.'

'There are still ten,' the corporal said.

'Who will hate you—until they forget you. Who will even curse you until they have forgot whom they cursed, and why. No no: close the window upon that baseless dream. Open this other one; perhaps you will—can—see nothing but grey beyond it—except for that bough, always; that one single bough which will be there always waiting and ready for that weightless and ephemeral burden. Take that bird.'

'Don't be afraid,' the corporal said. 'There's nothing to be afraid of. Nothing worth it.'

For a moment the old general didn't seem to have heard the corporal at all, standing a head below the other's high mountain one, beneath the seemingly insuperable weight of the blue-and-scarlet hat cross-barred and dappled with gold braid and heavy golden leaves. Then he said, 'Afraid? No no, it's not I but you who are afraid of man; not I but you who believe that nothing but a death can save him. I know better. I know that he has that in him which will enable him to outlast even his wars; that in him more durable than all his vices, even that last and most fearsome one; to outlast even this next avatar of his servitude which he now faces: his enslavement to the demonic progeny of his own mechanical curiosity, from which he will emancipate himself by that one ancient tried-and-true method by which slaves have always freed themselves: by inculcating their masters with the slaves' own vices—in this case the vice of war and that other one which is no vice at all but instead is the quality-mark and warrant of man's immortality: his deathless folly. He has already begun to put wheels

under his patio his terrace and his front veranda; even at my age
I may see the day when what was once his house has become a
storage-place for his bed and stove and razor and spare clothing;
you with your youth could (remember that bird) see the day when
he will have invented his own private climate and moved it stove
bathroom bed clothing kitchen and all into his automobile and
what he once called home will have vanished from human lexicon:
so that he won't dismount from his automobile at all because he
won't need to: the entire earth one unbroken machined de-moun-
tained dis-rivered expanse of concrete paving protuberanceless by
tree or bush or house or anything which might constitute a corner
or a threat to visibility, and man in his terrapin myriads enclosed
clothesless from birth in his individual wheeled and glovelike
envelope, with pipes and hoses leading upward from underground
reservoirs to charge him with one composite squirt which at one
mutual instant will fuel his mobility, pander his lusts, sate his
appetites and fire his dreams; peripatetic, unceasing and long since
no longer countable, to die at last at the click of an automatic
circuit-breaker on a speedometer dial, and, long since freed of bone
and organ and gut, leaving nothing for communal scavenging but
a rusting and odourless shell—the shell which he does not get out
of because he does not need to, but which presently for a time he
will not emerge from because he does not dare because the shell
will be his only protection from the hail-like iron refuse from his
wars. Because by that time his wars will have dispossessed him by
simple out-distance; his simple frail physique will be no longer able
to keep up, bear them, attend them, be present. He will try of
course and for a little while he will even hold his own; he will
build tanks bigger and faster and more impervious and with more
firepower than any before, he will build aircraft bigger and faster
and capable of more load and more destruction than any yet; for
a little while he will accompany, direct, as he thinks control them,
even after he has finally realised that it is not another frail and
mortal dissident to his politics or his notions of national bound-
aries that he is contending with, but the very monster itself which
he inhabits. It will not be someone firing bullets at him who for
the moment doesn't like him. It will be his own frankenstein
which roasts him alive with heat, asphyxiates him with speed,
wrenches loose his still-living entrails in the ferocity of its

prey-seeking stoop. So he will not be able to go along with it at all, though for a little while longer it will permit him the harmless delusion that he controls it from the ground with buttons. Then that will be gone too; years, decades then centuries will have elapsed since it last answered his voice; he will have even forgotten the very location of its breeding-grounds and his last contact with it will be a day when he will crawl shivering out of his cooling burrow to crouch among the delicate stalks of his dead antennae like a fairy geometry, beneath a clangourous rain of dials and meters and switches and bloodless fragments of metal epidermis, to watch the final two of them engaged in the last gigantic wrestling against the final and dying sky robbed even of darkness and filled with the inflectionless uproar of the two mechanical voices bellowing at each other polysyllabic and verbless patriotic nonsense. Oh yes, he will survive it because he has that in him which will endure even beyond the ultimate worthless tideless rock freezing slowly in the last red and heatless sunset, because already the next star in the blue immensity of space will be already clamourous with the uproar of his debarkation, his puny and inexhaustible voice still talking, still planning; and there too after the last ding dong of doom has rung and died there will still be one sound more: his voice, planning still to build something higher and faster and louder; more efficient and louder and faster than ever before, yet it too inherent with the same old primordial fault since it too in the end will fail to eradicate him from the earth. I don't fear man. I do better: I respect and admire him. And pride: I am ten times prouder of that immortality which he does possess than ever he of that heavenly one of his delusion. Because man and his folly—'

'Will endure,' the corporal said.

'They will do more,' the old general said proudly. 'They will prevail. —Shall we return?'

They went back to the waiting car and descended; they traversed once more the echoing and empty warrens concentric about the distant crowded *Place de Ville*. Then the alley again, the car slowing and stopping once more opposite the small locked gate in front of which, above a struggling group of five men the bayoneted rifles of four of them waved and jerked like furious exclamations. The corporal looked once at the struggling group and said quietly:

'There are eleven now.'

'There are eleven now,' the old general said as quietly; again one arresting gesture of the fine and delicate hand from beneath the cloak. 'Wait. Let us watch this a moment: a man freed of it, now apparently trying to fight his way back into what for all he knows will be his death cell.' So they sat for a moment yet, watching the fifth man (the same one who two hours ago had been taken from the cell by the same guards who came for Polchek) straining stocky and furious in the hands of his four captors apparently not away from the small gate but toward it, until the old general got out of the car, the corporal following, and said, not raising his voice yet either:

'What's wrong here, Sergeant?' The group paused in their straining attitudes. The prisoner looked back then he wrenched free and turned and ran across the pavement toward the old general and the corporal, the four captors following, grasping him again.

'Stand still, you!' the sergeant hissed. 'Attention! His name is Pierre Bouc. He didn't belong in that squad at all, though we didn't discover the mistake until one of them—' he glanced at the corporal '—you—condescended to produce his regimental order. We found him trying to get back in. He denied his name; he wouldn't even produce the order until we took it away from him.' Holding the short and furious man with one hand, he produced the dog-eared paper from his pocket. Immediately the prisoner snatched it from him.

'You lie!' he said to the sergeant. Before they could prevent him he ripped the order to shreds and whirled and flung the shreds in the old general's face. 'You lie!' he shouted at the old general while the scraps drifted like a confetti of windless and weightless snow or feathers about the golden hat, the calm incurious inscrutable face which had looked at everything and believed none of it. 'You lie,' the man shouted again. 'My name is not Pierre Bouc. I am Piotr—' adding something in a harsh almost musical Middle-Eastern tongue so full of consonants as to be almost unintelligible. Then he turned to the corporal, going rapidly on to his knees, grasping the corporal's hand and saying something else in the incomprehensible tongue, to which the corporal answered in it though the man still crouched, clinging to the corporal's hand, the corporal speaking again in the tongue, as if he had repeated himself but with a

319

different object, noun perhaps, and then a third time, a third slight alteration in its inflection, at which the man moved, rose and stood now rigid at attention facing the corporal, who spoke again, and the man turned, a smart military quarter-turn, the four captors moving quickly in again until the corporal said in French:

'You don't need to hold him. Just unlock the gate.' But still the old general didn't move, motionless within the cloak's dark volume, composed, calm, not even bemused; just inscrutable, saying presently in that voice not even recapitulant: not anything:

' "Forgive me, I didn't know what I was doing." And you said, "Be a man," but he didn't move. Then you said "Be a Zsettlani" and still no move. Then you said "Be a soldier" and he became one.' Then he turned and got back into the car, the soft voluminous smother of the coat becoming motionless again about him in the corner of the seat; the sergeant came rapidly back across the pavement and stood again just behind the corporal's shoulder; now the old general himself spoke in the rapid unvoweled tongue:

'And became one. No: returned to one. Good night, my child.'

'Good-bye, Father,' the corporal answered him.

'Not good-bye,' the old general said. 'I am durable too; I don't give up easily either. Remember whose blood it is that you defy me with.' Then in French to the driver: 'Let us go home now.' The car went on. Then the corporal and the sergeant turned together, the sergeant once more at and just behind his shoulder, not touching him, back to the iron gate which one of the sentries held open for them to pass through, and then closed and locked. Again, so grooved in old assumption, he had begun to turn down the corridor toward the cell when the sergeant once more checked and turned him, this time into a passage only wide enough for one and barely tall enough for any—a one-way secret duct leading as though into the very bowels of incarceration; the sergeant unlocked a solid door and closed it between himself and the corporal upon a cell indeed this time little larger than a big closet containing one endless man-width wooden bench for sleeping and an iron bucket for latrine and two men, all bathed in one fierce glare of light. One of them did have the swaggering face, reckless and sardonic, incorrigible and debonair, even to the thin moustache; he even wore the filthy beret and the knotted handkerchief about his throat, even the limp dead cigarette in the corner of his mouth, his hands in his pockets and one foot crossed negligently over the other as he had leaned against the wall of his narrow Montmartre alley, the other shorter man standing beside him with the peaceful and patient fidelity of a blind dog—a squat simian-like man whose tremendous empty and peaceful hands hung almost to his knees as if they were attached to strings inside his sleeves, with a small quite round simian head and a doughy face itself like one single feature, drooling a little at the mouth.

'Pray to enter,' the first said. 'So they tapped you for it, did they? Call me Lapin; anybody in the *Prefecture* will vouch for it.' Without removing his hand from the pocket, he indicated the man beside him with a nudge of his elbow. 'This is Casse-tête—Horse for short. We're on our way to town, hey, Horse?' The second man made a single indistinguishable sound. 'Hear that?' the first said. 'He can say "Paris" as good as anybody. Tell him again, Uncle— where we're going tomorrow.' Again the other made the thick wet sound. It was quite true; the corporal could recognise it now.

'What's he doing in that uniform?' the corporal said.

'Ah, the sons of bitches scared him,' the first said. 'I don't mean Germans either. You don't mean they are going to be satisfied to shoot just one of you out of that whole regiment.'

'I don't know,' the corporal said. 'He hasn't always been like this?'

'Got a fag?' the other said. 'I'm out.' The corporal produced a packet of cigarettes. The other spat the stub from his mouth without even moving his head, and took one from the packet. 'Thanks.' The corporal produced a lighter. 'Thanks,' the other said. He took the lighter and snapped it on and lit the cigarette, already—or still —talking, the cigarette bobbing, his arms now crossed in front of him, each hand grasping lightly the opposite elbow. 'What was that you said? Has he always been like this? Naah. A few flies upstairs, but he was all right until—What?' The corporal stood facing him, his hand extended.

'The lighter,' the corporal said.

'I beg pardon?'

'My lighter,' the corporal said. They looked at each other. Lapin made a slight motion with his wrists and up-turned his empty palms. The corporal faced him, his hand extended.

'Jesus,' Lapin said. 'Don't break my heart. Don't tell me you even saw what I did with it. If you did, then they are right; they just waited one day too late.' He made another rapid movement with one hand; when it opened again, the lighter was in it. The corporal took it.

'Beats hell, don't it?' Lapin said. 'A man ain't even the sum of his vices: just his habits. Here we are, after tomorrow morning neither one of us will have any use for it and until then it won't matter which one of us has it. Yet you've got to have it back just because you are in the habit of owning it, and I have to try to cop it just because that's one of my natural habits too. Maybe that's what all the bother and trouble they're getting ready to go to tomorrow morning is for—parading a whole garrison just to cure three lousy bastards of the bad habit of breathing. Hey, Horse?' he said to the second man.

'Paris,' the second man said hoarsely.

'You bet,' Lapin said. 'That's the one they're going to cure us of tomorrow: the bad habit of not getting to Paris after working for four years at it. We'll make it this time though; the corporal here is going with us to see that we do.'

'What did he do?' the corporal said.

'That's all right,' Lapin said. 'Say we. Murder. It was the old dame's fault; all she had to do was just tell us where the money was hidden and then behave herself, keep her mouth shut. Instead she had to lay there in the bed yelling her head off until we had to choke her or we never would have got to Paris—'

'Paris,' the second said in his wet voice.

'Because that's all we wanted,' Lapin said. 'All we were trying to do: just get to Paris. Only folks kept on steering him wrong, sending him off in the wrong direction, sicking the dogs on him, cops always saying Move on, move on—you know how it is. So when we threw in together that day—that was at Clermont Ferrand in '14—he didn't know how long he had been on the road because we didn't know how old he was. Except that it had been a good while, he hadn't been nothing but a kid then— You found out you were going to have to go to Paris before you even found out you were going to have to have a woman, hey, Horse?'

'Paris,' the second said hoarsely.

'—working a little wherever he could find it, sleeping in stables and hedgerows until they would set the dogs or the police on him

again, telling him to move on without even bothering to tell him
which way he wanted to go until you would have thought nobody
else in France ever heard of Paris, let alone wanted—had—to go
there. Hey, Horse?'

'Paris,' the second said.

'Then we run into one another that day in Clermont and
decided to throw in together and then it was all right, there was a
war on then and all you had to do was get yourself inside a government blue suit and you were free of cops and civilians and the
whole human race; all you needed was just to know who to salute
and do it quick enough. So we took a bottle of brandy to a
sergeant I knew—'

'The human race?' the corporal said.

'Sure,' Lapin said. 'You might not think it to look at him, but
he can move in the dark as quiet as a ghost and even see in it like
a cat; turn this light off for a second and he will have that lighter
out of your pocket and you won't even know it.— So he was in too
now—'

'He learned that fast?' the corporal said.

'Of course we had to be a little careful about his hands. He
never meant nothing, see: he just didn't know himself how strong
they were, like that night last month.'

'So you got along fine then,' the corporal said.

'It was duck soup.—So he was in too now and now he could
even ride sometimes, with the government paying for it, getting
closer and closer to Paris now; not much over a year and we were
all the way up to Verdun, that any boche will tell you is right next
door to Paris—'

'And still doing all right,' the corporal said.

'Why not? If you can't trust your money to a bank in peace
time, where else can you put it in a war except up the chimney
or under the mattress or inside the clock? Or anywhere else you
thought it was hidden for that matter because it didn't matter to
us; Horse here has a nose for a ten-franc note like a pig for a
truffle. Until that night last month and that was the old dame's
fault; all she needed to do was tell us where it was and then lay
quiet and keep her mouth shut but that didn't suit her, she had
to lay there in the bed hollering her head off until Horse here had
to shut her up—you know: no harm intended: just to squeeze her

throat a little until we could have a little peace and quiet to hunt for it in. Only we forgot about the hands, and when I got back—'

'Got back?' the corporal said.

'I was downstairs hunting for the money—got back, it was too late. So they caught us. And you'd have thought that would have satisfied them, especially as they even got the money back—'

'You found the money?' the corporal said.

'Sure. While he was keeping her quiet.—But no, that wasn't enough—'

'You found the money and had got away with it, and then turned around and came back?'

'What?' Lapin said.

'Why did you change your mind?' the corporal said. After a second Lapin said:

'Fag me again.' The corporal gave him another cigarette. 'Thanks,' he said. The corporal extended the lighter. 'Thanks,' Lapin said. He snapped it and lit the cigarette and snuffed the lighter, again his two hands began the rapid and involuted gesture then stopped and in the same motion one of the hands tossed the lighter back to the corporal, the arms crossed again, palms to opposite elbows, the cigarette bobbing while he talked. 'Where was I? Oh yes.—But that didn't suit them; just to take us out in a decent and peaceful way and shoot us wasn't enough; they had to take Horse here off in a cellar somewhere and scare the daylights out of him. Justice, see? Protecting our rights. Just catching us wasn't enough; we got to insist that we did it. Just me saying so wasn't enough; Horse too has got to holler it to high heaven— whatever that means. But it's all right now. They can't stop us now.' He turned and clapped the second man a hard quick blow on the back: 'Paris tomorrow morning, kid. Fasten on to that.'

The door opened. It was the same sergeant again. He did not enter. He said to the corporal: 'Once more' and then stood and held the door until the corporal had passed him. Then he closed and locked the door. This time it was the office of the prison com- mandant himself and what he—the corporal—assumed to be just another N.C.O. until he saw, arranged on the cleared desk, the utensils for the Last Sacrament—urn ewer stole candles and crucifix—and only then remarked the small embroidered cross on the coat of the man standing beside them, the other sergeant closing that door too between them so that he and the priest were alone, the priest lifting his hand to inscribe into the invisible air the invisible Passion while the corporal paused for a moment just inside the door, not surprised yet either: just once more alert, looking at him: at which moment a third person in the room would have remarked that they were almost of an age.

'Come in, my son,' the priest said.

'Good evening, Sergeant,' the corporal said.

'Can't you say Father?' the priest said.

'Of course,' the corporal said.

'Then say it,' the priest said.

'Of course, Father,' the corporal said. He came on into the room, looking quietly and rapidly again at the sacred implements on the desk while the priest watched him.

'Not that,' the priest said. 'Not yet. I came to offer you life.'

'So he sent you,' the corporal said.

'He?' the priest said. 'What he can you mean, except the Giver of all life? Why should He send me here to offer you what He has already entrusted you with? Because the man you imply, for all his rank and power, can only take it from you. Your life was never his to give you because for all his stars and braid he too is just one more pinch of rotten and ephemeral dust before God. It was neither of them who sent me here: not the One who has already given you life, not the other who never had yours nor any other life within his gift. It was duty which sent me here. Not this—' for an instant his hand touched the small embroidered cross on his collar '—not my cloth, but my belief in Him; not even as His mouthpiece but as a man—'

'A Frenchman?' the corporal said.

'All right,' the priest said. 'Yes, a Frenchman if you like—commanded me here to command—not ask, offer: command—you to keep the life which you never had and never will have the refusal of, to save another one.'

'To save another one?' the corporal said.

'The commander of your regiment's division,' the priest said. 'He will die too, for what all the world he knows—-the only world he does know because it was the one he dedicated his life to—will call his failure, where you will die for what you anyway will call a victory.'

'So he did send you,' the corporal said. 'For blackmail.'

'Beware,' the priest said.

'Then don't tell me this,' the corporal said. 'Tell him. If I can save Gragnon's life only by not doing something you tell me I already can't and never could do anyway. Tell him then. I don't want to die either.'

'Beware,' the priest said.

'That wasn't who I meant,' the corporal said. 'I meant——'

'I know whom you meant,' the priest said. 'That's why I said beware. Beware Whom you mock by reading your own mortal's pride into Him Who died two thousand years ago in the affirmation that man shall never never never, need never never never, hold suzerainty over another's life and death—absolved you and the man you mean both of that terrible burden: you of the right to and he of the need for, suzerainty over your life; absolved poor mortal man forever of the fear of the oppression, and the anguish of the responsibility, which suzerainty over human fate and destiny would have entailed on him and cursed him with, when He refused in man's name the temptation of that mastery, refused the terrible temptation of that limitless and curbless power when He answered the Tempter: *Render unto caesar the things which are caesar's.*—I know,' he said quickly before the corporal could have spoken: 'To Chaulnesmont the things which are Chaulnesmont's. Oh yes, you're right; I'm a Frenchman first. And so now you can even cite the record at me, can't you? All right. Do it.'

'The record?' the corporal said.

'The Book,' the priest said. The corporal looked at him. 'You mean you don't even know it?'

'I can't read,' the corporal said.

'Then I'll cite for you, plead for you,' the priest said. 'It wasn't He with his humility and pity and sacrifice that converted the world; it was pagan and bloody Rome which did it with His martyrdom; furious and intractable dreamers had been bringing that same dream out of Asia Minor for three hundred years until at last one found a caesar foolish enough to crucify him. And you are right. But then so is he (I don't mean Him now, I mean the old man in that white room yonder on to whose shoulders you are trying to slough and shirk your right and duty for free will and decision). Because only Rome could have done it, accomplished it, and even He (I do mean Him now) knew it, felt and sensed this, furious and intractable dreamer though he was. Because He even said it Himself: *On this rock I found My church*, even while He didn't—and never would—realise the true significance of what He was saying, believing still that He was speaking poetic metaphor, synonym, parable—that *rock* meant unstable inconstant heart, and *church* meant airy faith. It wasn't even His first and favourite sycophant who read that significance, who was also ignorant and intractable like Him and even in the end got himself also electrocuted by the dream's intractable fire, like Him. It was Paul, who was a Roman first and then a man and only then a dreamer and so of all of them was able to read the dream correctly and to realise that, to endure, it could not be a nebulous and airy faith but instead it must be a *church*, an *establishment*, a morality of behaviour inside which man could exercise his right and duty for free will and decision, not for a reward resembling the bedtime tale which soothes the child into darkness, but the reward of being able to cope peacefully, hold his own, with the hard durable world in which (whether he would ever know why or not wouldn't matter either because now he could cope with that too) he found himself. Not *snared* in that frail web of hopes and fears and aspirations which man calls his heart, but *fixed*, *established*, to endure, on that *rock* whose synonym was the seeded capital of that hard durable enduring earth which man must cope with somehow, by some means, or perish. So you see, he is right. It wasn't He nor Peter, but Paul who, being only one-third dreamer, was two-thirds man and half of that a Roman, could cope with Rome. Who did more; who, rendering unto caesar, conquered Rome. More: destroyed it, because where is that Rome now? Until what remains but that *rock*, that citadel. Render unto Chaulnesmont. Why should you die?'

'Tell him that,' the corporal said.

'To save another life, which your dream will electrocute,' the priest said.

'Tell him that,' the corporal said.

'Remember—' the priest said. 'No, you can't remember, you don't know it, you can't read. So I'll have to be both again: defender and advocate. *Change these stones to bread, and all men will follow Thee.* And He answered, *Man cannot live by bread alone.* Because

He knew that too, intractable and furious dreamer though He was:
that He was tempted to tempt and lead man not with the *bread*,
but with the *miracle* of that bread, the deception, the illusion, the
delusion of that bread; tempted to believe that man was not only
capable and willing but even eager for that deception, that even
when the illusion of that miracle had led him to the point where
the bread would revert once more to stone in his very belly and
destroy him, his own children would be panting for the opportunity to grasp into their hands in their turn the delusion of that
miracle which would destroy them. No no, listen to Paul, who
needed no miracle, required no martyrdom. Save that life. *Thou
shalt not kill.*'

'Tell him that,' the corporal said.

'Take your own tomorrow, if you must,' the priest said. 'But
save his now.'

'Tell him that,' the corporal said.

'Power,' the priest said. 'Not just power over the mere earth
offered by that temptation of simple miracle, but that more
terrible power over the universe itself—that terrible power over
the whole universe which that mastery over man's mortal fate and
destiny would have given Him had He not cast back into the
Tempter's very teeth that third and most terrible temptation of
immortality: which if He had faltered or succumbed would have
destroyed His Father's kingdom not only on the earth but in
heaven too because that would have destroyed heaven, since what
value in the scale of man's hope and aspiration or what tensile
hold or claim on man himself could that heaven own which could
be gained by that base means—blackmail: man in his turn by no
more warrant than one single precedent casting himself from the
nearest precipice the moment he wearied of the burden of his free
will and decision, the right to the one and the duty of the other,
saying to, challenging his Creator: *Let me fall—if You dare*?'

'Tell him that,' the corporal said.

'Save that other life. Grant that the right of free will is in your
own death. But your duty to choose is not yours. It's his. It's
General Gragnon's death.'

'Tell him that,' the corporal said. They looked at each other.
Then the priest seemed to make a terrible repressed and convulsive effort, whether to speak or not to speak was still not clear even

when he said, like a sort of gesture, a valedictory not to defeat nor despair nor even desperation, but as though to surrender itself:

'Remember that bird.'

'So he did send you here,' the corporal said.

'Yes,' the priest said. 'He sent for me. To render unto caesar—' He said: 'But he came back.'

'Came back?' the corporal said. 'He?'

'The one who denied you,' the priest said. 'That turned his back on you. Freed himself of you. But he came back. And now there are eleven of them again.' He moved until he was facing the corporal. 'Save me too,' he said. Then he was on his knees before the corporal, his hands clasped fist into fist at his breast. 'Save me,' he said.

'Get up, Father,' the corporal said.

'No,' the priest said. He fumbled a moment inside the breast of his coat and produced his prayer-book, dog-eared and stained too from the front lines; it seemed to open automatically on the narrow purple ribbon of its marker as the priest reversed it and extended it upward. 'Read it to me then,' he said. The corporal took the book.

'What?' he said.

'The office for the dying,' the priest said. 'But you can't read, can you?' he said. He took the book back and now clasped it closed between his hands at his breast, his head bowed still. 'Save me then,' he said.

'Get up,' the corporal said, reaching down to grasp the priest's arm, though the priest had already begun to rise, standing now, fumbling a little clumsily as he put the book back inside his coat; as he turned, stiffly and clumsily still, he seemed to stumble slightly and was apparently about to fall, though again he had recovered himself before the corporal touched him, going toward the door now, one hand already lifted toward it or toward the wall or perhaps just lifted, as though he were blind too, the corporal watching him, until the corporal said: 'You've forgotten your gear.'

The priest stopped, though he didn't turn yet. 'Yes,' he said. 'So I did.' Then he said, 'So I have.' Then he turned and went back to the desk and gathered the articles up—urn ewer stole and crucifix—and huddled them clumsily into or on to one arm and extended his hand toward the candles and then stopped again, the corporal watching him.

'You can send back for them,' the corporal said.

'Yes,' the priest said. 'I can send back for them,' and turned and went again to the door and stopped again and after a moment began to raise his hand toward it, though the corporal now had already passed him, to strike two or three rapping blows with his knuckles on the wood, which a moment later swung open and back, revealing the sergeant, the priest standing again for a second or two clasping to his breast the huddled symbols of his mystery. Then he roused. 'Yes,' he said, 'I can send back for them,' and passed through the door; and this time he didn't pause even when the sergeant overtook him and said:

'Shall I take them to the chapel, Father?'

'Thank you,' the priest said, relinquishing them: and now he was free, walking on; and now he was even safe: outside, out of doors with only the spring darkness, the spring night soft and myriad above the blank and lightless walls and between them too, filling the empty topless passage, alley, at the end of which he could see a section of the distant wire fence and the catwalk spaced by the rigid down-glare of the lights, these spaced in their turn by the red eyes of the Senegalese sentries' cigarettes; and beyond that the dark plain, and beyond the plain in turn the faint unsleeping glow of the sleepless city; and now he could remember when he had seen them first, finally seen them, overtook them at last, two winters ago up near the Chemin des Dames—behind Combles, Souchez, he couldn't remember—the cobbled *Place* in the mild evening (no: mild evening, it was only autumn yet, a little while still before there would begin at Verdun that final winter of the doomed and accursed race of man) already empty again because again he had just missed them by minutes, the arms the hands pointing to show him, the helpful and contradictory voices giving him directions, too many of them in fact, too many helpful voices and too many directions, until at last one man walked with him to the edge of the village to show him the exact route and even point out to him the distant huddle of the farm itself—a walled yard enclosing house, byre and all, twilight now and he saw them, eight of them at first standing quietly about the kitchen stoop until he saw two more of them, the corporal and another, sitting on the stoop in baize or oilcloth aprons, the corporal cleaning a fowl, a chicken, the other peeling potatoes into a bowl while beside, above them stood the farmwife with a pitcher and a child, a girl of ten or so, with both hands full of mugs and tumblers; then while he watched, the other three came out of the byre with the farmer himself and crossed the yard carrying the pails of milk.

Nor did he approach nor even make his presence known: just watching while the woman and the child exchanged the pitcher and the drinking vessels for the fowl and bowl and the pails of milk and carried the food on into the house and the farmer filled from the pitcher the mugs and tumblers which the corporal held and passed in turn and then they drank in ritual salutation—to peaceful work, to the peaceful end of day, to anticipation of the peaceful lamplit meal, whatever it was—and then it was dark, night, night indeed because the second time was at Verdun which was the freezing night of France and of man too, since France was the cradle of the liberty of the human spirit, in the actual ruins of Verdun itself, within actual hearing range of the anguish of Gaud and Valaumont; not approaching this time either but only to stand from a distance watching, walled by the filth- and anguish-stained backs from where the thirteen would be standing in the circle's centre, talking or not, haranguing or not, he would never know, dared not know; thinking *Yes, even then I durst not*; even if they did not need to talk or harangue, since simply to believe was enough; thinking. *Yes, there were thirteen then and even now there are still twelve*; thinking, *Even if there were only one, only he, would be enough, more than enough*, thinking *Just that one to stand between me and safety, me and security, between me and peace*; and although he knew the compound and its environs well, for a moment he was disoriented as sometimes happens when you enter a strange building in darkness or by one door and then emerge from it in light or by another even though this was not the case here, thinking in a sort of quiet unamazement *Yes, I probably knew from the moment he sent for me what door I should have to emerge from, the only exit left for me.* So it only lasted for a moment or two or possibly even less than that: one infinitesimal vertiginous lurch and wall stone and brick resumed once more its ordered and forever repudiated place; one corner, one turn, and the sentry was where he had remembered he would be, not even pacing his beat but just standing at ease with his grounded rifle beside the small iron gate.

'Good evening, my son,' the priest said.

'Good evening, Father,' the man said.

'I wonder if I might borrow your bayonet?' the priest said.

'My what?' the man said.

'Your bayonet,' the priest said, extending his hand.

'I can't do that,' the man said. 'I'm on parade—on post. The corporal will—the Officer of the Day himself might come along—'

'Tell them I took it,' the priest said.

'Took it?' the man said.

'Demanded it,' the priest said, his hand still steadily out. 'Come.' Then the hand moved, not fast, and drew the bayonet from the man's belt. 'Tell them I took it,' the priest said, already turning. 'Good night.' Or perhaps the man even answered; perhaps even in the silent and empty alley again one last fading echo of one last warm and human voice speaking in warm and human protest or amazement or simple unquestioning defence of an *is* simply because it *is*; and then no more, thinking *It was a spear, so I should have taken the rifle too*, and then no more: thinking *The left side, and I'm right handed*, thinking *But at least He wasn't wearing an infantryman's overcoat and a* Magazin du Louvre *shirt and so at least I can do that*, opening the coat and throwing it back and then opening the shirt until he could feel the blade's cold minuscule point against his flesh and then the cold sharp whisper of the blade itself entering, beginning to make a sort of thin audible cry as though of astonishment at its own swiftness yet when he looked down at it barely the point itself had disappeared and he said aloud, quietly: 'Now what?' *But He was not standing either*, he thought *He was nailed there and He will forgive me* and cast himself sideways and downward, steadying the bayonet so that the end of the hilt should strike the bricks first, and turned a little until his cheek lay against the still-warm bricks and now he began to make a thin sweet crying of frustration and despair until the pinch of his hand between the bayonet's cross guard and his own flesh told him better and so he could stop the crying now—the sweet thick warm murmur of it pouring suddenly from his mouth.

Beeping its horn steadily—not pettishly nor fretfully nor even irritatedly but in fact with a sort of unwearyable blasé Gallic detachment—the French staff-car crept through the *Place de Ville* as though patting the massed crowd gently and firmly to either side with the horn itself to make room for its passage. It was not a big car. It flew no general's pennon nor in fact any insignia of any kind; it was just a small indubitable French army motorcar driven by a French soldier and containing three more soldiers, three American privates who until they met in the Blois orderly room where the French car had picked them up four hours ago had never laid eyes on one another before, who sat two in the back and one in front with the driver while the car bleated its snaillike passage through the massed spent wan and sleepless faces.

One of the two Americans in the back seat was leaning out of the car, looking eagerly about, not at the faces but at the adjacent buildings which enclosed the *Place*. He held a big much-folded and -unfolded and -refolded map open between his hands. He was quite young, with brown eyes as trustful and unalarmed as those of a cow, in an open reliant incorrigibly bucolic face—a farmer's face fated to love his peaceful agrarian heritage (his father, as he would after him, raised hogs in Iowa and rich corn to feed and fatten them for market) for the simple reason that to the end of his eupeptic days (what was going to happen to him inside the next thirty minutes would haunt him of course from time to time but only in dreams, as nightmares haunt) it would never occur to him that he could possibly have found anything more worthy to be loved—leaning eagerly out of the car and completely ignoring the massed faces through which he crept, saying eagerly:

'Which one is it? Which one is it?'

'Which one is what?' the American beside the driver said.

'The Headquarters,' he said. 'The Ho-tel de Villy.'

'Wait till you get inside,' the other said. 'That's what you volunteered to look at.'

'I want to see it from the outside too,' the first said. 'That's why I volunteered for this what-ever-it-is. Ask him,' he said, indicating the driver. 'You can speak Frog.'

'Not this time,' the other said. 'My French don't use this kind of a house.' But it wasn't necessary anyway because at the same moment they both saw the three sentries—American French and

333

British—flanking the door, and in the next one the car turned through the gates and now they saw the whole courtyard cluttered and massed with motorcycles and staff-cars bearing the three different devices. The car didn't stop there though. Darting its way among the other vehicles at a really headlong speed, it dashed on around to the extreme rear of the baroque and awesome pile ('Now what?' the one in the front seat said to the Iowan who was still leaning out toward the building's dizzy crenellated wheel. 'Did you expect them to invite us in by the front?'

'It's all right,' the Iowan said. 'That's how I thought it would look.') to where an American military policeman standing beside a sort of basement areaway was signalling them with a flashlight. The car shot up beside him and stopped. He opened the door. Though, since the Iowan was now engaged in trying to refold his map, the American private in the front seat was the first to get out. His name was Buchwald. His grandfather had been rabbi of a Minsk synagogue until a Cossack sergeant beat his brains out with the shod hooves of a horse. His father was a tailor; he himself was born on the fourth floor of a walk-up, cold-water Brooklyn tenement. Within two years after the passage of the American prohibition law, with nothing in his bare hands but a converted army-surplus Lewis machine gun, he was to become czar of a million-dollar empire covering the entire Atlantic coast from Canada to whatever Florida cove or sandspit they were using that night. He had pale, almost colourless eyes; he was hard and lean too now though one day a few months less than ten years from now, lying in his ten-thousand-dollar casket banked with half that much more in cut flowers, he would look plump, almost fat. The military policeman leaned into the back of the car.

'Come on, come on,' he said. The Iowan emerged, carrying the clumsily folded map in one hand and slapping at his pocket with the other. He feinted past Buchwald like a football halfback and darted to the front of the car and held the map into the light of one of the headlamps, still slapping at his pocket.

'Durn!' he said. 'I've lost my pencil.' The third American private was now out of the car. He was a Negro, of a complete and unrelieved black. He emerged with a sort of ballet-dancer elegance, not mincing, not foppish, not maidenly but rather at once masculine and girlish or perhaps better, epicene, and stood not quite

334

studied while the Iowan spun and feinted this time through all three of them—Buchwald, the policeman, and the Negro—and carrying his now rapidly disintegrating map plunged his upper body back into the car, saying to the policeman: 'Lend me your flashlight. I must have dropped it on the floor.'

'Sweet crap,' Buchwald said. 'Come on.'

'It's my pencil,' the Iowan said. 'I had it at that last big town we passed—what was the name of it?'

'I can call a sergeant,' the policeman said. 'Am I going to have to?'

'Nah,' Buchwald said. He said to the Iowan: 'Come on. They've probably got a pencil inside. They can read and write here too.' The Iowan backed out of the car and stood up. He began to refold his map. The policeman leading, they crossed to the areaway and descended into it, the Iowan following with his eyes the building's soaring upward swoop.

'Yes,' he said. 'It sure does.' They descended steps, through a door; they were in a narrow stone passage; the policeman opened a door and they entered an anteroom; the policeman closed the door behind them. The room contained a cot, a desk, a telephone, a chair. The Iowan went to the desk and began to shift the papers on it.

'You can remember you were here without having to check it off, can't you?' Buchwald said.

'It ain't for me,' the Iowan said, tumbling the papers through. 'It's for the girl I'm engaged to. I promised her—'

'Does she like pigs too?' Buchwald said.

'—what?' the Iowan said. He stopped and turned his head; still half stooped over the desk, he gave Buchwald his mild open reliant and alarmless look. 'Why not?' he said. 'What's wrong with pigs?'

'Okay,' Buchwald said. 'So you promised her.'

'That's right,' the Iowan said. 'When we found out I was coming to France I promised to take a map and mark off on it all the places I went to, especially the ones you always hear about, like Paris. I got Blois, and Brest, and I'll get Paris for volunteering for this, and now I'm even going to have Chaulnesmont, the Grand Headquarters of the whole shebang as soon as I can find a pencil.' He began to search the desk again.

'What you going to do with it?' Buchwald said. 'The map. When you get it back home?'

'Frame it and hang it on the wall,' the Iowan said. 'What did you think I was going to do with it?'

'Are you sure you're going to want this one marked on it?' Buchwald said.

'What?' the Iowan said. Then he said, 'Why?'

'Don't you know what you volunteered for?' Buchwald said.

'Sure,' the Iowan said. 'For a chance to visit Chaulnesmont.'

'I mean, didn't anybody tell you what you were going to do here?' Buchwald said.

'You haven't been in the army very long, have you?' the Iowan said. 'In the army, you don't ask what you are going to do: you just do it. In fact, the way to get along in any army is never even to wonder why they want something done or what they are going to do with it after it's finished, but just do it and then get out of sight so that they can't just happen to see you by accident and then think up something for you to do, but instead they will have to have thought up something to be done, and then hunt for somebody to do it. Durn it. I don't believe they have a pencil here either.'

'Maybe Sambo's got one,' Buchwald said. He looked at the Negro. 'What did you volunteer for this for besides a three-day Paris pass? To see Chaulnesmont too?'

'What did you call me?' the Negro said.

'Sambo,' Buchwald said. 'You no like?'

'My name's Philip Manigault Beauchamp,' the Negro said.

'Go on,' Buchwald said.

'It's spelled Manigault but you pronounce it Mannygo,' the Negro said.

'Oh hush,' Buchwald said.

'You got a pencil, buddy?' the Iowan said to the Negro.

'No,' the Negro said. He didn't even look at the Iowan. He was still looking at Buchwald. 'You want to make something of it?'

'Me?' Buchwald said. 'What part of Texas you from?'

'Texas,' the Negro said with a sort of bemused contempt. He glanced at the nails of his right hand, then rubbed them briskly against his flank. 'Mississippi. Going to live in Chicago soon as this crap's over. Be an undertaker, if you're interested.'

'An undertaker?' Buchwald said. 'You like dead people, huh?'

'Hasn't anybody in this whole durn war got a pencil?' the Iowan said.

'Yes,' the Negro said. He stood, tall, slender, not studied: just poised; suddenly he gave Buchwald a look feminine and defiant. 'I like the work. So what?'

'So you know what you volunteered for, do you?'

'Maybe I do and maybe I don't,' the Negro said. 'Why did you volunteer for it? Besides a three-day pass in Paris?'

'Because I love Wilson,' Buchwald said.

'Wilson?' the Iowan said. 'Do you know Sergeant Wilson? He's the best sergeant in the army.'

'Then I don't know him,' Buchwald said without looking at the Iowan. 'All the N.C.O.'s I know are sons of bitches.' He said to the Negro. 'Did they tell you, or didn't they?' Now the Iowan had begun to look from one to the other of them.

'What is going on here?' he said. The door opened. It was an American sergeant-major. He entered rapidly and looked rapidly at them. He was carrying an attaché case.

'Who's in charge?' he said. He looked at Buchwald. 'You.' He opened the attaché case and took something from it which he extended to Buchwald. It was a pistol.

'That's a German pistol,' the Iowan said. Buchwald took it. The sergeant-major reached into the attaché case again; this time it was a key, a door key; he extended it to Buchwald.

'Why?' Buchwald said.

'Take it,' the sergeant-major said. 'You don't want privacy to last forever, do you?' Buchwald took the key and put it and the pistol into his pocket.

'Why in hell didn't you bastards do it yourselves?' he said.

'So we had to send all the way to Blois to find somebody for a midnight argument,' the sergeant-major said. 'Come on,' he said. 'Get it over with.' He started to turn. This time the Iowan spoke quite loudly:

'Look here,' he said. 'What is this?' The sergeant-major paused and looked at the Iowan, then the Negro. He said to Buchwald:

'So they're already going coy on you.'

'Oh, coy,' Buchwald said. 'Don't let that worry you. The smoke can't help it, being coy is a part of what you might say is one of his

337

habits or customs or pastimes. The other one don't even know what coy means yet.'

'Okay,' the sergeant-major said. 'It's your monkey. You ready?'

'Wait,' Buchwald said. He didn't look back to where the other two stood near the desk, watching him and the sergeant-major. 'What is it?'

'I thought they told you,' the sergeant-major said.

'Let's hear your angle,' Buchwald said.

'They had a little trouble with him,' the sergeant-major said. 'It's got to be done from in front, for his own sake, let alone everybody else's. But they can't seem to make him see it. He's got to be killed from in front, by a kraut bullet—see? You get it now? He was killed in that attack Monday morning; they're giving him all the benefit: out there that morning where he had no business being —a major general, safe for the rest of his life to stay behind and say Give 'em hell, men. But no. He was out there himself, leading the whole business to victory for France and fatherland. They're even going to give him a new medal, but he still won't see it.'

'What's his gripe?' Buchwald said. 'He knows he's for it, don't he?'

'Oh sure,' the sergeant-major said. 'He knows he's gone. That ain't the question. He ain't kicking about that. He just refuses to let them do it that way—swears he's going to make them shoot him not in the front but in the back, like any top-sergeant or shave-tail that thinks he's too tough to be scared and too hard to be hurt. You know: make the whole world see that not the enemy but his own men did it.'

'Why didn't they just hold him and do it?' Buchwald said.

'Now now,' the sergeant-major said. 'You don't just hold a French major-general and shoot him in the face.'

'Then how are we supposed to do it?' Buchwald said. The sergeant-major looked at him. 'Oh,' Buchwald said. 'Maybe I get it now. *French* soldiers don't. Maybe next time it will be an American general and three frogs will get a trip to New York.'

'Yeah,' the sergeant-major said. 'If they just let me pick the general. You ready now?'

'Yes,' Buchwald said. But he didn't move. He said: 'Yeah. Why us. anyway? If he's a Frog general, why didn't the Frogs do it? Why did it have to be us?'

'Maybe because an American doughfoot is the only bastard they could bribe with a trip to Paris,' the sergeant-major said. 'Come on.'

But still Buchwald didn't move; his pale hard eyes were thoughtful and steady. 'Come on,' he said. 'Give.'

'If you're going to back out, why didn't you do it before you left Blois?' the sergeant-major said.

Buchwald said something unprintable. 'Give,' he said. 'Let's get it over with.'

'Right,' the sergeant-major said. 'They rationed it. The Frogs will have to shoot that Frog regiment, because it's Frog. They had to bring a Kraut general over here Wednesday to explain why they were going to shoot the Frog regiment, and the Limeys won that. Now they got to shoot this Frog general to explain why they brought the Kraut general over here, and we won that one. Maybe they drew straws. All right now?'

'Yes,' Buchwald said, suddenly and harshly. He cursed. 'Yes. Let's get it over with.'

'Wait!' the Iowan said. 'No! I—'

'Don't forget your map,' Buchwald said. 'We won't be back here.'

'I haven't,' the Iowan said 'What you think I been holding on to it this long for?'

'Good,' Buchwald said. 'Then when they send you back home to prison for mutiny, you can mark Leavenworth on it too.'

They returned to the corridor and followed it. It was empty, lighted by spaced weak electric bulbs. They had seen no other sign of life and suddenly it was as though they apparently were not going to until they were out of it again. The narrow corridor had not descended, there were no more steps. It was as if the earth it tunnelled through had sunk as an elevator sinks, holding the corridor itself intact, immune, empty of any life or sound save that of their boots, the whitewashed stone sweating in furious immobility beneath the whole concentrated weight of history, stratum upon stratum of dead tradition impounded by the *Hôtel* above them— monarchy revolution empire and republic, duke farmer-general and sans culotte, levee tribunal and guillotine, liberty fraternity equality and death and the people the People always to endure and prevail, the group, the clump, huddled now, going quite fast until the Iowan cried again:

'No, I tell you! I ain't—' until Buchwald stopped, stopping them all, and turned and said to the Iowan in a calm and furious murmur:

'Beat it.'

'What?' the Iowan cried. 'I can't! Where would I go?'

'How the hell do I know?' Buchwald said. 'I ain't the one that's dissatisfied here.'

'Come on,' the sergeant-major said. They went on. They reached a door; it was locked. The sergeant-major unlocked and opened it.

'Do we report?' Buchwald said.

'Not to me,' the sergeant-major said. 'You can even keep the pistol for a souvenir. The car'll be waiting where you got out of it,' and was about to close the door until Buchwald after one rapid glance into the room turned and put his foot against the door and said again in that harsh calm furious controlled voice:

'Christ, can't the sons of bitches even get a priest for him?'

'They're still trying,' the sergeant-major said. 'Somebody sent for the priest out at the compound two hours ago and he ain't got back yet. They can't seem to find him.'

'So we're supposed to wait for him,' Buchwald said in that tone of harsh calm unbearable outrage.

'Supposed by who?' the sergeant-major said. 'Move your foot.' Buchwald did, the door closed, the lock clashed behind them and the three of them were in a cell, a cubicle fierce with whitewash and containing the single unshaded electric light and a three-legged stool like a farmer's milking stool, and the French general. That is, it was a French face and by its expression and cast it had been used to enough rank long enough to be a general's, besides the insignia and the dense splash of ribbons and the Sam Browne belt and the leather puttees, though the uniform which bore them were the plain G.I. tunic and trousers which a cavalry sergeant would have worn, standing now, erect and rigid as though enclosed by the fading aura of the convulsive movement which had brought him to his feet, who said sharply in French:

'Attention there!'

'What?' Buchwald said to the Negro beside him. 'What did he say?'

'How the hell do I know?' the Negro said. 'Quick!' he said in a panting voice. 'That Ioway bastard. Do something about him quick.'

'Right,' Buchwald said, turning. 'Grab the Frog then,' and turned on to meet the Iowan.

'No, I tell you!' the Iowan cried. 'I ain't going to—' Buchwald struck him skilfully, the blow seeming not to travel at all before the Iowan catapulted backward against the wall, then slid down it to the floor, Buchwald turning again in time to see the Negro grasp at the French general and the French general turn sharply face-to and against the wall, saying over his shoulder in French as Buchwald snapped the safety off the pistol:

'Shoot now, you whorehouse scum. I will not turn.'

'Jerk him around,' Buchwald said.

'Put that damn safety back on!' the Negro panted, glaring back at him. 'You want to shoot me too? Come on. It will take both of us.' Buchwald closed the safety though he still held the pistol in his hand while they struggled, all three of them or two of them to drag the French general far enough from the wall to turn him, 'Hit him a little,' the Negro panted. 'We got to knock him out.'

'How in hell can you knock out a man that's already dead?' Buchwald panted.

'Come on,' the Negro panted. 'Just a little. Hurry.' Buchwald struck, trying to gauge the blow, and he was right: the body collapsed until the Negro was supporting it but not out, the eyes open, looking up at Buchwald then watching the pistol as Buchwald raised it and snapped the safety off again, the eyes not afraid, not even despaired: just incorrigibly alert and rational, so alert in fact as apparently to have seen the squeeze of Buchwald's hand as it started, so that the sudden and furious movement turned not only the face but the whole body away with the explosion so that the round hole was actually behind the ear when the corpse reached the floor. Buchwald and the Negro stood over it, panting, the barrel of the pistol warm against Buchwald's leg.

'Son of a bitch,' Buchwald said to the Negro. 'Why didn't you hold him?'

'He slipped!' the Negro panted.

'Slipped my crap,' Buchwald said. 'You didn't hold him.'

'Son of a bitch yourself!' the Negro panted. 'Me stand there holding him for that bullet to come on through hunting me next?'

'All right, all right,' Buchwald said. 'Now we got to plug that one up and shoot him again.'

341

'Plug it up?' the Negro said.

'Yes,' Buchwald said. 'What the hell sort of undertaker will you make if you don't know how to plug up a hole in a bastard that got shot in the wrong place? Wax will do it. Get a candle.'

'Where'm I going to get a candle?' the Negro said.

'Go out in the hall and yell,' Buchwald said, swapping the pistol to the other hand and taking the door key from his pocket and handing it to the Negro. 'Keep on yelling until you find a Frog. They must have candles. They must have at least one thing in this . . . . ing country we never had to bring two thousand mile over here and give to them.'

FRIDAY * SATURDAY * SUNDAY

I T bade fair to be another bright and lark-filled vernal morning;
the gaudy uniforms and arms and jangling accoutrements and
even the ebon faces too of the Senegalese regiment seemed to
gleam in it as, to the cryptic tribal equatorial cries of its noncoms,
it filed on to the parade ground and formed three sides of a hollow
square facing the three freshly planted posts set in a symmetric row
on the edge of a long pit or ditch, almost filled and obliterated
now by four years of war's refuse—tin cans, bottles, old messkits,
worn-out cooking utensils, boots, inextricable coils of rusting and
useless wire—from which the dirt had been excavated to form the
railroad embankment running across the end of the parade, which
would serve as a backstop for what bullets neither flesh nor wood
absorbed. They came into position, then at rest and grounded
arms and stood at ease and then easy, whereupon there rose a
steady unemphatic gabble, not festive: just gregarious, like people
waiting for the opening of a marketplace; the pallid constant
almost invisible lighters winked and flared from cigarette to
cigarette among the babble of voices, the ebon and gleaming faces
not even watching the working party of white soldiers while they
tamped the last earth about the posts and took up their tools and
departed in a disorderly straggle like a company of reapers leaving
a field of hay.

Then a distant bugle cried once or twice, the Senegalese N.C.O.s
shouted, the gaudy ranks doused the cigarettes without haste and
with a sort of negligent, almost inattentive deliberation came to
alert and *at ease* as the sergeant-major of the city garrison, a
holstered pistol strapped outside his long buttoned-back coat, came
into the vacant side of the square before the three posts and
stopped and stood as, to the harsh abrupt ejaculations of the new
N.C.O.'s, the mutinied regiment filed into the empty rectangle
and huddled, pariahs still, hatless and unarmed, still unshaven,
alien, stained still with Aisne and Oise and Marne mud so that

343

against the gaudy arras of the Senegalese they looked like harassed and harried and homeless refugees from another planet, moiling a little though quiet and even orderly or at least decorous until suddenly a handful of them, eleven it was, broke abruptly out and ran in a ragged clump toward the three posts and had already knelt facing the posts in the same ragged clump by the time the sergeant-major had shouted something and an N.C.O.'s voice took it up and a file of Senegalese came rapidly out and around and across the empty parade and surrounded the kneeling men and pulled them, not at all roughly, back on to their feet and turned them and herded them back among their companions like drovers behind a small band of temporarily strayed sheep.

Now a small party of horsemen rode rapidly up from the rear and stopped just outside the square, behind it: they were the town major, his adjutant, the provost marshal adjutant and three orderlies. The sergeant-major shouted, the parade (save for the pariah regiment) came to attention in one long metallic clash, the sergeant-major wheeled and saluted the town major across the rigid palisade of Senegalese heads, the town major accepted the parade and stood it at ease, then back to attention again, and returned it to the sergeant-major who in his turn stood it at ease again and turned to face the three posts as, abruptly and apparently from nowhere, a sergeant and file came up with the three hatless prisoners interspersed among them, whom they bound quickly to the three posts—the man who had called himself Lapin, then the corporal, then the simian-like creature whom Lapin had called casse-tête or Horse—leaving them facing the hollow of the square though they couldn't see it now because at the moment there filed between them and it another squad of some twenty men with a sergeant, who halted and quarter-turned and stood them at ease with their backs to the three doomed ones, whom the sergeant-major now approached in turn, to examine rapidly the cord which bound Lapin to his post, then on to the corporal, already extending his (the sergeant-major's) hand to the *Médaille Militaire* on the corporal's coat, saying in a rapid murmur:

'You don't want to keep this.'

'No,' the corporal said. 'No use to spoil it.' The sergeant-major wrenched it off the coat, not savagely: just rapidly, already moving on.

'I know who to give it to,' he said, moving on to the third man, who said, drooling a little, not alarmed, not even urgent: just diffident and promptive, as you address someone, a stranger, on whom your urgent need depends but who may have temporarily forgotten your need or forgotten you:

'Paris.'

'Right,' the sergeant-major said. Then he was gone too; now the three bound men could have seen nothing save the backs of the twenty men in front of them though they could still have heard the sergeant-major's voice as he brought the parade to attention again and drew from somewhere inside his coat a folded paper and a worn leather spectacle case and unfolded the paper and put the spectacles on and read aloud from the paper, holding it now in both hands against the light flutter of the morning breeze, his voice sounding clear and thin and curiously forlorn in the sunny lark-filled emptiness among the dead redundant forensic verbiage talking in pompous and airy delusion of an end of man. 'By order of the president of the court,' the sergeant-major chanted wanly and refolded the paper and removed the spectacles and folded them back into the case and stowed them both away; a command, the twenty men about-turned to face the three posts; Lapin was now straining outward against his cord, trying to see past the corporal to the third man.

'Look,' Lapin said anxiously to the corporal.

Load!

'Paris,' the third man said, hoarse and wet and urgent.

'Say something to him,' Lapin said. 'Quick.'

Aim!

'Paris,' the third man said again.

'It's all right,' the corporal said. 'We're going to wait. We won't go without you.'

The corporal's post may have been flawed or even rotten because, although the volley merely cut cleanly the cords binding Lapin and the third man to theirs, so that their bodies slumped at the foot of each post, the corporal's body, post bonds and all, went over backward as one intact unit, on to the edge of the rubbish-filled trench behind it; when the sergeant-major, the pistol still smoking faintly in his hand, moved from Lapin to the corporal, he found that the plunge of the post had jammed it and its burden too into a tangled mass of old barbed wire, a strand of which had looped up and around the top of the post and the man's head as though to assoil them both in one unbroken continuation of the fall, into the anonymity of the earth. The wire was rusted and pitted and would not have deflected the bullet anyway, nevertheless the sergeant-major flicked it carefully away with his toe before setting the pistol's muzzle against the ear.

As soon as the parade ground was empty (before in fact; the end of the Senegalese column had not yet vanished into the company street) the fatigue party came up with a hand-drawn barrow containing their tools and a folded tarpaulin. The corporal in charge took a wire-cutter from the barrow and approached the sergeant-major, who had already cut the corporal's body free from the broken post. 'Here,' he said, handing the sergeant-major the wire-cutter. 'You're not going to waste a ground-sheet on one of them, are you?'

'Get those posts out,' the sergeant-major said. 'Let me have two men and the ground sheet.'

'Right,' the corporal said. The corporal went away. The sergeant-major cut off a section about six feet long of the rusted wire. When he rose, the two men with the folded tarpaulin were standing behind him, watching him.

'Spread it out,' he said, pointing. They did so. 'Put him in it,' he said. They took up the dead corporal's body, the one at the head a little gingerly because of the blood, and laid it on the tarpaulin. 'Go on,' the sergeant-major said. 'Roll it up. Then put it in the barrow,' and followed them, the fatigue-party corporal suddenly not watching him too, the other men suddenly immersed again in freeing the planted posts from the earth. Nor did the sergeant-major speak again. He simply gestured the two men to take up the handles and, himself at the rear, established the direction by holding one corner as a pivot and pushing against the other and then pushing ahead on both, the laden barrow now crossing the parade ground at a long slant toward the point where the wire fence died in a sharp right angle against the old factory wall. Nor did he (the sergeant-major) look back either, the two men carrying the handles almost trotting now to keep the barrow from running over them, on toward the corner where at some point they too must have seen beyond the fence the high two-wheeled farm cart with a heavy farm horse in the shafts and the two women and the three men beside it, the sergeant-major stopping the barrow just as he had started it: by stopping himself and pivoting the barrow by its two rear corners into the angle of the fence, then himself went and stood at the fence—a man of more than fifty and now looking all of it—until the taller of the two women—the one with the high dark strong and handsome face as a man's face is handsome—approached the other side of the wire. The second woman had not moved, the shorter, dumpier, softer one. But she was watching the two at the fence and listening, her face quite empty for the moment but with something incipient and tranquilly promising about it like a clean though not-yet-lighted lamp on a kitchen bureau.

'Where did you say your husband's farm is?' the sergeant-major said.

'I told you,' the woman said.

'Tell me again,' the sergeant-major said.

'Beyond Châlons,' the woman said.

'How far beyond Châlons?' the sergeant-major said. 'All right,' he said. 'How far from Verdun?'

'It's near Vienne-la-pucelle,' the woman said. 'Beyond St. Mihiel,' she said.

'St. Mihiel,' the sergeant-major said. 'In the army zone. Worse. In the battle zone. With Germans on one side of it and Americans on the other. Americans.'

'Should American soldiers be more terrible than other soldiers?' the woman said. 'Because they are fresher at it? Is that it?'

'No, sister,' the other woman said. 'That's wrong. It's because the Americans have been here so young. It will be easy for them.' The two at the fence paid no attention to her. They looked at each other through the wire. Then the woman said:

'The war is over.'

'Ah,' the sergeant-major said.

The woman made no movement, no gesture. 'What else can this mean? What else explain it? Justify it? No, not even justify it: plead compassion, plead pity, plead despair for it?' She looked at the sergeant-major, cold, griefless, impersonal. 'Plead exculpation for it?'

'Bah,' the sergeant-major said. 'Did I ask you? Did anyone?' He gestured behind him with the wire-cutter. One of the men released

347

the handle of the barrow and came and took it. 'Cut the bottom strand,' the sergeant-major said.

'Cut?' the man said.

'It, species of a species!' the sergeant-major said. The man started to stoop but the sergeant-major had already snatched the wire-cutter back from him and stooped himself; the taut bottom-most strand sprang with a thin almost musical sound, recoiling. 'Get it out of the barrow,' the sergeant-major said. 'Lively.' They understood now. They lifted the long tarpaulin-wrapped object from the barrow and lowered it to the ground. The woman had moved aside and the three men now waited at the fence, to draw, drag the long object along the ground and through the wire's vacancy, then up and into the cart. 'Wait,' the sergeant-major said. The woman paused. The sergeant-major fumbled inside his coat and produced a folded paper which he passed through the fence to her. She opened it and looked at it for a moment, with no expression whatever.

'Yes,' she said. 'It must be over, since you receive a diploma now with your execution. What shall I do with it? Frame it on the parlour wall?' The sergeant-major reached through the wire and snatched the paper from between her hands, his other hand fumbling out the worn spectacle case again, then with both hands, still holding the opened paper, he got the spectacles on his nose and glanced at the paper a moment, then with a violent gesture crumpled the paper into his side pocket and produced another folded one from inside his coat and extended it through the wire, shaking it violently open before the woman could touch it, saying in a repressed and seething voice: 'Say you don't need this one then. Look at the signature on it.' The woman did so. She had never seen it before, the thin delicate faint cryptic indecipherable scrawl which few other people had ever seen either but which anyone in that half of Europe on that day competent to challenge a signature would have recognised at once.

'So he knows where his son's half-sister's husband's farm is too,' she said.

'Pah,' the sergeant-major said. 'Further than St. Mihiel even. If at any place on the way you should be faced with a pearled and golden gate, that will pass you through it too.—This too,' he said, his hand coming out of his pocket and through the wire again,

348

opening on the dull bronze of the small emblem and the bright splash of its ribbon, the woman immobile again, not touching it yet, tall, looking down at the sergeant-major's open palm, until he felt the other woman looking at him and met the tranquil and incipient gaze; whereupon she said:

'He's really quite handsome, sister. He's not so old either.'

'Pah!' the sergeant-major said again. 'Here!' he said, thrusting, fumbling the medal into the taller woman's hand until she had to take it, then snatching his own hand quickly back through the wire. 'Begone!' he said. 'Get on with you! Get out of here!' breathing a little hard now, irascible, almost raging, who was too old for this, feeling the second woman's eyes again though he did not meet them yet, flinging his head up to shout at the taller one's back: 'There were three of you. Where is the other one—his *poule*, whatever she is—was?' Then he had to meet the second woman's eyes, the face no longer incipient now but boundless with promise, giving him a sweet and tender smile, saying:

'It's all right. Don't be afraid. Good-bye.'

Then they were gone, the five of them, the horse and the cart: rapidly; he turned and took the section of rusted wire from the barrow and flung it down beside the severed bottom strand.

'Tie it back,' he said.

'Isn't the war over?' one of the men said. The sergeant-major turned almost savagely.

'But not the army,' he said. 'How do you expect peace to put an end to an army when even war can't?'

When they passed through the old eastern city gate this time they were all riding, Marthe with the lines at one end of the high seat and the sister opposite with the girl between them, the seat so high that they seemed to ride not in the city's dense and creeping outflux but above it, not a part of it but on it like a boat, the three of them riding out of the city as on a float in a carnival procession, fluxed out of the anguished city on the fading diffusion of the anguish as on a legless and wheelless effigy of a horse and cart as though borne on the massed shoulders in a kind of triumph; borne along so high in fact that they had almost reached the old gate before the owners of the shoulders even appeared or thought to raise their eyes or their attention high enough to remark what they carried and to assume, divine or simply recoil from, what the cart contained.

It was not a recoil, a shrinking, but rather an effacement, a recession: a suddenly widening ring of empty space beginning to enclose the moving cart as water recedes from a float, leaving the float to realise, discover only then that it was not maritime but terrestrial and not supported by a medium but attached to earth by legs and wheels; a recession, as though the shoulders which for a time had borne it were effacing not only the support but the cognizance too of the weight and presence of the burden, the crowd pressing steadily away from the cart and even transmitting on ahead as though by osmosis the warning of its coming, until presently the path was already opening before the cart itself ever reached it, the cart now moving faster than the crowd, the faces in the crowd not even looking toward it until the second sister, Marya, began to call down to them from her end of the high seat, not peremptory, not admonitory: just insistent and serene as if she were speaking to children: 'Come. You owe him no obligation; you don't need to hate. You haven't injured him; why should you be afraid?'

'Marya,' the other sister said.

'Nor ashamed either,' Marya said.

'Hush, Marya,' the other sister said. Marya sat back into the seat.

'All right, sister,' she said. 'I didn't mean to frighten them: only to comfort them.' But she continued to watch them, bright and serene, the cart going on, the cleared space moving steadily before it as if the emptiness itself cleared its own advancing vacancy, so that when they came to the old gate the archway was completely clear, the crowd now halted and banked on either side of it for the cart to pass; when suddenly a man in the crowd removed his hat, then one or two more, so that when the cart passed beneath the arch it was as though it had quit the city enclosed in a faint visible soundless rustling. 'You see, sister?' Marya said with serene and peaceful triumph: 'Only to comfort them.'

Now they were out of the city, the long straight roads diverging away, radiating away like spokes from a hub; above them slowly crawled the intermittent small clouds of dust within which, singly, in groups, sometimes in carts also, the city emptied itself; the parents and kin of the mutinied regiment who had hurried toward it in amazement and terror, to compound between the old walls vituperation and anguish, now fled it almost as though in something not quite of relief but shame.

They didn't look back at it, though for a while it remained, squatting above the flat plain, supreme still, grey and crowned by the ancient Roman citadel and slowly fading until in time it was gone though they still had not looked once back to know it, going on themselves behind the strong slow heavy deliberate unhurryable farm-horse. They had food with them so they didn't need to stop save for a little while at noon in a wood to feed and water the horse. So they only passed through the villages—the silent arrested faces, that same faint visible soundless rustling as the hats and caps came off, almost as though they had an outrider or courier to presage them, the girl crouching in her shawl between the two older women, Marthe iron-faced, looking straight ahead and only the other sister, Marya, to look about them, serene and tranquil, never astonished, never surprised while the heavy shaggy feet of the horse rang the slow cobbles until that one too was behind.

Just before dark they reached Châlons. They were in an army zone now and approaching what five days ago had been a battle zone though there was peace now or at least quiet; still an army zone anyway because suddenly a French and an American sergeant stood at the horse's head, stopping him. 'I have the paper,' Marthe said, producing and extending it. 'Here.'

'Keep it,' the French sergeant said. 'You won't need it here. It is all arranged.' Then she saw something else: six French soldiers carrying a cheap wood coffin approaching the rear of the cart and even as she turned on the seat they had already set the coffin down and were drawing the tarpaulin-swaddled body from the cart.

'Wait,' Marthe said in her harsh strong tearless voice.

'It is arranged, I tell you,' the French sergeant said. 'You go to St. Mihiel by train.'

'By train?' Marthe said.

'Why, sister!' Marya said. 'In the train!'

'Restrain yourself,' the French sergeant said to Marthe. 'You won't have to pay. It's arranged, I tell you.'

'This cart is not mine,' Marthe said. 'I borrowed it.'

'We know that,' the French sergeant said. 'It will be returned.'

'But I must still carry him from St. Mihiel to Vienne-la-pucelle —You said St. Mihiel, didn't you?'

'Why do you argue with me?' the French sergeant said. 'Have I not told you one million times it is all arranged? Your husband will meet you at St. Mihiel with your own cart and horse. Get down. All of you. Just because the war has stopped, do you think the army has nothing else to do but cajole civilians? Come along now. You're holding up your train; it has a little more to do than this too.'

Then they saw the train. They had not noticed it before though the tracks were almost beside them. It was a locomotive and a single van of the type known as forty-and-eight. They got down from the cart; it was dusk now. The French soldiers finished fastening down the lid of the coffin; they took it up and the three women and the two sergeants followed to the van and stopped again while the soldiers lifted the coffin into the open door, then climbed in themselves and took up the coffin again and carried it forward out of sight and then reappeared and dropped one by one to the ground again.

'In with you,' the French sergeant said. 'And don't complain because you don't have seats. There's plenty of clean straw. And here.' It was an army blanket. None of the three of them knew where he had got it from. That is, they had not noticed it before either. Then the American sergeant said something to the French one, in his own language without doubt since it meant nothing to them, not even when the French sergeant said, '*Attendez*'; they just stood in the slow and failing light until the American sergeant returned carrying a wooden packing-case stencilled with the cryptic symbols of ordnance or supply, the American sergeant setting the box in place before the door and now they knew why, with a little of surprise perhaps, climbing in turn on to the box and then into the van, into almost complete darkness with only one pale shapeless gleam from the coffin's unpainted wood to break it. They found the straw. Marthe spread the blanket on it and they sat down; at that moment someone else sprang, vaulted into the van—a man, a soldier, by his silhouette in the door where there was still a little light, an American soldier, carrying something in both hands. Then they smelled the coffee, the American sergeant looming over them now, saying, very loud:

'*Ici café. Café*,' fumbling the three mugs down until Marthe took them and distributed them, feeling in her turn the man's hard hand gripping her hand and the mug both while he guided the spout of the coffee pot into the mug; he even seemed to anticipate the jerk, crying 'Watch it!' in his own language a second or two before the shrill peanut-parcher whistle which did not presage the lurch but rather accompanied it, bracing himself against the wall as the van seemed to rush from immobility into a sort of frantic celerity with no transition whatever; a splash of burning coffee leapt from the mug in her hand on to her lap. Then the three of them managed to brace themselves back against the wall too, the whistle shrieking again shrill as friction, as though it actually were friction: not a warning of approach but a sound of protest and insensate anguish and indictment of the hard dark earth it rushed over, the vast weight of dark sky it burrowed frantically beneath, the constant and inviolable horizon it steadily clove.

This time the American sergeant knelt, braced still, using both hands again to fill the mugs, but only half full now so that, sitting against the wall, they drank by installments the hot sweet comforting coffee, the van rushing on through darkness, themselves invisible even to one another in darkness, even the gleam of the coffin at the other end of the van gone now and, their own inert bodies now matched and reconciled with the van's speed, it was as though there were no motion at all if it had not been for the springless vibration and the anguished shrieks from the engine from time to time.

When light returned, the van had stopped. It would be St. Mihiel; they had told her St. Mihiel and this would be it, even if there had not been that sixth sense, even after almost four years, that tells people when they are nearing home. So as soon as the van stopped, she had started to get up, saying to the American sergeant: 'St. Mihiel?' because at least he should understand that, then in a sort of despair of urgency she even said, began, '*Mon homme à moi—mon mari*' before she stopped, the sergeant speaking himself now, using one or two more of the few other words which were his French vocabulary:

'No no no. *Attention. Attention*,' even in the van's darkness motioning downward at her with his hands as a trainer commands a dog to sit. Then he was gone, silhouetted for another instant

z

against the paler door, and they waited, huddled together now for warmth in the cold spring dawn, the girl between them, whether asleep or not, whether she had ever slept during the night or not, Marthe could not tell, though by her breathing Marya, the other sister, was. It was full light when the sergeant returned; they were all three awake now, who had slept or not slept; they could see the first of Saturday's sun and hear the eternal and perennial larks. He had more coffee, the pot filled again, and this time he had bread too, saying very loud: 'Monjay. Monjay' and they—she could see him now—a young man with a hard drafted face and with something else in it—impatience or commiseration, she anyway could not tell which. Nor did she care, thinking again to try once more to communicate with him except that the French sergeant at Châlons had said that it was all arranged, and suddenly it was not that she could trust the American sergeant because he must know what he was doing, since he had obviously come along with them under orders, but because she—they—could do little else.

So they ate the bread and drank the hot sweet coffee again. The sergeant was gone again and they waited; she had no way to mark or gauge how long. Then the sergeant sprang or vaulted into the van again and she knew that the moment was here. This time the six soldiers who followed him were Americans; the three of them rose and stood and waited again while the six soldiers slid the coffin to the door, then dropped to the ground, invisible to them now, so that the coffin itself seemed to flee suddenly through the door and vanish, the three of them following to the door while the sergeant dropped through the door; there was another box beneath the door for them to descend by, into another bright morning, blinking a little after the darkness in the sixth bright morning of that week during which there had been no rain nor adumbration at all. Then she saw the cart, her own or theirs, her husband standing beside the horse's head while the six American soldiers slid the coffin into the cart, and she turned to the American sergeant and said 'Thank you' in French and suddenly and a little awkwardly he removed his hat and shook her hand, quick and hard, then the other sister's and put his hat back on without once looking at or offering to touch the girl, and she went on around the cart to where her husband stood—a broad strong man in corduroy, not as tall as she and definitely older. They embraced, then all four of them turned

354

to the cart, huddling for a moment in that indecision, as people will. But not for long; there would not be room for all four of them on the seat but the girl had already solved that, climbing up over the shafts and the seat and into the body of the cart, to crouch beside the coffin, huddled into the shawl, her face worn and sleepless and definitely needing soap and water now.

'Why, yes, sister,' Marya, the older sister, said in her voice of happy astonishment, almost of pleasure as though at so simple a solution: 'I'll ride back there too.' So the husband helped her up on to the shaft, then over the seat, where she sat also on the opposite side of the coffin. Then Marthe mounted strongly and without assistance to the seat, the husband following with the lines.

They were already on the edge of the city, so they did not need to pass through it, merely around it. Though actually there was no city, no boudaries enclosing a city from a countryside because this was not even a war zone: it was a battle zone, city and countryside fused and indistinguishable one from the other beneath one vast concentration of troops, American and French, not poised, but rather as though transfixed, suspended beneath, within that vast silence and cessation—all the clutter of battle in a state of arrestment like hypnosis: motionless and silent transport, dumps of ammunition and supplies, and soon they began to pass the guns squatting in batteries, facing eastward, still manned but not poised either, not waiting: just silent, following the now silent line of the old stubborn four-year salient—so that now they were seeing war or what six days ago had been war—the shell-pocked fields, the topless trees some of which this spring had put out a few green and stubborn shoots from the blasted trunks—the familiar land which they had not seen in almost four years but which was familiar still, as though even war had failed to efface completely that old verity of peaceful human occupation. But they were skirting the rubble of what had been Vienne-la-pucelle before it seemed to occur to her that there still might be dread and fear; it was only then that she said to the husband in a voice that did not even reach the two others in the body of the cart: 'The house.'

'The house was not damaged,' the husband said. 'I don't know why. But the fields, the land. Ruined. Ruined. It will take years. And they won't even let me start now. When they gave me permission to come back yesterday, they forbade me to work them until they have gone over them to locate the shells which might not have exploded.'

And the husband was right because here was the farm, the land pitted (not too severely; some of the trees had not even been topped) with shell craters where she herself had worked beside her husband in the tense seasons and which had been the life of the brother in the cheap coffin behind her in the cart and which was to have been his some day whom she had brought back to sleep in it. Then the house; the husband had been right; it was unmarked save for a pock of small holes in one wall which was probably a machine-gun burst, the husband not even looking at the house but getting down from the cart (a little stiffly; she remarked for the first time how his arthritis seemed to have increased) to go and stand looking out over his ruined land. Nor did she enter the house either, calling him by name; then she said:

'Come now. Let's finish this first.' So he returned and entered the house; apparently he had brought some of the tools back with him yesterday too because he reappeared at once with a spade and mounted the cart again. Though this time she had the lines, as though she knew exactly where she wanted to go, the cart moving again, crossing the field now rank with weeds and wild poppies, skirting the occasional craters, on for perhaps half a kilometre to a bank beneath an ancient beech tree which also had escaped the shells.

The digging was easier here, into the bank, all of them taking turns, the girl too though Marthe tried once to dissuade her. 'No,' she said. 'Let me. Let me be doing something.' Though even then it took them a long time until the excavation was deep enough into the bank to contain the coffin, the four of them now shoving and sliding the box back into the cave they had made.

'The medal,' the husband said. 'You don't want to put that in too? I can open the box.' But Marthe didn't even answer, taking the shovel herself first until the husband relieved her of it and at last the bank was smooth again save for the shovel marks; after-noon then and almost evening when they returned to the house and (the three women) entered it while the husband went on to the stable to put the horse up for the night. She had not seen it in almost four years, nor did she pause to examine it now. She crossed the room and dropped, almost tossed, the medal on to the vacant

356

mantel and then turned, not really examining the room now. The house had not been damaged: merely eviscerated. They had moved out what the cart would carry that day in 1914, and the husband had fetched that back with him yesterday—enough dishes and bedding, the objects of no value which she had insisted on saving at the expense of things they would actually need when they returned; she could not even remember now what she had felt, thought, then: whether they would ever return or not, if perhaps that anguished day had not been the actual end of home and hope. Nor did she try to remember now, going on to the kitchen; the husband had brought food and fuel for the stove and Marya and the girl were already starting a fire in the stove; again she said to the girl:

'Why don't you rest?'

'No,' the girl said again. 'Let me be doing something.' The lamp was lighted now; it was that near to darkness before she noticed that the husband had not yet come in from the stable. She knew at once where he would be: motionless, almost invisible in the faint last of light, looking at his ruined land. This time she approached and touched him.

'Come now,' she said. 'Supper is ready,' checking him again with her hand at the open lamplit door until he had seen the older sister and the girl moving between the stove and the table. 'Look at her,' she said. 'She has nothing left. She was not even kin to him. She only loved him.'

But he seemed incapable of remembering or grieving over any-thing but his land; they had eaten the meal and he and she lay again in the familiar bed between the familiar walls beneath the familiar rafters; he had gone to sleep at once though even as she lay rigid and sleepless beside him she flung his head suddenly and muttered, cried, 'The farm. The land:' waking himself. 'What?'he said. 'What is it?'

'It's all right,' she said. 'Go back to sleep.' Because suddenly she knew that he was right. Stefan was gone; all that was over, done, finished, never to be recalled. He had been her brother but she had been his mother too, who knew now that she would have no children of her own and who had raised him from infancy; France, England, America too by now probably, were full of women who had given the lives of their sons to defend their countries and preserve justice and right; who was she to demand uniqueness for grieving? He was right: it was the farm, the land which was immune even to the blast and sear of war. It would take work of course, it might even take years of work, but the four of them were capable of work. More: their palliation and their luck was the work they faced, since work is the only anæsthetic to which grief is vulnerable. More still: restoring the land would not only palliate the grief, the minuscule integer of the farm would affirm that he had not died for nothing and that it was not for an outrage that they grieved, but for simple grief: the only alternative to which was nothing, and between grief and nothing only the coward takes nothing.

So she even slept at last, dreamless; so dreamless that she did not know she had been asleep until someone was shaking her. It was the older sister; behind her the girl stood with her worn dirty sleep-walker's face which might be pretty again with a little soap and water and a week of proper food. It was dawn and then she, Marthe, heard the sound too even before the older sister cried: 'Listen, sister!' the husband waking too, to lie for an instant, then surging upright among the tumbled bedclothing.

'The guns!' he cried, 'the guns!' The four of them were trans-fixed for another ten or fifteen seconds like a tableau while the uproar of the barrage seemed to be rolling directly toward them; transfixed still even after they began to hear above or beneath the steady roar of explosions, the whistle of the shells passing over the house itself. Then the husband moved. 'We must get out of here,' he said, lurching, plunging out of the bed, where he would have fallen if she had not caught and held him up, the four of them in their night clothing running across the room and then out of the house, quitting one roof, one ceiling only to run stumbling on their bare feet beneath that other one filled with thunder and demonic whistling, not realising yet that the barrage was missing the house by two or three hundred metres, the three women following the husband, who seemed to know where he was going.

He did know: a tremendous crater in the field which must have been from a big howitzer, the four of them running, stumbling among the dew-heavy weeds and blood-red poppies, down into the crater, the husband pressing the three women against the wall beneath the lip facing the barrage where they crouched, their heads bowed almost as though in prayer, the husband crying steadily in a voice as thin and constant as a cicada's: 'The land. The land. The land.'

That is, all of them except Marthe. She had not even stooped, erect, tall, watching across the lip of the crater the barrage as it missed the house, skirting the house and the farm buildings as neatly and apparently as intentionally as a scythe skirts a rosebush, rolling on eastward across the field in one vast pall of dust filled with red flashes, the dust still hanging in the air after the flashes of the shell-bursts had winked and blinked rapidly on, to disappear beyond the field's edge like a furious migration of gigantic daylight-haunting fireflies, leaving behind only the thunder of their passing, it too already beginning to diminish.

Then Marthe began to climb out of the crater. She climbed rapid and strong, agile as a goat, kicking backward at the husband as he grasped at the hem of her nightdress and then at her bare feet, up and out of the crater, running strongly through the weeds and poppies, dodging the sparse old craters until she reached the swathe of the barrage, where the three still crouched in the crater could see her actually leaping across and among the thick new ones. Then the field was full of running men—a ragged line of French and American troops which overtook and passed her; they saw one, either an officer or a sergeant, pause and gesticulate at her, his mouth open and soundless with yelling for a moment before he too turned and ran on with the rest of the charge, the three of them out of the crater too now, running and stumbling into the new craters and the fading dust and the fierce and fading stink of cordite.

At first they couldn't even find the bank. And when they did at last, the beech tree had vanished: no mark, nothing remained to orient by. 'It was here, sister!' the older sister cried, but Marthe didn't answer, running strongly on, they following until they too saw what she had apparently seen—the splinters and fragments, whole boughs still intact with leaves, scattered for a hundred metres. When they overtook her, she was holding in her hand a shard of the pale new unpainted wood which had been the coffin; she spoke to the husband by name, quite gently:

'You'll have to go back and get the shovel.' But before he could turn, the girl had already passed him, running, frantic yet unerring, deer-light among the craters and what remained of the weeds and the quenchless poppies, getting smaller and smaller yet still running, back toward the house. That was Sunday. When the girl returned with the shovel, still running, they took turns with it, all that day until it was too dark to see. The found a few more shards and fragments of the coffin, but the body itself was gone.

TOMORROW

ONCE more there were twelve of them, though this time they were led by a sergeant. The carriage was a special one, though it was still third class; the seats had been removed from the forward compartment and on the floor of it rested a new empty military coffin. The thirteen of them had left Paris at midnight and by the time they reached St. Mihiel they were already fairly drunk. Because the job, mission, was going to be an unpleasant one, now that peace and victory had really come to Western Europe in November (six months after the false armistice in May, that curious week's holiday which the war had taken which had been so false that they remembered it only as phenomenon) and a man, even though still in uniform, might have thought himself free, at least until they started the next one, of yesterday's cadavers. So they had been issued an extra wine and brandy ration to compensate for this, in charge of the sergeant who was to have doled it out to them at need. But the sergeant, who had not wanted the assignment either, was a dour introvert who had recluded himself in an empty compartment forward with a pornographic magazine as soon as the train left Paris. But, alert for the opportunity, when the sergeant quitted his compartment at Châlons (they didn't know why nor bother: perhaps to find a urinal; possibly it was merely official) two of them (one had been a fairly successful picklock in civilian life before 1914 and planned to resume that vocation as soon as he was permitted to doff his uniform) entered the compartment and opened the sergeant's valise and extracted two bottles of brandy from it.

So when the Bar-le-Duc express dropped their carriage at St. Mihiel, where the local for Verdun would engage it, they (except the sergeant) were a shade better than fairly drunk; and when, shortly after daylight, the local set the carriage on a repaired siding in the rubble of Verdun, they were even another shade better than that; by that time also the sergeant had discovered the ravishing of

361

his valise and counted the remaining bottles and, what with the consequent uproar of his outraged and angry denunciation, plus their own condition, they did not even notice the old woman at first; only then to remark that there had been something almost like a committee waiting for them, as though word of the time of their arrival and their purpose too had preceded them—a clump, a huddle, a small group, all men save one, of labourers from the town and peasants from the adjacent countryside, watching them quietly while the sergeant (carrying the valise) snarled and cursed at them, out of which that one, the old woman, had darted at once and was now tugging at the sergeant's sleeve—a peasant woman older in appearance than in years when seen close, with a worn lined face which looked as though she too had not slept much lately, but which was now tense and even alight with a sort of frantic eagerness and hope.

'Eh?' the sergeant said at last. 'What? What is it you want?'

'You are going out to the forts,' she said. 'We know why. Take me with you.'

'You?' the sergeant said; now they were all listening. 'What for?'

'It's Theodule,' she said. 'My son. They told me he was killed there in 1916 but they didn't send him back home and they won't let me go out there and find him.'

'Find him?' the sergeant said. 'After three years?'

'I will know him,' she said. 'Only let me go and look. I will know him. You have a mother; think how she would grieve for you if you had died and they had not sent you home. Take me with you. I will know him, I tell you. I will know him at once. Come now.' She was clinging to his arm now while he tried to shake her loose.

'Let go!' he said. 'I can't take you out there without an order, even if I would. We've got a job to do; you would be in the way. Let go!'

But she still clung to the sergeant's arm, looking about at the other faces watching her, her own face eager and unconvinced. 'Boys—children,' she said. 'You have mothers too—some of you—'

'Let go!' the sergeant said, swapping the valise to the other hand and jerking himself free this time. 'Gwan! Beat it:' taking her by the shoulders, the valise pressed against her back, and turning her and propelling her across the platform toward the quiet group which had been watching too. 'There ain't nothing out there any more by now but rotten meat; you couldn't find him even if you went.'

'I can,' she said. 'I know I can. I sold the farm, I tell you. I have money. I can pay you—'

'Not me,' the sergeant said. 'Not but that if I had my way, you could go out there and find yours and bring another one back for us, and we would wait for you here. But you ain't going.' He released her, speaking almost gently. 'You go on back home and forget about this. Is your husband with you?'

'He is dead too. We lived in the Morbihan. When the war was over, I sold the farm and came here to find Theodule.'

'Then go on back to wherever it is you are living now. Because you can't go with us.'

But she went no farther than the group she had emerged from, to turn and stand again, watching, the worn sleepless face still eager, unconvinced, indomitable, while the sergeant turned back to his squad and stopped and gave them another scathing and introverted look. 'All right,' he said at last. 'All of you that ain't seeing double, let's go. Because I don't want to mess around out there long enough to get one stinking carcass, let alone two.'

'How about a drink first?' one said.

'Try and get it.'

'Want me to carry your grip, Sarge?' another said. The sergeant's answer was simple, brief and obscene. He turned, they followed raggedly. A lorry, a closed van, was waiting for them with a driver and a corporal. They drew the empty coffin from its compartment and carried it to the van and slid it inside and got in themselves. There was straw for them to sit on; the sergeant himself sat on the coffin, the valise in his lap and one hand still gripping the handle as if he expected one or maybe all of them to try to snatch it from him. The lorry moved.

'Don't we get any breakfast?' one said.

'You drank yours,' the sergeant said. 'After you stole it first.' But there was breakfast: bread and coffee at a zinc bar in a tiny bistro for some inscrutable reason untouched by the shelling except that it had a new American-made sheet-iron roof, which stuck upward from the tumbled masses of collapsed walls surrounding and enclosing it. That was arranged too; the meal was already paid for from Paris.

A FABLE

'Christ,' one said. 'The army sure wants this corpse bad if they have started buying grub from civilians.' The sergeant ate with the valise on the bar before him, between his arms. Then they were in the lorry again, the sergeant gripping the valise on his lap, now; through the open rear door of the lorry as it crept between the piles of rubble and the old craters, they were able to see something of the ruined city—the mountains and hills of shattered masonry which men were already at work clearing away and out of which there rose already an astonishing number of the American-made iron roofs to glint like silver in the morning sun; maybe the Americans had not fought all the war but at least they were paying for the restoration of its devastation.

That is, the sergeant could have seen it because almost at once his men had entered a state resembling coma, even before they had crossed the Meuse bridge and reached the corner, where in time the five heroic-sized figures would stare steadily and indomitably eastward in bas-relief from the symbolical section of stone bastion which would frame and contain them. Or rather, the sergeant could have been able to, sitting with the valise huddled between his arms on his lap like a mother with a sick baby, watching them intently for perhaps another ten minutes where they lay sprawled against one another in the straw, the lorry well out of the city now. Then he rose, still carrying the valise; there was a small sliding panel in the lorry's front wall. He opened it and spoke rapidly and quietly for a moment with the corporal beside the driver; then he unlocked the valise and took all the bottles save one of brandy out of it and passed them to the corporal and locked the valise on the single remaining bottle and returned and sat on the coffin again, the valise huddled again on his lap.

So now, as the lorry climbed the repaired road to follow the curve of the Meuse Heights, the sergeant at least could watch beyond the open door the ruined and slain land unfold—the corpse of earth, some of which, its soil soured forever with cordite and human blood and anguish, would never live again, as though not only abandoned by man but repudiated forever by God Himself: the craters, the old trenches and rusted wire, the stripped and blasted trees, the little villages and farms like shattered skulls no longer even recognisable as skulls, already beginning to vanish beneath a fierce rank colourless growth of nourishmentless grass coming not tenderly out of the earth's surface but as though miles and leagues up from Hell itself, as if the Devil himself were trying to hide what man had done to the earth which was his mother.

Then the battered fort which nevertheless had endured, steadfast still even though France, civilization no longer needed it; steadfast still even if only to taint the air not only more than two years after the battle had ended and the mass rotting should have healed itself, but more than twice that many months after the war itself had stopped. Because as soon as the sergeant, standing now and clasping the valise to his breast, roused them with the side of his boot, they were already smelling it: who had not thought they would have to begin that until they were actually inside the fort; though once the sergeant had kicked and cursed the last of them out of the lorry, they saw why—a midden of white bones and skulls and some still partly covered with strips and patches of what looked like brown or black leather, and boots and stained uniforms and now and then what would be an intact body wrapped in a fragment of tarpaulin, beside one of the low entrances in the stone wall; while they watched two more soldiers in butchers' aprons and with pieces of cloth bound over their nostrils and lower faces, emerged from the low entrance carrying between them a two-man wheelless barrow heaped with more scraps and fragments of the fort's old 1916 defenders. In time there would be a vast towered chapel, an ossuary, visible for miles across the Heights like the faintly futuristic effigy of a gigantic grey goose or an iguanodon created out of grey stone not by a sculptor but by expert masons —a long tremendous nave enclosed by niches in each of which a light would burn always, the entrance to each arched with the carven names taken not from identity discs but from regimental lists since there would be nothing to match them with—squatting over the vast deep pit into which the now clean inextricable anonymous bones of what had been man, men, would be shovelled and sealed; facing it would be the slope white with the orderly parade of Christian crosses bearing the names and regimental designations of the bones which could be identified; and beyond it, that other slope ranked not with crosses but with rounded headstones set faintly but intractably oblique to face where Mecca was, set with a consistent and almost formal awryness and carved in cryptic and indecipherable hieroglyph because the bones here had been identifiable too which had once been men come this far from their hot sun and sand, this far from home and all familiar things, to make this last sacrifice in the northern rain and mud and cold, for what cause unless their leaders, ignorant too, could have explained some of it, a little of it to them in their own tongue. But now there only the dun-coloured battered and enduring walls of the fortress, flanked by the rounded sunken concrete domes of machine-gun placements like giant mushrooms, and the midden and the two soldiers in butcher's aprons dumping their barrow on to it, then turning with the empty barrow to look at them for a moment above the taut rags over their nostrils and mouths with the fixed exhaustless unseeing unrecognising glares of sleepwalkers in nightmares before descending the steps again; and over all, permeant and invincible, the odour, the smell, as though, victims of man and therefore quit of him, they had bequeathed him that which had already been invulnerable to him for three years and would still be for thirty more or even three hundred more, so that all that remained to him was to abandon it, flee it.

They looked at the midden, then at the low orifice in the dun stone through which the two soldiers with the barrow had seemed to plunge, drop as though into the bowels of the earth; they did not know yet that in their eyes too now was that fixed assuageless glare of nightmares. 'Christ,' one said. 'Let's grab one off that dump there and get the hell out of here.'

'No,' the sergeant said; there was something behind his voice not vindictiveness so much as repressed gleeful anticipation—if they had known it. He had worn his uniform ever since September 1914 without ever having become a soldier; he could remain in it for another decade and still would not be one. He was an office man, meticulous and reliable; his files were never out of order, his returns never late. He neither drank nor smoked; he had never heard a gun fired in his life save the amateur sportsmen banging away at whatever moved on Sunday morning around the little Loire village where he had been born and lived until his mother-land demanded him. Perhaps all this was why he had been given this assignment. 'No,' he said. 'The order says, "Proceed to Verdun and thence with expedition and despatch to the catacombs beneath the Fort of Valaumont and extricate therefrom one complete cadaver of one French soldier unidentified and unidentifiable either by name regiment or rank, and return with it." And that's what we're going to do. Get on with you: forward.'

'Let's have a drink first,' one said.

'No,' the sergeant said. 'Afterward. Get it loaded into the lorry first.'

'Come on, Sarge,' another said. 'Think what that stink will be down that hole.'

'No, I tell you!' the sergeant said. 'Get on there! Forward!' He didn't lead them; he drove, herded them, to bow their heads one by one into the stone tunnel, to drop, plunge in their turn down the steep pitch of the stone stairs as though into the bowels of the earth, into damp and darkness, though presently, from beyond where the stairs flattened at last into a tunnel, they could see a faint unsteady red gleam not of electricity, it was too red and unsteady, but from torches. They were torches; there was one fastened to the wall beside the first doorless opening in the wall and now they could see one another binding across their nostrils and lower faces what soiled handkerchiefs and filthy scraps of rag which they found on themselves (one who apparently had neither was holding the collar of his coat across his face), huddling and then halting here because an officer, his face swathed to the eyes in a silk one, had emerged from the opening; pressing back against the wall of the narrow tunnel while the sergeant with his valise came forward and saluted and presented his order to the officer, who opened it and glanced briefly at it, then turned his head and spoke back into the room behind him, and a corporal carrying an electric torch and a folded stretcher came out; he had a gas-mask slung about his neck.

Then, the corporal with his torch leading now and the foremost man carrying the stretcher, they went on again between the sweating walls, the floor itself beneath the feet viscous and greasy so that there was a tendency to slip, passing the doorless orifices in the walls beyond which they could see the tiered bunks in which in time during those five months in 1916 men had actually learned to sleep beneath the muted thunder and the trembling of the earth, the smell which above ground had had a sort of vividness, as though even yet partaking indomitably still of something of that motion which is life, not increasing so much as becoming familiar —an old stale dead and worn accustomedness which man would never eradicate and so in time would even get used to and even cease to smell it—a smell subterrene and claustrophobe and doomed to darkness, not alone of putrefaction but of fear and old sweat and old excrement and endurance; fear attenuated to that point where it must choose between coma and madness and in the intermittent coma no longer feared but merely stank.

More soldiers in pairs with masked faces and heaped barrows or stretchers passed them; suddenly more sweating and viscid stairs plunged away beneath them; at the foot of the stairs the tunnel made a sharp angle, no longer floored and walled and roofed with concrete; and, turning the corner behind the corporal, it was no longer a tunnel even but an excavation a cavern a cave a great niche dug out of one wall in which during the height of the battle, when there had been no other way to dispose of them, the bodies which had merely been killed and the ones which had been killed and dismembered too in the fort or the connecting machine-gun pits had been tumbled and covered with earth, the tunnel itself continuing on beyond it: a timber-shored burrow not even high enough for a man to stand erect in, through or beyond which they now saw a steady white glare which would have to be electricity, from which as they watched, two more hooded and aproned soldiers emerged, carrying a stretcher with what would be an intact body this time.

'Wait here,' the corporal said.

'My orders say—' the sergeant said.

'. . . . your orders,' the corporal said. 'We got a system here. We do things our way. Down here, you're on active service, pal. Just give me two of your men and the stretcher. Though you can come too, if you think nothing less will keep your nose clean.'

'That's what I intend to do,' the sergeant said. 'My orders say—' But the corporal didn't wait, going on, the two with the stretcher, the sergeant stooping last to enter the farther tunnel, the valise still clasped against his breast like a sick child. It did not take them long, as if there were plenty in the next traverse to choose from; almost at once, it seemed to the remaining ten, they saw the sergeant come stooping out of the burrow, still clasping the valise, followed by the two men with the burdened stretcher at a sort of stumbling run, then last the corporal who didn't even pause, walking around the stretcher where the two bearers had dropped

it, already going on toward the stairs until the sergeant stopped
him. 'Wait,' the sergeant said, the valise now clasped under one
arm while he produced his order and a pencil from inside his coat
and shook the folded order open. 'We got systems in Paris too. It's
a Frenchman.'

'Right,' the corporal said.

'It's all here. Nothing missing.'

'Right,' the corporal said.

'No identification of name regiment or rank.'

'Right,' the corporal said.

'Then sign it,' the sergeant said, holding out the pencil as the
corporal approached. 'You,' he said to the nearest man. 'About
face and bend over.' Which the man did, the sergeant holding the
paper flat on his bowed back while the corporal signed. 'Your
lieutenant will have to sign too,' the sergeant said, taking the pencil
from the corporal. 'You might go on ahead and tell him.'

'Right,' the corporal said, going on again.

'All right,' the sergeant said to the stretcher bearers. 'Get it out
of here.'

'Not yet,' the first stretcher bearer said. 'We're going to have
that drink first.'

'No,' the sergeant said. 'When we get it into the lorry.' He had
not wanted the assignment and indeed he did not belong here
because this time they simply took the valise away from him in one
concerted move of the whole twelve of them, not viciously,
savagely, just rapidly: with no heat at all but almost impersonal,
almost inattentive, as you might rip a last year's calendar from the
wall to kindle a fire with it; the ex-picklock didn't even pretend
to conceal his action this time, producing his instrument in plain,
view, the others crowding around him as he opened the valise. Or
they thought the rapidity and ease of the valise's rape had been
because they were too many for the sergeant, staring down at the
single bottle it contained with shock then outrage and then with
something like terror while the sergeant stood back and over them
laughing steadily down at them with a sort of vindictive and
triumphant pleasure.

'Where's the rest of it?' one said.

'I threw it away,' the sergeant said. 'Poured it out.'

'Poured it out, hell,' another said. 'He sold it.'

'When?' another said. 'When did he have a chance to? Or pour it out either.'

'While we were all asleep in the lorry coming out here.'

'I wasn't asleep,' the second said.

'All right, all right,' the ex-picklock said. 'What does it matter what he did with it? It's gone. We'll drink this one. Where's your corkscrew?' he said to a third one. But the man already had the corkscrew out, opening the bottle. 'All right,' the ex-picklock said to the sergeant, 'you go on and report to the officer and we'll take it up and be putting it into the coffin.'

'Right,' the sergeant said, taking up the empty valise. 'I want to get out of here too. I don't even need a drink to prove I don't like this.' He went on. They emptied the bottle rapidly, passing it from one to another, and flung it away.

'All right,' the ex-picklock said. 'Grab that thing up and let's get out of here.' Because already he was the leader, none to say or know or even care when it had happened. Because they were not drunk now, not inebriates but madmen, the last brandy lying in their stomachs cold and solid as balls of ice as they almost ran with the stretcher up the steep stairs.

'Where is it, then?' the one pressing behind the ex-picklock said.

'He gave it to that corporal riding up front,' the ex-picklock said. 'Through that panel while we were asleep.' They burst out into the air, the world, earth and sweet air again where the lorry waited, the driver and the corporal standing with a group of men some distance away. They had all heard the ex-picklock and dropped the stretcher without even pausing and were rushing toward the lorry until the ex-picklock stopped them. 'Hold it,' he said. 'I'll do it.' But the missing bottles were nowhere in the lorry. The ex-picklock returned to the stretcher.

'Call that corporal over here,' one said. 'I know how to make him tell where it is.'

'Fool,' the ex-picklock said. 'If we start something now, don't you know what'll happen? He'll call the M.P.'s and put us all under arrest and get a new guard from the adjutant in Verdun. We can't do anything here. We've got to wait till we get back to Verdun.'

'What'll we do in Verdun?' another said. 'Buy some liquor? With what? You couldn't get one franc out of the whole lot of us with a suction pump.'

'Morache can sell his watch,' a fourth said.

'But will he?' a fifth said. They all looked at Morache.

'Forget that now,' Morache said. 'Picklock's right; the first thing to do is to get back to Verdun. Come on. Let's get this thing into that box.' They carried the stretcher to the lorry and lifted the sheeted body into it. The lid of the coffin had not been fastened down; a hammer and nails were inside the coffin. They tumbled the body into it, whether face-up or face-down they didn't know and didn't bother, and replaced the top and caught the nails enough to hold it shut. Then the sergeant with his now empty valise climbed through the rear door and sat again on the coffin; the corporal and the driver obviously had returned too because at once the lorry moved, the twelve men sitting on the straw against the walls, quiet now, outwardly as decorous as well-behaved children but actually temporarily insane, capable of anything, talking occasionally among themselves, peacefully while the lorry returned to Verdun, until they were actually in the city again and the lorry had stopped before a door beside which a sentry stood: obviously the commandant's headquarters: and the sergeant began to get up from the coffin. Then Picklock made one last effort:

'I understand orders said we were to have brandy not just to go to Valaumont and get the body out, but to get it back to Paris. Or am I wrong?'

'If you are, who made you wrong?' the sergeant said. He looked down at Picklock a moment longer. Then he turned toward the door; it was as though he too had recognised Picklock as their leader. 'I'll have to sign some papers here. Take it on to the station and load it into the carriage and wait for me there. Then we'll have lunch.'

'Right,' Picklock said. The sergeant dropped to the ground and vanished; at once, even before the lorry had begun to move again, their whole air changed, as if their very characters and personalities had altered, or not altered but rather as if they had shed masks or cloaks; their very speech was short, rapid, succinct, cryptic, at times even verbless, as if they did not need to communicate but merely to prompt one another in one mutual prescient cognizance.

'Morache's watch,' one said.

'Hold it,' Picklock said. 'The station first.'

'Tell him to hurry then,' another said. 'I'll do it,' he said, starting to get up.

'Hold it, I said,' Picklock said, gripping him. 'Do you want M.P.'s?' So they stopped talking and just sat, immobile and in motion, furious in immobility like men strained against a pyramid, as if they were straining at the back of the moving lorry itself with the urgency of their passion and need. The lorry stopped. They were already getting out of it, the first ones dropping to the ground before it had stopped moving, their hands already on the coffin. The platform was empty now, or so they thought, would have thought if they had noticed, which they didn't, not even looking that way as they dragged the coffin out of the lorry, almost running again across the platform with it toward where the carriage waited on the siding; not until a hand began to tug at Picklock's sleeve, an urgent voice at his elbow saying:

'Mister Corporal! Mister Corporal!' Picklock looked down. It was the old woman of the morning whose son had died in the Verdun battle.

'Beat it, grandma,' Picklock said, twitching his arm free. 'Come on. Get that door open.'

But the old woman still clung to him, speaking still with that terrible urgency: 'You've got one. It might be Theodule. I will know. Let me look at him.'

'Beat it, I tell you!' Picklock said. 'We're busy.' So it was not Picklock at all, leader though he was, but one of the others who said suddenly and sharply, muttering it:

'Wait.' Though in the next second the same idea seemed to occur to them all, one end of the box resting now on the floor of the carriage and four of them braced to shove it the rest of the way, all of them paused now looking back while the speaker continued: 'You said something this morning about selling a farm.'

'Selling my farm?' the woman said.

'Money!' the other said in the same undertone.

'Yes! Yes!' the old woman said, fumbling under her shawl and producing an aged reticule almost as large as the sergeant's valise. Now Picklock did take charge.

'Hold it,' he said over his shoulder, then to the old woman: 'If we let you look at him, will you buy two bottles of brandy?'

'Make it three,' a third said.

'And in advance,' a fourth said. 'She can't tell anything from what's in that box now.'

'I can!' she said. 'I will know! Just let me look.'

'All right,' Picklock said. 'Go and get two bottles of brandy, and you can look at him. Hurry now, before the sergeant gets back.'

'Yes, yes,' she said and turned, running, stiffly and awkwardly, clutching the reticule, back across the platform.

'All right,' Picklock said. 'Get it inside. One of you get the hammer out of the lorry.' Luckily their orders had been not to drive the nails home but merely to secure the lid temporarily (apparently the body was to be transferred to something a little more elegant, or anyway commensurate with its purpose, when it reached Paris) so they could draw them without difficulty. Which they did and removed the lid and then recoiled from the thin burst of odour which rushed up at them almost visibly, like thin smoke —one last faint thin valedictory of corruption and mortality, as if the corpse itself had hoarded it for three years against this moment or any similar one with the gleeful demonic sentience of a small boy. Then the old woman returned, clasping two bottles against her breast, still running or at least trotting, panting now, shaking, almost as though from physical exhaustion because she couldn't even climb the steps when she reached the door, so that two of them dropped to the ground and lifted her bodily into the carriage. A third one took the bottles from her, though she didn't seem to notice it. For a second or so she couldn't even seem to see the coffin. Then she saw it and half knelt, half collapsed at the head of it and turned the tarpaulin back from what had been a face. They —the speaker—had been right; she could have told nothing from the face because it was no longer man. Then they knew that she was not even looking at it: just kneeling there, one hand resting on what had been the face and the other caressing what remained of its hair. She said:

'Yes. Yes. This is Theodule. This is my son.' Suddenly she rose, strongly now, and faced them, pressing back against the coffin, looking rapidly from face to face until she found Picklock; her voice was calm and strong too. 'I must have him.'

'You said just to look at him,' Picklock said.

'He is my son. He must go home. I have money. I will buy you a hundred bottles of brandy. Or the money itself, if you want it.'

'How much will you give?' Picklock said. She didn't even hesitate. She handed him the unopened reticule.

'Count it yourself,' she said.

'But how are you going to get it—him away from here? You can't carry it.'

'I have a horse and cart. It's been behind the station yonder ever since we heard yesterday what you were coming for.'

'Heard how?' Picklock said. 'This is official business.'

'Does that matter?' she said, almost impatiently. 'Count it.'

But Picklock didn't open the reticule yet. He turned to Morache. 'Go with her and get the cart. Bring it up to the window on the other side. Make it snappy. Landry'll be back any minute now.' It didn't take long. They got the window up; almost immediately Morache brought the cart up, the big farm-horse going at a heavy and astonished gallop. Morache snatched it to a halt; already the others in the carriage had the sheeted body balanced on the window sill. Morache handed the lines to the old woman on the seat beside him and vaulted over the seat and snatched the body down into the cart and vaulted to the ground beside it; at that moment Picklock inside the carriage tossed the reticule through the window, into the cart.

'Go on,' Morache said to the old woman. 'Get the hell out of here. Quick.' Then she was gone. Morache re-entered the carriage. 'How much was it?' he said to Picklock.

'I took a hundred francs,' Picklock said.

'*A hundred francs*?' another said with incredulous amazement.

'Yes,' Picklock said. 'And tomorrow I'll be ashamed I took even that much. But that will be a bottle apiece.' He handed the money to the man who had spoken last. 'Go and get it.' Then to the others: 'Get that lid back on. What are you waiting for, anyway: for Landry to help you?' They replaced the coffin lid and set the nails in the old holes. The absolute minimum of prudence would have dictated or at least suggested a weight of some kind, any kind in the coffin first, but they were not concerned with prudence. The ganymede returned, clasping a frayed wicker basket to his breast; they snatched it from him before he could even get into the carriage, the owner of the corkscrew opening the bottles rapidly as they were passed to him.

'He said to bring the basket back,' the ganymede said.

'Take it back then,' Picklock said: and then no more of that either; the hands snatching at the bottles almost before the corks were out, so that when the sergeant returned about an hour later, his outrage—not rage: outrage—knew no bounds. But this time he was impotent because they were indeed in coma now, sprawled and snoring in one inextricable filth of straw and urine and vomit and spilled brandy and empty bottles, invulnerable and immune in that nepenthe when toward the end of the afternoon an engine coupled on to the carriage and took it back to St. Mihiel and set it off on another siding, and waking them only because of the glare of yellow light which now filled the carriage through the windows, and the sound of hammers against the outside of it, which roused Picklock.

Clasping his throbbing head and shutting his eyes quickly against that unbearable glare, it seemed to him that there had never been so fierce a sunrise. It was almost like electricity; he didn't see how he could move beneath it to rise, and even on his feet staggering until he braced himself, he didn't see how he had accomplished the feat, bracing himself against the wall while he kicked the others one by one into sentience or anyway consciousness. 'Get up,' he said. 'Get up. We've got to get out of here.'

'Where are we?' one said.

'Paris,' Picklock said. 'It's already tomorrow.'

'O Christ,' a voice said. Because they were all awake now, waking not into remembering, since even comatose they had not really forgotten, but into simple realisation like sleepwalkers waking to find themselves standing on the outside of forty-storey window ledges. They were not drunk now. They didn't even have time to be sick. 'Christ, yes,' the voice said. They got up, staggering for balance, shaking and trembling, and stumbled through the door and huddled, blinking against the fierce glare until they could bear it. Except that it was electricity; it was still last night (or perhaps tomorrow night, for all they knew or for the moment cared even): two searchlights, such as anti-aircraft batteries had used against night-flying aeroplanes during the war, trained on the carriage and in the glare of which men on ladders were nailing long strips of black and funeral bunting along the eaves of the carriage. Nor was it Paris either.

'We're still in Verdun,' another said.

'Then they've moved the station around to the other side of the tracks,' Picklock said.

'Anyway it's not Paris,' a third said. 'I've got to have a drink.'

'No,' Picklock said. 'You'll take coffee and something to eat.' He turned to the ganymede. 'How much money have you got left?'

'I gave it to you,' the ganymede said.

'Damn that,' Picklock said, extending his hand. 'Come on with it.' The ganymede fumbled out a small wad of paper notes and coins. Picklock took and counted it rapidly. 'It might do,' he said. Come on.' There was a small bistro opposite the station. He led the way to it and inside—a small zinc bar at which a single man stood in a countryman's corduroy coat, and two tables where other men in the rough clothes of farmers or labourers sat with glasses of coffee or wine, playing dominoes, all of them turning to look as Picklock led his party in and up to the bar, where a tremendous woman in black said,

'Messieurs?'

'Coffee, Madame, and bread if you have it,' Picklock said.

'I don't want coffee,' the third said. 'I want a drink.'

'Sure,' Picklock said in a calm and furious voice, even lowering it a little: 'Stick around here until somebody comes and lifts that box, let alone opens it. I hear they always give you a drink before you climb the steps.'

'Maybe we could find another—' a fourth began.

'Shut up,' Picklock said. 'Drink that coffee. I've got to think.' Then a new voice spoke.

'What's the matter?' it said. 'You boys in trouble?' It was the man who had been standing at the bar when they entered. They looked at him now—a solid stocky man, obviously a farmer, not quite as old as they had thought, with a round hard ungullible head and a ribbon in the lapel of the coat—not one of the best ones but still a good one, matching in fact one which Picklock himself wore; possibly that was why he spoke to them, he and Picklock watching each other for a moment.

'Where'd you get it?' Picklock said.

'Combles,' the stranger said.

'So was I,' Picklock said.

'You in a jam of some sort?' the stranger said.

'What makes you think that?' Picklock said.

'Look, pal,' the stranger said. 'Maybe you were under sealed
orders when you left Paris, but there hasn't been much secret about
it since your sergeant got out of that carriage this afternoon. What
is he, anyway—some kind of a reformist preacher, like they say
they have in England and America? He was sure in a state. He
didn't seem to care a damn that you were drunk. What seemed to
fry him was how you managed to get twelve more bottles of brandy
without him knowing how you did it.'

'This afternoon?' Picklock said. 'You mean it's still today?
Where are we?'

'St. Mihiel. You lay over here tonight while they finish nailing
enough black cloth on your carriage to make it look like a hearse.
Tomorrow morning a special train will pick you up and take you
on to Paris. What's wrong? Did something happen?'

Suddenly Picklock turned. 'Come on back here,' he said. The
stranger followed. They stood slightly apart from the others now,
in the angle of the bar and the rear wall. Picklock spoke rapidly
yet completely, telling it all, the stranger listening quietly.

'What you need is another body,' the stranger said.

'You're telling me?' Picklock said.

'Why not? I've got one. In my field. I found it the first time I
ploughed. I reported it, but they haven't done anything about it
yet. I've got a horse and cart here; it will take about four hours to
go and come.' They looked at each other. 'You've got all night—
that is, now.'

'All right,' Picklock said. 'How much?'

'You'll have to say. You're the one that knows how bad you
need it.'

'We haven't got any money.'

'You break my heart,' the stranger said. They looked at each
other. Without removing his eyes, Picklock raised his voice a little.
'Morache.' Morache came up. 'The watch,' Picklock said.

'Wait now,' Morache said. It was a Swiss movement, in gold; he
had wanted one ever since he saw one first, finding it at last on
the wrist of a German officer lying wounded in a shell crater one
night after he, Morache, had got separated from a patrol sent out
to try for a live prisoner or at least one still alive enough to speak.
He even saw the watch first, before he saw who owned it, having
hurled himself into the crater just in time before a flare went up,

seeing the glint of the watch first in the corpse-glare of the magnesium before he saw the man—a colonel, apparently shot through the spine since he seemed to be merely paralysed, quite conscious and not even in much pain; he would have been exactly what they had been sent out to find, except for the watch. So Morache murdered him with his trench knife (a shot here now would probably have brought a whole barrage down on him) and took the watch and lay just outside his own wire until the patrol came back (empty-handed) and found him. Though for a day or so he couldn't seem to bring himself to wear the watch nor even look at it until he remembered that his face had been blackened at the time and the German could not have told what he was even, let alone who; besides that, the man was dead now. 'Wait,' he said. 'Wait now.'

'Sure,' Picklock said. 'Wait in that carriage yonder until they come for that box. I don't know what they'll do to you then, but I do know what they'll do if you run because that will be desertion.' He held out his hand. 'The watch.' Morache unstrapped the watch and handed it to Picklock.

'At least get some brandy too,' he said. The stranger reached for the watch in Picklock's hand.

'Whoa, look at it from there,' Picklock said, holding the watch on his raised open palm.

'Sure you can have brandy,' the stranger said. Picklock closed his hand over the watch and let the hand drop.

'How much?' he said.

'Fifty francs,' the stanger said.

'Two hundred,' Picklock said.

'A hundred francs.'

'Two hundred,' Picklock said.

'Where's the watch?' the stranger said.

'Where's the cart?' Picklock said.

It took them a little over four hours ('You'd have to wait anyhow until they finish nailing up that black cloth and get away from the carriage,' the stranger said) and there were four of them ('Two more will be enough,' stranger said. 'We can drive right up to it.')—himself and the stranger on the seat, Morache and another behind them in the cart, north and eastward out of the town into the country darkness, the horse itself taking the right road without

378

guidance, knowing that it was going home, in the darkness the steady jounce of jogging horse and the thump and rattle of the cart a sound and a vibration instead of a progress, so that it was the roadside trees which seemed to move, wheeling up out of the darkness to rush slowly backward past them against the sky. But they were moving, even though it did seem (to Picklock) forever, the roadside trees ravelling suddenly into a straggle of posts, the horse, still without guidance, swinging sharply to the left.

'Sector, huh?' Picklock said.

'Yeah,' the stranger said. 'The Americans broke it in September. Vienne-la-pucelle yonder,' he said, pointing. 'It caught it. It was right up in the tip. Not long now.' But it was a little longer than that, though at last they were there—a farm and its farmyard, lightless. The stranger stopped the horse and handed Picklock the lines. 'I'll get a shovel. I'm going to throw in a ground-sheet too.' He was not long, passing the shovel and the folded ground-sheet to the two in the back and mounting the seat again and took the lines, the horse lurching forward and making a determined effort to turn in the farmyard gate until the stranger reined it sharply away. Then a gate in a hedgerow; Morache got down and opened it for the cart to pass. 'Leave it open,' the stranger said. 'We'll close it when we come out.' Which Morache did and swung up and into the cart as it passed him; they were in a field now, soft from ploughing, the unguided horse still choosing its own unerring way, no longer a straight course now but weaving at times almost doubling on itself though Picklock could still see nothing. 'Dud shells,' the stranger explained. 'Fenced off with flags until they finish getting them out. We just plough circles around them. According to the women and the old men who were here then, the whole war started up again after that recess they took last May, right in that field yonder. It belongs to some people named Demont. The man died that same summer; I guess two wars on his land only a week apart was too much for him. His widow works it now with a hired man. Not that she needs him; she can run a plough as good as he can. There's another one, her sister. She does the cooking. She has flies up here.' He was standing now, peering ahead; in silhouette against the sky he tapped the side of his head. Suddenly he swung the horse sharply away and presently stopped it. 'Here we are,' he said. 'About fifty metres yonder on that bank dividing us, there used to be the finest beech tree in this country. My grandfather said that even his grandfather couldn't remember when it was a sapling. It probably went that same day too. All right,' he said. 'Let's get him up. You don't want to waste any time here either.'

He showed them where his plough had first exposed the corpse and he had covered it again and marked the place. It was not deep and they could see nothing and after this length of time or perhaps because it was only one, there was little odour either, the long inextricable mass of light bones and cloth soon up and out and on and then into the folds of the ground-sheet and then in the cart itself, the horse thinking that this time surely it was destined for its stall, trying even in the soft earth of the ploughing to resume its heavy muscle-bound jog, Morache closing the hedge gate and having to run now to catch the cart again because the horse was now going at a heavy canter even against the lines, trying again to swing into the farmyard until the stranger sawed it away, using the whip now until he got it straightened out on the road back to St. Mihiel.

A little more than four hours, but perhaps it should have been. The town was dark now, and the bistro they had started from, a clump of shadow detaching itself from a greater mass of shadow and itself breaking into separate shapes as the nine others surrounded the cart, the cart itself not stopping but going steadily on toward where the carriage in its black pall of bunting had vanished completely into the night. But it was there; the ones who had remained in town had even drawn the nails again so that all that was necessary was to lift off the top and drag the ground-sheeted bundle through the window and dump it in and set the nails again. 'Drive them in,' Picklock said. 'Who cares about noise now? Where is the brandy?'

'It's all right,' a voice said.

'How many bottles did you open?'

'One,' a voice said.

'Counting from where?'

'Why should we lie when all you've got to do to prove it is to count the others?' the voice said.

'All right,' Picklock said. 'Get out of here now and shut the window.' Then they were on the ground again. The stranger had never quitted his cart and this time surely the horse was going home. But they didn't wait for that departure. They turned as one, already running, clotting and jostling a little at the carriage door, but plunging at last back into their lightless catafalque as into the womb itself. They were safe now. They had a body, and drink to take care of the night. There was tomorrow and Paris of course, but God could take care of that.

Carrying the gather of eggs in the loop of her apron. Marya, the elder sister, crossed the yard toward the house as though borne on a soft and tender cloud of white geese. They surrounded and enclosed her as though with a tender and eager yearning; two of them, one on either side, kept absolute pace with her, pressed against her skirts, their long undulant necks laid flat against her moving flanks, their heads tilted upward, the hard yellow beaks open slightly like mouths, the hard insentient eyes filmed over as with a sort of ecstasy: right up to the stoop itself when she mounted it and opened the door and stepped quickly through and closed it, the geese swarming and jostling around and over and on to the stoop itself to press against the door's blank wood, their necks extended and the heads fallen a little back as though on the brink of swoons, making with their hoarse harsh unmusical voices faint tender cries of anguish and bereavement and unassuageable grief.

This was the kitchen. already strong with the approaching midday's soup. She didn't even stop: putting the eggs away, lifting for a moment the lid of the simmering pot on the stove, then placed rapidly on the wooden table a bottle of wine, a glass, a soup bowl, a loaf, a napkin and spoon, then on through the house and out the front door giving on to the lane and the field beyond it where she could already see them—the horse and harrow and the man guiding them, the hired man they had had since the death of her sister's husband four years ago, and the sister herself moving across the land's panorama like a ritual, her hand and arm plunging into the sack slung from her shoulder, to emerge in that long sweep which is the second oldest of man's immemorial gestures or acts, she—Marya—running now, skirting among the old craters picketed off by tiny stakes bearing scraps of red cloth where the rank and lifeless grass grew above the unexploded shells, already saying, crying in her bright serene and carrying voice: 'Sister! Here is the young Englishman come for the medal. There are two of them, coming up the lane.'

'A friend with him?' the sister said.

'Not a friend,' Marya said. 'This one is looking for a tree.'

'A tree?' the sister said.

'Yes, Sister. Can't you see him?'

And, themselves in the lane now, they could see them both—two men obviously but, even at that distance, one of them moving not quite like a human being and, in time nearer, not like a human being at all beside the other's tall and shambling gait, but at a slow lurch and heave like some kind of giant insect moving erect and seeming to possess no progress at all even before Marya said: 'He's on crutches': the single leg swinging metronome and indefatigable yet indomitable too between the rhythmic twin counterstrokes of the crutches; interminable yet indomitable too and indubitably coming nearer until they could see that the arm on that side was gone somewhere near the elbow also, and (quite near now) that what they looked at was not even a whole man, since one half of his visible flesh was one furious saffron scar beginning at the ruined homburg hat and dividing his face exactly down the bridge of his nose, across the mouth and chin, to the collar of his shirt. But this was only on the outside because the voice was strong and unpitying and the French he addressed them in was fluid and good and it was only the man with him who was sick—a tall thin cadaver of a man, whole to be sure and looking no less like a tramp, but with a sick insolent intolerable face beneath a filthy hat from the band of which there stood a long and raking feather which made him at least eight feet tall.

'Madame Dumont?' the first man said.

'Yes,' Marya said with her bright and tender and unpitying smile.

The man with the crutches turned to his companion. 'All right,' he said in French. 'This is them. Go ahead.' But Marya had not waited for him, speaking to the man on crutches in French:

'We were waiting for you. The soup is ready and you must be hungry after your walk from the station.' Then she too turned to the other, speaking not in French now but in the old Balkan tongue of her childhood: 'You too. You will need to eat for a little while longer too.'

'What?' the sister said suddenly and harshly, then to the man with the feather in the same mountain tongue: 'You are Zsettlani?'

'What?' the man with the feather said in French harshly and loudly. 'I speak French. I will take soup too. I can pay for it. See?' he said, thrusting his hand into his pocket. 'Look.'

'We know you have money,' Marya said in French. 'Come into the house.' And, in the kitchen now, they could see the rest of the first man: the saffron coloured scar not stopping at the hat's line but dividing the skull too into one furious and seared rigidity, no eye, no ear on that side of it, the corner of the mouth seized into rigidity as if it was not even the same face which talked and presently would chew and swallow; the filthy shirt held together at the throat by the frayed and faded stripes of what they did not know was a British regimental tie; the stained and soiled dinner jacket from the left breast of which two medals hung from their ribbons; the battered and filthy tweed trousers one leg of which was doubled back up and fastened below the thigh with a piece of wire; the Englishman propped on his crutches for a moment yet in the centre of the kitchen, looking about the room with that alert, calm unpitying eye while his companion stood just inside the door behind him with his ravaged insolent peaceless face, still wearing the hat whose feather now almost touched the ceiling, as though he were suspended from it.

'So this is where he lived,' the man with the crutches said.

'Yes,' Marthe said. 'How did you know? How did you know where to find us?'

'Now, Sister,' Marya said. 'How could he have come for the medal if he didn't know where we were?'

'The medal?' the Englishman said.

'Yes,' Marya said. 'But have your soup first. You are hungry.'

'Thanks,' the Englishman said. He jerked his head toward the man behind him. 'He too? Is he invited too?'

'Of course,' Marya said. She took two of the bowls from the table and went to the stove, not offering to help him, nor could the sister, Marthe, have moved fast or quickly enough to help him as he swung the one leg over the wooden bench and propped the crutches beside him and was already uncorking the wine before the whole man at the door had even moved, Marya lifting the lid from the pot and half-turning to look back at the second man, saying in French this time: 'Sit down. You can eat too. Nobody minds any more.'

'Minds what?' the man with the feather said harshly.

'We have forgotten it.' Marya said. 'Take off your hat first.'

'I can pay you,' the man with the feather said. 'You can't give me anything, see?' He reached into his pocket and jerked his hand out already scattering the coins, flinging them toward and on to and past the table, scattering and clinking across the floor as he approached and flung himself on to the backless bench opposite the Englishman and reached for the wine bottle and a tumbler in one voracious motion.

'Pick up your money,' Marya said.

'Pick it up yourself, if you don't want it there,' the man said, filling the tumbler, splashing the wine into it until it was overfull, already raising the tumbler toward his mouth.

'Leave it now,' Marthe said. 'Give him his soup.' She had moved, not quite enough to stand behind the Englishman but rather over him, her hands resting one in the other, her high severe mountain face which would have been bold and handsome as a man's looking down at him while he reached and poured from the bottle and set the bottle down and raised his glass until he was looking at her across it.

'Health, Madame,' he said.

'But how did you know?' Marthe said. 'When did you know him?'

'I never knew him. I never saw him. I heard about him—them —when I came back out in '16. Then I learned what it was, and so after that I didn't need to see him—only to wait and keep out of his way until he would be ready to do the needing—'

'Bring the soup,' the man with the feather said harshly. 'Haven't I already shown you enough money to buy out your whole house?'

'Yes,' Marya said from the stove. 'Be patient. It won't be long now. I will even pick it up for you.' She brought the two bowls of soup; the man with the feather did not even wait for her to set his down, snatching and wolfing it, glaring across the bowl with his dead intolerant outrageous eyes while Marya stooped about their feet and beneath and around the table, gathering up the scattered coins. 'There are only twenty-nine,' she said. 'There should be one more.' Still holding the tilted bowl to his face, the man with the feather jerked another coin from his pocket and banged it on to the table.

'Does that satisfy you?' he said. 'Fill the bowl again.' She did so, at the stove, and brought the bowl back, while again he splashed the wanton and violent wine into his tumbler.

'Eat too,' she said to the man with the crutches.

'Thanks,' he said, not even looking at her but looking still at the tall cold-faced sister standing over him. 'Only about that time or during that time or at that time or whenever it was afterward that I woke up, I was in a hospital in England so it was next spring before I persuaded them to let me come back to France and go to Chaulnesmont until at last I found that sergeant-major and he told me where you were. Only there were three of you then. There was a girl too. His wife?' The tall woman just looked down at him, cold, calm, absolutely inscrutable. 'His fiancée, maybe?'

'Yes,' Marya said. 'That's it: his fiancée. That's the word. Eat your soup.'

'They were to be married,' Marthe said. 'She was a Marseille whore.'

'I beg pardon?' the Englishman said.

'But not any more,' Marya said. 'She was going to learn to be a farmer's wife. Eat your soup before it is cold.'

'Yes,' the Englishman said. 'Thanks'—not even looking at her. 'What became of her?'

'She went back home.'

'Home? You mean back to the—back to Marseille?'

'Brothel,' the tall woman said. 'Say it. You English. The Americans too. Why did your French boggle at that word, being as good as it is with all the others?—She must live too,' she said.

'Thanks,' the Englishman said. 'But she could have stayed here.'

'Yes,' the woman said.

'But she didn't.'

'No,' the woman said.

'She couldn't, you see,' Marya said. 'She has an old grandmother she must support. I think it's quite admirable.'

'So do I,' the Englishman said. He took up the spoon.

'That's right,' Marya said. 'Eat.' But he was still looking at the sister, the spoon arrested above the bowl. Nor did the man with the feather wait this time to demand to be served, swinging his legs across the bench and carrying the bowl himself to the stove and plunging it, hand and all, into the pot before returning with the dripping and streaming bowl to the table where Marya had made the neat small stack of his coins and where the Englishman was still watching the tall sister, talking:

'You had a husband too then.'

'He died. That same summer.'

'Oh,' the Englishman said. 'The war?'

'The peace,' the tall woman said. 'When they let him come home at last and then the war started again before he could even put a plough in the ground, he probably decided that he could not bear another peace. And so he died. Yes?' she said. He had already taken up a spoon of soup. He stopped the spoon again.

'Yes what?'

'What else do you want of us? To show you his grave?' She just said 'his' but they all knew whom she meant. 'That is, where we think it was?' So did the Englishman merely say 'his'.

'What for?' he said. 'He's finished.'

'Finished?' she said in a harsh stern voice.

'He didn't mean it that way, sister,' Marya said. 'He just means that Brother did the best he could, all he could, and now he doesn't need to worry any more. Now all he has to do is rest.' She looked at him, serene and unsurprised and unpitying. 'You like to laugh, don't you?'

He did so, laughing, strong and steady and completely, with that side of his mouth still capable of moving, opening to laugh, the single eye meeting hers—theirs—full and calm and unpitying and laughing too. 'So can you,' he said to Marya. 'Can't you?'

'Why of course,' Marya said. 'Now, sister,' she said. 'The medal.'

So, in the lane once more, there were three of them now instead of the two he had brought with him—three bits of graved symbolic bronze dangling and glinting from the three candy-striped ribbons bright as carnivals and gaudy as sunsets on the breast of the filthy dinner jacket as, facing them, he braced the two crutches into his armpits and with the hand he still had, removed the ruined homburg in a gesture sweeping and invulnerable and clapped it back on at its raked and almost swaggering angle and turned, the single leg once more strong and steady and tireless between the tireless rhythmic swing and recover of the crutches. But moving: back down the lane toward where he and the man with the feather had appeared, even if the infinitesimal progress was out of all proportion to the tremendous effort of the motion. Moving, unwearyable and durable and persevering, growing smaller and smaller with distance until at last he had lost all semblance of advancement whatever and appeared fixed against a panorama in furious progressless unrest, not lonely: just solitary, invincibly single. Then he was gone.

'Yes,' Marya said. 'He can move fast enough. He will be there in plenty of time,' turning then, the two of them, though it was the sister who stopped as though it was only she who had remembered at last the other man, the one with the feather, because Marya said: 'Oh yes, there will be plenty of time for him too.' Because he was not in the house: only the stained table, the bowl and the overturned tumbler where he had fouled and wasted their substance, the stain of the wine and the soup making a little puddle in which sat the neat small stack of coins where Marya had arranged them; all that afternoon while the tall sister went back to the field, the sowing, and Marthe cleaned the kitchen and the soiled dishes, wiping the coins neatly off and stacking them again in that mute still pyramidal gleam while the light faded, until dark when they came back into the kitchen and lighted the lamp and he loomed suddenly, cadaverous and tall beneath the raking feather, from the shadows, saying in his harsh intolerable voice:

'What have you got against the money? Go on. Take it—' lifting his hand again to sweep, fling it to the floor, until the tall sister spoke.

'She has picked it up for you once. Don't do it again.'

'Here. Take it. Why won't you take it? I worked for it— sweated for it—the only money in my life I ever earned by honest sweat. I did it just for this—earned it and then went to all the trouble to find you and give it to you, and now you won't take it. Here.' But they only looked at him, alien and composed, cold and composed the one, the other with that bright and pitiless serenity until at last he said with a kind of amazement: 'So you won't take it. You really won't,' and looked at them for a moment longer, then came to the table and took up the coins and put them into his pocket and turned and went to the door.

'That's right,' Marya said in her serene and unpitying voice. 'Go now. It is not much further. You don't have much longer to despair': at which he turned, framed for a moment in the door, his face livid and intolerable, with nothing left now but the insolence, the tall feather in the hat which he had never removed breaking into the line of the lintel as if he actually were hanging on a cord from it against the vacant shape of the spring darkness. Then he was gone too.

'Have you shut up the fowls yet?' the tall sister said.

'Of course, Sister,' Marya said.

It was a grey day though not a grey year. In fact, time itself had not been grey since that day six years ago when the head hero whom the quiet uncovered throngs which lined both sides of the Champs Élysées from the Place de la Concorde to the Arch and the dignitaries walking humbly on foot who composed the cortege itself had come to honour, had driven all adumbration from the face of Western Europe and indeed from the whole Western world. Only the day was grey, as though in dirge for him to whom it owed (and would forever) for the right and privilege to mourn in peace without terror or concern.

He lay in his splendid casket in full uniform and his medals (the originals, the ones pinned to his breast by the actual hands of the President of his own motherland and the Kings and Presidents of the allied nations whose armies he had led to victory were in the Invalides; these which would return with him to the earth were replicas), the baton of his marshalate lying on his breast beneath his folded hands, on the gun caisson drawn by black-draped and pomponned horses, beneath the flag to which he in his turn and in its most desperate moment had added glory and eagles; behind him in the slow and measured procession colour guards bore the flags of the other nations over whose armies and fates he had been supreme.

But the flags were not first because first behind the caisson walked (doddered rather, in step with nothing as though self-immersed and oblivious of all) the aged batman who had outlived him, in the uniform and the steel helmet still pristine and innocent of war, the rifle through which no shot had ever been fired slung from the bowed shoulder in reverse and as gleaming with tender and meticulous care as a polished serving spoon or drawing-room poker or candelabrum, carrying before him on a black velvet cushion the sheathed sabre, his head bowed a little over it like an aged acolyte with a fragment of the Cross or the ashes of a saint. Then came the two sergeant-grooms leading the charger, black-caparisoned too, the spurred boots reversed in the irons; and only then the flags and the muffled drums and the unrankable black-banded uniforms of the generals and the robes and mitres and monstrances of the Church and the sombre broadcloth and humble silk hats of the ambassadors, all moving beneath the grey and grieving day to the muffled drums and the minute-spaced thudding of a big gun somewhere in the direction of the Fort of Vincennes, up the broad and grieving avenue, between the half-staffed grieving flags of half the world, in pagan and martial retinue and rite: dead chief and slave and steed and the medal-symbols of his glory and the arms with which he had gained them, escorted back into the earth he came from by the lesser barons of his fief hold and his magnificence—prince and cardinal, soldier and statesman, the heirs-apparent to the kingdoms and empires and the ambassadors and personal representatives of the republics, the humble and anonymous crowd itself flowing in behind the splendid last of them, escorting, guarding, seeing him too up the avenue toward where the vast and serene and triumphal and enduring Arch crowned the crest, as though into immolation or suttee.

It lifted toward the grey and grieving sky, invincible and impervious, to endure forever not because it was stone nor even because of its rhythm and symmetry but because of its symbolism, crowning the city; on the marble floor, exactly beneath the Arch's soaring centre, the small perpetual flame burned above the eternal sleep of the nameless bones brought down five years ago from the Verdun battlefield, the cortege moving on to the Arch, the crowd dividing quietly and humbly behind it to flow away on either side until it had surrounded and enclosed that sacred and dedicated monument, the cortege itself stopping now, shifting, moiling a little until at last hushed protocol once more was discharged and only the caisson moving on until it halted directly before the Arch and the flame, and now there remained only silence and the grieving day and that minute's thud of the distant gun.

Then a single man stepped forward from among the princes and prelates and generals and statesmen, in full dress and medalled too; the first man in France: poet, philosopher, statesman, patriot and orator, to stand bareheaded facing the caisson while the distant gun thudded another minute into eternity. Then he spoke:

'Marshal.'

But only the day answered, and the distant gun to mark another interval of its ordered dirge. Then the man spoke again, louder this time, urgent; not peremptory: a cry:

'Marshal!'

But still there was only the dirge of day, the dirge of victorious and grieving France, the dirge of Europe and from beyond the seas too where men had doffed the uniforms in which they had been led through suffering to peace by him who lay now beneath the draped flag on the caisson, and even further than that where people who had never heard his name did not even know that they were still free because of him, the orator's voice ringing now into the grieving circumambience for men everywhere to hear it:

'That's right, great general! Lie always with your face to the east, that the enemies of France shall always see it and beware!'

At which moment there was a sudden movement, surge, in the crowd to one side; the hats and capes and lifted batons of policemen could be seen struggling toward the disturbance. But before they could reach it, something burst suddenly out of the crowd—not a man but a mobile and upright scar, on crutches, he had one arm and one leg, one entire side of his hatless head was one hairless eyeless and earless sear, he wore a filthy dinner jacket from the left breast of which depended on their barberpole ribbons a British Military Cross and Distinguished Conduct Medal, and a French *Médaille Militaire*: which (the French one) was probably why the French crowd itself had not dared prevent him emerging from it and even now did not dare grasp him and jerk him back as he swung himself with that dreadful animal-like lurch and heave with which men move on crutches, out into the empty space enclosing the Arch, and on until he too faced the caisson. Then he stopped and braced the crutches into his armpits and with his single hand grasped the French decoration on his breast, he too crying in a loud and ringing voice:

'Listen to me too, Marshal! This is yours: take it!' and snatched, ripped from his filthy jacket the medal which was the talisman of his sanctuary and swung his arm up and back to throw it. Apparently he knew himself what was going to happen to him as soon as he released the medal, and defied it; with the medal up-poised in his hand he even stopped and looked back at the crowd which seemed now to crouch almost, leashed and straining for the moment when he would absolve himself of immunity, and laughed, not triumphant: just indomitable, with that side of his ruined face capable of laughing, then turned and flung the medal at the caisson, his voice ringing again in the aghast air as the crowd rushed down upon him: 'You too helped carry the torch of man into that twilight where he shall be no more; these are his epitaphs: They shall not pass. My country right or wrong. Here is a spot which is forever England—'

Then they had him. He vanished as though beneath a wave, a tide of heads and shoulders above which one of the crutches appeared suddenly in a hand which seemed to be trying to strike down at him with it until the converging police (there were dozens of them now, converging from everywhere) jerked it away, other police rapidly forming a cordon of linked arms, gradually forcing the crowd back while, rite and solemnity gone for good now, parade marshals' whistles shrilled and the chief marshal himself grasped the bridles of the horses drawing the caisson and swung them around, shouting to the driver: 'Go on!' the rest of the cortege huddling without order, protocol vanished for the moment too as they hurried after the caisson almost with an air of pell mell, as though in actual flight from the wreckage of the disaster.

The cause of it now lay in the gutter of a small cul-de-sac side street where he had been carried by the two policemen who had rescued him before the mob he had instigated succeeded in killing him, lying on his back, his unconscious face quite peaceful now, bleeding a little at one corner of his mouth, the two policemen standing over him, though now that the heat was gone their simple uniforms seemed sufficient to hold back that portion of the crowd which had followed, to stand in a circle looking down at the unconscious and peaceful face.

A FABLE

'Who is he?' a voice said.

'Ah, we know him,' one of the policemen said. 'An Englishman. We've had trouble with him ever since the war; this is not the first time he has insulted our country and disgraced his own.'

'Maybe he will die this time,' another voice said. Then the man in the gutter opened his eyes and began to laugh, or tried to, choking at first, trying to turn his head as though to clear his mouth and throat of what he choked on, when another man thrust through the crowd and approached him—an old man, a gaunt giant of a man with a vast worn sick face with hungry and passionate eyes above a white military moustache, in a dingy black overcoat in the lapel of which were three tiny faded ribbons, who came and knelt beside him and slipped one arm under his head and shoulders and raised him and turned his head a little until he could spit out the blood and shattered teeth and speak. Or laugh rather, which is what he did first, lying in the cradle of the old man's arm, laughing up at the ring of faces enclosing him, then speaking himself in French:

'That's right,' he said: 'Tremble. I'm not going to die. Never.'

'I am not laughing,' the old man bending over him said. 'What you see are tears.'

December, 1944
Oxford—New York—Princeton
November, 1953